FALLING FOR HER
RELUCTANT SHEIKH

BY
AMALIE BERLIN

MILLS
BOON®

Carol Marinelli recently filled in a form where she was asked for her job title and was thrilled, after all these years, to be able to put down her answer as 'writer'. Then it asked what Carol did for relaxation. After chewing her pen for a moment Carol put down the truth—'writing'. The third question asked: 'What are your hobbies?' Well, not wanting to look obsessed or, worse still, boring, she crossed the fingers on her free hand and answered 'swimming and tennis'. But, given that the chlorine in the pool does terrible things to her highlights, and the closest she's got to a tennis racket in the last couple of years is watching the Australian Open, I'm sure you can guess the real answer!

There's never been a day when there haven't been stories in **Amalie Berlin**'s head. When she was a child they were called daydreams, and she was supposed to stop having them and pay attention. Now when someone interrupts her daydreams to ask, 'What are you doing?' she delights in answering, 'I'm working!'

Amalie lives in Southern Ohio with her family and a passel of critters. When *not* working she reads, watches movies, geeks out over documentaries and randomly decides to learn antiquated skills. In case of zombie apocalypse she'll still have bread, lacy underthings, granulated sugar, and always something new to read.

THE BABY OF
THEIR DREAMS

BY
CAROL MARINELLI

MILLS &
BOON

Published in Great Britain 2015
by Mills & Boon, an imprint of Harlequin (UK) Limited,
Eton House, 18-24 Paradise Road, Richmond, Surrey, TW9 1SR

© 2015 Carol Marinelli

ISBN: 978-0-263-24735-0

Harlequin (UK) Limited's policy is to use papers that are natural,
renewable and recyclable products and made from wood grown in
sustainable forests. The logging and manufacturing processes conform
to the legal environmental regulations of the country of origin.

Printed and bound in Spain
by CPI, Barcelona

Dear Reader,

Some stories write themselves. Not all. Often I'm tearing my hair out. But I wasn't with Cat and Dominic. I actually had a plan with this story...my hero and heroine simply refused to stick to it.

I kept reminding them that *I* was the writer, but they refused to listen and I actually couldn't type fast enough some days to keep up with them. I simply loved them both, and I wanted to get to their happy-ever-after so that I could see for myself how *they* worked things out.

I hope you enjoy meeting them as much as I did.

Happy reading!

Carol x

Books by Carol Marinelli

Mills & Boon® Medical Romance™

London's Most Desirable Docs

Unwrapping Her Italian Doc
Playing the Playboy's Sweetheart

Bayside Hospital Heartbreakers!

Tempted by Dr Morales
The Accidental Romeo

Secrets of a Career Girl
Dr Dark and Far Too Delicious
NYC Angels: Redeeming the Playboy
200 Harley Street: Surgeon in a Tux
Baby Twins to Bind Them
Just One Night?

**Visit the author profile page at
millsandboon.co.uk for more titles**

PROLOGUE

THIS WASN'T HOW July was supposed to be.

'Hey, Cat!'

Catriona Hayes stood as her friend came out of her office but she was unable to return Gemma's smile. 'I've just got to go up to Maternity to see a patient and then we can…' Gemma didn't finish her sentence. Now she was closer she could see that her friend was barely holding it together—Cat's green eyes were brimming with tears, her long curly black hair looked as if it had been whipped up by the wind and she was a touch breathless, as if she'd been running. It quickly became clear to Gemma that Cat was not here at the London Royal for their shopping date.

She wasn't.

Cat had walked out of her antenatal appointment at the hospital where she worked and, like a homing beacon, had taken the underground to the Royal, where Gemma was an obstetrics registrar. She had sat in panicked silence on the tube and, despite being twenty weeks pregnant and wearing a flimsy wraparound dress and heels, she had been one of those people running up the escalator rather than standing and letting it take them to the top.

'You're not here for our shopping date, are you?' Gemma checked, and Cat vaguely recalled a date that they had made a couple of weeks ago. They were both supposed to finish at four today and the plan had been to hit the shops, given that Cat would know by now if she was having a boy or girl.

They had had it all planned—they were going to head off for a late afternoon tea and Cat would reveal the news about the sex of her baby. Then they would shop for baby things in the appropriate colours and choose shoes for Cat and Mike's wedding, which was just over three weeks away.

That was how it was supposed to be.

This was how it was.

'You know how we discussed keeping things separate?' Cat felt as if her voice didn't belong to her as she spoke to her closest friend. 'Can I change my mind about that?'

And, because she and Gemma had been friends since way back in medical school, she didn't have to explain what she meant.

'Of course you can,' Gemma said, battling a feeling of dread. 'Let's go into my office.'

When Cat had found out that she was pregnant she had discussed with her family doctor, and also her fiancé, the potential pitfalls of having your closest friend as your obstetrician.

Against her own gut instinct, an esteemed colleague of Mike's was now overseeing her pregnancy.

She had walked out on both of them today.

Now Cat walked into her friend's office on shaky legs and, for the first time as Gemma's patient, took a seat, wondering how best to explain what had been going on in her life. The past two weeks she had dodged speaking with Gemma as best she could.

Gemma poured her a glass of water and Cat took a long drink as her friend waited patiently. Finally she caught her breath enough to speak.

'I had an ultrasound a couple of weeks ago,' she started. 'There were some problems... I know I could have spoken to you but Mike wanted to wait for all the test results to be in before we told anyone. *If* we told anyone...' Tears were now falling thick and fast but she had run out of sobs and so was able to continue. 'The results are not good, Gemma. They're not good at all. I had an amnio and the baby has Edwards syndrome...' Cat elaborated further. 'Full-form Edwards syndrome.' She looked at her friend and saw Gemma's small swallow as she took in the diagnosis.

'What does Mike say?'

Not only had Cat found out her baby was terribly sick, but also in these past two weeks her relationship had crumbled.

'Mike says that it's not part of the plan... Well, he didn't have the guts to say it like that. He said that as a paediatrician he knows better than most what the baby would be up against and what we'd be up against—the anomalies are very severe. There really isn't much hope that it will survive the birth and if it does it's likely to live only for a few hours.' Her voice was starting to rise. 'He says that it's not our fault, that we've every chance of a healthy baby and so we should put it behind us and try again...' Cat's eyes flashed in anger. 'He's a paediatrician, for God's sake, and he wants me to have a late abortion...'

'What do you want, Cat?' her friend gently broke in. 'Do you even know what you want?'

'A healthy baby.'

Gemma just looked.

'And that's not going to happen,' Cat said.

Finally she had accepted it.

She sat there in silence. It was the first glimpse of peace she had had in two weeks. Since the first ultrasound, at Mike's strong suggestion, they had kept the findings to themselves and so she had been holding it all in—somehow working as an emergency registrar, as well as carrying on with their wedding plans and doing her best to avoid catching up with Gemma.

At first Cat had woken in tears and dread for her baby each morning. Today, though, she had woken in anger and, looking at the back of her fiancé's head and seeing him deeply asleep, instead of waiting for him to wake up, she had dug him in the ribs.

'What's wrong?' Mike had turned to her rage and she had told him they were through. That even if, by some miracle, the amnio came back as normal today, there was nothing left of them.

The amnio hadn't come back as normal.

Cat had known that it wouldn't; she'd seen the ultrasound and nothing could magic the problems away.

It had been confirmation, that was all.

Now Gemma gave her the gift of a pause and Cat sat, feeling the little kicks of her baby inside her as well as the rapid thud of her own heart. Finally both settled down as she came to the decision she had been reaching towards since the news had first hit.

'I understand that it's different for everyone. Maybe

if I'd found out sooner I'd have had a termination.' She truly didn't know what she might have done then; she could only deal with her feelings now. 'But I'm twenty weeks pregnant. I know it's a boy and I can feel him move. He's moving right now.' She put a hand on her stomach and felt him, in there and alive and safe. 'Mike keeps saying it would be kinder but I'm starting to wonder, kinder for whom?'

Gemma was patient and Cat waited as she rang through to the hospital where Cat was being seen and all the results were transferred.

Gemma went through them carefully.

And she didn't leave it there; instead, she made a phone call to a colleague and Cat underwent yet another ultrasound.

Her baby was imperfect, from his too-little head to his tiny curved feet, but all Cat could see was her son. Gently Gemma told her that the condition was very severe, as she'd been told, and she concurred that if the baby survived birth he would live only for a little while.

'I want whatever time I have with him,' Cat said.

'I'll be there with you,' Gemma said. 'Mike might—'

'I'm not discussing it further with Mike,' Cat said. 'I'll tell him what I've decided and it's up to him what he does, but as a couple we're finished.'

'You don't have to make any rash decisions about your relationship. It's a lot for any couple to take in…'

'We're not a couple any more,' Cat said. 'I told him that this morning—as soon as things started to go wrong with the pregnancy, even before things went wrong, I felt as if I didn't have a voice. Well, I do and I'm having my baby.'

* * *

It was a long month, a difficult month but a very precious one.

Cat cancelled the wedding while knowing soon she would be arranging a funeral but she pushed that thought aside as best she could.

Her parents were little help. Her mother agreed with Mike; her father just disappeared into his study if ever Cat came round. But she had Greg, her brother, who cleared out all her things from Mike's house.

He didn't hit him, much to Cat's relief.

Almost, though!

And, of course, she had Gemma.

At the end of July and at twenty-five weeks gestation Cat went into spontaneous labour and Gemma delivered her a little son. Thomas Gregory Hayes. Thomas because she loved the name. Gregory, after her brother. Hayes because it was her surname.

Cat would treasure every minute of the two precious days and one night that Thomas lived.

Most of them.

His severe cleft palate meant she couldn't feed him, though she ached to. She would never get out of her mind the image of her mother's grimace when she'd seen her grandson and his deformities—Cat had asked her to leave.

For two days she had closed the door to her room on the maternity ward and had let only love enter.

Her brother, Gemma and her new boyfriend, Nigel, a couple of other lifelong friends, along with the medical staff helped her care for him—and all played their part.

When Cat had no choice but to sleep, Greg, Gemma

or Nigel nursed him and Thomas wasn't once, apart from having his nappy changed, put down.

His whole life Thomas knew only love.

After the funeral, when her parents and some other family members had tried to tell her that maybe Thomas's passing was a blessing, it was Gemma who held Cat's hand as she bit back a caustic response.

Instead of doing as suggested and putting it all behind her and attempting a new normal, Cat took all her maternity leave and hid for a while to grieve. But as her return-to-work date approached she felt less and less inclined to go back, especially as Mike still worked there.

She applied for a position in the accident and emergency department at the London Royal, where her baby had been born and where Gemma worked.

Four months to the day that she'd lost her son Cat stepped back out into the world... Only, she wasn't the same.

Instead, she was a far tougher version of her old self.

CHAPTER ONE

Seven years later

'YOU'RE FAR TOO cynical about men, Cat.'

'I don't think that I am,' Cat answered, 'though admittedly I'd love to be proven wrong. But, no, I'm taking a full year off men.'

Cat was busy packing. Just out of the shower she was wearing a dressing gown and her long, curly black hair was wrapped in a towel. As she pulled clothes out of her wardrobe she chatted to her close friend Gemma, who was lying on Cat's bed and answering emails on her phone.

They were two very busy women but they usually managed to catch up a couple of times a week, whether at the hospital canteen, a coffee shop or wine bar, or just a quick drop-in at the other's home.

This evening Cat was heading to Barcelona for an international emergency medicine conference, where she was going to be giving a talk the following morning. She had got off early from her shift at the hospital to pack and Gemma had popped around to finalise a few details for the following weekend. Gemma and

Nigel's twin boys, Rory and Marcus, were being christened and Cat was to be godmother to Rory.

They were used to catching up on the run. Any plans
they made were all too often cancelled at the last minute thanks to Cat's position as an accident and emergency consultant and Gemma juggling being a mother
to two eighteen-month-old boys as well as a full-time
obstetrician.

Their lives were similar in many ways and very different in others.

'So you and Rick have definitely broken up?' Gemma
checked that Cat's latest relationship was really over.

'He's been gone a month, so I'd say so!'

'You're not even going to think about it?'

'Why would I consider moving to Yorkshire when
I'm happy here?'

'Because that's what couples do.'

'Oh, so if Nigel suddenly decided that he wanted
to move to…' Cat thought for a moment and then remembered that Nigel was taking French lessons. 'If
he wanted to move to France, you're telling me that
you'd go?'

'Not without consideration,' Gemma said. 'Given that
I'm the breadwinner there would have to be a good reason, but if Nigel really wanted to, then, of course, I'd give
it some thought. Relationships are about compromise.'

'And it's always the woman who has to be the one
to compromise,' Cat said, but Gemma shook her head.

'I don't agree.'

'You've never played the dating game in your thirties.'

'Yes, I have—Nigel and I only married last year.'

'Ah, but the two of you had been going out for ever
before then. It's different at our age, Gemma. Men

might say that they don't mind independent working women and, of course, they don't—just as long as you're home before them and have the dinner on.'

'Rubbish!' Gemma responded from her happily married vantage point. 'Look at Nigel—I work, he gave up teaching and stays home and looks after the children, and the house and me...'

'Yes.' Cat smiled. 'Well, you and Nigel are a very rare exception to my well-proven theory.'

But Gemma suddenly had other things on her mind when she saw what Cat was about to add to her case. 'Please don't take them,' Gemma said, referring to Cat's running shoes. 'They're ugly.'

'They're practical,' Cat said. 'And they are also very comfortable. I'm hoping to squeeze in a little bit of sightseeing on Sunday afternoon once the conference wraps up. There's a modern art museum, hopefully I'll get some inspiration for this room...'

She looked around at the disgusting beige walls and beige carpet and beige curtains and wished she knew what she wanted to do with the room.

Gemma got off the bed and went to Cat's wardrobe and took out some espadrilles.

'Take these instead.'

'For walking?'

'Yes, Cat, for walking, not striding...' She peered into her friend's luggage. 'Talk about shades of grey—that's the saddest case I've ever seen. You're going to Spain!'

'I'm going to Spain for two nights to catch the end of a conference. I'm not going on a holiday. I shan't even see the beach,' Cat pointed out. 'I wish that I *was* flying off for a holiday,' she said, and then sat on the bed. 'I hate July so much.'

'I know you do.'

It had been seven years since Thomas had died.

She didn't lug her grief around all the time but on days like today it hurt. Gemma smiled as her friend went into her bedside drawer and took out his photo. Cat kept it there; it was close enough that she could look at it any time and removed enough not to move her to tears. The drawer also meant she didn't have to explain the most vital piece of her past to any lovers until she was ready to.

She simply found it too painful.

'Rick asked how likely I was to have another one like him,' Cat admitted. It was what had really caused the end of her latest relationship. 'I told him about Thomas and then I showed him his photo…'

'He's not a doctor, Cat,' Gemma said. 'It's a normal question to ask. It's one you've asked.'

'I know that. It was more the way…' She was so hypersensitive to people's reactions when they saw her son but she smiled when Gemma spoke on.

'I loved how he smiled if you touched his little feet,' Gemma said, and her words confirmed to Cat that she was very blessed to have such a wonderful friend. 'He's so beautiful.'

He was.

Not to others perhaps but they had both seen his lovely eyes and felt his little fingers curve around theirs and they had felt his soft skin and heard his little cries.

And this was the hard part.

It was late July and she'd be away on *those* days.

The day of Thomas's birth and also the day that he had died.

'Do I take his photo with me?' Cat asked, and Gemma thought for a moment.

'I don't think you need his photo to remember him,' she said.

'But I feel guilty leaving him in the drawer.'

'Leave him with me, then,' Gemma said. 'I'll have a long gaze.'

Yes, she had the very best friend in the world, Cat thought as she handed over her most precious possession, and because she was going to start crying Cat changed the subject. 'Hey, did you have any luck tracking down that dress for the christening?'

'Nope.'

Gemma shook her head as she put the photo in her bag. 'I knew that I should have just bought it when I saw it. It was perfect.'

'It was very nice, but...' Cat didn't continue. A white broderie anglaise halter-neck with a flowing skirt was a bit over the top for Cat's tastes but, then, that was Gemma.

And this was her.

She pulled on some white linen pants and a coloured top *and* added the espadrilles.

'Am I girlie enough for you now?'

'You look great.' Gemma laughed. 'It's once you get there that worries me. With those clothes you'll just blend in with all the others...'

'Which is exactly my intention,' Cat said. 'I have to go soon.'

'But your flight's not till nine.'

'I know but I've booked in to get my hair blow-dried on the way.'

Her long black curls would be straightened, just as

they were twice a week. Cat always washed it herself before she went to the hairdresser's, though.

It saved time.

They headed downstairs, chatting as Cat did a few last-minute things. 'You're speaking in the morning?' Gemma checked.

'At nine.' Cat nodded. 'I'd have loved to have flown last night but I couldn't get away. Hamish isn't back till tomorrow and Andrew is covering me this weekend. Same old. It would have been nice to stay on for a bit and spend a few days in Barcelona…'

'Are you ever going to take some time off?'

'I'm off in October for three weeks.' Cat smiled. 'My exams will be done and I'm going to celebrate by decorating my bedroom. I can't wait to turn it into something that doesn't make me want to sleep downstairs on the sofa.'

'You've done an amazing job with the house.'

Last year, after a year of looking, Cat had bought a small two-bedroom home in a leafy London suburb. It was a twenty-minute drive to work at night, which meant, if Cat was on call, that she had to stay at the hospital. Yes, perhaps she could have bought somewhere just a little bit closer but the drive did mean that when she left the hospital, she really left the building.

Here, she could pull on tatty shorts and a T-shirt and get on with her second love—knocking down walls, plastering and painting. The house had been a real renovator's delight and Cat had delighted in renovating it.

The ghastly purple carpet had been ripped up to expose floorboards that, once sanded and oiled, brought a warmth to the house. A false wall in the lounge had been removed to reveal a fireplace and the once-purple-themed bathroom was now tiled white with dark wood fittings and had a gorgeous claw-foot bath.

'Will you sell it once you've decorated the bedroom?'

'I really don't know,' Cat admitted, tipping milk down the sink. 'Initially that was the plan, but now I love the place and want to simply enjoy it, but…'

'But?'

'I've really enjoyed doing it up bit by bit. I'm going to miss that.'

'After your bedroom you've still got the garden to make over.'

'Oh, no!' Cat shook her head. 'I'll get someone in to do that.'

As they headed out, Cat locked up and Gemma looked at the small front garden.

'It's the size of a stamp,' Gemma pointed out. There was just a rickety path and two neglected flower beds, and the back garden, Gemma knew, was a small strip of grass and an old wooden shed. 'You could have it sorted in a few days…'

'Nope!' Cat smiled. 'I have black thumbs.'

They said goodbye on the street.

'We'll catch up properly soon,' Cat promised. Both women knew that they wouldn't get much of a chance to gossip at the christening. 'I'll come over to yours after the conference. I haven't seen the twins for ages. I'll bring them a stuffed donkey each back from Spain.'

'Please, don't!' Gemma winced and glanced at her phone to check the time. 'Ooh, I might make it home in time to give them their bath before bed. Nigel's cooking a romantic dinner for the two of us tonight…'

'Lovely.'

'Enjoy Spain,' Gemma called. 'You might find your-self some sexy Spanish flamenco dancer or matador...'

'At an emergency medicine conference?' Cat laughed. 'I don't think there's much chance of that.'

'Well, a gorgeous waiter, with come-to-bed eyes and—'

'Oh, please!'

'Why not?' Gemma winked. 'If you can't manage a love life, then pencil a few flings into that overcrowded diary of yours.'

'There's another conference in Spain the following week that *you* might want to consider attending,' Cat said in a dry voice. 'Sexual health. You, as an obstetrician, better than anyone must know the perils of casual sex.'

'Of course I do, but sex *is* healthy.' Gemma grinned and then she looked at Cat. She wanted to pick up an imaginary sledgehammer of her own and knock down the wall that had gone up around her friend since her baby's death.

'Do you know what's brilliant about a one-night stand, Cat?'

'Gemma...' Cat shook her head. She really didn't have time to stand and chat but her friend persisted.

Gemma loved to talk about sex! 'He doesn't have to be perfect, you don't have to worry how you might slot into each other's lives and whether he leaves the toilet seat up or is going to support you in your career and all that stuff, because you're not looking for a potential Mr Right. He can be Mr Wrong, Mr Bad, Mr Whatever-It-Is-You-Fancy. God, but I miss one-night stands.'

'Does Nigel know your theory?'

'Of course he doesn't.' Gemma grinned. 'Nigel still thinks he was my second...' They both laughed for a moment but then Gemma stood firm. 'It's time for you to have some fun, Cat. Doctor's orders—you're to buy some condoms at the airport.'

Cat laughed and waved and got into her car and headed for the hairdresser's.

She adored Gemma.

And Nigel.

But…

What she hadn't said to her very good friend was that, as much as it might work for Gemma, she really didn't want a Nigel of her own. She didn't want someone asking what was for dinner every night, but nor did she want to be the one coming in after work and doing the 'Hi, honey, I'm home' thing.

Still, there wasn't time to dwell on it all.

She parked her car in her usual spot behind the church and grabbed her bag and walked quickly to the hairdresser's. She pushed on the door but it didn't open and she frowned and then she saw the 'Closed' sign.

'Don't do this to me, Glynn…'

He never forgot her appointments and Cat had been very specific about the time for today when she had seen him on Monday. Glynn knew that she had a plane to catch and that she would be pushed for time.

'Breathe,' Cat mumbled as she accepted that no amount of rattling the door was going to make Glynn suddenly appear.

It's a hair appointment, that's all, she told herself. There would be a hairdresser at the hotel. Only, her presentation was at nine in the morning and she'd wanted to have a leisurely breakfast in her room and calm herself down before that.

And it was Thomas's birthday tomorrow.

She was not going to cry over a missed hair appointment.

Cat wasn't crying over that as she drove to the airport. Instead, she was wishing the boot was full of presents and wrapping paper and that she was dashing to pick up a birthday cake...

Why was it still so hard?

So, as she could not get her thick curly hair smoothed into long, glossy and straight, she bought some hair serum at the airport, then checked in her luggage and headed through with ages to spare.

She went to the loos and sorted her hair as best she could, deciding she would straighten it tonight and again in the morning, but for now she tied it back and headed out.

She took a seat and read through her talk on her tablet. It was about palliative care and its place in the emergency department and, really, she knew it back to front and inside out. She had done hours of research and all her meticulous notes and patient studies now came down to one talk.

And then what?

Exams.

And then?

Cat blew out a breath.

Her career was a little like her house renovation.

The day she'd moved in Cat had stared at the purple carpet and the purple tiles that would take for ever to get off. It had seemed unlikely, near impossible, that she would ever get there and yet here she was, just a bedroom and a garden away from completion.

She had, through high school, always wanted to be a surgeon yet as a medical student she had stepped into the emergency department and had been quickly ushered into Resus to observe the treatment of a patient who had just come in.

A cyclist had lain there unconscious with a massive head injury. Cat had watched in silent awe as the staff had brought his dire condition under control. His heart, which hadn't been beating, had been restarted. His airway had been secured and the seizures that had then started to rack his body had been halted with drugs.

She had been sure at first that he would die and yet he had made it to Theatre and then on to Intensive Care.

She had followed him up and found out a week later that he had been transferred to a ward. She had gone in to see him, expecting what, she hadn't known. Certainly not a young man sitting up in bed, laughing and talking with his girlfriend, who was sitting by his side.

He should be dead, Cat had thought, though, of course, she didn't say that. Instead, she'd chatted to him for a few moments, unable to truly comprehend that here he was, not just alive but laughing and living.

Emergency medicine had become her passion right there and then. Yes, at twenty years old she had known she was a long way off being as skilled as the staff who had attended the cyclist that day.

Slowly she had got there, though.

And now here she was, coming to the top of her game.

So why the restlessness?

Cat glanced up at the board and rolled her eyes when she saw that her flight was delayed, and decided to wander around the shops.

Oh, there was Gemma's dress!

She was sure that it was, though looking at the price tag, not quite sure enough to buy it without checking, so she took a photo and fired a quick text to her friend.

Is this it?

It was, and Gemma promised to love her for ever and forgive any stuffed donkeys she might bring home for the twins if Cat would buy it for her.

She bought some duty-free perfume too, as well as her favourite lip gloss and...no—no condoms.

Finally the plane was boarding and Cat, along with her purchases, was on her way.

She didn't read through her talk again. She dozed most of the way, trying to drown out the sound of over-excited children and their parents. As they disembarked she almost forgot the dress but luckily she grabbed it at the last minute.

Very luckily, as it turned out.

Having spent hours watching an empty baggage carousel, seeing the shutters go down on all the airport shops and filling in numerous forms, she was doing her level best to hold it together as she climbed out of the taxi and walked into the hotel. It was close to midnight.

Her luggage was lost, her hair was a joke.

And tomorrow, at nine, she had to deliver the most important presentation of her life.

CHAPTER TWO

CAT WOKE BEFORE her breakfast was delivered and lay there.

She remembered a day seven years ago and wished, how she wished, that there was a seven-year-old waiting to open his birthday presents and to sing 'Happy Birthday' to.

It was a hard picture to paint and each year it got harder.

Was Mike in this happy family picture and did Thomas have brothers and sisters now?

No, she didn't miss Mike and the perfect world they had been building. She missed, on Thomas's behalf, all that he had been denied.

She couldn't afford to cry, especially given the fact she had no make-up with her and so she headed to the bathroom to set to work with the little she had.

With her heavy-duty hair straighteners neatly packed in her lost luggage, she was very grateful for the hair serum she had bought and applied an awful lot in an attempt to tame her long, wild curly hair.

When her breakfast was delivered she walked out onto the balcony and tried to calm herself with the spectacular view of the Mediterranean. It was just after seven but already the air was warm. The coffee was hot and strong and Cat tried to focus on her speech. *It will be fine,* she told herself, refusing to fall apart because she didn't have the perfect, *perfect* pale grey suit and the pale ballet pumps in the softest buttery leather to wear.

They were here to hear her words, Cat reminded herself.

Yet she couldn't quite convince herself that it didn't matter what she wore or how she looked.

Neutral.

That was how she always tried to appear.

There was nothing neutral about her today, she thought as she slipped on Gemma's dress.

Her rather ample bust was accentuated by the lace, the halter-neck showed far too much of her brown back—the tan was from painting the window frames on her last lot of days off, rather than lying on the beach. Her hair she tied back with the little white band that came with the shower cap in the bathroom and then she covered it with a thick strand of black hair.

A squirt of duty-free perfume, a slick of lip gloss and she would simply have to do.

Yet, she thought, having tied up her espadrilles, as she stood and looked in the mirror, while never in a million years would she have chosen this outfit for anything related to work, she liked how it looked. She wouldn't even have chosen it for anything out of work either. Generally she was in shorts or jeans when sorting out the renovations. Yes, she liked how she looked today. It reminded her of how she had looked before she'd had...

Cat halted herself right there.

She simply could not afford the luxury of breaking down.

Tonight, Cat told herself. Tonight she would order room service and a bottle of wine and reminisce.

Today she had to get on.

She had one last flick through her notes and then she headed out to register for the conference and also to check that everything was in place for her talk.

She was just putting her swipe card in her bag when the elevator doors opened and she looked up to an empty lift, bar one occupant.

Bar One was tall and unshaven with grey eyes and his dark hair was a touch too long yet he looked effortlessly smart in dark pants and a white shirt. All this she noted as she stood there and briefly wondered if she should simply let this lift go.

For some bizarre reason that seemed far easier than stepping in.

'Buenos días,' Bar One said, and then frowned at her indecision as to whether or not to enter.

'Buenos días,' Cat replied, gave him a brisk smile and stepped in. The floor number for the function rooms had already been pressed and as she glanced to the side and down, anywhere other than his eyes, she noted he too was an owner of the softest buttery leather shoes.

His luggage clearly hadn't been lost.

And neither was he wearing socks.

Three, Cat thought as his cologne met her nostrils and she found herself doing a very quick audit as to the number of garments that would remain on his lovely body once he'd kicked off those shoes.

Talk about thinking like a man!

She blamed Gemma, of course. It was her fault for

putting such ideas in her head, Cat decided as the lift opened at the next floor and unfortunately no one got in.

He said something else in Spanish and Cat shook her head. 'Actually, *buenos días* is as far as my Spanish goes.'

'Oh,' he said. 'I thought you were a local.'

His accent was English and he had just delivered a compliment indeed, because the locals, Cat had worked out during her prolonged time at the airport last night, were a pretty stunning lot.

'Nope.' She shook her head.

The lift doors opened and he wished her a good day as he went to step out.

'And you,' she offered.

'Sadly not,' he replied, and nodded to the gathering crowd outside the elevators. 'I'm working.'

'So am I,' she said, and he stood there a little taken aback as he let her out first.

Oh!

Dominic had thought she was on her way to some… Well, he'd had no idea really where she might have been on her way to but talk about a sight for sore eyes.

She had a very, very nice back, he decided as he followed her over to the registration desk, where there was a small line-up.

A very tense back, he noted as she reached into her bag and pulled out her phone.

'I'm Dominic…'

Cat had just had a text from the airline to say her luggage had been found. At Gatwick! It *should* be with her later this afternoon and could she confirm that she was still at the same hotel. She barely turned around as she fired back a text and told him her name. 'Cat.'

'Short for?'

She really didn't have time for small talk and she knew, just knew, because her back was scalding from his eyes, that it was more than small talk he was offering. 'I'm actually a bit busy at the moment…'

'Well, that's some name—no wonder you have to shorten it.'

Her fingers hesitated over the text she was typing and she gave a small, presumably unseen smile.

Dominic, even if he couldn't see her mouth, knew from behind that she'd smiled.

He watched as that rigid spinal column very briefly relaxed a notch and those tense shoulders dropped a fraction.

Still, he left things there. He certainly wasn't going to pursue a conversation that had been so swiftly shut down.

Instead, he looked at the brochure with only mild interest. He loathed this type of thing. He'd only put his hand up because he'd needed the update hours and because his parents and sister lived nearby—it would be a good chance to catch up. As well as that, he was seriously considering moving here.

He kept himself up to date and found these presentations pointless, or rather bullet-pointed—most speakers had everything on slides and it was rather like being read a bedtime story out loud. At thirty-two years of age, he would rather read for himself.

'Dominic!'

He glanced over at the sound of his name and gave a smile when he saw that it was someone he had studied with in London.

'How are you, Hugh?'

Cat stood there, trying not to notice the delicious depth to his voice. Not that he spoke much; it was his friend who did most of the talking.

She registered and was told that one of the organisers would be with her shortly to take her to where her talk was being held.

'This way, Dr Hayes...'

Dominic stopped in mid-sentence as Cat was led away. She must be speaking, he realised, and, quite shamelessly, he glanced through the list of speakers and found out her name for himself.

Catriona Hayes.

And then he saw the topic of her talk.

Palliative Care and its Place in the Emergency Department.

Absolutely *not* what he needed.

So, instead of hearing her speak, he took himself off to listen to a disaster management panel but his mind wasn't really there. Half an hour later he slipped out unnoticed and slipped into where she was talking.

She noticed him come in.

There was a tiny pause in her talk as she glanced at the opening door and saw *him* enter.

He didn't take a seat but leant against the back wall with arms folded. There was a small falter in her flawless talk as he took his place but then she continued where she'd left off.

'Of course, it's great for the patient when they receive a terminal diagnosis to take that break, that trek, that overseas trip. It can just be a touch inconvenient for us when they present, minus notes, diagnosis, information and family. And so, because that's what we do, we leap in and do our best to save them.' She looked out at the room. 'Of course, it's not so great for the patient either when they come around to our smiling faces… It's hard on the staff when a four-year-old presents on Christmas Eve. It's our instinct to do all that we can. There isn't always time to speak at length with the family when they come rushing in with their child but listen we must…'

It wasn't like a bedtime story with everything spelt out. Yes, there were bullet points, but they were only brief outlines and, for Dominic, a lot of her words felt like bullets as she filled in the gaps.

Brusque was her delivery as she covered things such as legalities, next of kin, patient rights. For good measure, staff, relative and patient guilt was thrown in too.

He listened, he felt, yet his face never moved a muscle.

As she finished, he left the room and went off to lunch but, even if it smelt fantastic, food didn't appeal and instead he took some water and went out onto a large balcony.

Unlike others who had been at her talk Dominic didn't go up and congratulate her. Neither did he tell her that her talk had touched a nerve.

He could have walked over and said how his wife had got up in the night and wandered off. He could have said how angry she had been to wake up two days later in ICU and that he could still see the reproach in her eyes, as if Dominic had somehow failed her because she'd lived.

No, he didn't need or want *that* look from Cat and he was tired, so tired of women who gave out sympathy and understanding.

He'd prefer something lighter.

Or darker, perhaps! Hopefully, Dominic thought, heading back in, so too would she.

CHAPTER THREE

IT WOULD BE an absolute lie to say the attraction hadn't been as instant as it was mutual.

All through the lunch break there was a knot high in Cat's stomach and tension in her muscles and she knew that she was bracing herself for him to come over.

Except he didn't.

Ouch!

She wasn't sure if she even wanted him to.

There was an arrogance to him, not that she couldn't handle arrogant men; she'd dealt with more than her share of them.

No, it was something else about Dominic that had her seriously rattled—the presumption of sex.

From the briefest conversation she had gleaned that much. From the roam of his eyes on the bare skin of her back, from the sullen, one-sided conversation with his friend that had told her his mind was on her.

From the corner of her eye she watched as he came in from the balcony and then went over and chatted to a group.

She was incredibly aware of his presence and it had been a long time since she had felt anything close to that.

Not that it mattered.

She was being ignored.

Funny, but she knew that it was deliberate and what was stranger still it made her smile. 'Excellent talk…' A middle-aged blond man came over and introduced himself. 'Gordon.' He smiled.

'Cat.'

It was a very long thirty minutes.

Gordon simply didn't let up and Cat couldn't really make her excuses and leave because he was talking about his wife who had died and the total hash that had been made in the emergency department.

It was a busman's holiday for Cat as she lined up for the lovely buffet lunch and Gordon followed her with his plate.

'Two hours, we waited, Cat,' he said, and she glanced up and met those gorgeous grey eyes and saw that Dominic was now unashamedly watching her.

Rescue me, her green ones said, but he looked away.

'And then…' Gordon continued to tell her about his wife's IV coming out and the drugs that didn't go in. Yes, it was a sad story, but it was a story she dealt with every day and it was her lunch break.

'Paella, please.' Cat held out her plate to the waiter but he shook his head.

'We're waiting for some more…'

Cat chose some odd noodle salad, just to get away, but Gordon chose the same and he was off again. He sat next to her at a high table and droned on and on.

She met Dominic's eyes again and this time he smiled.

You missed your chance, his eyes said.

I've changed my mind, was her silent plea.

Well, you're too late!

He yawned and pulled out his pamphlet and with a very small smirk walked off.

What a bastard.

Cat laughed and then turned to Gordon's confused expression.

'I said, then she died…'

'Sorry, I thought you said then she…' Cat let out a breath. 'What a terrible time you had.'

She just didn't need to hear about it today of all days.

She didn't see Dominic again all afternoon, not that it mattered by then. At 5:00 p.m. when she got back to her room to find that her luggage still hadn't arrived, it wasn't the Spanish-speaking English doctor who was on her mind.

It was Thomas.

She didn't want to go down for dinner in an hour and be sociable.

Room service seemed a far better idea.

A huge plate of paella.

A bottle of wine.

She wished she'd brought his photo.

But there had been too many sad birthdays and, suddenly realising that she had a very small window if she didn't want to spend tomorrow dressed in Gemma's dress or linen pants that were more suitable for travel, she headed out.

She found herself in a large department store, explaining to an orange woman that, apart from a lipstick, she had no make-up with her.

'My luggage was lost,' she said.

The woman was so horrified on her behalf that Cat actually smiled. 'It's fine…'

It was.

So much so that instead of buying loads of make-up and then heading upstairs to the *ropa de señora* section to purchase a chic Spanish outfit Cat wandered out and found herself drawn to a busy market. There were gorgeous dresses blowing in the late-afternoon breeze and they were nothing like what she usually wore.

If she walked into work dressed as she was today, it would draw comment. Here, apart from a couple of vaguely familiar faces from conferences of long ago, no one knew her.

It was incredibly freeing—she could be whoever she chose to be.

Cat took her time with her purchases. She chose a loose long dress in lilac and shorts that were very short, along with a top and a stringy-looking bikini. And, she decided, instead of the museum on Sunday afternoon she was going to the beach.

She liked Barcelona.

Far more than she had expected to.

It was cosmopolitan, busy yet friendly, colourful and hot.

Walking back into the hotel, she was about to take her purchases up and get changed and, instead of hiding in her room, perhaps head out for dinner by herself when she saw him.

Dominic.

'I was wondering where you were,' he said by way of greeting, and Cat liked it that he was direct.

'I went shopping…' She was about to explain that her luggage was lost but then decided she didn't have to explain anything.

'Cat!' a voice boomed, and she turned and saw that

Gordon was bearing down on her. 'There's a group of us heading to the hotel restaurant. Why don't you join us?'

'Oh, I'd love to but I can't,' Cat said. 'I'm expecting a call. A conference call. I—'

'Maybe after?' Gordon checked.

'I'll try.'

Gordon smiled over to Dominic. 'Do you have plans or would you like to join us?'

Dominic dealt with things far more effortlessly than Cat. 'I've already got plans, but thank you for asking.'

As the group walked off they were left standing.

'Liar,' Dominic said. 'You don't have a conference call you have to get to.'

'Was it obvious?' she groaned.

'To me it was.' Dominic nodded. 'Liars always have a need to elaborate. You'd know that, working in Emergency.'

'I know,' she said. 'So would Gordon.'

'Is he a friend?'

Cat shook her head.

'A colleague?'

'No.'

'So why not just say no if it's something that you don't want to do?'

'I know that I should. I just feel bad…'

'Well, don't—he's far too busy banging on about his late wife to notice what others are feeling.'

She felt her nostrils tighten. 'That was mean.'

'No,' Dominic refuted. 'He tried to run the whole sorry story by me yesterday. What's mean is buttonholing a relative stranger and completely ruining their lunch.'

He shrugged.

He was dismissive.

She didn't like that and she was about to head off when he halted her in her tracks.

'Do you want dinner away from the hotel?'

'I've got a conference call to make,' she said, and gave him a tight smile.

'Sure?' he said.

Usually, yes.

She didn't like his dismissal of Gordon but, apart from that, he was, well, deliciously overwhelming.

Gemma's words were ringing in her ears. He didn't have to be perfect, he didn't have to be anything other than…

God, but she fancied him.

She could have left it there, just walked off and it would have been over. There were no games, no pretence, just his question, which she now answered truthfully. 'Dinner away from the hotel sounds great,' she said. 'I'll just…' She held up her bags and was about to suggest that she take them up and meet him back here in…half an hour, or however long it took to get showered and dressed.

But by then she'd have changed her mind, she knew.

Half an hour from now she'd be calling Reception to pass on a message to him.

Or she could just go with how she felt now.

'I'll just ask Reception if they can take my bags up.'

The streets were noisy and he navigated them easily and took her to a place that Cat would never have found had she explored on her own—a few streets along from the strip the hotel was on. They walked down a stone stairwell and to an *asado* restaurant that was noisy and smoky, even with the open area out the back.

'So, are you pleased your talk is over?' he asked when they were tucked away at a table.

'Very,' Cat said. 'I can relax now.'

And relax she did, admitting she had no clue about Spanish wine and letting him choose.

'Are you staying till Monday?' he asked, and she shook her head.

'No, I fly out tomorrow evening—I'm back at work on Monday. I wish…'

'Wish what?'

'Well, I was really only thinking of my talk when I booked the flights. I wasn't actually expecting to like Barcelona so much. I should have tagged on a couple of days' annual leave and done a bit of exploring.'

'You always could.'

It sounded very tempting but it was a little too late for that now. 'We're pretty short on staff at the moment. My colleague Andrew is going on leave and Hamish, he's the other consultant…' She rolled her eyes. 'I'm sure you know how it is.'

'Remind me,' he said.

'Remind you?' she checked. 'Where do you work?'

'Scotland.'

She waited for him to elaborate, which he did but it was vague rather than specific. 'I work a little bit here and a longer bit there,' Dominic said, and Cat then felt the scrutiny of his gaze and the message behind his words as he spoke on. 'I don't like to be tied to one place.' And then he elaborated properly. 'Or one person.'

Well, that certainly told her.

In part, Cat was tempted to simply get up and leave. It wasn't a meal, they both knew that. This wasn't two like-minded colleagues sharing a dinner after a busy day at a conference.

This was exactly what the dear Dr Gemma had ordered.

Cat was old enough to know it.

Their knees were nudging and suddenly her lips felt too big for her face without the resting place of his mouth.

She felt his eyes glance down as she reached for her drink and from the sudden weight in her breasts she knew where his glance had been. Only, it wasn't sleazy. Or, if it was, it came from both of them because she'd been doing the same to his bum a little earlier as he'd walked down the stairs.

No, this wasn't just dinner.

'Do you have a problem with that?' he said, and she blinked as she tried to remember the conversation. Oh, yes, the not-tied-to-one-person thing, he was asking if she had a problem with that.

Did she?

Yes, a part of her did.

Very much so.

A part of her wanted to tell him where he could shove his arrogant, presumptuous offer and head back to her hotel room and bury herself in the grief of today.

Yet the other part of Cat thrummed in suspense. Could she simply let loose and enjoy a night of passion with a very beautiful man with the cast-iron guarantee of no future?

It was refreshingly tempting.

He was seriously beautiful. Far more so than she was used to.

He was also rather more brusque and arrogant than she would choose, just rather too alpha for her.

She was tired, so tired of the inevitable let-down in relationships, the starting gun of hope, the numerous false starts and then the sprint that turned into an exhausting jog, and then standing bent, hands on thighs, and admitting defeat, because the two of you were just not going to make it to the finish line.

She was surprised at the ease of her decision.

'No.' Cat finally smiled. 'I have no problem with that.'

'Good.'

Housekeeping sorted, she tried to focus on the menu but, at thirty-four, she felt she'd just passed her driving test and been given the keys but was far from skilled enough to drive.

'Están listos para ordenar?'

The waiter came over and presumably asked if they were ready to order.

'I'll have paella.' She handed back the menu.

'The chicken here,' Dominic said, 'is the best you'll ever taste…'

Her eyes narrowed. Usually she'd say that she'd like the paella, thank you for interfering. She certainly didn't need a man choosing her food and yet as she glanced around, sure enough, the locals were eating the chicken.

Oh, he was so far from her usual fare but, no, he didn't need to be perfect tonight.

'When in Spain…' She shrugged.

She had the chicken and, as he had promised, it was amazing.

'Lemony, herby and so fat and juicy,' Cat commented on her second mouthful.

'And salty,' Dominic said. 'We'll be up all night, guzzling water…'

He was presumptuous.

She knew, though, that he was right.

The rest of the world, the past, the future, was like rain as they huddled, as if under some imaginary umbrella, and enjoyed now—the spectacular food, the music that filled the restaurant.

They barely talked about work. She said something about being the only female consultant and how they gave every gynae patient to her. He mentioned how he'd lived in London till a couple of years ago, just half an hour or so away from her.

But then work got left behind and she found out how he loved the architecture in Edinburgh but was fast falling in love with Spain.

And she told him about her passion for renovation, and her obsession with wallpaper, how she could spend hours leafing through sample books but, even then, you could never quite know how it would look once up.

Usually she never got to that part as eyes had long since glazed over with boredom.

His glazed with lust.

'Do you put it up yourself?' Dominic asked.

'I do.' She smiled.

'I feel emasculated.'

'Oh, I doubt you could ever be that.'

It was Dominic who then smiled.

Was it wrong? she wondered as they danced.

Was it wrong to be dancing and happy on his birthday?

Tonight it felt right.

A sexy flamenco dancer was kicking his heels and strumming away and then, when he slowed things down,

Cat felt her cheeks blaze with fire for sins not yet committed as Dominic pulled her into him.

His fingers ran lightly down her bare back and it felt utterly blissful.

'Fourteen hours later than I'd have preferred,' Dominic said into her ear, because that was how long it had been since he'd first itched for the feel of that sexy spine beneath his fingers.

'Well, I'm glad for your sake that you waited,' she said, imagining her reaction had he been so bold.

His touch didn't feel bold now; it felt right.

When the music ended they made it back to their table and when the bill came Cat did her usual and put her card down.

'We can go halves,' she said as he picked up the card to hand it back to her.

'Don't do that, Cat.'

'What?'

'Ruin a perfectly good night.'

If she were setting the ground rules for the future, she'd have insisted on paying her way.

Instead, they were setting the ground rules for tonight and she shivered in the warm night air as they headed for the hotel.

They walked back along the beach. It was after eleven but not really dark thanks to a near full moon and, despite the hour, the beach was far from deserted.

'There are some gorgeous beaches not far from here,' he said. 'Are you still determined to head back without seeing the place?'

'I am, though I wish I'd known just how much I'd like it,' she admitted. 'I'm going to come again but next time for a holiday. You're here a lot, then?'

'Quite a bit,' Dominic said. 'I have family here.'

'Oh.'

She ached to know more about him but Reticent was possibly his middle name because, apart from long conversations about everything and nothing, he gave away little.

The only thing she was sure of was their attraction.

'Which is why,' he continued, 'when I saw the conference was being held this year in Barcelona I decided to combine both. I'm very glad now that I did.' He turned her around and she looked into his dark eyes and his face. He was unreadable. 'I wish you had got here on Thursday.'

'Why?' she asked, her brain a bit sluggish with his mouth so close. She was far too used to focusing on work and she assumed that she must have missed some spectacular talk, or some cutting-edge revelation. The answer was far more basic than that.

'We could have had three nights instead of one.'

Still, he didn't kiss her, though she ached, *ached* for him to do so, but he just smiled in the dark like a beautiful devil and then they walked on.

Back at the hotel Cat was breathless, though not from walking, as they stepped into the foyer. They went through Reception and there was a lot of noise coming from the bar from their fellow attendees.

'Did you want to go to the bar?' Dominic offered.

'Yes.'

'Again,' he said, 'she lies.'

Cat smiled. 'She does.'

They headed for the elevators.

No, he didn't ask her for her floor.

He pressed his.

They stood backs against opposite walls facing each other as the lift groaned its way up, letting people in, letting people out.

And his eyes never left her face.

With three floors remaining they were finally alone and still he did not beckon.

Stay, Cat told herself, though she felt like a Labrador waiting for Christmas dinner.

Ping!

She walked slowly only because he did.

And his very steady hand swiped the card and opened the door to his room.

Would he offer her a drink? Cat wondered as she looked around.

The room was the same as hers, except it smelt of his cologne and there was a suitcase on the floor.

And then there was no time for further observation because he turned her to him and finally there was the bliss of his mouth. It was the roughest ever kiss and tasted divine. His tongue, his lips, his hands, the hunger in him was so consuming that there was no room for thought. She hadn't been kissed like this since—well, since for ever. His tongue was wicked, his hands pressing into her head and his body just primed and ready, because she could feel him.

She ached to feel him, so much so that the three garments of clothing she'd assumed he was wearing—was it only this morning?—were being unbuttoned and unzipped by Cat as his mouth never left her face.

He halted her briefly, long enough to retrieve his wallet, because of course he carried condoms, and she watched as he deftly put one on and so thick and hard was he that she played with him for a moment as he removed her dress.

She heard a brief tear and knew she would be up all week sewing Gemma's dress as it was now a white puddle on the floor.

She'd think about that later. Right now she was concentrating on him as his tongue met with her ear and she just about came in midair at the thought of him inside her.

Her bra was gone. She knew that because his mouth was on her breast as his hands slid her panties down.

And then she felt herself being lifted.

Not just onto him, but lifted out herself.

Out of grief, out of control, out of everything she knew.

Her shoulders met the wall and then he entered her and filled her, so rapidly and completely that it hurt enough to shout.

'Yes,' he said, and his mouth moved under her hair and his fingers met the back of her neck as he ground into her.

Cat wasn't used to being so thoroughly taken. A bit of foreplay might have been nice, but then she'd never been so close to coming in her life.

She was thoroughly rattled in the nicest of ways. He just kept thrusting in and she held on to her own hands behind his neck and then of her own accord was grinding down.

It felt amazing.

Just that.

It felt so amazing that he knew, more than she did herself, about what she liked.

Oh, she liked it rough.

She liked the intensity of him and the deep, rapid

thrusts and the way he stopped kissing her and stared her down.

He felt the tension and thank God for that because he was past consideration. He could feel the clamp of her thighs around him and the heat of her centre and had moved to the point of no return just as she started to pulse.

He loved orgasms, he met them regularly, but there was something so intense about hers, something so intrinsically matched to his, that she drove him on to more.

To get back to her mouth and rougher kisses and deeper thrusts and then he felt it, the slight collapse of her spinal column and the slump of her shoulders as she rested her head on his and he knew she was smiling.

Even as he shot the last of himself into her, he knew she was smiling and somehow that made him smile too.

No guilt, no regret, they met each other's eyes and kissed again but without haste this time.

Then he took her to bed and they lay there a moment before she was back to his mouth, down to his hips, and they did it all over again.

And again.

CHAPTER FOUR

DESPITE HAVING SLEPT for all of an hour, Dominic woke before sunrise.

Just as he always did.

Even if he went back to sleep afterwards, his body clock still dictated that he watch the sun come in.

He glanced at the clock and it was just after four and he knew where he needed to be.

Where they needed to be.

'Cat,' he said. 'Cat…' He watched her slowly stretch like her namesake. 'Get dressed…'

She could have, given the circumstances, assumed her use-by date had expired and she was being thrown out, but he gave her a kiss to awaken her and told her to hurry as he picked up the phone.

Her Spanish was…well, it wasn't, but she knew the word 'coffee' when she heard it in any language.

'Where are we going?' she asked as, doing up her espadrilles in the elevator, they made their way down.

'You need to see more of this city.'

'At 4:30 a.m.?'

'We could do it tomorrow if you'd stay another night.'

He hoped she would stay another night but they both knew that that wasn't happening.

Cat blinked as the doorman handed them two take-out coffees and Dominic took her hand and they walked to a car.

'You've hired a car.'

He didn't answer and when she got in she realised that it wasn't a hire car because there were coffee cups and papers and it looked pretty much like the inside of hers.

'Just how long are you here for?' she started to ask.

'Ask no questions,' he said.

Yes, she reminded herself, that was what they were about—fun, freedom...

And yet he intrigued her.

He spoke Spanish and he drove like a local through the dim city streets and she drank her coffee and tried to get her brain into gear.

'Come on.' He parked the car and took her hand and she was happy to just go with the adventure.

Without him she'd still be asleep.

Instead, she was wide-awake, walking up a hill and wondering just what the hell was going on, and then she remembered it was one of *those* days.

There was a tiny fracture to her mind, an angry inward curse that she could have made it through almost forty minutes of being awake without remembering the day that it was.

'This is Collserola,' Dominic explained. 'It is a national park—the green jewel of Barcelona...'

And it wasn't exclusively here for them because, as they climbed the hill, Cat found herself behind a group of tourists and it became clear as they chose their spot and sat on mossy ground that this was the place to be at sunrise.

And it was.

The city twinkled its night lights, the cars weaved in orange lines and beyond that, slowly, the dark ocean started to turn to blue as around them woodland came to life.

'It's amazing,' she said, and then turned to him but Dominic didn't answer.

He sat watching and tried to tell himself that he shouldn't have brought her, that he should feel guilt. Oh, there it was, this clutch of guilt in his chest had arrived. He had no issues with last night; it was the morning he was wrestling with.

And Cat didn't notice his lack of answer because as the world came to light she was on the edge of crying.

I miss you every single day.

I miss you this very second.

Just not every second.

Not every moment.

And sometimes moments run into hours but I still miss you every single day and will for ever.

How can that be? both wondered.

When did the seconds start to join up? When did that first full minute devoid of grief arrive and your leaving go unthought-of for an hour?

At what point did a cruel world start to turn beautiful again?

'To think I could have left without seeing this.' Cat broke the strange silence they were wrapped in and he turned then and looked at her.

And the clutch of guilt in his chest released.

It just went.

He would regret it later, Dominic decided.

Right now they shared a kiss.

A deep kiss that chased her softly to the ground and she could feel damp grass beneath bare shoulders and for them both all was right with the world.

It was a kiss unlike last night's, soft and tender, and she opened her eyes in the middle and saw his closed and wondered how it might be to be loved by this man.

It felt as if she was, it was the strangest glimpse of it. Her hands were in his hair and his mouth was still over hers, and if there hadn't been a lot of tourists present and two hundred cameras clicking, he would have made love to her, Cat knew.

He would have peeled off her dress and just slipped inside her.

She'd never come to a kiss, but the deep, sensual press of his mouth persisted. The roam of his hands was gentle, pressing into the side of her. In public, somehow shielded, she just came to private thoughts that she dared not examine and he nearly did too just feeling her slight rise and then the stillness in his arms.

It was a long, lingering kiss that had to stop and as his lips left hers she looked up into his eyes and she wished she could stay here for ever.

So did he.

Of course they couldn't.

'We have to get back,' he said, and waited for the clutch of guilt to return but it had escaped.

'We do.'

It was rather odd to step back into normality.

This time she pressed the lift button for her floor and there were others in there with them. When they arrived at her floor they shared a sort of odd wave as Cat got out.

Oh, my, she thought as she saw the damage to Gemma's dress. There were grass stains up the back, a tear near the bust, and then she looked at her face.

Yikes.

She looked as if she had spent the night having torrid sex with a stranger.

She had!

It was this morning that disconcerted her, though in the very nicest of ways.

She had a shower, wearing a shower cap, and then got out and picked half a forest out of her hair.

She had love bites on her breasts and she remembered his mouth there and suddenly she wanted him all over again.

She put on her lilac dress and went downstairs and took her seat in a talk she had been very much looking forward to.

But how did you concentrate on extracorporeal membrane oxygenation? Cat thought. Dominic was off doing whatever he was doing but he might as well have been sitting next to her because that's where her thoughts were.

She felt the buzz of her phone in her bag and she sneakily pulled it out.

Of course it couldn't be him, suggesting they sneak away, she reminded herself.

He didn't even know her number.

It just felt as if he should.

Instead, it was Gemma.

Are you okay?

Yes, but your dress isn't, Cat was tempted to reply.
She thought of the tear he had made in it last night and
the grass stains today.

She just hoped they had another one at Gatwick.

All good, Cat answered without thought, and then
she guiltily fired another text.

It seems wrong to say that today.

She smiled when Gemma replied.

You awful person. Go to your room and be miserable
this very minute. xxx

No, Cat didn't want to go to her room and cry away
the day.

She closed her eyes.

She flew at seven and it seemed far, far too soon.

He wasn't around at lunchtime and thankfully Gordon
was telling his story to someone else. There was a sag of
disappointment in Cat, though, as she lined up for lunch,
for the few remaining hours they were missing out on.

Still, there was always something to smile about and
smile she did when she saw a lovely full silver platter of
delectable paella and she held out her plate to the waiter.

'My room, now...'

She hadn't even heard him come up behind her and the
low whisper in her ear was like an audible hallucination.

'I'm not going to get my paella, am I?' she said, but
he'd gone.

No, she wasn't going to get her paella.

Two minutes later, with only sixteen minutes to spare
before the afternoon session started, she was kneeling

on the floor, hands splayed on his bed as he took her from behind.

He wasn't a considerate lover, just a very, very good one.

If they'd had time, Cat would have turned her head to tell him that usually she wouldn't...

Wouldn't what?

She did turn, though, and she saw his look of intense concentration, felt his fingers on her clitoris, urging her to come, and then she didn't even bother thinking. She just closed her eyes to the pleasure of being taken.

Her head was on her forearm and he was pounding her from behind and, Cat thought as she started to come, it was blissful to be that woman, even if just for a little while.

His.

They skipped the afternoon sessions.

Like bunking off school, they took his car again and drove for half an hour to a beach and sat there, eating ice cream and then rubbing suntan lotion into each other with sticky hands.

And on one of the saddest days in her calendar year she found bliss.

'So your parents are both doctors?' Dominic said as they lay on towels and stared at each other, and she nodded.

'Were they high achievers?'

'God, yes. They still are. It's easier to ring their secretaries to schedule lunch than try to do it myself.'

'You are joking?' he checked.

'Half.' She smiled. 'What about yours?'

He seemed to think before answering.

He was.

They really hadn't spoken about anything other than themselves but it felt quite normal to have her ask.

'I don't really know where to start,' he admitted. 'Well, my mother never worked. Her sole job was to look beautiful for my father. He was an arrogant bastard. Growing up, I hardly ever saw him—he worked on the stock market and would bring his stress home, worrying about the yen or the pound dropping a quarter of a percentage point.' Her eyes were so patient, Dominic thought. She didn't ask questions; she just lay there, staring.

Because she loved his voice.

Because anything he said she wanted to hear.

'Anyway, then he had the absolute fortune of collapsing with a heart attack and going into full cardiac arrest.'

'Fortune?'

'We always joke now that he had a personality transplant because, while his illness made me switch from physics to biology and suddenly become very interested in medicine and saving the world, my father completely changed. He was very depressed at first and he had to see a psychologist and things but then he completely turned his life around. He sold up, got out of the money game, and he and my mother fell in love all over again, and now...'

He hesitated. He didn't want to give too many specifics. He didn't want to say that he was looking forward to Monday and heading over to see his slightly eccentric parents or rather, disconcertingly, he did want to tell her just that.

There was a part of Dominic that wanted to extend this conversation, which meant extending them, and that wasn't what this weekend was about so he kept things light.

'They started an internet dating service. Or rather it wasn't by internet initially, it was more a word-of-mouth thing. They used to set up their friends and anyone coming over to Spain…'

'Stop!' Cat laughed.

'It's true, though. Now they run this very exclusive dating site for the over fifties…'

To hear this rather detached man talking about his crazy parents made Cat start to *really* laugh.

Oh, she laughed at times, of course she did.

Just not like this.

They lay then in silence and Dominic thought about the six months after Heather had died.

After the funeral, instead of throwing himself into work, as had been his initial plan, he had accepted his parents' suggestion to come and stay in Spain with them.

At first they had infuriated him with their calm acceptance of the terrible facts. Of course they had been upset but not once had they matched his anger.

As he had raged and paced around the villa, or slept in well past midday, they had simply accepted him and whatever place he was in—providing conversation when needed and meals that appeared whether he felt he needed them or not.

And finally, when the anger had gone, Dominic had been very grateful for their presence and calm, which had allowed him to heal in his own time.

He had spent days walking and watching the ocean as he slowly come back to join a world that had altered for ever. Yet move on he had, catching himself the first time he'd found himself laughing along at a joke or smiling at a thought that had popped into his head.

And a smile stretched his lips as he thought of them now.

'They're amazing people,' he admitted. 'So, yes, what seemed like the most terrible disaster at the time turned out to be a blessing.'

They stared at each other, they found each other, right there in that moment.

'Don't leave tonight...' he said, but even before the words were out he was changing his mind and even as she heard them there was confusion in her eyes because it was supposed to be a one-night stand.

'Come on,' he said. 'Let's go in the water.'

There they could be apart and think.

There she could work out how to articulate the million reasons that she had to go back. How did she tell him that the woman he had met this weekend didn't actually exist, that she wasn't floaty and feminine and spontaneous?

She was rigid and brittle and meticulous.

And Dominic too, as they ran to the water, was wondering what had possessed him to ask her to stay.

But not even the sea could keep them apart because ten strides in they were waist deep in water, limbs around each other, kissing in the sun, out on display, and there was no reason in the world why she should leave.

The water was idyllic, just a shade cooler than the temperature of skin, and she could feel the sun beating on her shoulders.

She'd heard about the magical seven. Seven waves in, seven out, seven years since love had died and today it felt as if it was being born again.

They said nothing but their kisses were deep and tender but whatever they were finding was invaded, whatever the moment had meant it was gone.

'*Ayuda!*'

No, Cat didn't know Spanish, but a cry for help she was familiar with and she swung around.

'*Necesito ayuda...*'

Dominic was already swimming over to an elderly man who was waving his arms. Beside him on a pedalo there was a woman who was sitting up but even from here Cat could see she was in trouble. She was clutching her chest and leaning forward.

Others were coming over to assist and Dominic was calling out to a woman standing on the beach to call for an ambulance.

He called for Cat to go to shore. 'In my backpack!' he shouted. 'There's a pack...'

At least someone was organised today.

Cat raced up the beach as a group of men steered the pedalo in and then carried the woman to the shore.

She was still sitting up, Cat noted as she shook the contents of his backpack out.

There it was, a small pack, but as she went to stuff the contents she had tipped out back inside, her hand closed on a small bump in his wallet.

A circular bump.

She shook her head and ran back towards the gathered crowd.

'Thanks...'

She opened the pack. There were gloves, a mouth-guard and airway... There was even a small kit for IV access and she watched his very steady hands slip a needle in, all the while reassuring the woman, who was clammy and sweaty, that she would be okay.

It should feel very different to be out in the middle of nowhere rather than in the calm efficiency of the emergency department, yet he had everything under control—a few beachgoers were holding their towels to shade the woman from the fierce afternoon sun and Dominic wiped her face with a cloth soaked in bottled water and spoke calming words in Spanish.

Cat noticed he was holding the woman's wrist as he spoke, keeping a constant watch on her pulse. As she glanced down at Dominic's hand Cat wondered if she had been blind or simply not looked, because now she could see the slight pinkness of a ring mark on his suntanned skin.

She felt a bit sick.

In the distance she could hear sirens and, even if the worst happened now and the lady went into cardiac arrest, assistance and equipment were just a few moments away.

The paramedics were just as efficient as they were back home and rather more used to retrieving heavy patients from a sun-drenched sandy beach than they would be in London.

They spoke at length with Dominic as they did the ECG tracing and administered analgesia and generally made the woman more comfortable before transferring her onto the stretcher.

The men all carried the stretcher up the beach until they let the legs down on the stony ground.

Her heart was racing, not from the mild drama but from what she had thought she had felt.

A wedding ring?

Surely not, Cat thought.

But why not? another voice in her head asked.

Why the hell not?

'Let's grab our things and head back,' Dominic said, and she nodded and tried not to shrug him off as his arm went around her waist.

She didn't know what to say to him. She just didn't know how to speak.

'You've caught the sun,' he commented as they drove back to the hotel.

'I know,' she said. Her shoulders were stinging but not as much as her thoughts.

'Are you okay?' Dominic checked.

'Of course.' She cleared her throat. 'It was just a bit upsetting.'

'What?' He glanced over. 'She had chest pain.'

Oh, that's right. Cat remembered the man she had disliked before she had completely fallen under his spell. He was arrogant, dismissive and rather mean.

'It's different without all the equipment...'

He didn't comment. Chest pain was such a routine part of his day and he'd assumed it was the same for her.

'She'll be fine,' he said, but she couldn't answer.

They were back in the elevators and she went to push the button for her floor but his hand stopped her and he pushed his.

Arrogant bastard, Cat thought this time.

Still, she wanted to be sure so she went with him to his hotel room and, completely at ease, he dropped his clothes and headed for the shower.

She didn't join him.

He washed off the sand and was glad that she hadn't come in. He needed to think.

Was he going to ask again that she stay awhile longer?

And if she couldn't, was he going to ask to see her again?

'What time is your flight?' he called from the shower.

'Seven,' she answered, and then she did something most uncharacteristic for her. She wasn't a nosy person yet she was about this.

She went into his bag and pulled out his wallet and opened it, and she didn't need to dig for the ring to find her answer. She pulled out a photo instead.

Cat knew her fashion and, yep, this was pretty recent.

Dominic made a lovely groom.

He also made a very dark lover because she jumped when she heard his voice.

'I wish you hadn't done that, Cat.'

He stood with a towel around his waist, watching as she tucked the photo back in. In his mind he was conflicted.

Tell her.

No.

Because then the bubble burst and everything they had found this weekend dispersed.

Yes, he could explain.

He simply wasn't ready to.

If he was going to tell her, then it would be in his own time.

And their time had run out.

He didn't like a snoop.

'Do you know what, Dominic?' She looked up at him. The delicious scent of him, fresh from the shower, was reaching her now and she practically held her breath as she gave a grim smile. 'I wish I hadn't done that either.'

She tossed the wallet on the bed and walked past him.

And he held open the door and let her out.

CHAPTER FIVE

CAT ARRIVED BACK at Gatwick Airport and, of course, because she didn't need it now, her suitcase was amongst the first to come out.

Instead of driving home, though, she found herself on a search of the shops and thankfully found Gemma's dress.

They met in the canteen on Monday morning and Cat got back her photo while Gemma received the second version of the white dress.

'Thank you so much for this.' Gemma beamed as she peered into the bag. 'It's beautiful, isn't it? I know I probably shouldn't wear white for the christening…'

'It's not a wedding,' Cat said. 'You don't have to worry about offending the bride.'

She looked at the dress as Gemma pulled out a corner and she felt her throat go tight. Hers, she knew, should have been thrown straight into the garbage but instead she'd thrown it into the back of her wardrobe.

No, she wanted to say to Gemma, *I did not have sexual relations with that married man.*

Oh, help.

She most certainly had.

'So how was it?' Gemma asked.

'It was great,' Cat said. 'Very informative.'

'About what?'

'Well,' Cat attempted, 'about things.'

'And how was your talk?'

'It went really well,' she said, but all she could really remember of it was the moment Dominic had walked into the room and how he had stood with his arms folded at the back.

'And how was the museum?'

Cat frowned.

'You said you were going to do some sightseeing and go to the museum, maybe get a bit of inspiration for your bedroom.'

As Cat's cheeks burned pink, she wondered if her friend was a witch.

'Well, did you?'

'Did I what?'

'Get inspiration for the bedroom?'

'No.'

'Oh.'

'And no shopping for stuffed donkeys, I see.'

'I was working, Gemma.'

'Of course you were.' Gemma smirked.

She knew, Cat was quite sure.

Had she examined things more carefully at the time, some flags might have been raised. Perhaps it should have been obvious, Cat thought, that he was married. Yet his reluctance to share personal information hadn't been an issue at the time; instead, it had felt as if they were chasing the same thing—fun, pleasure, grabbing the moment and running with it.

It had started to feel different at Collserola, though.

Cat couldn't properly explain it but there she had

started to want more than just the weekend. There, watching the sunrise, there had been a shift and she had felt him pensive beside her and for a moment, just a moment, she had felt as if time might not have been running out for them.

And that night, her second without him, Cat did what she'd tried not to because it hurt too much—she recalled their kiss in the sea. For a while there she'd thought she'd be staying.

Not for ever.

Just that something had been starting.

Something far bigger than either had expected to find.

Yet, as guilty as she felt about the weekend, Cat didn't feel used—after all, she had gone along with the anonymity that had been offered. She had enjoyed embracing her femininity, going out and doing things she never would have done had Dominic not been there.

And, even though she did her level best to forget him, their time together could not be undone and it was as if he had set off a little chain reaction, because colour started coming back into her life.

The following Sunday Cat wore another new dress to the twins' christening, a burnt orange and red paisley wraparound dress, and her hair was worn down and curly.

Glynn had rung to apologise and explain that his mother had been taken ill and Cat had had a difficult time explaining to him that, no, she wasn't not coming to see him because of what had happened. 'I like it curly, Glynn,' Cat said. 'Of course I'll be in again...'

Just not yet.

For now she enjoyed having those two extra hours a week not having her hair yanked and blown smooth.

She stood at the font, looking at Gemma's dress as she and Nigel juggled the twins, and wondering who on earth she was to offer guidance as a godmother, while knowing if that day ever came, then she would.

Oh, she doubted she would ever marry but she did believe in the sanctity of it and to think about what had happened made a curl of shame inside her that meant it was something she wouldn't be discussing with Gemma.

She loved Gemma and Nigel and their little family and she remembered Thomas's christening and when they had been there for her.

Gemma must have been thinking of it too, because she gave her friend the nicest smile and later pulled her aside.

'My parents are driving me crazy,' Gemma said. 'They want to know when we're having the cake. I'm sure they want to go home.'

Cat smiled. Gemma's parents loathed any change to their routine.

'Are you okay, Cat?'

'Of course.'

They told each other everything and she could have come up with some airy excuse, that today was hard because…

Only, she wouldn't use Thomas as an excuse for not being able to meet her friend's eyes.

'What are you up to, Cat?'

'I'm not up to anything.'

'Is there something you're not telling me?'

For the first time since they'd been teenagers she lied properly to her friend.

'Don't be daft.'

And she got on with smiling and enjoying this very special day.

But over the next few weeks Cat threw herself into her work and studying for her exams, which were tough but no tougher than expected. It meant there was no time to catch up with Gemma.

And even when three weeks' annual leave stretched ahead of her, she still avoided her friend.

Though she was starting to realise that she wouldn't be able to avoid her for long.

Gemma texted.

Is everything okay?

Cat didn't answer.
Gemma persisted.

Did we have an argument that I didn't notice?

Finally Cat texted back.

Can I tell you when I'm ready?

Because she wasn't just yet.

Of course.

No, she wasn't quite ready, so she stripped walls and sanded back a mantelpiece and tried to face something she was avoiding.

When it proved too hard, she took herself to her

favourite shop and spent a morning turning pages of wallpaper samples.

'I think a silver grey,' Cat said to Veronica, the owner, who was as obsessed with wallpaper as she was. 'Perhaps with one wall in silver and the rest in a matt finish…'

Silver moonlight hues had appealed but as Veronica went to clear some space so they could put together samples she moved a book and suddenly it wasn't those colours that Cat wanted.

'I haven't seen this,' she said.

'It's only just in…'

'Oh, my,' Cat said. She could almost feel the pulse from the sample book as she turned the pages. It was like being walked blindfolded and then having it removed and finding herself standing in a spring park. Birds, butterflies and tree branches that stretched and flowers, endless flowers…

It reminded her of Collserola and that one magical morning and she certainly didn't need such a constant reminder, except…

'Would this be a feature wall?' Cat checked, and then almost winced when the assistant pulled up some images on her computer screen.

Every wall was covered. In some of the images even the ceilings were papered. It was a sort of cross between a cheap Paris hotel and an enchanted wood.

'This is so far removed from what I was planning,' Cat said, and Veronica nodded.

'You don't want to know the price.'

'I don't,' Cat said, and tried to get back to silver grey. 'Have you got it in?'

'I do, though it's incredibly hard to get hold of. It

was on a special order but the buyer couldn't wait and went for something less…'

'Less what?' Cat asked. 'Less migraine inducing, less…?' She let out a breath. 'Less sexy…?'

Yes, somehow it was sexy.

'Just less,' Veronica said.

It was sold to the guilty conscience that just wanted to revisit that gorgeous morning over and over again.

A time when the world had been absolutely beautiful.

Magical even.

The strange thing, Cat thought as she stepped back a full week later and surveyed her handiwork, the world still was.

Magical.

Instead of the muted tones for the bedroom she had chosen colour. And now, in autumn, she stood in the middle of summer and imagined this being her haven when winter came in.

Yes, that weekend had changed her in a way she was finally accepting.

'Hey, Gemma.' Cat called her friend, who had so patiently waited for the morose mood to pass by. 'The bedroom's finished.'

Gemma really was a brilliant friend. She came over within an hour, clutching a bottle of champagne and two glasses, and they did a walk through the house. Cat had a photo in each room of what it had looked like before she'd set to work and it was hard to believe now just how bad it had once been.

As she opened the bedroom door she watched her friend's jaw drop in absolute amazement as she stepped in.

'I want to live in your bedroom for ever,' Gemma said.

'Nigel might not be too pleased.'

'He can come too,' Gemma said. 'Oh, my, it is beautiful. It's just stunning. I can't believe you've finished the house.'

'I haven't yet.'

'Well, it looks pretty perfect to me. What do you still have left to do—the garden?'

'No.'

Gemma followed Cat out of the master bedroom and down the hallway that no longer creaked when you walked, and she frowned as Cat opened up the guest bedroom.

It had a dark wooden bed that was dressed in white linen. There was a gorgeous bookcase next to the open fire. On the mantelpiece were beautiful ornaments. Every last piece had been chosen with care.

'But it's already perfect,' Gemma said.

'I'm going to make it into a nursery.'

'Will it sell better if you do?'

'No, I've decided against selling.'

'So why are you making it into…?' The penny was slowly dropping and a rather stunned Gemma halted and turned to her friend.

Yes, there was magic in nature.

'You're pregnant?'

There was a long stretch of silence.

Gemma was an obstetrician and she was used to women finding themselves rather unexpectedly pregnant.

It seemed today, though, that it was the doctor who was more surprised.

She was.

Cat had spent the past few weeks fighting the idea and then getting used to it. A private person, she revealed only when she was ready.

And tonight she was.

'How long have you known?' Gemma asked.

'A couple of weeks after the twins were christened,' Cat said. 'I tried to put it out of my mind, what with my exams and everything. I decided to work out how I felt when I was on leave.'

'And how do you feel?' Gemma asked, struggling to put back on her obstetrician's hat.

'Well, I'm going to be terrified until I have the tests and get all the results back...'

'The chances of it happening again are minimal,' Gemma said.

'I know they are.'

'But you shan't relax till they're in.' Gemma smiled gently and Cat nodded. 'Apart from that, how do you feel?'

'I still don't know,' Cat admitted. 'I don't know if I'm happy or worried or anything really.'

'You know that I'm here for you, whatever you decide.'

'I do and even if I haven't been ready to speak about it till now, it's helped a lot to know that.'

Gemma opened the champagne.

For herself.

She didn't even bother with a glass!

'What about Rick? How did he take it?'

'It isn't Rick's.'

'Then who—'

'I don't want to discuss that.'

'Now, hold on a minute,' Gemma said. 'You're not my patient yet—you're my friend so we *are* going to discuss that. What happened in Spain?'

'How do you know that it was in Spain?'

'Because you've been different since then, and also you don't top up your tan by sitting in a hotel room.'

'Yes, it was then,' Cat admitted. 'I met someone but it was never going to be going anywhere. It was supposed to be a bit of fun, a weekend of no consequence...' She gave a wry smile. 'We were careful...'

'You have no idea how many times I hear that a day,' Gemma said.

'We used condoms.'

'Note the plural,' Gemma said. 'Was it a sex-fest, then?'

'I guess.'

'You dirty girl.' Gemma grinned.

'Okay, I can tell you what happened now.' And so she told Gemma all about the hair appointment that hadn't happened and the missing luggage. 'I ended up wearing your dress for the presentation,' Cat explained. 'I felt like a fish out of water at first but then I started to enjoy myself. I felt a bit like my old self. Anyway, he made it very clear from the start that he was only interested in the weekend and nothing more...' Cat thought about the moment when he had asked her to stay on for longer but she shoved that aside. It didn't matter now. 'At first I was going to tell him to get lost, he's not my usual type at all, but then...' She shrugged. 'I decided that a weekend of no-strings fun was better than six months of starting out all hopeful and then slowly finding out that a relationship wasn't working.'

'And was it?'

'For a while,' Cat said.

'So, what's his name?'

'Dominic,' she replied.

'And have you told him about the baby?' Gemma asked.

'He's married.' Cat made herself say it. They stood

in the spare room that would soon be a nursery in silence. It was Cat who broke it. 'I'm sorry, Gemma…'

'You don't have to say sorry to me,' Gemma said. 'After all, it wasn't Nigel who you slept with.'

'I know, but even so.' There were tears in Cat's eyes. She still couldn't quite believe how careless she'd been. 'I didn't know that he was married right until the end— the bastard had taken off his ring and tucked it in his wallet. I probably didn't ask enough questions,' she admitted. 'He seemed very direct to me. He didn't seem the sort of person who would cheat, which says a lot about my gauge for guys…'

'Well, whether he's married or not,' Gemma said, and Cat knew that her friend's doctor's hat was firmly on now, 'Dominic still has a responsibility towards the baby…'

Cat shook her head. 'It might be a bit late to be thinking of it but I'm not tearing a family apart. I'm not going to contact him just yet. I don't even know where he works, I don't even know his surname…'

'Come off it, Cat.'

'Okay, I looked up the conference attendees and I do know his surname but I can manage—'

'It's actually not about you and whether or not you can manage,' Gemma said. 'And it's not about his wife and how she'll react. It's about the baby, Cat.' Gemma was as firm as Cat had known she would be. The very questions that she had been wrestling with for weeks were now being voiced by her friend. 'It's about your baby, who will grow up and will want to know, and has a right to know, who their father is. Whether or not you want him to be, Dominic has a right to be involved, or not, in his baby's life.'

'I know all of that,' Cat said. 'And I shall tell him, just not yet. Gemma, I'm eleven weeks pregnant. I'm doing my very best to simply get used to that fact. I'm not going to upend his life while I'm still in my first trimester…'

'Oh, but you'll upend yours. Why the hell should he get away with a few weeks of stress—'

'I'm not stressed,' Cat said. 'I was at first but I'm not now. I want this baby and I'm going to do the very best that I can by it. I shall look up Dominic at some point but not now. Not now while I'm still trying to work things out. I need to find out the test results before I tell anyone. I need to know that it's not going to be happening again…'

Cat knew she had Gemma's support and, yes, she could tell her most things but there was something she couldn't explain to her friend just yet because she didn't actually understand it herself.

She missed Dominic.

Yes, it had been but one weekend and, yes, she was angry, not just with him but herself.

It was how she would react when she saw him that terrified Cat.

She knew that she wouldn't cry and break down if he told her he wanted nothing to do with them—it would come as a relief, in fact.

And she didn't want a penny from him either.

There were two things that terrified her—how he might react to the news if their baby was less than perfect, which was understandable given all that had gone on.

And how she might react if he took the news well.

Or, rather, how she might react when she saw him again.

What if that spark blew all her scruples away?

The mere thought of his kisses terrified her.

His smooth talk too.

She had this awful glimpse of life as a mistress.

Tucked away in England with her baby.

And she'd never be that.

If he was to be in their baby's life, then it would be without lies.

Which meant someone was going to get hurt.

CHAPTER SIX

CAT DID LOOK him up.

At twenty weeks gestation, when her scan and amnio had come through as clear, Gemma told her that she had no excuse not to.

It really had been an excuse because whatever the outcome of the tests it wouldn't have changed the course of the pregnancy for Cat.

But the results came in before Christmas and Cat had visions of Dominic and his fraught wife and the triplets she had now assigned to him, and decided she couldn't ruin Christmas for them.

Or New Year.

Still, she had looked him up and it had taken about fifteen minutes to find out where he worked.

She recalled him saying that he liked the architecture in Edinburgh and after a few false starts she found someone who knew him and was told he was now working at a large teaching hospital in Glasgow.

Ah, that's right, Cat remembered, he didn't like to be tied to one place for too long.

Or one person.

And so Cat had sat on that knowledge for another month.

Her second pregnancy threw up so many memories

of her first. There were so many thoughts and fears and she wanted to get past the milestone she had reached with Thomas.

Finally, though, she plucked up the courage to make the call.

'You're looking for Mr Edwards?' A cheery female voice, with a heavy Glaswegian accent, checked.

'Dominic Edwards—he's an emergency consultant.'

'Oh, you mean Dom!' There was a long pause. 'No, he was only here for a couple of months… Sorry, I've no idea where he is now.'

And that ended that.

Though, not quite, of course.

Now into February and thirty weeks pregnant Cat and Gemma caught up one Monday morning for breakfast in the canteen. They were interviewing for Cat's maternity leave position and she didn't want to be around for that.

Pregnancy suited her and she was enjoying this one. Colour had continued to come back into her life since that weekend and she was wearing the paisley dress that she had bought for the twins' christening, along with chocolate-brown high-heeled boots. Her hair hadn't been straightened since and hung over her shoulder in a thick, long ponytail.

'I really don't want to see who's replacing me,' she admitted as she peeled the lid of her yoghurt and, having licked it, added, 'Temporarily, of course! I'll be back.'

'Full-time?' Gemma checked.

'That was the plan,' Cat admitted, 'and I've told Andrew that I shall be returning full-time but I'm starting to really wonder how on earth I'm going to manage it.'

'Have they had many applicants for the role?' Gemma asked.

'There have been a few, but only two standouts—two women who are looking at job share,' Cat said.

'You could think about doing that,' Gemma suggested.

'I don't like sharing at the best of times and especially not my job,' Cat said. 'Still, I'm going to have to work something out. I can't believe how quickly my due date is coming up.'

Cat had always heard women saying that their pregnancy seemed to drag on for ever, yet hers seemed to be galloping along at breakneck speed.

Work was as unrelenting as ever and she did her level best not to bring any aches and pains with her, but by the end of the day she was exhausted. The nursery hadn't been sorted out; instead, her days off were spent looking at child-care centres. All to no avail. Even the crèche at the hospital wasn't geared to a baby whose single parent worked such erratic hours.

'If I'm going to work, then I'm going to have to get a nanny,' Cat conceded as she added sugar to her tea. 'But even that comes with its own set of problems.'

'Such as?'

'I have a two-bedroom home.' She sighed. 'A small two-bedroom home.'

'And you don't like sharing.' Gemma smiled. 'Can't you get somewhere bigger?'

'I'm going to have to at some stage but the thing is, I love my home. I've just got it exactly how I want it but, yes, I guess I'm going to have to look at moving. Not yet, though,' she said. 'I think I'll stay put for now and once I've had the baby I'll think about putting the house on the market. I'll have six months to move...'

'So you're planning to have your house on the market, find another one *and* move, all with a new baby?'

'It's a baby,' Cat said. 'I'm not going to be working...' She let out a sigh. 'I haven't got a clue, have I?'

'Well, if anyone could do it all, then it would be you,' Gemma said. 'Though I just can't imagine how I'd have managed when the twins were tiny. Just having people viewing the house when you're trying to feed or you've just got...' Gemma hesitated '...*it* off to sleep...'

'You were about to say *him*.' Cat smiled.

'No, I wasn't,' Gemma refuted. 'What I'm actually trying to say is that I wouldn't count on getting too much done during those six months of maternity leave. It's isn't an extended holiday, Cat. If you are considering moving to somewhere bigger, it might be a good idea to start that ball rolling now...'

'I guess.' She sighed. 'Even if the new place does need some work, I could do that while I'm...' She stopped when she saw Gemma's small eyebrow rise and then laughed. 'Okay, I'm going to accept that I have no real idea as to the disruption this small person is going to make to my life when *he* arrives.' Cat waited for Gemma to comment but she didn't. 'I want to find out what I'm having.'

'Well, then, it's good that you've got an appointment to see me this evening.'

'Gemma!' Cat protested, because now that she had made up her mind, she wanted to know straight away. 'Tell me.'

'No, I won't tell you here and I'm serious about that. We agreed that catch-ups were for friend talk and my office was for official baby talk...'

'Fair enough,' she grumbled.

'And speaking as a friend and not a doctor, have you—'

'I need to get back,' Cat interrupted. She didn't want to get into that conversation with Gemma *again*, and explain that she still hadn't spoken with Dominic.

She knew, though, that she needed to contact him.

Tonight, she decided, she'd deal with it tonight but almost immediately she changed her mind.

It was surely better to ring around hospitals during the day. It would sound far more professional to any of his colleagues than calling at night, and she certainly didn't want to create gossip for him.

Gemma started to head to Outpatients, where she was holding antenatal clinics all day, and Cat would be her last patient. 'I'll see you at five. Hopefully I shan't be running late. Come and have dinner after,' she suggested. 'We might even make it in time to see the twins before they go down for the night.'

'I'd love that. I honestly don't know how you do it,' Cat admitted. 'Do you feel like you're missing out?'

'Sometimes.' Gemma nodded. 'I worry more, though, that they're missing out on me and so I completely over-compensate when I do see them and rot up all of Nigel's routines. I know I'm lucky, though. I don't have to worry about them while I'm here and I can concentrate on work, knowing that they're at home with their dad.' She gave her friend a smile. 'You need your own Nigel.'

Cat smiled back but the thing was, she didn't want her own Nigel.

She wanted… Cat halted her thoughts right there. Dominic wasn't the man she thought she had met. And even if he was, it was supposed to have been a one-night stand. He had said to her face that he didn't want to be tied to any one person or place. She couldn't really imagine his reaction when he found out that she was having his baby.

She didn't want his reaction.

Cat slowed down her walking. There was a flutter of panic in her chest as she remembered her last pregnancy and the disappointment of Thomas's father, the silent suggestion of blame for daring to mess up his perfect life.

She didn't want that for herself again and she couldn't stand it for her baby.

Yet she had to.

She was tired of the guilt that came with putting it off and she decided that, bar an emergency coming into the department, she wasn't leaving her office until she had found out where he was working and had contacted him.

Did she tell him outright? Cat wondered.

Suggest that they meet?

So deep in her thoughts was she that at first she didn't notice the tall suited man walking alongside Andrew.

He noticed her, though.

In fact, at first sight she barely looked pregnant.

She was wearing a tight dress and high boots and looked somehow sexy and elegant but then she turned to speak with one of the nurses and he saw the tight, round swell of her stomach and, attempting a detached professional guess, he would put her at...

Yes, there was something that they needed to discuss. That was why he was here after all.

He watched as she turned from the conversation she was having and startled as she glanced towards him, but then she gave a small shake of her head and strode on.

Then she looked over towards him again and he

watched as not only did her face pale but she stood frozen to the spot.

Frozen.

For a foolish moment Cat considered darting into a cubicle—it would be a futile game of hide-and-seek, though, because it would appear that she'd already been found.

And so, as Andrew called her over, somehow she did her best to pretend that the walls of the emergency department weren't shaking and that the ground wasn't opening up between her feet.

She walked towards him.

Dominic.

Her one-night stand.

The father of her child.

'Cat.' Andrew beamed. 'Did you have nice days off?'

'I did.'

'Excellent! I tried not to worry you, but on Friday one of the job share applicants pulled out and the other wasn't interested in pursuing the position if she couldn't be guaranteed regular part-time hours.'

'I see,' Cat said, even though she didn't.

'I've still got two more interviews to complete,' Andrew went on, although Cat knew those two were really more of a formality and would be a rather poor choice. 'However,' Andrew said, 'we had a late applicant. Cat, this is Dominic Edwards. He's been working in Scotland for the last two years but we're hoping to lure him back south of the border.'

For now, Cat knew, she would simply have to go along with the polite small talk. Whatever the reason Dominic was here, whatever the outcome when she told him her news, at the first opportunity she would have a

quiet word with Andrew. Hopefully she wouldn't have
to reveal to her colleague that Dominic was her baby's
father, but if she had to, then she would. There was no
way this could happen.

No way!

Thankfully there was a call for help from one of the
cubicles and Cat was just about to flee in relief and go
and assist when Andrew halted her. 'I'll go,' he said. 'If
you could carry on showing Dominic around.'

'I can deal with the patient,' Cat said. 'You're in the
middle of conducting an interview.'

'I know, but the patient happens to be my mother-in-
law.' Andrew rolled his eyes. 'The interview has already
been interrupted twice. My apologies again, Dominic…'

'It's no problem at all,' Dominic said. 'Take your time.'

As Andrew walked off Cat stood there and she truly
didn't know what to say.

She kept praying that the alarm clock would buzz, or
that there would be a knock on the door to the on-call
room and she'd find out she was having a bad dream.

A vaguely sexy bad dream, though, because rather
inappropriately, given the circumstances, she couldn't
help but notice how amazing he looked.

When in Spain, the times that he'd had clothes on,
Dominic had dressed smartly, though somewhat more
casually than he was now. Today, on a Monday morning, he seemed too beautiful for the rather scruffy emergency department. Dressed in a dark grey suit and tie,
his hair was shorter than she remembered but it still
had enough length that it fell forward. Clean shaven,
he smelt as he had the last time she had seen him, the
moment he had stepped out of the shower.

The moment she had walked away and he hadn't stopped her—in fact, he had held the door open.

And, just like that day, she could feel his contained anger.

'Has the cat got your tongue, Cat?' he asked as she stood in silence.

It would seem that it had because still she said nothing.

'Well, I'll make this very simple for you, then,' he pushed on. 'A, B or C?'

Cat could feel her eyelashes blink rapidly as he sped through the multi-choice he had created just for her.

'A—mine, B—not mine, or C—not sure.'

'Dominic…' she said, and how strange it felt to be saying his name while looking at him again. How odd it felt that he was here, terribly beautiful, terribly cross. 'It's not that simple…' Cat attempted. But it was to him.

'A, B or C, Cat?'

She couldn't meet his eyes as she delivered the answer. 'A.'

'Mine.'

Yours.

His.

Dominic said nothing at first. He tried to stare her down but she refused to look at him as she now attempted to speak.

'I was going to try to find out where you were working. Today, in fact,' Cat said.

'I don't believe you for a moment.'

She couldn't blame him for that.

'What time to do you finish work?' Dominic asked.

'I've got plans tonight,' Cat said to his shoulder, because she still couldn't meet his eyes.

'Tough,' he said. 'Cancel them.'

'I've actually got a doctor's appointment.'

He hesitated but he refused to be fobbed off. 'What time is your appointment?'

'Five,' Cat said. 'But my obstetrician is a friend of mine and I'm going there for dinner afterwards...' She was floundering for excuses. She would far prefer to have had this conversation over the phone or via email. There at least she could have hidden from his angry gaze.

And, yes, he was angry—even if she was doing her best not to see it, she could feel it from his stance and she could hear it in his terse voice.

'I'm quite sure that your obstetrician friend will understand that you can't make dinner because you're going to be having a long overdue conversation with your baby's...' He halted and glanced over her shoulder, and Cat guessed that Andrew was making his way back.

'Name somewhere,' Dominic said, 'and I'll be there.'

She hesitated a beat too long for his impatient mood.

'Name somewhere,' he said again, 'or I'll just keep right on talking until you do and your boss will quickly realise that I have a rather vested interest in this maternity leave position.'

'Oliver's,' Cat said, referring to a small wine bar that a lot of staff at the hospital frequented. 'It's just down the—'

'I'm sure that I'm capable of working it out.'

The conversation ended as Andrew joined them again.

'How's your mother-in-law?' Dominic asked politely.

'Thankfully, she's about to head off to the ward.' Andrew gave a sigh of relief. 'Would you like to come and take a look at the radiology department, Dominic?'

'I'd love to,' he said, and then he addressed Cat. 'It was nice to meet you.'

'And you.' She gave him a tight smile.

For the next couple of hours Dominic remained in the department, being shown around, observing a clinic and being introduced to staff. It was clear to Cat that Andrew had decided that he had the role.

She was busy enough to avoid him and Dominic seemed fine with that for he made no attempt to catch her eye or talk.

He did let her know, though, when he was leaving. She was sitting on a high stool, trying to write up some notes, but had just put her hands on her hips to curve her aching back and stretch it when he came in.

'I'm heading off,' he said, and Cat glanced around and saw that they were alone.

'You don't have to tell me your movements,' she responded in a very crisp voice. Now that the shock of seeing him was starting to wear off, her own anger with him was making itself known and she let a little of it out. 'You knew full well that I worked here. What on earth were you thinking?'

'We'll speak tonight,' he said. 'Take as long as you need for your appointment but don't even think of not showing up afterwards. I want this sorted before we start working together.'

'Working together?' she checked. 'I thought you were applying for the maternity leave position.'

'I am but Andrew mentioned that you were short-staffed and wanted to know how I'd feel about doing a few locum shifts prior to commencing full-time.'

'*If* you get the job.'

'Why wouldn't I get it? The interview went very

well,' he said. 'I happen to be very good at what I do. Andrew seems to think I'd be an asset…'

He'd be an emotional liability, though, Cat thought. Well, she'd soon see about him working here, she decided as Dominic stalked off, though she didn't get a chance to speak to Andrew for the rest of the day.

Instead, she sat in Gemma's office at a quarter to six, having her blood pressure taken. Given who had just arrived on the scene, neither Gemma nor Cat were surprised to find that it was a smudge high.

'I can't believe that he'd just show up like that,' Cat said as her friend undid the cuff.

'Well, I think it's a good thing that it's all being brought to a head,' Gemma said. 'Go and lie down so I can have a feel.'

They carried on chatting as Cat did so and she opened up her wrap-over dress.

'Ooh,' Gemma said as Cat's stomach danced away while she lay there. 'Someone's wide-awake.'

'I just grabbed a glass of orange juice,' Cat said. 'I think it's woken him up.'

Gemma examined her bump as they chatted and this evening she made an exception to their rule and was both doctor and friend.

'He's furious.' Cat sighed.

'Which makes two of you,' Gemma said. 'Ask him if he's told his wife yet! That might knock him off his high horse a touch…' Then she was kind. 'Cat, you had many reasons for not telling Dominic. Given all you've been through and Mike's reaction to the bad news, of course you're protective of this baby…'

'I just wanted to know it was okay before I said anything to Dominic.' Cat admitted what Gemma already had guessed. 'Then I wanted to get further along than I had with Thomas…' She closed her eyes for a moment because tears were on the verge of spilling out. Getting past twenty-five weeks had been a huge milestone. 'The last few weeks I've had no excuse, though.'

'So why didn't you tell him?'

'It was supposed to be a one-night stand. I don't want to discuss Thomas with a man I spent one night with. Do you know, I didn't even particularly like him? I thought he was a bit mean and dismissive.'

Gemma said nothing.

'Arrogant,' Cat said. 'Chauvinist… He wouldn't let me pay half for dinner.' She mimicked a deep voice. '"Why would you ruin a perfectly good night?" He's all the things I don't want in a man.'

Cat frowned as a blob of warm jelly was squirted onto her stomach. 'What are you doing?'

'An ultrasound.'

'I'm not due for one. Is there a problem?'

'No problem at all,' Gemma said, 'I just thought it might be nice for you to have a peek at your gorgeous baby. I'm recording it,' she added. 'Maybe Dominic might want to see it too.'

'Do you think?' Cat frowned. She loved having Gemma doing her ultrasounds—all her ultrasounds with Thomas had been fraught affairs. Mike had actually taken the probe out of the radiologist's hand once in an attempt to take over.

'I think that it might be a very nice olive branch,' Gemma said. 'It must be a shock for him and this might help him get used to the idea. When things get tense between the two of you, this might serve as a little reminder that it's your baby you're discussing…'

Cat nodded and looked over at the screen.

It was a fun ultrasound. Gemma wasn't taking measurements, just a brief check that all was okay, which it was, and then they took a lovely long look.

There it was, opening its little mouth like a fish, and it was the most beautiful thing Cat had ever seen. 'What am I having?'

'You're sure you want to know?'

'I already know,' Cat said. 'I just want to hear it.'

'You're having a little girl,' Gemma said, and Cat felt as if the examination couch had dropped from beneath her, a little like turbulence on a plane.

'I was convinced it was a boy!'

'I know that you were,' Gemma said. 'She's beautiful. Look at those cheeks…'

It felt so different to look at the screen and to know it was her daughter that she was seeing. There she was, wiggling, waving and content in her own little world.

'Happy?' Gemma asked as Cat lay there.

Yes, she was dreading facing Dominic, yes, her life had been turned upside down and inside out but 'happy' was the right word.

Here, now, seeing her little girl, Cat was exactly that— happy.

'You're going to be a brilliant mum,' Gemma said, 'and, no matter how awkward things are between you and Dominic, I'm sure that you'll sort it out as best you can.'

After Cat had stood up and done up her dress, Gemma handed her the recording of the ultrasound and Cat put it in her bag.

'Good luck.' Gemma smiled.

'I'll need it.' She glanced at the clock. 'He's going to think I've stood him up.'

'He knows you've got an antenatal appointment?' Gemma checked, and Cat nodded. 'Well, surely he knows they don't run like clockwork...'

'Mike was always—'

'That was Mike,' Gemma said.

And this was Dominic.

'Hey, Cat,' Gemma said as she went to go. 'When you saw him again, did you still fancy him?'

'Moot point—I don't fancy married men.'

'Did you still fancy him?' Gemma persisted.

'Yes,' she admitted, 'but that's for this office only. The day I sit crying to my friend about whether or not I sleep with him because, of course, he and his wife never do it, or I start saying, he's going to leave his wife after Christmas...you have my permission to shoot me.'

'I shall and can you tell him from me that he's an utter bastard,' Gemma said.

'Oh, I shall.'

Trust Gemma to make her laugh, Cat thought as she walked the short distance to Oliver's. She was calmer than she'd expected to be as she stepped inside.

There was Dominic, sitting with a glass of wine and looking rather more rumpled than he had that morning. His tie was off, the top button of his shirt undone and his eyes were black with loathing as Cat made her way over.

She didn't expect him to stand for her.

Very deliberately he didn't.

It was a bit like walking into the headmaster's office, Cat thought, but refused to be rattled. She shook off her coat and put it on the low bench opposite him and then took a seat.

'Sorry, I'm a bit late. Gemma was running—'

'It's fine.'

Cat blinked at the ease of his acceptance.

It wasn't her timekeeping that was Dominic's concern!

'How was the appointment?'

'All's well,' Cat said.

'She's a good friend?' Dominic asked, and Cat nodded as she bristled in instant defence.

'Are you going to ask if that's wise?' she checked.

Dominic said nothing and she continued.

'Everybody seems to question whether or not I'm sensible to be seeing a friend, but—' Only then did he interrupt.

'You're a consultant and, from everything I heard at my interview and everything I've seen, you're meticulous and thorough, possibly a bit obsessive about certain details. I'm quite sure you've given your choice of obstetrician very careful thought. I'm sure your friend and you both discussed the pros and the cons of having her. I don't think there's anything I can add that you haven't already thought through.'

Cat felt the little bubble of indignation that she had around that topic deflate a touch.

'She's excellent.'

'I'm sure she is.'

'Have you heard from Andrew?' Cat asked.

'Nope,' Dominic said. 'I'm not really expecting to hear positive news. I'm quite sure you've had, or will be having, a quiet word in his ear…' He watched the colour mount on her cheeks as a waiter poured Cat some water and gave them menus. 'Though, if you haven't already, please think long and hard before you do. I assume you live close to work?'

'Sorry?'

'I'm just thinking for handovers and things.'

'Handovers?'

'Access visits, or whatever they're called.' Then he raised his voice just a fraction and the pink on her cheeks moved to a burning red. 'If we work at the same place, then it might make it a little easier when I want to spend time with *my* child!'

'I was going to tell you—' Cat attempted, but she didn't get very far.

'When it turned eighteen?' He shook his head. He clearly didn't believe her and she couldn't really blame him a bit for that. 'I don't think for a moment that you were going to tell me. In fact, I'm quite sure you'd already got what you needed from me that weekend.'

Cat's mouth gaped open. 'You think I deliberately got pregnant? What? That I'm some psycho going around pricking holes in condoms?' She shook her head and then met his eyes. 'I shouldn't be surprised. My mother thinks the same. Well, not quite that scenario but she seems to think I got bored one weekend and popped off to the sperm bank.' She dragged her eyes from his and looked at the menu as she spoke.

'I never set out to get pregnant.'

Dominic sat there and images of them making love danced before him—her hand rolling on a condom, another time, about to take her from behind, it had been Cat who had grabbed one and handed it to him.

If anything, it had been he who had been about to be careless, so ready had he been to take her.

It wasn't the best thought to be having right now and he reached for a wine and gave a small nod.

'Fair enough.

'And I did try to contact you. I spoke to some cheery woman in Glasgow who said that Dom had moved on…'

'It would have taken an hour tops to find me if you'd really wanted to,' he said.

'Have you told your wife yet?' She smirked as she read through the menu. 'Or were you hoping it wasn't yours?'

'Well, given my wife is all seeing and knowing now, I'd assume that she already knows.' He watched her frown. 'She's dead.'

Cat looked up.

'She's been dead for more than two years.'

'And you didn't think to tell me?'

'Don't even go there, Cat. You're the one keeping the big secret. Anyway, I *chose* not to tell you.'

'Why?'

'Because I didn't want *that* look.'

He didn't get to elaborate—the waiter was back and Cat ordered steak and a tomato salad and rolled her eyes because she really wanted seafood but it was on the list of noes that Gemma had given her. 'I'm never going to get my paella.'

'I'll have it for you,' he said, and ordered it.

'Bastard,' Cat said, even if she managed a small smile, but it soon faded as they got back to the serious talk once the waiter had gone.

'I didn't tell you at first because I wanted to make sure all the tests were okay…' The water she took a sip of seemed to burn as it went down. 'They were.'

'That's a poor excuse, Cat, because if they hadn't been

okay, a bit of notice that I'd be arranging my life around a special-needs child would have been appreciated.'

Again, his reaction surprised her. He didn't jump on results or demand facts. He had but one question.

'When's your due date?'

'The nineteenth of April.'

'Cat, I nearly bought a house in Spain last month. I was offered a job and that was going to be the starting date.'

'You can still take it,' Cat said, but rather quickly wished that she hadn't as his finger pointed in her direction and he shot out one word.

'Don't!'

He was doing his very best to stay level and calm but that she'd happily wave him off to Spain incensed him. 'I was pointing out how bloody late you've left it. I know!' Dominic said. 'How about you have the baby, I take it to Spain and you can see it during your annual leave?' He watched as her pink tongue bobbed out and she licked nervous lips. 'Yeah, not a nice thought, is it, Cat, so don't suggest the same for me. You need to get used to the idea that I'm not going to be some distant figure in my child's life. I'm going to be there, not just for Christmas and birthdays. I'm going to be doing the school pick-up and homework and I'll be there each and every parent-teacher night. You might not want me there and I fully get that we can't stand each other, so we can do it through lawyers if you prefer...'

'When did we get to not being able to stand each other?'

'Oh, about the time you started snooping through my wallet, about the time I found out that you'd deny me knowledge of my own child...'

'I thought you had a wife, maybe a family...'

'Even if I had, I still should have been told.'

Their food came then and she stared at his rather than hers.

'That was really horrible of me,' he admitted as he looked at his large plate of paella, especially as it looked seriously nice.

'Hopefully you'll have a massive allergic reaction.' Cat, less than sweetly, smiled.

'Yes, and no doubt you'll take ages to find the adrenaline pen so I'll be dead and that will take care of that...'

There was a tiny silence.

'When you said you didn't want to tell me you were a widower because of *that* look,' Cat said as she cut her steak. 'What did you mean?'

'Things change when you tell people that you're a widower...' He scooped out a mussel and then pulled a misty-eyed face that made her smile reluctantly. 'I can't really explain it. Honestly, since Heather died I've had more offers for sex than a rock star. Which sounds good but women seem to think I want to make love, or that I'm comparing them to my poor late wife, or even that I must want a wife... They don't get I just want to get down and dirty.'

'So we weren't making love?' Cat pouted and he smiled. 'Dominic, it was supposed to be a one-night stand.'

'And now we have to deal with the consequences.' He got back to his food. 'Did you find out what *we're* having?'

The 'we're' was very deliberate.

'I only just found that out now,' she said. 'A girl.'

She watched as his fork paused midway to his mouth and then he put it down.

The past ten days, since he had seen the maternity cover position being advertised, since he'd started to suspect she might be pregnant, had been spent in a whir of fury and concern. Now, in the midst of anger and change, he got a moment in the quiet centre of the storm.

A girl.

A daughter.

He just sat there as the news sank in and somehow, he had no idea how, it changed things, because, in that moment, he went from none to having not just one but two ladies to take care of and he looked at the bump of the little one and then into the eyes of her mum.

'Oh.'

'I know,' Cat said. 'I thought I was having a…' She was about to say *another boy* but she quickly changed. 'A boy.'

Yes, she understood Dominic a little better than he knew because she didn't want to be the recipient of *that* look.

Baby two after such a turbulent baby one was a private pain, one she could barely share with Gemma, let alone a man whose bed she'd been in for a single night.

No, he didn't need to know all about her.

There was a lot to talk about but they finished their meal in silence, lost in their own private thoughts.

'Have you thought of names?' Dominic asked as they put their cutlery down.

'I was leaning towards Harry till tonight.'

'I never thought I'd be running through baby names,' Dominic said.

'Didn't you and…?' She hesitated. It was none of her business whether or not he and his wife had planned on having children.

Dominic was grateful that she didn't finish the question. No, he and Heather hadn't got around to thinking of children. And he didn't want to share his wife with this virtual stranger.

'Do you want a quick coffee? Then I'm going to have to go,' he said, 'if I want to make my flight.'

'You're going back to Scotland tonight?'

'No, I'm going to Spain for a few days. As I said, I'm in the middle of relocating there and I've been looking at homes. Given that the baby is mine, there's a lot to do there. I'll have to withdraw my application and I'd like to do that in person, and I want to tell my parents face-to-face what's happening.'

'Will they be disappointed that you're not moving there now?'

'I don't think so. I wasn't exactly going to be living next door to them or anything. I expect they'll be surprised about the baby and then pleased.'

'Where are you flying out from?'

'Gatwick.'

'Good luck with your luggage,' Cat said, and gave a low laugh. 'I'll drive you.'

'I can take a taxi.'

'You're the one banging on about how we need to talk.'

He conceded with a nod.

'And no coffee for me, unfortunately.' Cat sighed. 'It gives me hiccoughs. I'm stuck with tea. I miss champagne, I miss coffee, I miss seafood…'

'I'll buy you the biggest bottle of champagne and

have paella delivered to your hospital bed once the baby is here.'

It was a very nice thing to say, Cat thought. It was a nice thought to have because, even if they were the odd couple and doing this on the run, at least they weren't at each other's throats now.

'How did you find out about the baby?' Cat asked a little later as they walked to her car.

'Well, I keep an eye on jobs and things and I saw one come up in your department. I remembered something you said about being the only female consultant...'

She flashed the lights of her car and they walked over to it.

'I told myself that I was being ridiculous. You could have been married or anything...'

'Would you have cared if I was married that weekend?' she asked.

'No,' he admitted.

'I don't like you,' Cat said, but he just laughed.

'You don't have to like me. Anyway, I'd never have cheated on my wife, but that weekend, had you been cheating...' Dominic shrugged. 'Anyway, it's all hypothetical.'

'But very telling.'

'Do you want me to lie to you, Cat, just say the right thing?'

'No.'

'Anyway, back to how I tracked you down—the dates for the leave all added up and...' They stopped talking as they got in but once they were pulling out of the car park the conversation resumed. 'I was going to call you but then I decided to surprise you.'

'That wasn't very nice.'

'No, I know that it wasn't,' he said. 'I wasn't feeling very nice at the time, but…' He didn't continue, they just drove in silence, but as the airport came into view conversation started again. 'You haven't chosen badly, Cat. I might have been a bit of a bastard the way I landed on you and some of the things I've said tonight but I'm not going to be a negative in your baby's life. And,' he added, 'I'm sure you don't need my opinion of you but when I think of some of the women that I could have been having this conversation with, I'm very happy that it's you. I think you'll be a brilliant mum and I'm quite sure we'll do this right. We've still got a couple of months to work things out…'

'We do,' Cat said.

He went into his wallet, pulled out a business card and wrote a few things on the back and Cat frowned when she read them.

'Why would I need your social network details? I'm not going to be checking up on you…' Then she went pink when she recalled how he'd caught her going through his wallet.

'Or me you,' Dominic said. 'But if you update about the baby and things…'

'I'll call you if there's a problem.'

'I meant for day-to-day stuff,' he said. 'I don't need formal emails and progress updates. Soon you might want the same…'

'Sorry?'

'Well, she won't stay a baby. My family lives in Spain.'

'You'd take her on holiday? No.'

She was adamant, her response was instant. 'You're not taking her out of the country.'

And Dominic was about to respond that his lawyer

would see to it but he held that in. He could see the conflict in her eyes and he knew that she was struggling with the concept.

Cat was. She had glimpsed the future.

There would be pictures of her child with her father in houses she never set foot in. Holidays spent apart.

'I just sent a friend request,' Dominic said. 'Up to you whether or not you accept it.'

'Here…' She went into her bag and wrote down her number, then she remembered the recording.

'What's this?'

'I had an ultrasound today. If you want to see her…'

'Thanks.'

He went to get out of the car. 'I am sorry for not telling you, Dominic.'

He gave her a grim smile. 'Yeah, well, I don't accept your apology—I'm not that magnanimous. Call me when you need to…'

'I shan't.'

'Oh, I'm sure you'll have questions.'

'I won't.'

But even before she got home Cat had found several.

Would he want to be at the birth?

The very thought filled her with horror!

Cat did her best to stay in control and the one place she was guaranteed to lose it was in the labour ward.

No, she did not want arrogant, surly Dominic seeing her swearing like a sailor and breaking down.

No way!

And what were they going to tell people at work?

Her mind was darting as she stepped back into her home.

She put some washing on and, completely wrecked

from a long and difficult day, wrestled off her boots, which was very hard with a stomach like a basketball, and then had a very quick bath and went to bed.

Except, though tired, she couldn't sleep and she picked up her phone and, sure enough, there was his friend request, which she accepted.

His status was given as single and Cat frowned, wondering why he didn't say he was widowed.

Oh, that's right, he loathed *that* look.

Then she smiled when she read his status. A little cryptic note that she was sure was aimed at her.

You can run but you can't hide.

She carried on reading and looking at photos of his eccentric parents and terribly beautiful sister and then there she was.

Heather.

She knew it was her from the photo she had glimpsed in the hotel.

Now she felt as if she was snooping, so she went back to Dominic and saw a picture of him all wet and gorgeous coming out of a swimming pool. At thirty weeks pregnant and not wanting to be, she was terribly, terribly turned on.

'So not happening,' she said, and turned off her phone.

His body was still there, goading her to have another glimpse, at six the next morning when she drank her tea and switched her phone back on.

But then she smiled when she saw what he had changed his relationship status to.

It's complicated.

It most certainly was but, the funniest thing was that as she dressed for work and headed out to face the day, even if they weren't together, they were on the same side—her baby had a father and that sat right with Cat. She didn't feel quite so alone.

CHAPTER SEVEN

DOMINIC'S PARENTS WERE, though initially surprised, completely delighted with the news.

There was too much wine drunk and they spoke late into the night, and they kept making the most ridiculous suggestions.

'Why don't you bring her here so we can get to know her and she can have a little holiday?'

'She's thirty weeks pregnant,' Dominic said, and looked over at Kelly for some help.

'Mum, they're not a couple,' his sister said.

'Perhaps, but I'd still like to meet her. We could come over.' His mother, Anna, was warming to the idea. 'We could fly over for the birth. I'd love to see my grand-daughter being born.'

Dominic swore under his breath before answering. 'I don't even know if I'm going to be present at the birth…'

'You could film it,' Anna said. 'Live-stream it.'

'And then you could set it to music and forward it to your hippy friends…' Dominic sarcastically responded, and when his father nodded this time Dominic swore out loud. 'You weren't even there when we…' he gestured to Kelly '…were born.'

'And I regret it to this day,' James said. 'That's the beauty of being a grandparent, you get to do things right the second time around.'

What planet were they from? Dominic wondered.

Even if they made him laugh, they drove him mad at times, and this was one of those times. He could only imagine how well that suggestion would go down with the cool and rather distant Cat.

Yes, they made him laugh, because he was doing that now as he pictured her shocked expression as he told her he wanted to film the birth.

'Cat and I are going to sort things out between us.' Dominic told his parents how it would be. 'Preferably without lawyers. You guys need to stay back.'

'From our grandchild?'

He closed his eyes for a brief moment. He'd never considered having a baby but now that he was he wanted his parents in his child's life, so he thought long and hard before answering.

'From Cat and me,' he said. 'We've got two months to work things out. You're to stay out of things.'

Anna didn't answer. In fact, Dominic was sure she shook her head.

After his parents had gone to bed, he sat, listening to the trickle from the pool filter and enjoying sitting with his sister outside. It was cool and they had the gas heaters on but after a cold Scottish winter it was blissful.

'I love it here,' Dominic said.

'Would Cat?'

'Oh, we are so far from that, Kelly,' he said. 'It was a one-night stand, a weekend conference…'

'That's completely changed your life,' Kelly said. 'You were all set to move here.'

'I was *almost* all set,' he said.

'Almost?'

'I don't want to talk about it.'

He didn't.

He didn't want to tell his sister that, despite the seriousness of his plans, since August they had started to change. Unable to get that night out of his mind, and furious at how the weekend had ended, he had considered calling Cat to explain things. And if he was thinking about calling her, it had seemed a bit nonsensical to be considering moving further away than he was already.

Yes, he hadn't been idly flicking through jobs in London.

He'd been wondering how he could ask her to give them a chance.

'Is there any hope for the two of you?' Kelly asked. 'You obviously fancied each other and you said things went well when you saw her again…'

'Kelly, the stakes are a lot higher now. Surely we should be concentrating on how we're best going to be as parents rather than trying to establish a relationship.'

'I guess.'

'What if it doesn't work? What if we give it a go and one of us wants to end it? God, we don't need hurt feelings and resentment added to the mix. I hardly know anything about her.'

'Does she know about Heather?'

'I told her tonight that I was a widower.'

'Tonight?' Kelly checked.

'Yep.'

'So what were you two talking about that weekend?'

Dominic rolled his eyes. 'We weren't really talking.'

Except that wasn't entirely true.

They had talked, they had shared more than sex. That was the reason he had wanted to look her up.

'I took her to Collserola Park,' Dominic said. 'We watched the sun come up. You know how Heather had a thing about sunrise?' he asked, and Kelly nodded. 'Not once, when I've been with someone, have I felt guilty. It's always just been sex and I knew Heather would get that but that morning, sitting watching the sun come up with someone who wasn't Heather, was the most unfaithful I'd ever felt.'

'It sounds like you two have something to build on…'

'Maybe,' he said. 'But it would be foolish at best to rush this. I've had one brilliant marriage, Kelly. I'm not downgrading for the second one. Right now Cat and I need to sort out how we're going to be for the baby. The two of us as a couple will just have to wait. I'm not going to see her for another three weeks and that's if I even get the job.'

'Won't she see to it that you do?'

Dominic managed a wry laugh. 'You have a far sweeter mind than I do, or Cat come to that. I'm quite sure she'll be seeing to it that I don't.'

They said goodnight and as he lay in bed he took out his laptop and plugged in the recording and saw for the first time the life they had made.

She was beautiful, so beautiful that it actually brought tears to his eyes.

It should feel like a mistake—surely this was something he should have been doing with Heather—and yet, seeing his baby on the screen, thinking of Cat…

It didn't feel like a mistake.

It felt right.

Was there a chance for them?

Could strangers who had shared just a night have got it so right that they could spend the rest of their lives together?

Cautious with his emotions, it had taken years to get around to getting engaged to Heather.

They had gone out for more than two years before they'd moved in together.

Another three years before they'd got married.

And they hadn't been ready to even start trying for a baby before Heather had been taken ill.

He flicked on his social media site and saw that Cat had accepted his friend request and it was Dominic who snooped.

She had the most boring page ever.

He found out nothing new about her, other than that her star sign was Virgo and that her friends wrote on her wall more than she did.

No mention of Spain, no lovers' names.

Nothing.

He wanted to know more, though, and even if they needed to be concentrating on the baby, somehow they had to make time for them, and that was why he changed his status.

Not single.

Not in a relationship.

It's complicated sounded about right, so that, for now, would do.

CHAPTER EIGHT

'You sound out of breath,' Dominic commented.

It was Thursday night, a few days since they'd met, and Cat had only just arrived home when she answered her phone and it was him.

'That's because I just took my boots off.' She sighed. 'Which is no mean feat these days.'

'I'm just calling to let you know what you probably do already—Andrew called this afternoon while I was flying back from Spain and left a cheery message, asking me to call him. So it sounds like I got the job.'

'You did,' Cat said, flicking on the kettle.

'Do you have an issue with that?'

'I did,' she admitted, 'but I don't now.'

'He's also asked if I can start a couple of weeks before I officially take up your position. Do you have an issue with that?'

'A bit,' she admitted, 'but I'll get over it. How was Spain?'

'Still beautiful.'

'How were your parents with the news?'

'Elated.'

'Oh!'

'Invasive.'

'Okay.' She let out a laugh. 'It's not just them. Honestly, people think they can ask me the most personal questions and as for touching my bump…' She shuddered.

'I promise not to touch your bump uninvited.'

'Thank you.'

'I'm coming down this weekend and I'll be looking at houses. I'm just checking you're not planning on moving in the near future…'

Cat was silent. He really had meant it when he'd said he wanted to be around for his child.

'No, I have no plans to move. Well, I might need a bigger house but I shan't be leaving the area.' She thought for a moment. 'You're not going to move too close, though? I mean…'

'I don't want to be your neighbour, Cat. Just close enough to make things easier on both of us. I was going to rent but I've been doing that for a couple of years. I want to give her a proper base.'

'Sounds good. While I've got you on the phone I actually do have a couple of questions,' she said.

She had quite a list actually.

'Can they keep till the weekend?' he asked. 'I'm a bit swamped right now.'

'Sure.'

'We can go out for dinner and discuss things.'

And if he could be so brusque and direct, without apology, then so too could she.

'I don't want to go out,' she said, because she'd had to swap to get this weekend off and there was a lot to be done. By evening all she would be ready for was a night flopped on the sofa. 'I don't want to discuss my private life in a restaurant. You can come here.'

'Okay, don't worry about cooking, though.'

'Oh, I shan't.'

'Saturday, about six?' Dominic checked. 'I'll come when I've finished looking through houses.'

'Whenever,' Cat said.

She heard a voice in the background.

A female voice.

'I have to go.'

He was probably at work, she told herself as she ended the call.

And even if he wasn't, it was none of her business.

Cat really didn't have time to dwell on her feelings, if she even had feelings for Dominic. Aware she was only going to get bigger and that there weren't too many days off between now and her maternity leave starting, when Saturday came she found herself back in the wallpaper shop. This time she had Gemma in tow and her brother's offer to come and help this afternoon when the cot was being delivered.

'We have the softest pink,' Veronica said. 'It actually feels like candy floss...'

'The last time I ate candy floss I vomited,' Cat said to Gemma.

'It's gorgeous,' Gemma insisted as she ran her hands over it, but Cat shook her head as she opened up another sample book.

'That,' Cat said, 'is what I call gorgeous.'

'It's blue!'

It was *so* blue, the paper was every shade of night and brushed with dandelions that looked as if they could blow away in the night wind.

And so Cat found herself up a ladder as her brother, Greg, hovered nervously. He had no idea how to hang wallpaper so he held the ladder instead and handed her the glued sheets to put up.

'It's very dark,' Greg offered, when she was done.

'It's supposed to be for sleeping,' Cat said. 'You don't like it?'

'I don't know,' Greg admitted. 'Maybe when the cot's in and you've got the right furniture and light fittings...'

'You have no imagination, Greg.'

'I'm an accountant,' Greg said. 'What time's the cot arriving?'

'It's a p.m. delivery, that's all they'd say.' A knock at the door had Cat smiling. 'You can help set it up while I go and get changed.'

'Help?'

Cat laughed as Greg went down to get the door and then she looked around the bedroom. 'A brave choice' had been Veronica's words when she had made her selection. Gemma had looked worried and Greg was sitting on the fence...

'Cat!' Greg called. 'The cot's here and so is the reason for its purchase.'

Dominic gave a wry grin as Cat's brother announced his early arrival.

He had surprised himself with his own reaction when he had seen a man waiting for the delivery of the cot.

A good-looking man around Cat's age.

It had taken only a moment to work out it was probably her brother, and as he introduced himself the same green eyes had confirmed that fact.

Dominic, though, was unsettled by his brief two-bulls-in-one-paddock moment.

Another thing that needed to be discussed, he thought.

No, he wasn't particularly looking forward to tonight.

Then he changed his mind because, wearing khaki trousers and with a vest top on, Cat came down the stairs and he noticed that between now and earlier this week her belly button had poked out.

'Dominic.' Cat gave a wary smile at the strange air of hostility in her hallway. 'This is my brother, Greg.'

'We've already introduced ourselves,' Greg said as the delivery man dragged cardboard boxes up her stairs. 'Right, I'm off.' Greg gave his sister a brief kiss on the cheek.

'I thought you were going to stay and help with the cot.'

'Er...Cat,' Greg said, 'I'm sure Dominic can manage that much at least...so long as it's not too much responsibility for him...'

Oh, no!

She groaned inwardly as Greg got all big brother and angry and tried to somehow equate putting up a cot with men who impregnated helpless virgins and left them heavy with child.

'I've got this, thanks, Greg,' she said, but only as her brother shot Dominic a filthy look and then stalked off did it dawn on her what the problem was.

'Oh, God,' she said to Dominic. 'I forgot to tell him you weren't married.'

'Remind me never to take over a multi-trauma patient from you,' he said.

'What?'

'Well, you're not very good at passing on pertinent information.' He smiled. 'Anyway, the mood he's in, it wouldn't have made a difference. I'm still the one-night stand who left his precious little sister pregnant.'

'He hasn't been like that...' she was about to say,

since she'd broken down on Greg about Mike, but now wasn't the time and anyway she had to sign for the delivery, so she finished with a lame '…in ages.'

He waited till she'd signed for the cot and the door was closed before he continued speaking.

'Well, next time you're talking, if you could slip into the conversation that I'm not cheating on my wife, it would be appreciated.'

'I shall.'

Dominic doubted it.

He assumed he was way down on her list of topics of conversation.

He assumed rightly.

But he was up at the top of her thoughts.

Inappropriate thoughts for a heavily pregnant woman about a man she didn't particularly like.

'Lovely hallway,' he said.

'Come through.' She opened the door to the lounge and Dominic stood there for a moment.

'This is such a sight for sore eyes after some of the dumps I've seen today.'

'Did you find anything you liked?'

'One that I liked.' He told her the address and it was close but not too close. 'It needs far too much work, though.'

'Ooh,' Cat said. 'Tell me.'

And so he told her about the dodgy plumbing, the ancient kitchen, fireplaces, cornices and the disgusting bathroom with green carpet and a study that was completely covered in cork tiles.

'That sounds like my idea of heaven,' Cat said, and she went to her perfect mantelpiece and took down a photo. 'This was what this room looked like when I bought the place.'

'Oh, my God, it's worse than the one I saw today.'

'We can do a tour if you like,' she said. 'I love showing off my handiwork.'

'You renovated it?'

'Every last bit of it.'

'Oh, my...' he said as they walked down her hallway and to the kitchen. 'We could swap houses,' he said. 'You could renovate mine while you're on maternity leave...'

'I might be a bit busy, Dominic,' she said.

'I'm sure you could fit it in,' he teased, and yet it made Cat smile because everyone else told her how zoned out and incapable she was going to be once the baby was here.

He seemed to know her better than everyone else.

It was strange, it was nice.

It was unexpected.

She took down a picture from the fridge and showed Dominic the absolute disaster the kitchen had once been.

'I didn't have a sink for the first three months. I had to do my dishes in the purple room of pain upstairs.'

'Show me your purple room of pain, Cat...'

Whoops, were they flirting?

Up the stairway they went, admiring the wooden bannister as they did so. 'There were about twenty layers of gloss paint,' Cat told him, and then she opened the bathroom door and took a photo from a small dark wooden chest so he might understand just how painful purple could be.

'Everything was purple,' Cat said, 'even the toilet seat cover...'

'But it's like something you'd find at a yoga retreat now,' he said. 'Not that I frequent them, but if I did…' he looked at the rolled white towels on the dark wood and the gorgeous claw-foot bath '…well, I'd demand a bathroom like this.'

'It's fabulous, isn't it?' she said. 'But the place is tiny. No room for a nanny.'

'A nanny?'

'I'm going to be working full-time, Dominic.' She didn't look to see his expression. 'Do you want to see her room?'

'The nanny's?'

'The baby's.'

'I would.'

She was a little nervous about opening the door, she wasn't sure why, but as she did and he stepped in, she found she was holding her breath. Dominic looked around.

'It's like…' he started, and she braced herself for 'a brave choice' or to be told how dark it was, or for Dominic to point out that it was dark blue when they were having a little girl. 'It's like a magical night-time,' Dominic said. 'It's amazing. You just want to…'

'Say it!'

'Sleep!'

'Yes.' Cat was delighted. 'That's what I thought. It's just so dark and peaceful and once the curtains are in and the light fittings…'

'And the cot,' he said, looking at it all piled against the wall. 'Do I have to do that?'

'You'd look a right bastard if you left it for me to do.'

'Fair call,' Dominic said. 'Right, shall I go and get dinner?'

Cat nodded.

'Anything in particular?'

'I'd love a hot curry,' she said. 'And mango chutney…'

'How hot?'

'Very hot.'

'Okay.' Dominic frowned. 'But I thought pregnant women would avoid curries…'

'What's the population of India?' Cat asked as they walked back down the hall. 'I'd like a beef curry and lots of naan. You get dinner and I'm going to have a bath and get changed.'

'What's in there?' Dominic asked, fully knowing they were passing her bedroom door.

'Something you'll never see.' She smirked as he headed off.

But as Dominic got into the car and Cat stripped for the bath, she wondered if she should just run it cold to put out the fire down below. They'd both known she was lying.

Her bedroom was *yet* to be seen.

Which was a problem.

A very real one.

Sex would only make things complicated.

And they were complicated enough already.

CHAPTER NINE

HE WAS GONE for ages.

Ages.

So much so that when Cat came out of the bath and peered out of her bedroom window and saw that there was no car coming down the street, instead of quickly dressing, she took a few minutes to put on moisturiser. As she rubbed it into her stomach she wondered just how much bigger she could get.

She put on a long grey tube dress and then combed through her hair.

Still no car.

Was he shopping for ingredients? she wondered.

She didn't bother with make-up.

Instead, she poured a nice big glass of iced water, her latest favourite drink, and then she put the door on the latch and went back upstairs and started taking the cardboard off the cot.

'It's open,' she called, when he finally arrived. 'I'll be down soon.'

Dominic was serving up dinner when she came down five or so minutes later, carrying a pile of cardboard.

'Come and eat.'

She did so, but first she poured herself a small glass

of antacid for her inevitable heartburn and he smiled as she took a seat on the floor at the coffee table, where he had set up.

'If I'm going to get heartburn, I want it to be worth it,' she said. 'It smells fantastic. Where did you go?'

'About fifteen minutes away. I worked near here a few years ago and I was guessing this curry house wouldn't have closed down.'

She could see why it hadn't when she tasted the curry.

'We can put the cot up after dinner,' he suggested, and Cat nodded.

'It will be good to have that room done.'

'You had some questions for me.'

'I do,' she agreed, and took a breath. 'Are you going to tell people at work that, well, that you're going to be a father?'

'I don't know.'

'And if you do, are you going to say that the mother is me?'

Dominic pondered for a moment. He hadn't thought this through properly. 'I guess not. Well, not at first. Maybe once you've gone on leave, or you've had the baby. Has anyone actually asked who the father is?'

'Not at work,' Cat said. 'Well, not directly. I keep my personal life to myself pretty much.'

'Okay,' he said. 'Well, you don't have to worry about me saying anything. What else?'

She was rather nervous to ask the next one. 'Are you going to want to be there at the birth?'

This question Dominic had thought about. 'I think that depends on what you want, and I would guess that you might not want me there…' He gave a tight shrug and then he looked at Cat for her response.

'I don't want to rob you of anything, but…'

'Just the first six months of the pregnancy,' he sniped, and then he stopped trying to score points. 'Sorry, go on.'

She didn't really know how best to say it. 'If you add it all up, we've probably spent less than forty-eight hours together.'

'I get that.'

'And I just think I'd do better on my own.'

'Fair enough.'

She was grateful for his words but she knew that it wasn't completely fine with him, that she was denying him being present at the birth of his daughter.

Well, tough, she thought, scooping some curry onto her naan. Surely some things were better unseen!

'My parents both want to be there, though,' Dominic said suddenly, and she nearly choked on the water she was drinking. She looked at his expressionless face and she had no idea if he was joking. 'I pointed out that I didn't even know whether I'd be there and they suggested that you film it…'

'For them?' she croaked, and he nodded. 'I know we don't know each other very well,' she said, 'but I trust we know each other enough that you said an emphatic no.'

'I did,' he said. 'While I wouldn't normally presume to speak on your behalf I delivered that no for you and reminded my father that he was away on business when I was born and didn't see me till I was six weeks old.'

'Really?'

'This apple fell very far from that tree. I'll be seeing her very soon after she's born.'

'Of course.'

He got up then and Cat waited as he went out to the car and when he came back he handed her a bag. 'I wasn't going to give this to you.'

'What is it?'

'My mother's been shopping.'

She most certainly had. Wow, the Spanish had amazing taste in baby clothes. There were tiny little sleepsuits and little hats and cute socks and a thick envelope, which Cat opened with a frown.

'I've no idea…' Dominic said.

'They just wanted to say congratulations,' she said as she read the letter, 'and to let me know that whatever goes on between us two, I'm welcome any time in their home.'

'Too much?' he checked.

'No,' she admitted. 'That's actually very nice of them.' She thought for a moment—it really was. Suddenly her baby had a whole other family and, aside from Dominic, they included her.

'Don't expect the same from my family,' Cat warned.

'Oh, I don't.' Dominic smiled. 'Next question.'

'I'm hoping to breastfeed. I know that you'll want to see her and have her stay over, but…'

'Not till she's old enough,' he said. 'I understand that she'll need her mum. Maybe we play that one by ear, trust that we'll work out what's right for her.'

'Okay.'

It sounded a lot better than trying to work out some neat arrangement with a lawyer.

'Any more questions?'

'I think that's it,' she said. She'd had loads but, really, now that he'd said they'd play things by ear she felt soothed by that.

'You're sure?' he said, as if he expected there to be more, but Cat nodded.

'Do you?' she asked.

'Well, I guess that I do… Are you seeing anyone at the moment? I mean, is there someone who's going to…?' He couldn't really admit that he didn't like the idea of another man being more of a constant in his child's life than he was but Cat had started to laugh.

'I have no idea why, Dominic,' she said, 'but I can't seem to pull lately. It's like I've got two heads or something.' Then she was serious. 'No, I'm not seeing anyone.'

It didn't fully answer the sudden questions that filled both their minds, how they'd feel about the other dating, but they decided to drop that hot coal for now.

After dinner they headed upstairs and between them they put up the cot.

'This is about as far as my DIY skills go,' Dominic warned. 'I only know how to use a drill from my orthopaedic rotation.'

It was more a fiddly job than a difficult one, though it was easier with two, but after a few attempts it was up. Cat put in the mattress and then Dominic checked that the side slid up and down.

'Do you think,' Dominic asked as they surveyed their handiwork, 'that I should maybe get the same wallpaper for her room at my place?'

'I think that would be really nice for her.'

For the first time she glimpsed the two of them getting this right, not just able to manage but that their daughter's future would be better for having him in her life.

'I'm sorry I didn't let you know,' she said. 'I had my reasons.'

'You thought I was married,' he said. 'I really wish you hadn't gone snooping that day. I don't like snoops.'

'I don't usually. Remember on the beach, when I went to get the mouthguard?'

He frowned in recall as Cat spoke on.

'I saw a ridge in your wallet that felt like a ring and then I kept seeing a pink line on your ring finger, and the more you stayed out in the sun the pinker it got. When you were having a shower I let curiosity get the better of me.'

'Fair enough,' he said. 'I'd only just started to take the ring off.'

'Why didn't you tell me you were widowed?'

'I wasn't ready to share her with you,' Dominic said. 'That might sound odd...'

'No, no, I get it.'

That part Cat did, because she still wasn't ready to share Thomas.

'Heather had several brain tumours and that's all I want to say about it.'

'Okay,' she said, and she glanced over and saw how uncomfortable he was with the topic. 'We didn't sign up for this, did we?'

He understood what she was trying to say. 'The baby's actually the easy part.'

It was opening up and sharing your life with another person that was the difficult bit.

He looked down at her stomach and the mini-gymnast within, because in her tight dress you could see the baby moving. Cat did the right thing.

She took his hand and he felt the solid bulge of their child's head trying to climb into Cat's ribs, and then she guided his hand down past her belly button to a foot, and then she left him free to roam.

And that lump of hot coal that they had dodged was back, it had to be, because she was terribly hot and for once it had nothing to do with the extra person she was carrying.

It had more to do with the reason her baby was there.

'Haven't you got another question, Cat?'

Her cheeks were pink and she wondered how to broach the most difficult question of all.

'Us.' Dominic did it for her. 'Dating.'

She swallowed.

'My parents and sister all seem to think we should give us a go,' he said. 'I've told them that it's the most terrible idea I've ever heard.'

'Terrible?'

'Well, we know the sex part would be fine…'

'You assume it would be fine,' Cat corrected.

'I know it would be fine for me,' he said. 'I've never found a pregnant woman attractive till now…' His hand was on her stomach and it wanted to move up to the thick nipple and stroke it, he wanted that dress off, and from the loaded silence between them he guessed that she did too. 'From my perspective,' he said with a low, sexy huskiness, 'I'd have no problem doing you on the floor right now.'

'You could,' she admitted.

'But then what?' He looked at her and met eyes that glittered with lust. 'What if we break up? What if it doesn't work out between us?'

'I don't know.'

'So,' he said, when he'd far rather not, 'no sex for

us, none of the easy part. What I'm proposing is six months…'

'Of what?'

'No dating anyone else…just us, getting to know each other, working out how we can be friends, concentrating on the baby…'

It was the most sensible thing she had ever heard.

She should be cheering really.

No pressure, no stepping on the roller-coaster, no promises made that might prove impossible to keep.

No sex.

It was the last part she was wrestling with.

'Sure.' She smiled. 'Can you remove your hand, please?'

'Yep.' He did so. 'I'm going to go,' he said.

'Where are you staying?'

He didn't answer her question. 'I start work in three weeks on Monday…'

'Where will you stay? I mean, even if you put in an offer on the house…'

'Not your problem, Cat,' he said, though he said it nicely. 'You worry about yourself and the baby. I'll sort out things at my end.'

He did.

The next day he had another look at the house before heading for home. It was a ten-minute walk from Cat's.

Two weeks later, driving home, Cat found herself slowing the car down as she always did when she drove past it.

Actually, she had no need at all to be driving past.

She just did these days.

SOLD.

She tried to imagine the future.

Stopping the car at this very spot and getting her baby and its bags out and handing her heart over to him.

She couldn't.

And it was even harder to imagine driving off.

Going home alone to an empty house when the people she loved were in another one.

No, Cat corrected, the baby she loved…

No, a little voice told her, *you are crazy about him and have been since the moment you met him.*

They just didn't know each other at all.

CHAPTER TEN

THERE WASN'T REALLY the chance to get to know each other.

Cat's pregnancy continued to gallop along at breakneck speed and for Dominic, seeing the bank, sorting out the purchase of his house, working his notice and arranging to move his stuff to England had his blood boiling about how hard Cat had made it by not telling him.

Then he'd remember the reason he was moving his life several hundred miles and *not* in the planned direction of Spain and he chose to let it go.

He didn't move in on the weekend before he started working at the Royal. Cat knew that because, after a long weekend on call, she drove home on the Monday morning and the house was still untouched.

And even if their paths didn't cross during those first few days at work she certainly knew that he had started because she heard the nurses discussing the sexy new doctor.

'Is he seeing someone?' Cat heard Marcia asking Julia on their coffee break early one evening. 'He doesn't have a ring.'

'I don't know,' Julia said. 'I'm going to ask him when

he comes on.' She smiled at Cat, who was taking a seat. 'How many weeks now?'

'Thirty-four,' Cat said.

'When do you finish up?' Marcia asked.

'Just next week to go.'

If she lasted that long.

She ached, her stomach was huge and she felt as if she was wearing some awful fake pregnancy outfit. She was all boobs and belly and even though it was cold and just coming into spring, she was permanently too hot and felt as if she was wrapped in a blanket.

She was dressed in her grey tube dress with her hair worn up just to keep it off her neck and a small cotton cardigan to stop people asking her if she was cold. 'You're on nights next week, aren't you?' Julia groaned in sympathy. 'I am too. I can wheel you around in one of the wheelchairs.'

Cat smiled. 'I might just take you up on that!'

They'd all tried to subtly prise out of her who the father was but had accepted that she didn't want to tell. Apart from that, though, she was getting on better with everyone. Yes, she was more than back to her old, pre-Mike self.

Cat was sipping on iced water and trying not to fan herself when Dominic walked in and Marcia and Julia perked up.

'How's the move?' Julia asked.

'Not happening till the weekend,' Dominic said, and took a seat and nodded to Cat.

'Are you on tonight?' Cat checked, and glanced at the clock. It was only seven and he wasn't due to start till nine.

'I am. I'm here now if you want to finish up.'

Cat shot him a warning look. She did not need him babysitting her and so she said nothing.

She didn't need to; Julia took care of that.

'So, is it just you moving in?' she fished. 'Or have your whole family relocated?'

'Just me,' Dominic said.

'So you're not married?'

'No.'

'Girlfriend?' Marcia asked.

'Nope.'

'So you're single!' Julia beamed.

She wasn't smiling for long.

'Julia?' Dominic asked. 'Why would you assume that just because I haven't got a girlfriend that I'm not in a relationship?'

She watched Julia frown as she tried to work it out and Dominic got up and left.

'Does that mean he's gay?' Marcia asked. 'Does that mean…?'

Cat left them to it but she did have to smother her smile as she tapped him on the shoulder in the kitchen. 'Don't start coming in early so you can cover for me. If I need help…'

'Oh, for God's sake,' he said. 'I'm staying with friends at the moment and they've got three children all under five. Believe me, I would far rather be at work.'

'Oh.'

'So stay if you want to, go home if you like…'

She stayed, but it was only on principle.

By 8:00 p.m. the department was quiet and the few patients they had were all either waiting to go to the ward or waiting for their lab work to come back.

'So you're moving at the weekend?' she asked.

'Yep.' Dominic rolled his eyes. 'I knew I was buying a bomb but when I got the keys... You should see it.'

She'd like to see it. Only, he didn't offer.

The only solace she had was the exclusion zone he'd put around dating, so she knew he wasn't busy with someone else.

She just sensed his dark mood.

'I'm going home,' she said.

''Night.'

Yes, his mood was dark.

It was two years to the day since Heather had died.

Last year at this time he had realised he had to move on.

He'd just never expected his life to head in this direction, and moving in at the weekend was going to be hell.

It was.

All the furniture he'd had brought down proved to be an expensive mistake, because it ended up being donated. He watched the charity truck drive off with half of his life on board and as he took delivery of a cot he felt as if he were on Pluto.

He was back in London minus a wife.

And about to become a father by a woman he barely knew.

It was time to rectify that.

Cat came in from work on Sunday evening and there was a note on her door, inviting her to dinner.

She stopped at the supermarket and bought flowers, which was very back to front, but, then, every part of them was back to front. Seeing her standing there, holding a bunch of daffodils, made him smile when he opened the door.

'I was lying to Marcia and Julia. I'm not gay.'

'Yes, well, I'd worked that one out. You can still like flowers, though.'

Spring had sprung and he looked in a box to find a glass because he didn't own a suitable vase.

He chose not to explain that he had once owned a heavy crystal vase that had been a wedding present but he'd got rid of it and there was a little hand-blown glass one they'd bought on their honeymoon. He couldn't bear to part with it or put Cat's flowers in it.

Then he chose to open up a little.

'It was Heather's two-year anniversary the other day...'

'I'm sorry.'

'And I've just got rid of a truckload of our stuff. Not everything, but...' Yes, he was bad at sharing and so the daffodils got a beer mug, which felt a whole lot better than placing them in *their* vase.

She knew there was nothing she could say and Dominic was very glad that she didn't try.

'Do you want a tour?' he offered.

'I thought you'd never ask.'

He saw disaster, Cat saw potential.

'This house is going to be amazing,' she said as she walked through.

'It smells,' Dominic said. 'It didn't the last time I walked through it.'

'They'd have sprayed something.' Cat laughed. 'You've got damp...'

He knew that from the surveyor's report.

'Not much, though,' she said. 'And you could just get rid of this wall...'

'Sure you don't want to swap houses?'

'I'm very sure.' She smiled. 'I've got enough to do

at mine. I think I'm nesting. I keep washing things and folding things—it's really disconcerting.'

'Here.' He opened up a cupboard and pulled out a jumble of laundry. 'If you feel the need.'

'I shan't.'

Dinner was nice.

A lovely lamb roast he had made, better than the frozen meal Cat would have managed before falling into bed.

'I start nights tomorrow,' she said. 'Four of them, and then I'm out of that place.'

'Are you looking forward to stopping work?'

'Now I am,' she admitted. 'At first I wanted to work right up to the last minute but not now.'

She was now thirty-five weeks, soon to be thirty-six, and the thought of four weeks or more of this was daunting, to say the least.

'I got a cot,' Dominic said.

'I saw.'

'I'm quite sure you don't want to put up another one…'

Actually, she did.

'I know she won't be here much at first, but if she is, it's better she has somewhere she can sleep,' Dominic said. 'I'll get around to decorating it…' He looked at the woman who wasn't the woman he was supposed to have been doing this with and then he looked away.

'I'm really sorry you're hurting,' she said.

'It's not your fault. It just is what it is. Tomorrow's the anniversary of her funeral. There are just all these bloody dates in March…'

July was her horrible month.

This one would be as hard as the first for she'd be

telling Thomas that he was a big brother now. She'd be at her happiest and saddest at the very same time and she didn't quite know how she'd deal with it.

And, yes, perhaps then she could have told him but she found it impossible to share that most painful part of herself.

She didn't trust his reaction.

The death of a child was agony.

The death of a child, when it was suggested by the people you love most, even her own parents, that it might be a blessing, made it a place you chose not to go with others.

One wrong word from Dominic, she knew, would kill her inside.

'I'm going to go,' Cat said, because they were too new to be too close. 'Give you some time.'

He nodded and saw her downstairs and to the door.

'I want to be there, Cat.' He said what was on his mind. 'For the birth.'

'I know you do.'

'I'm not going to push it. I'm not going to demand or anything, I'm just telling you how I feel. I know I said that it didn't matter but it's starting to matter more and more to me. I don't think I'll be having any more children. I think this little one will be it.'

He went to touch her stomach and then remembered he couldn't, uninvited.

'You can,' Cat said, and he felt the little life when he was so cold today on the inside. Guilt dimmed a touch because how could this be wrong?

How could falling in love be wrong?

If, indeed, that was what he was doing.

'Go,' Dominic said. 'I need to think.'

And so too did she.

CHAPTER ELEVEN

'Dominic wants to be at the birth,' Cat said as Gemma finished examining her.

'What do you want?' Gemma asked.

'I don't know,' she admitted. 'I wish we had longer to work this all out…'

'You'd have had longer if you'd told him sooner.'

'Yes, well, I'm sure Dominic is thinking the same. I nearly told him about Thomas,' Cat admitted. 'And I know that at some point I'll have to. I'm just missing him more and more with each passing day. I'm missing all the things he missed out on and I know if I tell Dominic I'm going to start howling.' She looked up and she'd thought Gemma might be cross but her lovely friend had tears in her eyes.

She hadn't just delivered Thomas; Gemma had been his godmother. She had held him and loved him when Mike hadn't. Nigel too had been there, cuddling her baby and not grimacing at his imperfections, the way even her own mother had.

'I'm here for you, Cat,' Gemma said. 'As I am for all my mothers. If you don't want Dominic to be there, you can just say no and I'll see that it's enforced. If he is going to be there, he has to know you're going to be very emotional.' She gave her a smile. 'You finish up work this week?'

Cat nodded. 'Yes, I'm back here tonight for four nights and then I hang up my stethoscope for six months.'

'Are you okay to work?' Gemma checked.

'Is there a problem?'

'No,' Gemma said. 'If you feel up to it, that's fine. Your blood pressure is normal, everything looks good. You just look tired, Cat. I mean, really tired. I'm more than happy to sign you off for these last few nights.'

It was incredibly tempting but Cat shook her head.

'I don't think it's just the pregnancy that's causing sleepless nights,' she admitted. 'I'll see these nights through and then I'll concentrate on Dominic and me and try to decide what the hell I'm going to do about the birth.'

'Come on, then,' Gemma said. 'Let's get out of here. You're my last patient today and I need to get home. Nigel's got his French class tonight.'

'He's still learning French?'

'He is.' Gemma smiled as she put on her jacket. 'You know how we had to cancel the honeymoon because of my blood pressure with the twins? Well, he's determined we're going to have one. Though why he has to learn French to take me to Paris is beyond me.'

Cat waited as Gemma handed all the files over to the receptionist and wished her goodnight and then popped in to thank the midwife who had worked with her in the antenatal clinic today. They were out in the corridor and heading for home when Gemma stopped walking and turned to her. 'Friends now,' she said.

'Of course.' Cat frowned and then realised she was about to get a lecture.

'Let him in.'

'I don't know how,' Cat said. 'It's not just me. He never talks about Heather, or rarely. All I know is that she had a brain tumour, or rather tumours.'

'Why don't the two of you go away for a couple of days and talk things out while you're still able to?' Gemma suggested. 'You're thirty-five weeks now. There's still time. The best day of Nigel's life was seeing the twins being born. He cut the cords, he held them first…'

'I know,' Cat said, and then she smiled. 'Dominic's parents asked him to film it.' She thought Gemma would laugh but she just rolled her eyes.

'Tell me about it! I had a father ask if I could move a little to the left the other week so he could get a better shot.' They both laughed for a moment but then they were serious.

'If Dominic is going to be there at the birth, then he has to know about Thomas. If he's in the delivery room, he needs to be told that this baby isn't your first. He'll find out as soon as you get there.'

Gemma was right, Cat knew as she got ready to go to work that night.

She had a shower to wake her up and, thank goodness, Cat thought, she no longer had to worry about straightening her hair.

She massaged conditioner into the ends and then stood there for a good ten minutes, letting the water wash over her, holding her big fat belly and loving the life within.

He didn't get to do that, Cat thought as she looked down at the little foot or knee that pressed her taut stomach out.

Dominic didn't get to enjoy this simple, beautiful treasure of a moment.

Perhaps they should go away for a couple of days.

Talk.

Or not.

Just find out a little more about each other before the baby arrived and they attempt to co-parent. They were pretty much on opposite shifts at work, so they didn't really see each other there. Dominic was busy trying to get the house sorted on his days off and Cat was busy trying to catch up on sleep on hers.

She got out of the shower and combed through her hair. Everything was an effort and she wondered if she shouldn't have taken Gemma up on her offer to take these last nights off.

Despite it having been a nice clear day, it was cool and drizzling outside and the house was cold. She shivered as she crossed the hall and went into her bedroom. Turning on the light, she let out a small curse as the light bulb popped. Yes, she loved her high ceilings but it would be foolish to attempt to get out a ladder in the dark and climb it.

She'd ask Greg to come and change it for her.

She needed a Nigel, Cat thought, and then sat on her bed in the dark and surprised herself by bursting into tears.

No, she didn't want her own Nigel and she didn't want her brother dragging himself here on his way home from work just to sort out her light.

She wanted Dominic.

Cat laughed at herself, sitting there crying over a light bulb, but it was the very simple things that rammed the big things home.

She wanted the ease of asking him and didn't know whether she could or not.

It was time to find out.

She used the flashlight on her phone to choose what to wear, knowing that when she got to work she would be changing into scrubs and flat shoes. For now she grabbed her boots. She pulled out a small cami and the now well-worn paisley dress and went downstairs to put them on.

As she went to pull on her boots she remembered the hell of getting them off, but she'd deal with that later. Right now she couldn't be bothered to trudge back upstairs and rummage through her wardrobe in the dark.

Stop crying, Cat told herself as she drove to work, but the tears kept trickling out.

What the hell is wrong with you? she scolded herself. She parked in her usual spot and walked into Emergency.

There was Dominic, coming out of a cubicle, and he gave her a brief nod.

A colleague's nod.

Well, what did you want him to do? Cat asked herself. *You told him to stay back at work.*

But then he called her back.

'How come you're here?' he checked. 'You're not due to start till ten.'

'Oh!' That's right, she was on ten till eight instead of the more usual nine till seven. Her brain was so scrambled she kept forgetting the littlest thing.

Not at work.

At work she was fine but in all things domestic and mundane her memory was like a sieve.

She didn't tell him she'd mixed up her shifts. Instead, she just shrugged and walked into the changing room.

There was a knock at the door and Cat frowned and opened it.

'You've been crying.'

'Yes.'

'Can I come in?'

'It might look a bit odd if you're seen in the female changing rooms.'

'Not really. I'm checking on a heavily pregnant colleague who's clearly been crying.'

Cat went and sat on the bench as he came in and he stood against the closed door, like a security guard.

'So?'

She sat there for a moment. 'Can't I just be having a bad day?'

'Of course,' he said. 'How did the appointment go?'

Ah, that's right, Cat thought, he was worried about the baby, not her. 'All good,' she said. 'Head down. Gemma offered to sign me off work but only because I'm tired. Everything else is fine.'

'But you're here.'

'Yes.'

'And tired and teary.'

'My light bulb blew in my bedroom,' she said.

'You didn't try to change it?'

'I'm not stupid,' she answered quickly. 'No, I didn't try to change it.'

She looked up at him and he smiled, then spoke. 'You won't ask, will you?'

'I don't know if I can.'

'For God's sake, Cat, do you really think you can't even ask me that?'

'I know I can but what happens next time one blows? I mean, do I call you...?'

'Well,' Dominic said, 'from my light-bulb experience, when one goes the others tend to follow, so for the next few weeks I will be on light-bulb duty.'

'Thank you.'

'Give me your key and I'll go and do it on the way home and then drop the key back to you when I come on in the morning.'

She looked in her bag to get it.

'Is there anything else?'

Say it, Cat.

She took a big breath.

'Do you want to go away?'

'Sorry?' Dominic's eyes widened, clearly taken back by her suggestion.

'Well, I'm finishing up this week and I presume you'll get some days off. I thought it might be nice to get away before the baby comes along, sort out a few things…'

'Separate rooms?' he asked, and she laughed.

'I haven't thought that far ahead.'

'I have,' he said, and came over. She thought it was to take the key but having pocketed it he bent down.

'What are you doing?' she asked as he lifted one of her legs.

'Helping you off with your boots,' he said. 'And it's no to separate rooms.'

God, he was sexy. He lifted one leg and his eyes never left her face as, far more easily than she ever could, he pulled the boot off. 'But you said—'

'I know that I did but, as you know, I'm prone to changing my mind.' He had her other leg up and was pulling off the other boot, and if there had been a lock on the door he'd have turned it.

'I think,' Dominic said, 'we should celebrate the one uncomplicated thing about us and have loads and loads of sex and then, maybe then, it might be a bit easier to talk…'

'Easier?'

'I can't think very straight at the moment.'

'Sounds like a plan,' she said. He was holding one leg and she was possibly in the least flattering position. Her dress gaped open, and she glanced down and thanked the sock gods that she'd lost them in the washing machine and her feet were bare.

She could see his erection and she was just as ready.

'I'll book somewhere nice,' she said, but Dominic wasn't waiting till next week.

'I could always arrange to come in late to work tomorrow,' he said. 'I'm on with Andrew,' he clarified, because she was frowning. 'Maybe I might need a little lie-down in your bed after I exert myself changing your bulb.'

'I might be a bit tired in the morning.'

'You won't be too tired, Cat.'

No, she wouldn't be.

Exhausted perhaps but as his hand stroked her calf she imagined it higher and she needed that now.

His pager was going off and it was possibly just as well, or they might be found in the most compromising of situations and their cover would be well and truly blown.

He leant over and gave her a kiss, a rough, wet one, and then pulled her to standing. Her stomach was hard and his hands were wild with possession but then his pager went again.

'You need to go,' she said.

'I need to come.' He grinned and gave her the briefest kiss but then he did the right thing and went to work.

Cat was way too early for her shift.

She could have let Dominic go early but was quite sure that he'd say no. Anyway, the thought of sitting down for an hour was terribly appealing so she made a mug of tea, took herself off to the break room and started to watch the news.

Her tea remained untouched, and within two minutes of sitting down she was out for the count.

Dominic popped in once to speak to one of the nurses about a patient he had in cubicle two and saw her there, dozing, and the dark smudges under her eyes.

He felt a bastard that in a few minutes he'd be waking her so that he could go home.

'Hey, Dominic.' Julia popped her head around the door. 'We've got a guy found unconscious outside a pub. He's talking now, but very confused…'

'Okay, I'll come now.'

His patent was in cubicle five.

'Hello, sir,' he said. 'I'm Dominic, one of the doctors on tonight.'

He was told, far from politely, where he could go.

'Okay, what's your name?' Dominic asked.

It was a swear word, apparently.

Dominic saw that the patient's blood pressure was high and when he checked it again, it was even higher.

'Does he have any ID with him?' Dominic asked, and Julia gave a worried shake of her head.

'He's got no phone, no wallet, nothing. I think he might have been mugged.'

Dominic couldn't smell alcohol on the patient, and while he had all the signs of being a belligerent drunk,

Dominic was very relieved to have been called promptly. He was growing increasingly sure that this man was suffering from a serious head injury.

'Come on, sir…' He tried to calm the man down and then glanced over to Julia. 'Can you call Radiology for me? And Mr Dawson.'

The patient spat.

'And an anaesthetist. I think we'll have to sedate him.'

Thank God Cat wasn't dealing with this, Dominic thought as he blocked a punch from the irate man.

He just wanted her safe at home.

CHAPTER TWELVE

CAT WOKE AND stretched and went to take a sip of her tea, then pulled a face when she realised it was stone cold.

She gave a small yelp when she saw that it was a quarter past ten.

Yes, she might need help with a light bulb but she didn't need help with her shifts at work. She had a long drink of water in the kitchen and then walked quickly to the department, retying her long hair as she did so and trying to convince herself that she wasn't too tired to work.

She heard a raised voice coming from a cubicle and frowned as somebody told Dominic incredibly inappropriately just where he could go and to please get away from him. Cat had this sinking feeling in her stomach as she recognised the voice.

'Sir.' Dominic's voice was crisp and calm. 'I'm very concerned about you. I want you to lie down. I'm going to get you a scan now. I believe that you have a serious head injury.'

He looked up as Cat came into the cubicle and she realised he hadn't been covering for her. He'd been busy trying to calm a very agitated patient.

'Nigel.' Cat went over and she knew instantly just

how serious this was. She was grateful that Dominic had recognised this wasn't a drunken man. This was gentle, kind Nigel, who at first didn't recognise even her.

'Nigel, it's Cat, you're at the hospital.'

He told her what she could do with that information and then he frowned as the familiar face came near him and he started to cry, angry, frustrated tears.

'Cat, what the hell is going on?' Nigel begged. 'Cat, help me.'

'We're going to help you, Nigel,' she said, and he finally lay down. She glanced up at Dominic. 'What happened?'

'We think he was mugged,' Dominic told her. 'We're just taking him to be scanned now. You know him?'

Cat nodded. She was trying not to cry herself as she held Nigel's heaving shoulders. 'This is my friend Gemma's husband. Nigel Anderson,' Cat said. 'He's thirty-two.'

'Any medical history?'

'I don't think so,' Cat said. 'This is nothing like him.'

'I get that,' Dominic said, his voice grim.

Nigel had given up fighting now. He had finally lain down but then he suddenly sat up and started vomiting.

'I'm going to go with him,' Dominic said. 'The neurosurgeon and on-call anaesthetist are meeting me there.' Joe, the porter, was running over.

Everything was under control, Cat realised. No, Dominic hadn't been covering for her. He'd been busy trying to give Nigel the acute care he needed.

'Call his wife,' Dominic said as he headed off with the patient.

For a moment Cat stood there, simply stunned, but

then she went to the nurses' station and pulled out her own phone.

She had made many difficult calls in her life, it was part of her job, but this would be, by far, the hardest she had made.

'Hey, Gemma,' Cat said.

'Cat!' Gemma answered, and then she must have realised the time, or perhaps heard the distress in her friend's voice, even though Cat was doing her best to sound calm. 'Is everything okay?'

'Gemma…' She took a breath.

'Is the baby…?'

Oh, poor Gemma, she was busy putting her doctor's hat on and now Cat had to put on hers. 'I've just started my shift. Nigel's been brought in.'

Gemma gave a shocked gasp. 'He's at his French lesson.'

'He was found in the street, Gemma. He has a head injury and is having a CT scan now.'

'Is he unconscious?'

'No,' Cat said, but she didn't want to offer too much reassurance because Cat knew that Nigel's condition was serious. 'He's very confused, Gemma.'

'How confused?'

'He was agitated.'

'Yes, well, he hates hospitals.' Gemma pushed out a nervous laugh. 'He doesn't even like coming in to have lunch with me and—'

'Aggressive,' Cat broke in, and she knew that in saying that Gemma would understand just how serious this was.

'How long will the scan take?'

'Not long at all,' Cat said. Fortunately, they had one

of the newest machines and the results would be in very quickly, though she was quite sure that Nigel wouldn't be returning to the department. He would, she guessed, be going straight up to either Theatre or ICU. 'Can you get someone to watch the twins and come here?'

'I'll call my parents.'

Cat looked up and saw that the light that meant there was an emergency in the radiology department was going off.

'Ask Gill to come in and watch them,' Cat said, referring to Gemma's neighbour. 'Andy can drive you in. I have to go now, Gemma.'

She loathed leaving her friend hanging. She knew the panicked state she had placed her friend in, but there wasn't time to wait for Gemma's parents. They were slow and annoying and would ask five hundred questions before they even started to reach for their car keys.

She rushed to the radiology department but the anaesthetist had arrived already and was intubating Nigel.

'He's got a small subdural,' Dominic explained. 'He started seizing and has just blown a pupil. We're going to race him up to Theatre.'

Nigel was now sedated and Dominic told her that the neurosurgeon had gone ahead to scrub as they started to move Nigel out. It was calm and controlled, the only panic in the room internal, and Cat looked at her friend's husband, perhaps the kindest man she knew, lying there fighting for his life.

She held his hand as they ran along the corridor. 'I'll look after Gemma and the twins,' she said to him, and at the elevators she gave an unconscious Nigel a very brief kiss as they went to move him in. 'You look after you and get well.'

She was breathless from her brief run and wanted to sit down on the cold tiled floor and cry but instead she pushed herself to turn around and head back down.

She could only guess at what was about to greet her.

'Where is he?' Gemma was frantic, running towards Cat just as she got back to the emergency department.

'I've asked at Reception…'

'Come in here,' Cat said, leading her to a small interview room.

'I want to see him now.'

'He's in Theatre, Gemma.'

Her friend simply crumpled. She just lost it.

She stood there and folded over and it dawned on Cat she had never seen Gemma anything other than calm before. Even when there had been a scare about the twins Gemma had remained upbeat and positive. Now, though, she couldn't even make it to a chair and it was Cat who held her up.

Thankfully, Dominic, back from taking Nigel to Theatre, came in and took over. He explained what was going on.

'They're operating on him now. He has a small subdural haematoma.' Dominic explained that Nigel was bleeding on his brain and that he had been rushed to Theatre to evacuate the bleed and relieve the pressure that was building. 'Mr Dawson is the one doing the surgery and he's one of the best.'

'He's brilliant,' Cat said.

'I don't understand what happened, though,' Gemma wept. 'He was at his French class.'

'It would seem he got jumped,' Dominic said. 'He had no wallet with him, no phone or ID. A passer-by found him lying down outside a pub. Luckily they called for an ambulance instead of just assuming he was drunk.'

'Nigel doesn't drink.'

'When he arrived here he was confused, he said that he needed to get home. His blood pressure was high and I arranged for an urgent CT scan. At that point Cat came on duty and of course she knew who he was. It all happened that quickly. He was drowsy during the CT and only at the last minute did he become unconscious.'

All poor Gemma could do now was wait.

'Cat will go with you to wait,' Dominic said, and Cat gave a grateful nod.

It was only as she walked out of the department that she started to realise she wouldn't be coming back to work until she was a mother.

Just as Nigel and Gemma had dropped everything for her when she'd had Thomas, it was time for Cat to do the same.

'Will you speak with Andrew and explain I won't be able to come in?' Cat said to Dominic.

'Of course,' he said. 'Just take care of your friend.'

She did.

It was the longest night.

Nigel came through Theatre and Mr Dawson was cautiously optimistic but he explained that Nigel would remain in an induced coma for the next forty-eight hours at least.

'I can't believe someone would do this for a wallet.' Gemma sat, holding his hand. 'He's got two little boys who need him. I need him.'

And Cat, who had sworn she'd never need anybody, knew what she meant.

She needed the breakfast that Dominic bought them

when he dropped in in the morning, having finished his shift.

She needed his support and she got it.

Her shifts were covered, Gemma's parents moved in to take over the twins and Cat went home at lunchtime and packed a bag for herself, then went to Gemma's and did the same for her friend.

When she got back to the hospital, they holed up as the world went on.

Just as Thomas had never been left alone, she and Gemma took turns to sit by Nigel's bed while the other slept. Even when his parents and brother visited, either Cat or Gemma were there.

Gemma trusted Cat to notice things she wasn't sure anyone else would, and it was the only way she'd consider getting some rest herself.

'How is he?' Dominic came into Cat's line of vision late on the second afternoon.

'The same,' Cat said. 'It's just a matter of waiting.'

'How's Gemma?'

'She's just gone home to check in on the twins. She's all upbeat and positive now. She's talking as if he's just had his wisdom teeth out.'

'How are you?'

Cat shrugged.

'Are you getting any sleep?'

'Some. Gemma and I have taken over one of the on-call rooms.' She looked up and smiled as her friend came back and Dominic spoke for a moment with Gemma and then left.

'How were the twins?' Cat asked.

'Teary and clingy. Mum and Dad keep asking when

I'll be back. I know that the twins are too much for them but what else can I do?'

'I can look after them,' Cat offered.

'I need you here, though.'

'Have you managed to get hold of your sister?' Cat asked. Gemma's sister was in the army and not immediately accessible.

'Finally, and she's asking for urgent leave and should be back in a couple of days.'

It was another long night and as Gemma slept through the morning part of it Cat sat with Nigel.

They were going to try to extubate him later and it was scary, to say the least.

'You have to be okay, Nigel,' Cat said. 'Your family needs you.'

'They do,' Gemma said, and Cat looked up and smiled at her friend. 'Thanks for being here.'

'Where else would I be?'

'And I must thank Dominic.'

'For what?'

'Covering all your shifts, bringing me decent coffee. He's gorgeous,' Gemma said, and took her seat by Nigel. 'I don't blame him for not saying he's a widower.' She took Nigel's hand. 'See, Nigel, you have to get well or I'm going to be getting loads of offers for sympathy sex…seriously,' she said to her comatose husband. 'I'll have all the single dads lining up to fix the car or the leaky roof. I'll have to fend them off.' She turned to Cat and smiled. 'Go and have a sleep. I'm going to talk dirty to my husband and remind him of all he'll be missing out on if he dares to leave.'

Cat slept.

The very second she lay down in the on-call room

she fell asleep and awoke with a jolt only when the door opened and there was Dominic.

'What's happened?'

'Good news, well, cautiously good.' He was holding a large mug and he waited for her to sit up, which was rather difficult to achieve, and then he handed it to her and brought her up to date.

'He was fighting the tube and they've extubated him.'

'Is he speaking?'

'No.'

'Has he opened his eyes?'

'No, but he responds to voices and is moving all limbs.'

'I should go…' Cat went to get out of the bed but he took her shoulder and pushed her back.

'No, no. Gemma's in with him. I've just come from speaking with her. Her mum's not well. Well, she's got a cold…'

'They're useless,' Cat hissed.

'I said that you'd go and watch the twins.'

'What did Gemma say?'

'She was relieved, I think.'

Cat let out her own sigh of relief. If Gemma was happy for her to go, then, really, things must be starting to look better for Nigel.

'I thought he was going to die,' she admitted.

'I know you did.'

For the past couple of days, since the moment she'd heard Nigel swearing and cursing, she had honestly thought he would die, or that the Nigel she'd known was gone.

Now there was hope that he was on his way back.

'Have your tea, then I'll drive you. There's no need to rush.'

'Are you working?'

'Just till five. Hamish worked last night and again tonight. I'm back in at nine tomorrow, but I can take half an hour to drop you at Gemma's.'

Cat nodded. She was way too tired to drive.

He sat on the edge of the bed and she looked at him—unshaven and exhausted—and she could see the strain in his features, and whether or not she was allowed to ask, she did.

'Is this hard on you too?' They both knew she was referring to his late wife.

'Yep.' He took a drink of her tea and then handed it back to her.

'Heather ended up in ICU and she hated me for it. She never said it, of course, but it was something she dreaded and not how she wanted it to be...' He didn't tell her any more and Cat sat there, not feeling slighted in the least. The sharing part was so incredibly hard at times. They'd been sort of thrust on each other by the baby.

That hurt Cat.

It was a niggle in her heart, a wound that gnawed.

That day when she'd thought he was cheating, instead of correcting her he had simply let her go—that was how much she had meant to him then, which made it hard to confide in him now.

'I'm going to see Nigel,' she said, 'and get Gemma's keys and things.' She looked around the room—in two days she'd accumulated quite a lot of stuff. Toiletries, clothes, towels...

'I'll pack it up,' he offered.

'Thanks.'

She buzzed and was let into ICU, where Gemma sat with Nigel's mum, but she stood up and gave Cat a hug.

'How is he?' Cat asked.

'Well, he didn't exactly open his eyes but he did sort of screw them up when I spoke to him,' Gemma said. 'He knows we're all here.'

Cat went over and gave Nigel a kiss. 'Hurry up and wake up,' she whispered into his ear, 'or she'll start talking dirty to you again.'

'He moved his eyes,' Gemma said. 'What did you just say?'

Cat laughed but she gave Nigel's hand a big squeeze. 'You keep getting better, okay?' She turned to her friend. 'Right, I'll go and watch the twins…'

'I feel awful, asking,' Gemma said, because she could see how exhausted Cat was.

'Please, don't,' Cat said.

'My sister will be here tomorrow, I hope.'

'It's fine. Just stay with Nigel and don't worry about anything else.' She smiled at Nigel's mum and headed out to where Dominic was waiting for her.

'How old are the twins?' Dominic asked as they walked to his car.

'Two,' Cat said.

'Good luck!' He smiled.

It felt strange, getting into a car with him again.

It was a different car from the one in Spain but there were coffee cups and papers and she looked around for a moment, remembering him taking her to Collserola and that morning.

She hadn't known him then.

She didn't really know him much better now.

Maybe Dominic was thinking the same thing, because

he turned on the engine and reversed out of his parking space and, just when she was least expecting him to, he told her about the very moment his world had fallen apart, the split second that he'd known everything was about to change.

CHAPTER THIRTEEN

'HEATHER WAS A VET,' Dominic said, and Cat turned and looked at him but didn't respond, and he remembered that he liked that about her—she didn't butt in or say unnecessary words.

'We met at university. She was crazy about animals. Horses, dogs, cats, cows…but mainly horses. She was a staunch vegetarian. She'd given up trying to get me to be one. Almost. Really, I think she would have been vegan by now.'

Still, Cat said nothing.

'We went out for years before we got engaged and it was a couple of years after that before we got married. I knew her very well, that's the point I'm making.'

He turned briefly and Cat nodded.

'One night she got up and, I don't know why, I came downstairs and I found her eating a steak sandwich. It was one of my steaks that I'd cooked and was taking for lunch the next day.' He managed a small laugh at the odd detail, yet it had been so very strange, just so completely out of character that he could remember to this day his confusion. 'Heather got all cross when I pointed out that she was eating steak, and said she was starving and she'd just fancied it and when she saw it in the fridge she couldn't resist it. I got that but it was bizarre, so unlike Heather. I thought maybe she had some sort of iron deficiency, or even that she was pregnant, perhaps. It was just a tiny thing that didn't make sense but then there started to be more and more tiny things. A couple of days later we had an argument that came from nowhere. She was furious about something and to this day I can't remember how it started. I just know that I had never seen her more angry. I knew then there was something very wrong.'

He gave a wry smile. 'It's very hard to say in the middle of an argument that I thought there might be something wrong with her... It would be like asking if she'd got PMT. But I knew that I wasn't arguing with her. I could reason with Heather but she was suddenly like a stranger. Anyway, she huffed off to bed and went for a sleep and woke up and was back to being Heather.'

The satnav announced they had reached their destination and Cat looked up and realised they were outside Gemma's, but she made no move to go in.

He'd told her more than she needed to know, but it was what he'd needed to tell her, so she understood.

'The row scared me and it must have scared her enough that she went to a doctor, who took her seriously. She called me at work and said she was about to have a head CT and would I come down.' He turned and looked at Cat. 'I knew,' Dominic said. 'I knew even before she had the scan and so did Heather. We went from normal to dying in one week.'

'No treatment?'

'Chemo,' Dominic said. 'But it was dire and really with little prospect, so after four rounds she pulled the plug. She always said we treated animals with more dignity than humans and she was very clear about what she wanted.'

Bizarrely, Cat thought, even though she wanted to know, she also wanted to tell him to stop.

She wanted to put up her hand and say, 'She died, I get it. I don't need the details. I cannot bear your pain,' but she sat there and looked at him and there wasn't a tear on his face, just a depth in his voice, and she understood now his quip about Gordon.

He wasn't mean at all—he was in agony and trying to hold on as he did what he had to.

Talk.

'Well,' Dominic said, and he reminded her a bit of Gemma, chatting away, as if she wasn't dying inside. 'We went on holiday, we thought we had a couple of months' grace. She wanted to go to Stonehenge. I don't know if it was a tumour making her wacky or just the way people go when they're dying—you know, the universe, God and living in the moment—but Heather got obsessed with sunrises. We were staying in a little cottage and I woke up one morning and she wasn't in bed. At first I thought she must have gone to get a drink or to the toilet but then I went looking for her. The front door was open. I drove around the streets and I met some guy who said he'd seen a woman being taken off in an ambulance...' He stopped talking then because there was a tap at the window and it was Gemma's mother, so cheery that the cavalry had arrived and she could go home.

Cat pressed open the window.

'Not now!' she snapped, and closed it again. 'Sorry about that,' she said to Dominic as Gemma's mum did an indignant, affronted walk back inside.

'The ambulance…' Cat said, and Dominic nodded, very glad Cat had told the woman to go. He just had to tell this story all in one hit.

'I called the local emergency department as I drove there but I never told them that she didn't want any active resuscitation.' He took a very big breath and his eyes silently begged her to say something.

'I doubt they'd have listened to someone calling in over the phone. I wouldn't have,' Cat said. 'I mean, I'd have listened and taken it in, but…' She shook her head.

'I didn't even tell them, though. I still feel like I let her down there.'

'You just weren't ready for her to die.'

'No, but I wish for her sake she had that morning. She got another three weeks and they were hell.' He gave her a grim smile. 'I could have told you all this at that lunch, nailed you to a wall like Gordon did…'

'You couldn't, though,' Cat said. 'I get why.'

Did she say it now?

Did she say, 'Well, guess what happened to me!'

Of course she couldn't. Anyway, Gemma's dad was heading towards them.

'I want to tell him to…' Dominic said, and that made her smile.

'So do I,' Cat said. 'But we won't.'

'No, we won't. I'm going to go back to work,' Dominic said. 'You're going to look after the twins and when you have time I'd like you to look up somewhere amazing for us to escape to the very second Nigel gets the all-clear.'

'I shall.'

'Go,' he said, 'and don't give me *that* look.'

'I shan't,' she said, and gave him a kiss on the cheek instead and then headed inside.

'Sorry about that.' Cat smiled at Gemma's very offended mum. 'That was a colleague from work and he'd just had some difficult news.'

Gemma's parents were already putting on their coats.

Cat soon understood that possibly it wasn't because she'd caused offence that they practically ran out of the house.

Two two-year-olds missing their parents and their routines.

Two two-year-olds who threw down their sandwiches because they didn't know how to say they liked them cut in squares, not triangles.

Two two-year-olds who were like wriggling eels in the bath as Cat knelt on the floor beside them that night.

Yes, they *all* needed Nigel, Cat thought as she got them into pyjamas and started to shepherd them down the stairs for some milk.

She wasn't a very good shepherd. One would go down, the other up, and she was too aching to carry them again.

'Daddy!' Rory squealed, when the key turned in the door.

'Mummy!' Marcus shouted, and the three of them stood there in slightly stunned surprise as Gemma came through the door.

'Gemma!'

Cat's heart just about stopped in terror as the twins thundered down the stairs and into their mum's arms. Gemma burst into tears and dropped to her knees and cuddled them.

'Is he...?'

'He's fine!' Dominic came in, carrying an awful lot of bags, only to look up and see Cat frozen on the stairs.

'Sorry,' Gemma said. 'I didn't meant to scare you. I just lost it when I saw the boys.'

'I wasn't expecting you,' she managed.

'Nigel told me to come and get some rest.'

'He's talking?'

'A bit.' Gemma nodded. 'Really, he's asleep most of the time but he's managing a few words and they've moved him out of Intensive Care.' Gemma, after her little meltdown, was trying to sound all calm in front of the boys but Cat could hear the wobble in her friend's voice. 'It's all looking good.'

'Thank God.'

'My sister should be here soon,' Gemma said. 'She's in a taxi on her way from the airport, so I thought I'd have a night to settle these two a bit before I head back there again.'

Cat stayed and helped her with the boys and Dominic sat half-asleep in a chair. Finally the twins looked as if they might be ready to crash.

Gemma and Cat carried them up and put them in their little beds and stood watching them for a while.

'I don't know how I could do this without Nigel,' Gemma said.

'Well, you're not going to have to find out.'

They went back down the stairs and Gemma told Cat to go home.

'You'll call me if you need me, though,' Cat said, her hands on her back, trying to stretch her spine.

'I shall, but once Angela gets here I should be fine. Thank you so much, Cat, and you too, Dominic.' As they went to head out Gemma called into the night, 'You'll call me if you need me, won't you, Cat?'

'I shan't be needing you for a while yet.' Cat laughed but Dominic saw the slight frown on Gemma's face.

'Cat…' Gemma strode towards them. 'You and Dominic need to sort this out.'

'Gemma!' Cat warned.

'No!' Gemma was practically shouting. Wrung out, emotional, she just spilled out her thoughts right there on the street. 'I just about lost my husband, and I'm telling you that there are moments in life that you can never get back, and if you don't let him in—'

'Gemma!' Cat broke in. 'We've got this, okay?'

'Well, make sure you have,' Gemma said, 'because life changes in a second.'

Then she burst into tears again and Cat and Dominic saw her back to the house.

'Sorry, sorry,' she kept saying.

'It's fine.'

Cat just about drooped in relief when she saw the taxi pull up and Angela get out.

Finally they got into the car and Cat let out a tense breath. 'God…'

'She's upset, she's tired,' Dominic said.

'She's interfering.'

And she knew she had to talk to him.

Just not tonight.

'Are you coming in?' she asked as they pulled up at her house.

'Well, if I do, it's for the night,' he warned, 'but that's only because if I sit down I won't get up again.'

'And me.'

'No wild sex,' he said. 'Because I don't want you to be disappointed.'

'You're safe.'

They were so tired they didn't even bother going through the motions of sitting down or making a drink. Instead, they scaled the stairs as if it were Everest.

'Is your back sore?'

'It's killing me,' Cat said. 'The twins wanted to be carried all the time, they were so clingy...'

They got to the bedroom and she went to turn on the light but, of course, it didn't work.

'You had one job to do,' she said, and they both laughed. It would keep.

She went for a shower and came back into her dark bedroom, where Dominic was already in bed. The street-light cast a slight orange glow and it was nice, so nice, to drop her towel and to get into her own bed, and she let out a lovely moan.

'That feels good,' she said.

'You have a very comfortable bed,' he commented.

'I know.' She sighed. Only, it didn't feel very comfortable tonight. She lay on her back and then turned and faced away from him.

'Rub my back.'

'I'm too tired,' he said, but he rolled over and obliged.

It wasn't sexual. It was intimate and blissful.

His fingers got right into the ache at the bottom of her spine and then moved up to the tight shoulders and then into her neck, and he remembered the spine that had greeted him on the day they'd met. He spoiled the thoughtful massage thing by getting a huge erection.

Cat kept feeling it, even as she tried to pretend not

to notice the brush of it against the back of her thigh now and then.

Then it stopped being a massage and his mouth came onto her shoulders and she closed her eyes at the bliss.

Not too tired at all, as it turned out.

His fingers came around the front as he kissed her neck and explored breasts that were twice as large as the last time he'd felt them.

He examined the changes. The thick, ripe nipples and then down to the taut swell of her naked stomach, and he got to feel the baby move and kick into his palm. It was a treasured moment.

Then his hand moved down to the curve of fuller hips and Cat let out a moan.

She wasn't too tired to move; she simply didn't want to. She liked it that all she had to do was nudge her bottom back a fraction to deliver her consent and he slipped in and his own moan told her it was bliss for him as he was drawn into that wet warmth.

'When I think of all those condoms I wasted on you,' Dominic said. They had deep, lazy sex and she turned her head and their tongues mingled for a very long moment. Then he got back to the easy task of making her come.

Very easy, because with each measured thrust she felt him tense more, and pressing back on him, giving in to him, the pleasure meant Cat was over and about to be done with. He came very deep inside her and she gripped him back and dragged out more. All tension left them.

'Now I'm comfortable,' Cat said.

'And me.'

They'd worked hard these past days for that long sleep.

But Dominic woke, as he once used to, just before sunrise.

He hadn't done that in months.

On this morning, though, Cat's long exhalation of breath and stirring of discomfort moved him from deeply asleep to half-awake and he lay there, feeling her stomach, which had been hard beneath his hand, soften.

Okay.

Light was starting to filter into the bedroom as he recalled Gemma's slightly odd demand that Cat ring her if needed, and he knew he was going to be a father today.

He already was, he thought.

From the moment in Oliver's when Cat had told him they were having a daughter he had become a father in his mind.

Soon he'd officially be one.

Thin rays started to stretch and strengthen and the black turned to grey and the room started to emerge. A chest of drawers, a large bookshelf and then grey dispersed and colour came in.

It was like waking up in some enchanted woodland.

There were trees, flowers, knotted wooden trunks and branches holding nests, and he half expected ivy to sneak across the bed and coil around them. He felt Cat's stomach tighten again beneath his hand and she stirred in discomfort.

'I lied to you,' he said.

Cat woke to those words and his kiss on her shoulder.

'When?'

'The second time we met,' Dominic admitted. 'I

didn't just happen to see the maternity leave position. I was already thinking of moving to London.'

'Not Spain?' Cat's brain was all foggy.

'I was thinking of moving to Spain, I almost was moving to Spain, but I couldn't quite get that weekend out of my head and I was wondering, before I cut all ties here, whether it might be worth...'

Cat lay there in silence as he continued.

'I regretted how it ended and I wondered if we stood a chance. I kept waiting to get over you but I didn't so I was looking at jobs in London. I was thinking of taking a temporary one before I moved to Spain and catching up with you to see...'

'See what?'

'If what we'd found that weekend still existed.'

Cat felt his hand stroking her stomach and his lovely long body melded with hers and, yes, what they'd found still existed.

'I haven't been honest with you,' Cat said, but tears tripped her words and he kissed the back of her head.

'That's okay,' Dominic said. 'You were stepping into my hotel room, not a confessional.'

Her stomach tightened and Cat stretched her legs out because it hurt, not just in her stomach but her back too and right down to her toes. 'Oh...' Cat breathed her way out of it. 'I think...'

'You are,' Dominic said. Her contractions were coming about five minutes apart.

'It's too soon.'

'You're thirty-six weeks, it's fine.'

'I mean, it's too soon for us,' she said, and started to cry. 'I was going to talk to you. I wanted to tell you things when we went away.'

'We've got ages to talk,' Dominic said. 'First labours take...' And he stopped then, halted at his own presumption as realisation hit.

'Second.'

She started to really cry.

It wasn't supposed to be like this.

They should be sitting in some lovely mansion, having afternoon tea, and she would be selecting a cupcake and mention Thomas, and Mike, oh, so casually and bypass the agony it had been. Instead, her stomach was in spasm and her knees were coming up and, ready or not, this baby was coming today.

'I want a bath,' she said. 'Oh, my God, we had sex...'

She was frantic for her bath and to arrive all clean and shiny in the labour ward.

No, it wasn't supposed to be like this.

He ran the bath, she rang the hospital and it was just as well she'd told him because the tired midwife asked if it was her first.

'No, it's my second.'

Dominic closed his eyes as he checked the water and then Cat came in.

'They said to come straight in.'

'Have your bath,' Dominic said. 'Your waters haven't broken...'

He helped her in and she got another contraction and from the strength and speed of them now she wasn't going to be sitting in the bath for very long. She looked at Dominic sitting on the toilet lid and there would be no Gemma delivering her. It would be a stranger. She had no choice but to confess how scared she was today.

And so she told him a little, about the happy person

she had once been and the baby and husband-to-be she'd had, and he sat, as she had for him, quietly.

She told him about the ultrasound and the Edwards syndrome and he didn't start demanding if she'd been thoroughly tested this time around, he just sat. And he didn't insist that it was unlikely to happen again and that his brilliant sperm couldn't possibly be at fault, he just sat.

'Thomas,' Cat said. 'Thomas Gregory Hayes.'

And he wanted to put his hand up and tell her to stop. *You had a baby, I get it.*

But they had to share themselves.

'Thomas, because I love the name. Gregory, after my brother, and Hayes because I didn't want Mike to be attached to him. He didn't want him…'

And still he sat there as Cat, angry, pregnant, lay in the bathtub.

'He's in the drawer.'

Dominic gave a slightly startled look as if she was telling him to go and fetch a dead baby or an urn of ashes from her bedside.

'His photo,' Cat said.

He went and fetched it and came back.

And, no, it wasn't how it was supposed to be. Where were her cupcakes, where was her cup of tea and something to distract her as he looked closely at her child.

Dominic sat on the loo seat as she breathed through another contraction, and when she finally opened her eyes it was to see the man who had told her with little emotion about the death of his wife crying.

He did not recoil in horror. He was looking at her son and then he looked at her and finally, only then, he spoke.

'A few weeks ago I couldn't imagine having a baby and now I'm sitting here trying to imagine how I'd feel if I lost one.'

Oh, my God! Cat was stunned. *He's crying!*

'Sorry, Cat.'

'It's fine.'

'No, I'm really sorry. I should be…'

What?

Stronger?

A touch more dismissive?

That he cried for her son and her loss meant the world.

'I wanted to get to twenty-five weeks,' Cat said. 'And then…' She told the truth. 'I didn't trust you enough to tell you about him.'

'I understand why you didn't.'

They trusted each other now. Their hearts always had but finally their minds had caught up.

'We need to get to the hospital,' she said, and as she stood her waters broke.

'Some one-night stand you turned out to be,' he said as he helped her out of the bath.

A drive that took twenty minutes at night was markedly longer at 7:00 a.m. and Cat was having visions of delivering at the kerb when thankfully the hospital came into view.

'Argh, I'm supposed to be working,' Dominic said, and made a very rapid call but then started to laugh.

'Poor Julia, she's really confused now. I just told her my partner's about to deliver a baby.'

They walked down the long corridor and gathered a few double takes along the way as some of the staff saw that snooty Cat was in her dressing gown *and* with the new sexy doctor.

That this was Cat's second pregnancy was on her chart, mentioned in every phone call made, and then the lovely doctor who came asked about Thomas as he went through Cat's notes.

'You had him at twenty-five weeks?'

Cat nodded.

'Normal vaginal delivery?'

'Yes,' Cat said. 'Well, it didn't feel very normal at the time.'

'Okay, I'm just going to take a look…' The doctor's voice trailed off as the doors opened and Gemma walked in.

'Thanks, Chand.' She smiled. 'This special delivery is mine.' And then she gave Cat a very severe frown. 'I told you to call me…'

'So you did,' Cat said. 'How did you find out I was here?'

'I told the ward that if you came in they were to let me know.'

'You knew I was going to have her.'

'Sort of,' Gemma said. 'But I was here anyway.' She started to pull on gloves. 'I couldn't sleep, I wanted to see Nigel.' Gemma looked over at Dominic and tested the water. 'Can you step out while I examine her, please?'

'He's staying.'

'I can have him removed.' Gemma grinned, delighted by the turn of events.

'There's no need for that,' Cat said.

'Has she finally told you?' Gemma asked, looking up at Cat's puffy face.

'Yep.'

'And so you know that this going to be very emotional for her,' Gemma checked. 'I mean, above and beyond.'

'I do.'

'How's Nigel?' Cat asked as Gemma pulled the sheet back.

'Talking,' Gemma said. 'He knows who I am, he knows the year we're in if not the month…he's doing really well,' she said as she examined her friend. 'As are you.'

Cat found out then that she was already fully dilated.

'Can you give me a push…?'

'I don't want to push.'

Oh, maybe she did.

'I'm not ready to push.'

'Yes, Cat, you are,' Gemma said, and nodded to the midwife, who was busily getting equipment out.

'Come on, Cat,' Gemma urged, when she lay there, fighting her own body and refusing to bear down.

'I can't.' She was starting to lose it. The lights were too bright, the voices too loud, and she'd never known pain like it. She wanted ten minutes to get used to the idea that her baby was on the way and when Gemma told her to push, right down into her bottom, she told her just what she could do with that notion.

'Come on, Cat…' Gemma's voice, Cat noticed for the first time, was really annoying. 'You can do this…'

'I can't,' she said.

She was scared to push, as scared as she had been the last time, but then Dominic spoke.

'Yes, you can,' he said, and she was about to argue when his lovely deep voice spoke on. 'You've done this before, Cat, you know what to do.'

He let Thomas in.

All the fear she'd had the last time, fear she still held on to, left, and she started to push her baby into the world.

She'd done this before, she had been a mother for seven years, just a lost one, but now the world was turning that around.

Gemma moved one leg back and Dominic the other. 'Just getting a better angle for the live-stream to my parents,' Dominic said, and that made her laugh.

'Come on, Cat...' Gemma said, and her voice wasn't annoying any more. 'Hold it...'

And there was a silence, a pause, and then she arrived. A little scrawny thing, very red and with a mass of black hair, she lay on Cat's stomach too stunned to cry, her little mouth open, her eyes screwed closed.

'Hey, kitten,' Dominic said.

'Don't,' Cat said. 'That's cheesy...'

But Cat and Dominic's kitten she was. Tiny and mewing and there, ready or not.

Dominic cut the cord and Cat just lay there, gazing down at her tiny, perfect baby and her funny-shaped head, little dark red lips. She had never been happier or sadder at the same time, because this was how it should be.

'It's okay...' Gemma was there when Cat folded. She'd known it was coming and she wrapped up her daughter and handed her to her dad, who had to juggle the two loves of his life. One arm full of baby, the other full of Cat as she cried for Thomas.

It was such a cry, one she had been dreading and the reason she hadn't wanted him near her for the birth. The midwife took away their daughter for a little while and

Gemma disappeared and she was alone with her heart and with him until the grief that would be present for ever faded enough to let life in.

Somehow they coexisted.

'Thank God I told you,' Cat said, because she couldn't imagine him not being here, not just for himself or their baby but for her.

'That's how I felt when I told you,' he admitted. 'Just relief.'

'Where is she?' Cat asked, when she peered out from the shield he had provided and wanted her little girl.

'Do you want her back in?'

She did.

Cat fed her for the first time and it soothed not just the baby but the baby's mum.

The midwife left and Gemma went to write up her notes and then it was the three of them.

'What are we going to call her?' Cat asked.

'I've no idea,' Dominic said.

For now she was Baby Hayes.

He didn't much like that.

When she finished feeding Cat handed their little daughter to her dad and she watched as he held her. She saw his expression falter and she knew that Heather was on his mind.

It didn't threaten her, not a bit. She knew he wasn't thinking that he wished Cat was Heather, more that Heather should have got to know this bliss.

'She'd be so proud of you,' Cat said, and let the other love in his life in, just as he had with Thomas.

'She would be,' he agreed, because Heather had known what a closed-off bastard he was and how long it had taken him to even commit to getting engaged. Yet here he was a dad and in love, not just with his baby but with the woman who'd given birth to her. Yes, she'd be so proud of him for pushing through, for showing up to each day and having the guts to fall in love again while knowing more than most just how much it could hurt.

Gemma came back in for a last-minute check before she headed back to visit Nigel.

'She's beautiful,' Gemma said. 'Just so gorgeous. I think I need to have another baby.'

'Don't tell Nigel that yet.' Cat smiled as her best friend got to hold her tiny daughter. 'You want to keep his blood pressure down.'

'I went over and told him you'd had a little girl and he smiled and said, "That's good." I'm starting to really think that he'll be okay.'

'Go and be with him,' Cat said. 'Thank you for being here today.'

'I couldn't not be,' Gemma said. 'I'm hardly going to miss out on delivering my own goddaughter…'

'Er…Gemma…' Cat said, and looked at Dominic. 'We haven't quite got around to discussing religion yet.'

'I don't even know how old Cat is,' Dominic said, and peered at Cat's observation chart and saw her date of birth. 'You're two years older than me!'

'Oh.' Gemma pouted, her doctor's hat clearly well and truly off. 'Well, bear me in mind when you do get around to it.'

'Tell you what,' Dominic said, 'if you can't be godmother, how about you be bridesmaid?'

'Really?' Gemma beamed.

'Well, I have to ask her,' Dominic said, 'and then she has to say yes…'

'You'd better,' Gemma said, and handed back the baby, and when she'd gone Cat turned to Dominic.

'You don't have to marry me.'

'I know that I don't but I want to.'

'She can have your surname if that's what you want.' But, no, from the way Dominic was looking at her Cat was starting to realise that he loved her.

'I want you to have my name.'

'Not professionally, though,' Cat checked.

'Oh, yes,' Dominic said. 'I want my name on everything.'

'You are so completely not my type.'

'Well, you're not mine either,' he admitted. 'You stood outside that elevator in your lovely floaty dress, with your girlie curly hair, all blushing, shy and nervous…'

'Is that your type?'

'It was for a while.'

'Well, for your information, I wasn't shy and I wasn't nervous.'

'I know that now,' he said. 'You were turned on.' But then he was the most serious he had ever been. 'I never thought I'd do this again, Cat. I never thought I could get so lucky twice, but I have. So you're going to marry me, Gemma's going to be the bridesmaid and that's settled. Now all we have to do is choose a name for our baby.'

It was the best day ever.

And made more so by Dominic going out while Cat slept at lunchtime and returning with a very big ring. He then scratched out 'Baby Hayes' and changed it to 'Baby Edwards'.

'I don't think she's old enough to know,' Cat said.

'I know.'

They still couldn't decide on her name.

Her parents came, and then Greg and his wife and children.

A little later in the afternoon Eloisa was dressed in a little Spanish sleepsuit that had been bought a few weeks ago and had been sent along with a letter without judgment, just offering love.

And so they did live-stream with his barking-mad parents, though thankfully not the birth, and showed off their daughter to them and his sister, Kelly, as well as Cat's ring.

'She's beautiful,' Anna said.

'I know.' Dominic smiled. 'I think she looks like me.'

'I was talking about Cat!'

They were gorgeous!

And then a rather bemused Andrew popped in for a visit and did a double take when he saw Dominic sitting there by the bed and holding Cat's hand.

'I thought it was just a coincidence that your partner had gone into labour, Dominic. Then the rumours started flying and it would seem that they're true.' He just stood there bemused. 'You two?'

'Yep,' Dominic said.

'But why did you go to such lengths to hide it? You could have said at the interview.' Andrew frowned. 'Cat, you know it wouldn't have affected his chance at the role.'

Cat just smiled and chose not to tell Andrew that even she hadn't known he'd applied for the job and Dominic decided not to reveal he hadn't known for sure then if it was even his baby.

'I wonder,' Dominic said, when Andrew had left,

'what he'd have to say if he knew just what went on at the conference that the department sent you to.'

It was exhausting, being so happy.

So much so that when she'd fed her tiny baby again and put her down for a sleep Cat chose to take the midwife's advice to rest when the baby did. She didn't even notice that Dominic left, but awoke to the sound of the meals trolley. It rolled past her door.

'You're nil by mouth,' the midwife said, when Cat buzzed her to ask where her food was.

'Why?' Cat asked, but the midwife had gone.

She was starving and there was absolutely no reason for her to be nil by mouth, but then the midwife came back smiling, holding the door for Dominic, who was carrying a tray along with a big bucket holding champagne.

'Paella.' Cat licked her lips as he removed the lid and she saw the saffron rice and gorgeous seafood.

'Oh, and coffee...' She picked up the cup and inhaled. 'You remembered.'

'Of course,' Dominic said. 'I might not know an awful lot about you but I remember the little I do.'

Dinner in bed, her baby sleeping by her side and Dominic pouring champagne. It was time to get to know each other a whole lot more.

From the luxurious place of love.

EPILOGUE

They were possibly the most frazzled bride- and groom-to-be ever.

On the plane the five of them took up a full aisle.

There was Cat on one end, Dominic on the other, Eloisa in her bassinet and Rory and Marcus creating havoc between them.

Nigel and Gemma were on a delayed honeymoon and were, about now, taking a leisurely drive from Paris to Barcelona. They would be there to meet them at the airport.

'Did you pack your pills?' Dominic checked, when they finally got off the plane. 'Because I'm not coming near you otherwise.'

'Oh, yes.' Cat nodded, very happy to have only one child.

The twins were adorable but, absolutely, Dominic agreed, they all needed Nigel.

And there he was with Gemma, smiling and waving. Cat's friend was very happy to see the twins and relaxed after a full week away from her beloved terrors.

She was also ready for a girls' night out before the big day, she told Cat as they walked to the car.

Cat and Gemma had a room booked for the night, her hen night, but for now Gemma was with Nigel, unsettling the twins and his routines, while Cat was in Dominic's room, sneaking in one last feed with Eloisa.

She was gorgeous, a smiley, happy baby who had her father's dark eyes and her mother's thick black hair.

'I *can* give a bottle,' Dominic said, holding his hands out to take her.

'I know,' Cat said. 'I just feel guilty,'

'Why would you feel guilty?' came Dominic's sarcastic response. 'I get the family buffet with Nigel and co. and you get to eat wherever you choose with adults and get as drunk as you please.'

'I know, I can't wait,' Cat said.

'Again she lies,' Dominic said. 'I assume it's not me and the family buffet you're feeling guilty about?'

'No.'

She *was* looking forward to her night out, she really was. She'd managed to breastfeed for only six weeks and now, at three months old, Eloisa happily took her bottle and Dominic often got up to feed her at night.

It was just…

'It's just…' Cat said. 'It's not just one night that I'm leaving her but two.'

'Cat.' Dominic was firm. 'If we hadn't got our problems sorted then about now, I might be having Eloisa to stay at my house for the night. And when you went back to work, there would have been no nanny, it would have been me.'

'I know.'

'And,' Dominic added, 'if you're worried about leaving her with my parents tomorrow, don't be. They are a bit odd but they will look after her as if she's made of glass.'

'I know all that.'

Cat loved his parents. She and Dominic had taken Eloisa to Spain when she was six weeks old and had stayed at the villa. Anna had been brilliant when Cat had been upset that her milk had dried up. She had been far more understanding about Cat's tears than her own mum would have been. Now they were back again just a few weeks later. Cat was looking forward to the next couple of weeks. After their wedding night they would stay at the villa again and she would get to know his parents better.

'I'd have brought her here without you,' Dominic pointed out. 'Not just yet, of course, but I always wanted her to be close to my parents. So just thank God we grew up and spoke to each other and that you're not crying your eyes out, driving back from Gatwick Airport, having just waved her goodbye.'

'Okay.'

'So go and enjoy your night out.' He smiled. 'And I'll see you tomorrow.'

She had the best night with her friend and her family. They went to the restaurant Dominic had first taken her to, and though she would tell him she'd had the paella he'd know she was lying.

'This chicken,' Gemma said, 'is amazing.'

'There's a lot of salt,' Cat's mum replied, and reached for a glass of water.

They laughed a lot, drank a bit much and danced into the small hours.

Well, Cat's mum and dad went off to bed but the two best friends had a brilliant time.

And then it was back to the hotel and she stayed up late into the night, chatting with Gemma.

'It was bliss,' Gemma said about their honeymoon. 'It was so nice to be able to talk to each other without being interrupted and to go for a walk without having to sort out hundreds of shoes.' She turned and looked over at Cat, who lay on her side in bed, listening to Gemma. 'I've got something to tell you.'

Cat both smiled and frowned. 'Well, I hope you're not pregnant, given the amount of champagne consumed tonight.'

'No, and I know both Nigel and I said never again when I had the twins, but we are going to try for another,' Gemma said.

'Yes!' Cat grinned. 'I knew you would.'

But that wasn't all.

'Remember when you joked about Nigel moving to France? Well, as it turns out, he wants to move there for a while and teach English.'

Cat's jaw gaped. 'And?'

'I want to take some time off with the next baby. Some real time off. I've loved working but before I know it the twins will be at school and I want some mummy time with them… So home might be France for a while.'

'It sounds brilliant,' Cat said, though she held on to news of her own until she could run it by Dominic.

'It does.' Gemma sighed. 'Though it's a terrible shame I did German at school! You know, a few months ago, as much as I said I'd give it every consideration, I'd still have freaked. We probably can't afford it, but…'

'You can't afford not to?'

Gemma nodded. 'Things were a bit tense between Nigel and I for a while,' she admitted. 'Nothing terrible but I was tired of working and felt I was missing out on the twins. But then his head injury happened and I thought I was going to lose him and, believe me, that changed an awful lot of things.'

Cat lay there remembering being with Dominic on the beach and his words—*'What seemed like the most terrible disaster at the time turned out to be a blessing.'*

There were so many blessings to be had.

'Spa day tomorrow.' Gemma broke the silence. 'I do love late weddings. There's ages to get ready and none of that hanging around between the service and party.' She looked at her friend. 'How come you chose sunset instead of sunrise, if that's when you two knew it was serious?'

'We just thought it would be easier to get everyone there in the evening,' Cat said. 'Greg isn't arriving till tomorrow.'

Gemma frowned but Cat changed the subject.

Just as Gemma hadn't told her till now about tense times with Nigel, she too didn't tell Gemma everything.

As she drifted off to sleep Cat thought about what sunrise had meant for Dominic and Heather, how she was quite sure that it had been that morning at Collserola that Heather had handed him over to Cat.

And sunrise was, for Cat, one of those times when you lay in bed with your baby feeding, and sometimes shed a tear for the one that you never got to feed.

Sunsets belonged to them, sitting outside in the garden, as Cat liked to now she had finally done it up. Sunsets were the time when she thought about Dominic driving home from work and the night to come, which was always precious.

Their wedding day dawned and Cat and Gemma

awoke to breakfast in bed and then shared a spa day, getting massaged and oiled. Cat's hair was done and make-up applied and then late afternoon Gemma headed off to get Eloisa.

She was all smiles, blowing bubbles, happy to see her mother, and together Cat and Gemma dressed her in her little outfit and Cat's dad knocked on the hotel room door and July was about to become beautiful again.

Oh, there were sad days in it but there were very happy ones too.

They drove the short distance to Collserola.

'How far is it?' Gemma asked, once they were out of the car and walking up the hillside, with Cat's dad puffing behind.

'Nearly there,' Cat said, and then she saw her tribe all waiting and she saw Dominic's smile when he noticed how they were dressed.

The bride and the bridesmaid both wore white.

Two broderie anglaise dresses. Cat's one had spent three days at the dry cleaner's having grass stains removed, and two being expertly repaired, but she refused to wear anything else for this very special wedding.

And, no, Gemma did not outshine the bride. No one could for her smile was so wide as they stood at sunset at Collserola Park, with their families beside them.

Gemma held Eloisa, who was dressed in white broderie anglaise too, and at three months of age was going to spend her second night away from Mummy.

She was going to get to know her rather eccentric grandparents on her father's side, of course.

Her rigid maternal grandparents were flying back to England at the crack of dawn.

Still, they were here tonight and that was all that mattered for now.

Or rather she and Dominic were all that mattered right now.

He put a ring on her finger and Cat's eyes filled with tears as he told her how much he loved her.

And then she put a ring on his finger, a finger that had worn one before, and Cat's eyes filled up again.

'I love you,' she said.

'I know you do.'

Their vows were said as the sun went down and life together carried on.

They had a party at his parents' villa.

Greg's children swam in the pool and Nigel took the twins inside for a sleep.

Cat dived into the paella and looked up to see Anna holding her granddaughter and smiling down. Kelly asked her something and Anna stood and handed little Eloisa over to her husband, who took the baby with a smile.

It reminded her of that precious time with Thomas when he had never been put down and had been surrounded only by love.

'She'll be fine,' Anna said, bringing out a tray of desserts and placing them on the table.

'I know she will.'

They had their priorities right, Cat thought, glancing at her own parents, who were both checking their phones.

She thought about the letter James and Anna had sent her, inviting her, with or without Dominic, into their home. Cat understood better now why Dominic would have fought, legally if he'd had to, to have his parents in his daughter's life.

It hadn't come to that, though.

They partied into the night and then it was time to head back to the conference hotel for Dominic and Cat, though to the luxury suite this time.

'She's sound asleep,' Dominic said as they crept in to whisper goodnight to their daughter.

'How lucky are we?' Cat said, remembering how it might have been.

Dropping the baby off.

Picking her up.

Doing this apart, instead of together.

'Come on,' he said. 'I guess we have to go and do what newlyweds do now.'

'I suppose.' Cat sighed.

They couldn't wait!

They left the people they loved and were driven to the hotel.

They walked through the foyer. 'Do you want a quick drink at the bar?' Dominic nudged.

'No.'

The elevator door opened and together they stepped in and this time there was no hugging the wall and wondering where the night might lead.

It was straight to his arms and a blistering kiss and it would be straight to bed, except Cat had something on her mind.

'I've been thinking,' Cat said as they stepped into the suite and Dominic poured champagne.

'Have you?'

'How's my job?'

'Do we have to talk about work tonight?'

'Please.'

'It's busy,' Dominic said. 'Are you still thinking about job-sharing with me?'

Cat shook her head. It was something they'd both considered but Cat had other plans.

She loved him.

No question.

'I was thinking of selling my house,' Cat said, which made sense, given they spent most of their time at his. 'I'm going to make a nice profit. Enough to maybe take a year off work.'

'What are you going to do?' Dominic asked. 'Renovate mine?'

'No.' Cat laughed at the hope in his voice and she closed her eyes at his kiss and his hands that were, more tenderly this time, removing her dress. 'I think I want to learn Spanish.'

Dominic stopped in mid-kiss.

'Er…why?'

'I'd like to be able to speak with the locals,' Cat said. 'You said you wanted to spend some time here.'

'I did.'

'Then do,' Cat said. 'You've already upended my life, so why not a little bit more?'

'When did you decide this?'

'I started thinking about it last time we were here. I can see how much you love it and I think it would be amazing to live here for a while, and then…' She thought of life here with him and smiled when she thought of her best friend just a leisurely drive to Paris away, and she gave a small shrug. 'Who knows?'

She loved him and love deserved careful consideration at times.

He had made her so happy, had given her back her dreams, and she wanted to make all his come true too.

She had been far too cynical about men, about love, about hope.

'You're sure?' he checked.

She was now.

Absolutely, Cat was sure of this love.

* * * * *

FALLING FOR HER
RELUCTANT SHEIKH

BY
AMALIE BERLIN

MILLS
BOON®

Published in Great Britain 2015
by Mills & Boon, an imprint of Harlequin (UK) Limited,
Eton House, 18-24 Paradise Road, Richmond, Surrey, TW9 1SR

© 2015 Amalie Berlin

ISBN: 978-0-263-24735-0

Dear Reader,

In my mind, there are three kinds of sheikh heroes:

1. The kind of sheikh I like.

2. The kind of sheikh I want to shake to death.

3. The hybrid sheikh—the one I want to shake to death, but who eventually wins me over by learning from his mistakes and giving me some good grovelling at the end.

Number threes are my favourite. Throw some sleep therapy into the concept, and I'm hooked. Of all the books I've written, this one's probably my favourite— maybe even surpassing my debut.

Before I got started, I got to do loads of super-fun 'research' (note the ironic quotes).

I watched every documentary on sleep and dreaming I could get my hands on. As an unrepentant nerd, this made me completely happy. ('Research.')

I read some smoking-hot sheikh books—you know…for mood. (More 'research'.)

And I spent hours naming fictional countries— something I'd never done before. It was surprisingly difficult but, like most of my brainstorming, I turned it into a fun game and then spent way too much time debating the best locations of the 'e' and the 'a'. 'E' and then 'a' won, because 'Merirach' sounded better than 'Marirech'. (See? Yet more important 'research'!)

I'd say I hope you have as much fun reading Khalil and Adalyn's story as I had writing it, but that just seems impossible to me. So instead I'll say, if you get one quarter of my 'pleasuretainment', I'll consider all those hours of 'research' well worth the effort. :)

Amalie X0

To Laurie Johnson, my second editor.
She once suggested I tackle a sheikh book,
something I hadn't considered before and probably
wouldn't have considered for a good long while
without her planting the seed.

To Laura McCallen, my current editor,
for supporting my tendency to run around naked
in public. Okay, that's a lie. But she does support
my tendency to go off on wild story tangents,
something I'm extremely grateful for. :)

Books by Amalie Berlin

Mills & Boon® Medical Romance™

Craving Her Rough Diamond Doc
Uncovering Her Secrets
Return of Dr Irresistible
Breaking Her No-Dating Rule

**Visit the author profile page at
millsandboon.co.uk for more titles**

Praise for
Amalie Berlin

'A sexy, sensual, romantic, heartwarming and purely
emotional, romantic, bliss-filled read. I very much look
forward to this author's next book and being transported
to a world of pure romance brilliance!'
—*GoodReads* on *Craving Her Rough Diamond Doc*

CHAPTER ONE

BOBBING ON WHIPLASH desert winds, Dr. Adalyn Quinn's helicopter dropped and paused, dropped and paused, descending in the aeronautical equivalent of two steps forward, one step back, each jostle adding another crack to her already brittle nerves.

Digging her nails into her seat base, she pitched forward, stiff and straining against the seat belts across her hips and torso. The overly snug belts, while uncomfortable, felt illogically safer than wobbling about like week-old gelatin, as she had been.

Her older brother tried but had never quite understood the cold, black pit of fear that sank in her middle when she even thought of travel, so there was no way for him to comprehend the abyss that had been trying to swallow her sanity during the long hours of this godforsaken journey. The one he'd tossed her into.

He'd thought himself helpful when he'd said, "Take those antianxiety medicines you never take, to help your trip."

Because remaining calm while dying a fiery death? So much better than feeling acute terror without pharmacological filters. Sure, she could concede that point. But having her wits artificially addled when she'd probably need them to escape burning, twisted wreckage—supposing she lived that long? Less brilliant.

The idea that one of the vehicles *wouldn't* crash was the thought that sounded like fantasy. Naturally, her airborne catastrophe would happen on this last leg of her trip, worlds away from lace balconies and her safe, quiet life.

Her stomach curdled as they fell another few feet. She just had to hold on a little while longer.

The pilot's voice crackled in her headphones, alerting her to their landing at the former airport site for the Kingdom of Merirach. As if she couldn't feel it. As if every shift of the wind didn't brutalize her mind with images of crashes and broken, twisted bodies. After nearly twenty-four hours of this self-inflicted mental torture it would be easy to think she'd become numbed to it, but that primal fear still had the ability to tighten her body until her shoulders stretched stiffly, like old boot leather. She wouldn't have been surprised if at any second her skin cracked and her collarbone snapped in half.

Broken.

Twisted.

Body.

They touched down with a jolt, bounced twice and settled. She immediately began fumbling with the latches on her belts, trying to get free. To get out of the flying death trap. To get to him.

Adalyn had a rule about putting her life or well-being into someone else's hands. A simple rule really...*don't do it!* But right now it comforted her to think that the distance between her and safety could be measured in feet. He'd be waiting for her.

Jamison's best friend.

The one she'd never met because she didn't travel, but to whom Jamison had sent her.

He'd be there, and he'd take her to a nearby hotel where she could eat the protein bars she'd brought for sustenance, drink water purified by her special tablets and sit in the dark with the earplugs she'd brought to create the illusion of solitude.

She could rest. Sleep. Sleep was what she needed. Sleep and alone time somewhere without wheels attached. If she had all that, it might lower her blood pressure enough that she couldn't see her clothing move from the force of each beat of her heart…

"Door," she said, dragging the headphones off and hanging them from the armrest on her seat. And then again, "Door."

Why were they moving so slowly?

She needed out.

Tomorrow she would officially see her patient, work on diagnosing and outlining a treatment plan, then go the heck home.

End of adventure.

The only thing she had going for her now was the darkened interior of the helicopter. No one could see her expression. She didn't have to work so hard to keep it all hidden as she had on the other planes and vehicles. The last thing she wanted was to put her issues on display and have someone label her hysterical—one of the most offensive words she'd ever learned and had heard daily in the months after the crash.

Outside the chopper, in the not-too-far distance, a ring of headlights provided the only light source, aside from the blinking things on the helicopter controls.

Even she—the Queen of Never Ever Traveling—knew what an airport looked like at night. Runways. Dual bands of lights. A big building with lots of people inside. Lots of light.

Here there was only darkness and the cars. One more dangerous vehicle for her to climb into before she reached her assignment.

It really wasn't any wonder that someone living in a country so recently torn apart by civil war would have sleep difficulties, but she was here anyway.

Seconds later, the door slid open and a blast of cold air surprised her lungs, sending her into a coughing fit. But with the help of her black-suited entourage, she still scrambled from the helicopter. Once her feet hit solid ground she hunched forward and ran toward the cars, clueless as to whether or not the men followed.

Only when she reached the cars, far outside the reach of the rotating blades of death, did she straighten and look back. Two of her escorts—men in suits who'd met her at the airport of the neighboring kingdom—had made the run with her and the rest now gathered her embarrassing amount of luggage and followed.

Should she tip them? Was that expected? Insulting? Her travel book had said nothing about how to treat the servants of a royal house.

The man who had been her translator reached her side and herded her toward one of several identical sport utility vehicles with darkened windows. Though he was careful not to touch her, he wrenched open the back door of the vehicle and gestured to her with such force that she climbed in.

Unlike when he'd retrieved her, the man didn't even attempt English this time. With so little sleep and such a terrible grasp of the language, Adalyn couldn't even tell where the words started and stopped in whatever he'd said. He could've even said one of the couple of hundred words she'd managed to learn, and she wouldn't have known it.

How much farther would they have to go?

Once she stopped moving, her body caught up with her lungs—recognizing the cold finally—and she folded her arms across her chest and rubbed them to try to increase their warmth.

"You should've worn a jacket."

The low male voice broke through the sound of her pounding heart and shivering breaths, the first indication she wasn't alone in the car. She turned and as her eyes adjusted to the low lighting after the blinding headlights she could make out a traditionally robed figure not two feet away in the seat beside her.

"I thought I was coming to a hot place. I was told that it was chilly at night, but I thought that just meant I needed long sleeves, not a parka."

A soft sound—trapped somewhere between a sigh and a chuckle—answered her. Like strained amusement.

"Are you Khalil?" *Please, say yes.* She'd made it all the way to his country—surely he would meet her at the airport?

Loud voices outside the vehicle cut through the air and her fellow passenger's voice dropped to a sharp whisper. "Yes. We will speak further at the palace, Adalyn. It isn't far."

"Palace? I thought we would be working in a clinic environment. And I'd stay at a hotel."

"I do not sleep at a clinic."

"Right... Sorry..." Of course he wouldn't sleep at a

clinic. Why had she thought that? Because it was familiar. Because that's how things worked where she practiced…at her clinic. But this place was not New Orleans.

"Later I will explain." His words clipped the frosty air with short, abrupt sounds. If she could still see her breath, his words would've probably floated away in blocky cubes, formed by hard right angles and razor edges.

The front car doors opened, the suited men climbed in and for seconds she could see him under the light of the dome, but he'd already turned away, cutting off the conversation with body language. It was a technique she often used, or had used enough to recognize it.

He fixed his gaze out his window, though at what she couldn't guess. Nothing, unless he had the night vision of a cat.

The status of her rescue mission suddenly seemed like a charade, as capricious and dangerous as a ride in anything with wheels. Like the large vehicle she was in. It started rolling and banished all other thoughts from her mind—just as cars always did for her. Even now, years later, having to ride in a car felt like a forced march to her own execution.

The only thought that stayed with her as she analyzed every bump and turn for the telltale feeling of a wreck in progress was: What had Jamison gotten her into?

It couldn't have been more than a couple of miles' travel, but it took ages. By the time they stopped, her jaw hurt from clenching and she felt just a little light-headed from her breathercise.

Khalil climbed out as soon as the vehicle stopped rolling, before Adalyn could even really get a glimpse

of him. "See her settled in the suite adjoining mine."
All she could make out was a tall man with dark robes
and the traditional dress that by turns intrigued and
worried her.

Once those words were out—and in English, no
less—he immediately switched over to his native
tongue, leaving no doubt that he wasn't speaking to
her. Well, the sooner she got to her suite, the sooner she
could sleep and, she prayed, stop shaking...

Khalil tugged on a clean shirt. A dress suit. At this
hour... Since he'd been in Merirach, he hadn't worn
much but the robes, at least when he was in the palace
and bound to the demands of his position, but Western
dress would probably set her more at ease.

If he was honest, it was more than that. The robes
that tradition dictated reminded him what he was doing
there, and the responsibility he carried. Of who he was
supposed to be. Not himself. But now, dealing with her,
he didn't want to be Sheikh Khalil of Akkari, Regent of
Merirach, he wanted to be Dr. Khalil Al-Akkari—the
son not born to rule. Maybe it would help them both deal
with the situation if they came at it as equals.

Tomorrow he'd have to go back to the robes that
helped people in his host kingdom identify him as the
current regent, and she'd have to become used to seeing him in them.

Knowing Jamison's history meant he knew the history of his chubby little sister, too. Jay always referred
to her as the world's biggest introvert. A homebody
who considered a trip to the library or bookstore to be
her portal to all things exotic. Anyone would be leery
of traveling to a country so recently out of a civil war,

but someone who never traveled—not even on the best of circumstances—compounded the size of the favor he'd owe her for agreeing to come such a long way to help him out.

It was late so he skipped the tie—he wanted familiarity, not formality. Just to be courteous.

The other courteous thing would've been to send one of the family jets to retrieve her, at least then she would've arrived sooner and had an easier journey, but that would've just triggered questions from his elder brother. Malik always had questions. The sort of questions Khalil had no desire to answer. And if things worked out with Adalyn, questions he'd never have to answer.

He stepped through the door to the adjoining room where she'd been settled, and froze in his tracks. Her back was to him, all supple skin on display, so pale he'd swear she'd never even heard of the sun. The only thing covering her was a scrap of white cotton panties stretched over the plump little cheeks on display as she bent over the bed and dug around in the suitcase for clothes.

She'd had the same idea to change.

She just hadn't been as quick about it as he had.

She really wasn't the chubby little girl he'd seen in pictures...

Khalil's mouth watered so sharply that his jaw ached.

He swallowed, shocked by the pang of want that shot through him.

Smooth, slender and curved...she looked like a cool, life-giving oasis in a barren landscape.

Not yet aware that he'd entered, she continued by

straightening with another scrap of white cotton she shook out and pulled over her head.

Khalil closed his eyes, a baby first step that allowed him a small measure of control of his body, control he needed to force a half turn away from her. When he knew he'd be facing the wall, he opened his eyes again, but he could still see her in his peripheral vision.

Damn.

He closed them again. It was either that or give in to the powerful urge to look. Clearing his throat was the best warning he could think of to soften the surprise of his arrival. "I apologize, I should've knocked."

She squawked and then there was a thump, along with some other commotion he couldn't identify. If it had taken effort to look away, it took even more not to look back.

"Should I come back?" he asked, because he had to do something...

"Yes!" The word erupted from her and set him in motion. As he reached for the door, a more tentative babble came from behind him, "No, wait. You can stay, just don't turn around for a minute."

She muttered something beneath her breath, disgruntled words he couldn't make out. If she was anything like her brother, those words wouldn't be fit for company anyway.

Khalil stayed in place and stared hard at the carved wooden door.

Count the lines in the wood grain.

Don't think of the mostly nude woman behind him.

And for God's sake, don't look.

He lost track of the lines and had to start again. Keeping control of his mind and actions was easier when he wasn't tired, but he'd been in the palace for nearly a week this time around… *Tired* wasn't a strong enough word for what he was—he was exhausted in a way that even heart-accelerating doses of caffeine couldn't help.

"You can turn around. I guess I'm decent." She didn't sound at all certain.

When he turned back, it was to overly bright eyes and pink cheeks. He locked his gaze to hers in another effort to exert control over his baser impulses. "You don't look like your picture…" Which was not the way he'd intended to start this conversation.

"Sorry."

Why was she apologizing? He was the one who'd barged in.

She tugged at the bottom hem of her short dressing robe, the fidgeting making clear her response: sorry was a verbal fidget.

In the picture he'd seen, she'd been at least thirty pounds heavier and the victim of an unfortunate complexion issue. She'd worn glasses and had kept her hair pulled back in a haphazard ponytail. She'd looked like someone studious and intelligent. And now…she looked like a dark-haired pixie with large green eyes. And breasts he could clearly see the shape of through the slinky blue material of her robe.

Eyes! Look at her eyes!

He'd had a reason to come into the room…

"Your equipment…" He grasped for his train of thought.

She clutched the robe tighter, eyes widening further as her voice hitched. "My equipment?"

"Not that equipment…" It was all he could do not to

groan at yet another verbal misstep. It didn't help that he'd put her one door away from him, like a shiny-new mistress. And, sweet mercy, did she ever look the part of timid virgin, blushing and stammering the first time her body was exposed to a man's eyes.

For the first time in Khalil's life he wished he could take advantage. Tear that robe off her, coerce and tease until she lay back on the thick bed behind her...and welcomed him with open arms. And legs. His eyes wandered down, past the hem of the silky material to the smooth, pale, shapely legs...

For God's sake, look her in the eye.

"My men have brought your *medical* equipment to the palace." He cleared his throat, which had gone dry again. "Where would you like it delivered?"

"Oh." She shifted around again, fidgeting with the belt and the hem again, anywhere the material folded or covered her. "I assumed that I was placed in this room so that I would have access to your room to monitor you as you sleep."

With a quick hop—which sent too many interesting places jiggling—she rounded the suitcase and perched on the corner of the bed. Her knees clamped together and she resumed smoothing the fabric down her thighs, willing it to cover more of her body than it had when she'd been standing. "Monitors here, but the camera equipment in your room. I know that sounds really creepy, but it is recorded so I can review it the next day to make sure that I didn't miss anything, but after that it gets erased. Otherwise I'd just have to hover at your bedside and watch you sleep."

A short nervous laugh escaped her before she clamped her lips shut, the very picture of distress despite the laugh. "I doubt anyone would be able to get any rest if they felt like someone was standing there, leering at them. My aunt's cat used to do that in the morning when she wanted me up. Just sit there and stare… And it always worked. Woke me right up."

Babbling, a sign of nerves. Definitely nervous. Maybe shy, too, if the way she worked to keep him from even seeing her knees was anything to go by. And all that wasn't what he should be focusing on.

He'd known she would need to monitor him, he was familiar with the method in which sleep studies were conducted, but the way she described watching him sleep only made him think of that long dark hair spread across cool white cotton pillows…and the slinky robe slipping over pale, soft flesh.

She added, "It'll take several hours to set up all the equipment so I thought maybe we would do it tomorrow. I really won't be of any use to anyone until I've had at least eight hours."

Right, she was tired. He should say something, stop her babbling.

"Of course."

Had he ever dated a woman so shy and modest? If he had, he should probably remember her if that appealed to him so much. He'd think less of any man who confessed this sort of reaction to innocence. To think himself capable of it. That emotion could be named by the taste of bile at the back of his throat.

But the sudden, intense aversion to the thought of accepting her help disgusted him even more.

Help was the whole reason for her to be there. He should just tell her everything right now. That would replace the sweet, nervous innocent with something uglier, a reflection of the blackness devouring him from the inside out. She'd give him her pity, at best, and she sure as hell wouldn't sit there, barely clothed, trusting him to fake his way through the actions of a good man.

"I doubt the equipment is going to be very helpful. My problem is I don't sleep. I've got insomnia. And when I fail to fall asleep, I don't tend to stay in bed for hours, trying. Not a lot to monitor when that happens. Which happens a great deal of the time." He'd opened his mouth, said words, but not the right ones. His throat refused to let those words pass.

"Well, you have to sleep sometime. I mean, you're not a drooling idiot right now, and after you miss enough sleep—well, I'm sure you've noticed the effects. But there are also other effects that are actually quite dangerous. We all have a maximum amount of time we can go without sleep and then our brains start taking micro-sleeps when we're trying to work. Or trying to drive. Insomnia sounds like a pain in the butt, but really it can be very dangerous."

Dangerous, like his reaction to her. "So your solution to it is?"

Solution? The only one he needed right this second was the one that would keep him from ogling his oldest friend's little sister.

"There are a lot of different treatments, and sometimes that means a sleeping pill if you're at a state where it's gotten very dangerous for you to stay awake."

He'd never consciously liked the idea of innocence before. Before he'd come into the room and been tantalized by the nearly nothing she'd had on—coupled with his weakened state—this was certainly a natural reaction. Not just another flaw in his character.

"Lose this battle so you can live to keep fighting the war. On another day. Night."

He just had to remember who she was and what she was to him. It shouldn't matter to him what she thought of him, so he should be able to tell Adalyn the truth and actually get the help he'd dragged her around the globe for, not send her to treat imaginary illness.

"You know," she continued, "if the battle is a desire to sleep the natural way. Sleep aids aren't the greatest thing in the world, but sometimes they are necessary as you're trying to retrain yourself and your bed habits." She yawned, reminding him that she was tired, too. Probably jet-lagged.

And she'd stopped smoothing her robe closed. Definitely tired.

He remained standing as stiff as his suit by the door. "I have sleep aids but, as you said, I try not to use them. I may have dragged you across the world for nothing, Dr. Quinn." Doctor. Not Adalyn. Speak to her professionally, and perhaps his thoughts would follow that lead.

"Am I getting that you don't want me to be here? Did Jamison twist your arm into agreeing to this?" Her gaze sharpened and she stood, her head tilting and those pretty green eyes fixing on him with an intensity that faked alertness. And a little bit of hope. "Because if you really don't want me here, we could take a day or two and just diagnose and prescribe a treatment and I could go home, rather than sticking around to see you through whatever you need to get right. Jamison could be satisfied with that."

"It's not that I don't want you here," he said before it became clear she was offering him an out. She didn't want to be there any more than he wanted her there. They could put on a brief show of his treatment, enough to satisfy Jay, and then she would happily go home. "I just don't sleep well at the palace. Or at all. I sleep…" He rubbed his brow, pausing as he paced to a chair and sat. Her fatigue amplified his own. "I sleep better when I'm not in the palace."

"Do you keep an apartment somewhere else? Or are you referring to before you came to this kingdom to do the regent thing?"

"I don't keep an apartment. It's a tent." Why was he telling her this? Letting her witness his trouble would lead to questions, the bane of his existence. The prospect of her finding out seemed worse than the whole world finding out, and he couldn't even bring himself to care how sexist that seemed to him—not wanting to be treated or rescued by the sweet creature his inner caveman salivated over. He didn't want her to know any of it, his weakness, his shame.

"I take short medical missions out into the desert to treat those who live in camps far from medical assistance. I'm a doctor, it is just who I am, and I want to hold on to that part of myself while I'm doing my duty for my country and my family, and not let my skills grow rusty for lack of use, as they would if I stopped practicing and became a full-time bureaucrat."

"And when you're on your medical missions in a tent, you sleep better?" she said, fixating on that part.

What she should be fixating on was the fact that he didn't sleep here in the palace. If she were to continue to treat him, she'd have to go, too. "I can't explain it, but I should've thought about that before you came all this way. I know you have no desire to come out into the desert with me, and the equipment would be useless there anyway. Apologies, Adalyn."

She sat back down on the edge of the bed, thoughtful frown firmly in place. "How long are the missions?"

"Many days." Not that many, but more than two. He would disappear for weeks on end if he could get away with it.

"And people don't know you're doing this?"

She should sound less interested, not more.

"I keep a small staff here, and I'm always available via satellite phone. Since this is not my home country—it's my mother's kingdom—the people here, especially those out in the desert camps, don't know what I look like. I go by a different name. We have a fake logo sprayed onto the trucks. It's…"

"Tricky." She grinned as she said the word and then yawned wider than she had before. "Well, I have a theory about the sleeping in the tent thing. But if you only take a short trip when you go, I'm assuming it's fairly frequent short trips?" She stopped, shifted on the bed some more and tried again. "I can go…on one trip. And that would be a few days of monitoring when you're actually sleeping. And then we can tell Jamison that we worked on a treatment plan for you to implement."

"The sun is brutal, Adalyn. You will burn to a crisp. And the heat, if you're unused to it…"

"Where I live it gets very hot. And humid. Super-humid. So humid that mold is a massive problem. I can handle heat. And wear sunblock. We'll be going in a vehicle anyway, right? Something with a roof?" She frowned momentarily, eyes sliding to the side beneath pinched brows. That was the kind of look he wanted from her. Uncertainty.

Uncertainty her words did not share. "I can go from the vehicle to the tent and not have to be in direct sunlight too much." She stood and wandered toward him but passed by to reach for the doorknob. "I hate to kick you out of a room in your home, but I'm really very tired. I think I have jet lag. Jamison never adequately described it to me before. It's awful."

He took the hint and rose to move that way. "The way my schedule is arranged, I really should head out in the morning." Before she had time to rest up.

She opened the door and held it patiently for him. "What time?"

"It's best to travel in the morning, before the heat of the day."

"What does that translate to in numbers?"

"Six to ten, give or take."

She looked at the clock, no doubt calculating just how few hours of rest she'd be getting if she actually went through with the plan. "Okay. I'll be ready at six." Another yawn and then she wandered back to the bed, leaving him at the door. "Try to rest if you can. We'll start tomorrow."

Pulling down the blankets, she crawled in—robe and all—and reached for the clock to set it.

She'd never go. In the morning, after she'd had a few hours to reset her brain and remember how much she hated to travel, she'd come to her senses and he could trundle her back off to the helicopter pad and send her home. "Good night, Adalyn. Thank you for being willing to try."

"No offense, Khalil, but I did it for Jamison. I'm sure you're a nice man and that you deserve help—it's torture to be kept awake, like real torture, and I wouldn't wish it on anyone—but if anyone else had asked me to come, you'd be on your own."

She clicked off the light and he allowed himself a tiny smile. He'd probably do anything for Jamison, too; he was closer than Khalil's real brothers had ever been. "Duly noted. And you have tried to do that by coming all the way here to meet with me."

"I'll see you at six," she said again, then sat up so he could see her only by the light spilling through the door to his chamber. "And, Khalil? Knock first next time. I wouldn't want to cause you years of therapy."

What did that mean? She'd already lain back down and burrowed into the pillow, effectively shutting him out. "Sleep well, little sister," he murmured, shutting the door behind him. Calling her "Doctor" hadn't done anything for his libido. Maybe calling her "little sister" would be able to keep him from thinking about the lush flesh he'd seen on display.

Jay needed a talk about sending his innocent, pretty little sister off to foreign countries and men who might take advantage of her.

Men of weaker constitution than Khalil.

CHAPTER TWO

COLLEAGUES LIKED TO JOKE that Adalyn had chosen sleep medicine as her specialty in a direct reaction to how badly she'd longed for sleep during medical school and residency.

'Sleep is for the weak' was practically a motto of the twenty-first century. A crutch to help people get by in this competitive world and all its requirements for productivity, to prove they weren't beholden to the hours of vulnerability almost every living creature had to succumb to daily. The concept of sleep as a luxury.

Sacrificing sleep meant compromising health. Physical. Mental. Emotional. And she was doing it again in order to keep up with Khalil's schedule and not let her brother down. Her brother, who would want her to be healthy! Ah, more contradictions of modern living.

Sleep-deprived, but clean, mostly upright and dressed—unlike the last time she'd seen Khalil—Adalyn knocked on the door to his suite while looking at her watch. Ten to six—she was tired and only passably functioning, but she'd made his hour of departure. She'd even managed to pack a small bag with the bare minimum she'd need for three days in the desert.

No answer.

He'd said he never slept in the palace, though she doubted that was true unless he had been out in the desert as recently as a couple of days ago. Being tired could explain his forgetting to knock before he'd entered her bedroom the previous night, but if he'd gone more than forty-eight hours without any sleep he wouldn't be nearly as coherent as he had been in their short conversation. But if he was sleeping in after she'd managed to get up and get ready...

He'd been so adamant he wouldn't sleep.

Truly, insomnia wasn't what she'd expected she was coming to treat. One of the ways that Jamison had talked her into coming, his strongest method, had been guilt. What did you do when a hero was wounded? You treated them. And by the story he'd told, with bold strokes, Jamison had painted Khalil as a wounded hero. Not two months ago the country had been in revolt, the royals murdered, except for the heir—who was underage and too young to take the throne. Khalil and his brother had undertaken a mission to rescue the boy and the brother hadn't made it back. But Khalil had, with the boy—the heir who was too young to rule and now away at some school somewhere.

After all that? Well, if she'd had to guess, she'd have said his problem would've been nightmares. But then again, that was her specialty.

If he'd heard her knock, plenty of time had passed for him to throw pants on and answer the door. Adalyn knocked again. Still no answer.

Well, two knocks were warning enough. She grabbed her bag—the smallest she'd brought—and marched into Khalil's bedroom suite.

Coming from a bright room to a dark one, all she

could see was the outline of heavy drapes over the bedroom windows. She couldn't even begin to guess where light switches would be in the chamber, so she marched to one of the windows and pulled open the heavy brocade curtain. And then she could see. Empty. Khalil wasn't sleeping in. Khalil wasn't there.

But at least now she could see the door leading out.

He'd all but screamed last night that he didn't want her there. She'd just expected that once they made a plan he would stick with it. Propelled by the sick feeling she'd been left, she hurried out of the room, just shy of a run.

For once her travel paranoia had done something good for her—despite her exhaustion, when the men had marched her to the suite, she'd still been able to memorize the route out of the palace in case of another sudden civil war—who knew how often those things happened in this place? Or fire. Fire was something she'd want to be able to escape without a map or a guide. One turn, another long hallway, more gilded opulence and crystal light fixtures…doors, doors, doors…another turn. She finally made it to a courtyard, having passed not a single person along the way, and stepped out just in time to see two large trucks pulling away.

Not knowing what else to do, she shouted, "Khalil!"

He sat in the driver-side window of the first truck, and when she'd shouted the name she probably shouldn't even be using at the palace he did nothing but make eye contact with her through the side-view mirror. He'd heard her but didn't take his foot off the gas.

A surge of frustration rode a wave of irritation, and before she even knew it she'd broken into a dead run after the truck.

Leaving without her? Make her travel all the way to this place, make her lose sleep and get on dangerous vehicles on land and air and then abandon her where she could be of no help to him, for no danged reason? If they made travel guide recommendations for the perfect time to shout at or make rude gestures at a royal, this would be at the top.

The trucks moved slowly enough in the courtyard to give the illusion that she might catch up with them, but the closer the gate came, the more that hopeful thought evaporated.

Muttering expletives under her breath wasn't enough, either.

The trucks slowed, making a sharp turn for the gate—too far to reach, and what was she going to do if she got there? Climb on a moving vehicle? Yeah, right.

She'd never been moved to violence by anyone before, but she dropped her bag and grabbed the nearest rock—small enough to throw but big enough to express her frustration—and channeling her anger she let the rock fly with as much force as a really tired nerdy chick could muster.

She didn't aim for him. She didn't really aim. She probably couldn't aim if she tried, at least not beyond the general intention to hit the truck somewhere, but the rock sailed strong and true, impacting the side window of the rear seat of the truck, right behind where Kahlil sat. It immediately spiderwebbed.

That stopped the truck.

That stopped both trucks.

Khalil got out, looked at the window and slammed his door. A couple tiny fragments of glass in the center of the impact rattled and fell out from the force of his gesture. He shook his head minutely at the men in the truck behind and stormed toward Adalyn, red crawling up his neck and over his face. "What the hell was that?"

Right then Adalyn remembered that she was pretty much afraid of everything. Including confrontation. Having big angry men yell at her was also on her Do Not Do list.

But if she backed down now, he'd probably just send her back inside and go on his merry way to wherever he was going.

"Emergency call button." Adalyn's short words came out with a grunt, the sound of exertion…mental if not physical. Before he reached her she jogged for the other side of the trucks to the passenger-side door. As she wrenched it open and climbed the running board to step in, strong hands locked on her hips and set her back on the ground.

There, in the relative seclusion of the side door area, he gave her a spin and forced her to face him. He was close. Too close, all but plastering her to the side of the truck, his arms forming a cage around her that kept her in place so he could effectively loom over her. "I know how you Quinns are fond of bucking authority figures, but in this country—and while still at this palace—you can't behave like that toward me."

It hit her how he was dressed. No robes today. No suit, either. He wore khakis and a light linen shirt with the collar unbuttoned, something that made him look almost like a normal person, not the autocrat he sounded like.

Their cozy little passenger-door alcove blocked the early-morning breeze and cocooned her in a heady scent of cedar, hints of citrus and something utterly masculine. Looking up into his golden-brown eyes, she felt entirely too vulnerable suddenly, as if he'd see the white flag waving in her pupils and know how close she was to backing down. She squinted at him, relying on the decreased area to make her intentions harder to read. And if it worked, she'd have to remember to use it the next time she got the harebrained idea to yell and throw rocks at a royal.

And she still couldn't hold his gaze.

Looking at his mouth? That was just as bad, but for more confusing reasons.

Her gaze tracked farther down. His neck was safe, though a vein stood out there, pulsing, and seeing how fast his heart beat caused a little flutter in her belly. Even in her worst imaginings related to this trip, they had all been about accidents, explosions and possibly drowning at sea after a water crash... Never once had she thought she'd have to fight her patient to be able to treat him. The small amount of backbone she'd found quickly faded. All she wanted to do was get her bag and go back inside, but she muttered, "You were leaving me behind on purpose."

Khalil dropped his arms and stepped back, needing to put some distance between himself and the woman who was supposed to be sleeping through his departure. Distance would help him keep from shaking some sense into her or just putting his hands back on her.

Even after he'd grabbed places on the truck and forced himself to focus on her, his palms still tingled with the memory of firm, curvy hips.

With a slow breath in through his nose, he took a few seconds to look over the courtyard. At least no one but

the small private crew who traveled into the desert with
him had witnessed the rock showdown.

"I assumed you wouldn't want to go." That was true,
at least until he'd seen her outside with the overnight
bag. After that, he really had no clue why he hadn't
stopped. Maybe the idea that one more hurdle would
make her give up… Only, it hadn't.

She looked him in the eye again, but he could tell
from the color in her cheeks and the way her hands now
gripped the door frame that her bravery was faltering.
"I told you I would come last night."

"Yes, and then you had a little time to sleep on it and
think more clearly. At least, I'd hoped that would be the
case." He managed to calm his voice when he said it, a
small victory considering he wanted to shout, *Go back
inside. Go home. Go anywhere else.*

"So you really don't want me here. You let me come
all this way and…" As she spoke, her words came more
and more slowly, and those soft green eyes he'd so ad-
mired hardened to bare slits. She might be tired, she
might not enjoy confrontation and she might be a little
intimidated by him, but she was still angry. "I'm not
at my best today, but I do still have a little bit of functioning gray matter working for me. You're sabotaging
this on purpose."

"Adalyn—"

"No. I'm the one talking now!" She released the
frame of the door and reached up to jab him once in
the chest. "You didn't just let me come all this way,
you assured that I would have the roughest trip possible, right? You have loads of planes—you and Jamison
have gone to practically as many countries as the Peace
Corps on them—but I had to arrange transport and ship

the equipment…and all that. You sent your black-suited henchmen to retrieve me at the last possible minute, but that's it. You made my journey as hard as you could possibly make it in order to make me be the one who broke a promise to my brother. Didn't you?"

And he wouldn't defend it or deny it.

But if she poked him in the chest again, he was going to…

No, there would be no feeling up his best friend's irritating little sister. He crossed his arms to keep his hands under control and said instead, "You really want to go into the desert? It's nothing like you read in books. No rest stops between here and where we're going. Poisonous creatures that sting and bite. Dust, sun, heat—this isn't some glorified field trip."

She stepped up on the running board and turned to face him, now somewhat closer to eye level, and used that added height to glare at him, her chin tilting to match the challenge in her posture. "Say it," she demanded, the tiniest wobble in her voice breaking through his resistance more than the bravado she put on. "Tell me I can't go. I'll tell Jamison that I did all I could, but, whatever you promised him, you broke your word. Go ahead, Khalil. Tell me I can't go. I'm happy to go pack my bags and find a way out of your gilded palace in the sand and go home. But you have to say it, because I came all this way for Jamison, and I'm not going to be the one who lets him down."

Son of a…

"Just sit down and shut up already," he muttered, shaking his head.

Adalyn drew a deep, satisfied breath, and at the second her lungs felt filled to capacity the true meaning of her victory pushed the air back out again in a rush. She'd just had a fight in order to be *allowed* to ride out into the scorching desert in a big dangerous truck with a man who really didn't want her with him.

So not a victory.

She edged onto the seat and closed the door. He rounded the truck and climbed back in at the driver's side, slamming his own door and bringing down another shard of glass from the window she'd broken and that now had a tiny hole in the center. The window that now looked…really dangerous.

"Aren't we going to change to a truck without a broken window?"

"No. Want to change your mind and go back inside?" He pulled on his seat belt and started the truck.

Yes!

"No, I'm going with you unless you order me not to." And now that she thought about it, that was a really stupid idea.

The trucks started rolling forward, continuing on… Without her bag! "Are we going to turn around and fetch my bag?"

If she'd eaten anything in the past several hours, she'd have been sick. No bag meant no protein bars, no water purification tablets… She was going out into the desert where they probably only had water sources of questionable cleanliness…

"No. Want to change your mind?"

Yes. *Yes.*

"Is that all you can say?" She grit her teeth and fixed her gaze in front of her. "I'm coming with you. But if I start to stink in the next couple of days I'm going to roll around in your fresh clean clothes so you can bask in my stench just as much as I'll have to."

"Good. Someone as irritating as you are shouldn't smell so good."

The urge to take off one shoe so she could better beat him with it nearly overwhelmed her limping self-control. Yet more evidence that being sleep-deprived in a foreign land brought out the worst in her.

Could someone get motion sickness if they were only going a few miles per hour? Her stomach thought so. "You're the one who's all sultan-like, but I wouldn't think it kingly to tuck tail and run when confronted with a problem. You *should* put off your trip and stay home to get treatment."

"Amazingly enough, this isn't just something I can put off. I'm not going into the desert because you don't want me to. I'm also not going just because I'm tired and want to sleep, though honestly I am really looking forward to that part. In the other truck is a cool box with vaccinations to be given. The tribes don't have the best access to clean water, and though we've put measures into motion to change this they still struggle with disease because of it."

Okay, that deflated her anger balloon a little. Except that bit about the unclean water, and her not having the tablets… "Maybe not, but you're not going to get my bag because you want to put me out. So don't get too smug and superior just because you have a valid reason for going on this trip."

She pretended he hadn't said she smelled good, because she really didn't know what to do with that information. Thank him? Give him the name of her favorite perfume?

"Fine." He grabbed the radio handset and said something she didn't understand as the truck rolled on.

The other truck hadn't yet passed through the gate, and she turned to look over her shoulder, trying to work out what he'd just done. "Why did you agree to my coming in the first place if you're so all fired against it?"

"I was tired, Jay was persistent," Khalil answered, hanging the radio handset back in its place.

With how stringently he wanted her to not go with him, Adalyn had no illusion he would wait if she climbed out of the truck and ran to pick up her bag. Resigned, she dragged on her seat belt.

Looking at him made her angrier. Looking out the side window made her feel sick. Looking out the front terrified her. She went with angry and twisted slightly under the confines of her overly tightened seat belt to look at Khalil.

Even scowling, as he was, he was handsome. That probably played into his privileged air. Royalty, doctor, handsome… It all added up to *spoiled* and used to getting what he wanted. He probably had insomnia because his bed was too lumpy, like the princess and the pea.

"I don't buy it," she said, trying to ignore the way her stomach squeezed and rolled with every creak and crackle from the window she'd broken. The wind tore at the shards, barely holding together. What if the bits flew up and got in his eyes and blinded him and he crashed them into something deadly? She chanced another glance back at the hole, mentally calculating what was safest—for the windows up front to be up or down. If she rolled down her window, would the air flow drag the shards into the cab or push them out of the truck rather than in? Maybe they wouldn't fly around at all.

Maybe this was just another paranoid scenario playing out in her mind, like the thousands of fiery deaths she'd imagined on the way there.

Stay on topic.

Khalil was the topic. And narrating all her bloody imaginings to him wouldn't inspire any sort of confidence that she could help him. "I can't believe that with this level of aversion you left the situation to chance. You're too domineering and controlling to leave this up to fate. You fit the alpha-male mold even without the royalty stuff added on, but without even knowing me you counted on me chickening out. That's dumb. Maybe you should try to sleep more."

Antagonizing him probably wouldn't inspire confidence in her, either.

He looked sideways at her, his eyes off the road long enough to increase her worry. She took a deep breath and tried to relax her arms and shoulders. With the road rushing at her, she couldn't even release a fraction of that tension. She closed her eyes and tried again, channeling the physical manifestation of her fear to her right hand, where she could at least grip and abuse the armrest on the door and he might not see.

"You should try to sleep now," he said, his voice remarkably level.

"Yeah, that won't happen. I tried to sleep all the way here. It didn't work at all."

"Try again." Whatever anger she'd roused in him earlier was now gone. He could've been telling her the time of day for all the emotion reflected in his tone. Maybe she hadn't antagonized him so much after all. "We have a few hours' drive ahead of us."

"That may be, but…" But. But how much should she

reveal? Would it make him act like less of a jerk if he knew what she was putting herself through for him? Or, more accurately, for Jamison? Or would he just use it as ammunition to get her back out of the truck and his presence? "I can't sleep in a moving car. Or plane. You should be able to understand someone not being able to sleep when they want to. I would love to go to sleep and block all this out, but I can't."

"The truck scares you?"

"All vehicles scare me," she muttered, and laid her head back, eyes still closed and arms now folded. "They're dangerous. People die all the time in car accidents."

Her voice became small and thready with the last statement, reminding him of her history in a way that left him feeling unaccountably exposed and irritated. When their parents had died, Jamison had been away at school with him, and Khalil had witnessed firsthand how destructive it could be to lose both your parents in your formative years. He'd pulled Jamison back from his more destructive actions, distracting him in whatever way he'd been able to…including a couple of fistfights just because picking a fight and making Jay mad at him had been the better alternative to the things he'd been about to do.

Had anyone helped her with her grief? If she really was scared of all vehicles, she must have felt put through the wringer to get here.

And that thought didn't help, either. He wanted her to go, but using a fear born of the death of her parents to make her do what he wanted seemed like the worst kind of evil.

CHAPTER THREE

ADALYN WHITE-KNUCKLED HER way through the desert trek. Now and then Khalil talked to her, and she knew it for what it was—distraction. However much he didn't want her there, when it mattered he was kind.

When they reached the camp location he turned and looked at her. "Take a few minutes to collect yourself before you get out, but don't take too long—the sun is reaching its zenith and the heat will rise very quickly now that the air-conditioning isn't running." Nevermind the now somewhat larger hole in the back window…

She nodded, finally letting herself look out the dusty windows at the little tent village. "Khalil?"

Saying his name stopped him from climbing down, though the door was open. He closed it enough to dampen their voices and kept his low. "Don't call me Khalil. I'm Zain while we're here. The people know me by one name—having you use another will confuse things."

"Right." She nodded, still not thinking all that clearly. "Zain? There's a man running toward the truck."

That effectively took his attention from her. Zain-not-Khalil climbed down immediately and closed the door. Through the broken window she could hear them speaking, but that didn't mean she understood the words. What she did pick up on was the urgency in the man's voice. She leaned over to get a better view of him gesturing quickly toward one of the nearby tents.

"Adalyn, I need your help." Zain still sounded as authoritarian as Khalil had, but it made her move despite the earlier order to stay until she'd collected herself.

Adalyn climbed out and rounded the truck, meeting him at the back. "What's wrong?"

"His son is sick, and they've not been able to even keep water in him for two days."

Adalyn looked at the man and then at Khalil, nodding. "What do you want me to do?"

He'd already pulled open the back doors of the truck and climbed in. "I want you to assist me. My medics aren't here yet, they went back to get your bag. So you're my nurse for now." In the back, he dug into a couple of different trunks and one cooler, pulling out supplies and stuffing them into an actual old-time doctor's bag.

"Nurse. Okay." She nodded, even if she wasn't sure what he wanted. "My clinical skills are rusty. I haven't actually treated injuries and illness since residency." Wait, what had he said? "Did you say that they went to get my bag?"

"Yes." He answered her question first, then added, "If you can follow instructions, you'll be fine."

"I can follow instructions." That probably wasn't the correct word for it, considering he was more giving orders than helpful instructions. But she could follow orders, too, when it suited her to do so.

"Get the doors. Then catch up." He jumped down, ushering the worried father with him off in the direction of the nearby camp.

Adalyn climbed into the truck, closed the trunks and

flipped latches, then jumped down and did the same with the double doors at the back. Without the prospect of the vehicle moving, it lost its ability to scare her. Just having the chance to move and focus on something aside from imminent death let her compose herself. By the time she rounded the truck Khalil had reached a tent and she barely caught sight of him ducking to enter through the flap. Five more seconds and she might not have even known which tent he'd gone to.

As she hurried across the sandy expanse, the sun heated her dark hair to temperatures it never saw outside styling appliances. The long, thick, chestnut fall of hair carried that heat down her back so that by the time she reached the tent and called a greeting, she wished she'd pulled it up. Or cut it. Or maybe that she'd just let him head off into the desert on his own, rather than fighting to come with him. The man hadn't been wrong in warning her that she wasn't built for this kind of adventure. New Orleans heat was a different creature entirely.

"Zain?" She said his fake name, not knowing what the protocol was to enter someone's tent. You couldn't exactly knock or ring the bell.

"Come." He had that autocratic edge to his voice again.

She pulled open the flap and stepped inside. It smelled like a sick ward, but it was somewhat cooler than the air outside, something she was thankful for.

In the center of the tent a woman covered in layers of undoubtedly uncomfortable cloth held a small child in her lap. From the sweat matting his short hair and the color of his face, Adalyn could tell his fever had reached worrisome levels. Without asking any other questions, she stepped over and knelt with Khalil.

"Rotavirus," he said. "I need to set up an IV and get some fluids into him."

Khalil hadn't had much time to diagnose or examine before she'd gotten there, and that meant no time to sort out his supplies. When she opened the satchel and pulled out a bag of saline, she looked at him. "You expected rotavirus?"

"They had an outbreak of it a few weeks ago, and that's actually the vaccines I'd intended to give."

Rotavirus… What did she remember about this? Not usually deadly, but it could be. Poor drinking water and sanitation usually caused outbreaks.

"Are any other children ill?" While she quietly asked for updates—just making sure that her rusty information wasn't going to cause tetanus—she fished out other supplies. The IV kit. Alcohol preps. Tourniquet.

"Not right now. But we're not going to be able to give the vaccine to him for a couple of days, just to make sure." The more he talked, the longer he was within the small tent, the more like a regular man he seemed… and less like an angry dictator. "They should be healthy before it's given."

Though he looked somewhat severe still, tension no longer stood out in cords down his neck. No matter what kind of edge he had in his voice when he spoke to her, when he spoke to these people…his people… Khalil's voice became much gentler. She didn't even need to understand the words to know what he was doing. Comforting. Reassuring. Explaining treatment. The things a good doctor did. Was this the man that Jamison called his best friend?

Adalyn waited for a lull in the conversation to ask, "How can we keep the other children from getting it?"

"My medics have a new purification system they'll set up when they get here. And we'll see what we can do for other interventions." He looked at her, his honey-brown eyes taking on the quality of examination, and before he even said anything she knew what he was looking at. Inside the tent, sheltered from the sun, her skin still burned. She was going pink. Her sunburn had already started. And she'd probably have freckles before they got back to the palace.

"I didn't swim in sunblock before I left this morning, which I should have done. I will remedy that when they get here with my bag." It still shocked her that he'd given in on that. She kind of wished she'd been nicer to him in the truck, and she hadn't thanked him yet… "I misunderstood. When you said 'Fine,' I thought you just meant you weren't going to quarrel with me, but you meant the bag, right?"

He nodded and tied the band around the unconscious boy's arm, then began prodding for a vein.

"Thank you…Doctor." She'd almost called him Khalil, it had been on the tip of her tongue. She should probably stop thinking of him as Khalil if she wanted to maintain his cover. Which she did. He'd done something kind for her in getting her bag, maybe she could turn this situation around and still get him to let her help him. Maybe tomorrow after he'd had a night of sleep he'd be more reasonable about it. Maybe she could win him over, get his cooperation…and shorten the length of time she'd need to stay there, away from home.

Despite feeling and feeling for a vein, he still hadn't picked up the needle or alcohol prep.

"It's hard to find a vein when they're very dehydrated," Adalyn said. This was actually something she was good at.

"I know."

"Of course you do. I'm sorry. I didn't mean to insinuate you didn't. I was thinking out loud. But, as rusty as most of my clinical skills are, I'm actually really good at IVs." He looked at her, the weight of his gaze settling on her, considering. He'd let her do it if she convinced him. "I can hit it. If you like. It's actually something that I do regularly for an elderly neighbor. She's not a child, but she's got tiny veins."

"Your neighbor needs you to set up an IV for her?"

"I do blood draws for her weekly to take with her to her anticoagulation appointment. I draw in the morning when I get in from work, we put it into a thermos and she takes it with her. They can never hit the vein without several stabs, so she prefers it if I do it." Rather than give a fuller recitation of her most recent IVs, she figured she'd said enough for him to decide and quieted to let him work it out.

"I appreciate the offer."

The woman who held her child hadn't said anything, and Adalyn didn't know how much English she understood, if any. So she did what she could and smiled, reaching over to pat the woman's arm. "It'll be okay. We're going to help him." And then asked Khalil, "What's his name?"

"I don't know," he answered, but ignored her offer in favor of palpating the tiny arm for a vein.

"Upper arm might be better. I'd say leg, but they can kick those out pretty easy."

He flipped off the tourniquet and moved to the boy's other arm, starting over again.

Her keys…

Adalyn patted the many pockets on her pants, un-snapped a thigh pocket and fished out the set, then snatched the little laser she played with her neighbor's cat with.

"What are you doing?"

"This will help." She pressed the button to turn on the cheap little laser pointer and pressed it to the boy's arm where he was palpating for a vein. Through the thin layer of baby fat the light illuminated the dark pathways that were blood vessels. "That help?"

"What the…?" He blinked and let her track the light over the boy's skin. There were special infrared lights he'd heard of for illuminating veins, but he'd never seen such a cheap-looking gadget do it. "Is that infrared?"

"Wee sight illuminators are best, and I have one for Mrs. Stiverson's sticks, but I didn't bring it with me. I've used this in a pinch before, though. I probably should have left my keys at the p—" She stopped herself before *palace* came out of her mouth. "At home." A slightly flummoxed shake of her head and she moved past it. "But I'm kind of afraid something will happen and I'll be separated from something important if I don't have it with me at all times."

If he kicked her out of the country, she meant. Khalil could read between those lines easily enough.

The thought had occurred to him.

Rather than comment, he reached for another alcohol prep, swabbed the skin and then lifted her hand to swab the tip of the light and the area she'd pressed against the small boy's arm. When he was certain that it was all disinfected and the skin illuminated, he felt right over one of the larger, dark vessels. "It's not all that deep," he murmured, getting a nod from her.

"And there's a small amount of thickness on the edges, probably the walls of the vessel, but if you aim for the center you'll be fine."

After a few more words of reassurance for the mother, he asked the boy's name and gave instructions on holding him snugly in case he woke up and began to struggle.

"His name is Nadim, and he's three," Khalil said in quiet English, since Adalyn had wanted to know. "If he wakes up, drop the light and hold his legs. She'll have his top half, but if he has use of his legs he'll be able to put up more of a fight."

"Of course." She kept the light against the boy's skin, but with her other hand reached down and wrapped her fingers around the tiny ankle closest to Khalil.

So, she could follow orders.

Carefully, he threaded the line into the boy's vein and when rewarded with a blood return attached a saline flush to double-check. Sometime in all this she'd dropped the light and had taken over holding the line so it didn't slip out.

When he'd confirmed that the vein was indeed intact still, he taped down the cannula and she hooked the tubing up to the bag and stood, letting gravity feed the fluid down to the end before he attached it to the needle.

"How are we going to hang it?" she asked.

"We'll have a stand when the medics get here."

"I made them late."

"No. Well, yes, but you're earning your keep." Her little cheap key chain light had saved him a lot of headache. Khalil might not want her there to help him, but he could appreciate the help she provided for the people in his care. "I might not have hit that vein without your trick, and most assuredly would not have on the first try. Where'd you learn that?"

"It's something I always check on pretty much every light I get my hands on." She smiled at him, her first honest, unguarded smile. Her cheeks bunched, bringing the pink closer to her green eyes so that they seemed all the greener, and gave that suggestion again of innocence. Beneath her aggravation at him there was a sweetness about her.

"My dad and I used to put flashlights to our cheeks, noses, whatever…then turn off the lights and make faces at one another with glowing cheeks and black hollow-looking eyes. Got me in the habit of checking different lights against my skin."

He spoke again with the mother, giving her instructions and explaining what he was going to do. When he stopped speaking and looked at her again, Adalyn continued her story. "I had to give a presentation in college and got my own pointer because I wanted to be the best. I was nervous talking in front of everyone, but I managed to get through the whole thing by distracting myself by pressing it against my arm or hand and watching the veins get illuminated. Coping mechanism that turned into a trick that helped me in residency. I was all about tricks that might make me better able to do the job. I'm not a natural, like Jamison."

"That why you went into sleep medicine?"

"No." She turned off the light and stashed it in her pocket again, then began cleaning up the garbage left behind from the containers.

Clearly she wasn't going to give him more information than that. Not unless he dragged it out of her.

For the time being he hung the bag on a bit of wood at the top of the tent, and when it didn't cause the thing to bow or collapse, he turned his attention back to Adalyn. "Why did you pick sleep medicine?"

"Because it was a good fit for me. I understand sleep problems."

"Are you an insomniac?"

"No." She stuffed the trash into one of the bigger bags and then set it beside his, where it would be easy to dispose of. When her task was finished she rubbed the boy's leg in a way that comforted the mother, who was clearly so worried that she didn't even have anything to ask or talk about. Her attention entirely focused on her son and the line now feeding life-giving fluids into him that he couldn't vomit back up, but she seemed reassured simply by their presence.

Adalyn might be rusty, but she did have the touch.

"I had nightmares when my parents died." Her words came so softly he could have missed them if he'd not been looking at her. "It took me a long time to learn how to manage them. I think that's why I find sleep so interesting. Everyone shrugs off the importance of rest, but it's fascinating how much the body does while you're sleeping. And that's not even counting what the mind gets up to in dreams…"

Bad things, that's what his mind got up to in dreams.

Maybe she would understand if he just told her the basics. That he had nightmares and his insomnia was more of a choice than a symptom.

Not that he wanted to even go that far with his explanations. She'd want to know why he had nightmares—it didn't take a mental leap to give significance to the lack of sleep as being preferable to the nightmares. And dreams that bad…she'd want to know details. What were they about? What did they make him feel? Things he just couldn't bring himself to talk about. He didn't even like to think about them.

"Jay never mentioned that about you." Or maybe he had and Khalil hadn't been paying sufficient attention when they'd spoken on the phone. He certainly hadn't been able to come up with a reason not to keep her from coming—at least one that Jay would buy. He hadn't bought the one about the country having recently been in a civil war, and that had seemed like a given.

"I never really let Jamison know how bad they were, so please don't tell him." She shrugged, but not a hint of the earlier smile remained, even in her eyes. "I didn't let anyone but my therapist know. My aunt and uncle sent me to therapy to deal with the deaths, so I talked to her about it all. And we worked on it together."

"She was a sleep specialist?"

"No. Not in any way, but she understood enough to get us started, and she dug into any studies she could find as well, learned all she could to help me."

Voices outside the tent alerted him. "They're here." He looked down at the woman and her son and crouched back down. He made a quick introduction between Adalyn and the mother—since he'd neglected it before— and repeated the instructions he'd given earlier.

Afterward he turned to Adalyn and went through the list with her again in English and in more detail.

"You're leaving me here?"

"I'm going to help them set up the tents, and I'll send someone in with the stand for the IV. Be careful when you transfer it from where I've got it standing. The last thing they need is for the tent to collapse on them while they're trying to get the little guy well."

"What if she says something to me? I don't understand…" He could tell she was trying to keep the alarm out of her voice, but the way she turned to keep her face hidden from the mother but remained entirely visible to him let him know.

Was there anything the woman wasn't scared of?

Travel.

Cars.

Planes.

Letting her brother down.

Being alone with a woman she couldn't understand.

Unclean drinking water. Actually, he couldn't blame her for that one. But, really, how had she managed the backbone required to launch that rock at his truck?

"I'm not going far, Adalyn. I'll have them bring you a walkie-talkie, too. If you need anything, just call me on it and I'll come. You need to stay out of the sun—you've already begun to burn, and that will no doubt feel worse when the sun goes down. Setting up means a lot of heavy labor and today we're doing the tents and setting up the purification system for the water. It would be better if you stayed inside."

Somewhere in his list of reasons she'd started to look less alarmed and worried. Either that or she was getting control of her eyebrows, since they were in more or less a neutral position now. "Just make sure that they get the walkie-talkies and the stand in here quickly."

He nodded and she turned back to the woman, rubbing her arm through the layers of fabric.

"Remember who you are calling on the radio." He

tried to give her the kind of reminder that wouldn't give away his charade, and would make sure she didn't give it away, either. He hoped. Zain. Not Khalil.

She nodded and murmured, "I'll remember, Dr. Zain." A small comfort at least. Maybe she'd even remember it if she had to call him in an emergency situation.

He headed out and, after he relayed the orders for what she needed to one of his men, grabbed a walkie-talkie and strapped it to his belt, then went to help unload the trucks.

Even with the heat and the heavy labor, Khalil didn't mind helping set up. It was such a different situation than at the palace that it calmed him. Routine, blending in with everyone else. Anonymity wasn't something he'd ever really had—even when he'd been away in England at school, people had known who he was. They were just less likely to be cowed by it than those in his home country. But before coming to Merirach, when he and Jay had gone on medical missions into other countries—places where no one had known or cared who he was or what he did—it had been heaven.

As they pounded long rods deep into the ground and started pitching the tent, some of the village men came over to help them get it lifted.

They started quietly, but as they worked their normal comraderie came swinging into full force and soon one of the young men had asked about Adalyn. Dark hair. Pale skin. Green eyes. Of course she'd attracted attention. But beyond the coloring that gave her an exotic edge, she had something else that took her from pretty to the kind of looks that'd hang in any man's mind. It couldn't be the innocent way she had, and it really

couldn't be how many things frightened her, though
that did somewhat rouse a protective instinct in him. It
was something else.

But how could he explain who she was?

If he said she was there to treat him, they'd think he
wasn't capable of being a good doctor to them.

If he said she was just a colleague, then at least a
couple of the young men would think about her in a
way that made him instantly tense. Jamison wouldn't
want her having a surprise desert marriage, no matter
what goods she got in exchange for her hand.

Khalil wouldn't like it, either.

Even Zain wouldn't like it.

He had to say something...

"She's my mistress." He said the only thing he could
think of, with the hot sun beating down on him and the
hours of not sleeping behind him.

For the first few seconds after the words had come
out a kind of ominous quality lingered around them and
he couldn't put his finger on why, but his inner caveman woke up again, entirely too pleased with this lie.

He felt his pulse increase, but before he got the pole
he'd been working on placed a riot of laughter broke out
among the men. They all had their ideas about American
women, and that just confirmed the worst of it.

They might not entirely condone it but, as his mistress, she'd sleep in his tent and none of the men would
question it. He hadn't thought about where she'd sleep
before, but that certainly had to be what would need to
happen. As his colleague, there wouldn't be any sort
of ownership. She might still be up for grabs, but if he
claimed her as his own in some fashion, they'd respect

that boundary. They respected him, so no matter what they thought about her morals she'd be protected.

The more he thought about it the better he liked the idea.

Actually, it might work out even better than that. She didn't even like him seeing her knees, so how would she feel about being thought of as his mistress? Would that be enough to convince her to let him call the chopper and send her home? If he had learned one thing about Adalyn, it was that she didn't like surprises. Well, she didn't like much of anything—except maybe illuminating her skin with different lights and talking about sleep—but surprises were probably right at the top of her list of things she didn't like. Right there with motor vehicles.

CHAPTER FOUR

THIS WAS NOT exactly how Adalyn had expected the trip to go.

Granted, she hadn't had that much time to contemplate what she was getting herself into. Last night all she'd really been able to think had been *sleep*. Then this morning and in the truck she'd been too preoccupied with everything else to wrap her mind around what the little tent village was going to be like.

She couldn't liken the situation to anything she'd experienced. The only quasi-normal part was watching Nadim sleep, as well as the other medical aspects returning to her. She'd focus on those things. That would make everything seem less foreign and scary.

When Nadim woke, she got him to drink some liquid antinausea medicine. When that stayed down, she got a little fever-reducing medicine into him, too. Khalil had… No. She had to call him Zain, think of him as Zain. Back in the palace she probably had to call him by a title, so maybe the only place to call him Khalil was when sleep was near.

Zain might want a report on treatment, but she went into his satchel for the stethoscope instead and listened to little Nadim's belly first.

Zain hadn't told her to call with any good news, only emergencies, but a quick look at the IV they'd been giving him confirmed that they'd be in need before much longer. He'd taken nearly the whole bag already and still hadn't needed to relieve himself. Not that she could ask, but he didn't seem as if he needed to.

Right. She needed her translating dictionary. She should also get that other bag and hang it, though perhaps on a lower titration rate.

"I need to get more." She said the words in English because she just didn't have the words to communicate properly.

Her words had two sets of dark eyes looking at her. Adalyn stood and pointed to the bag, and with a series of gestures led the mother through the fluids situation. Almost out, easy to see in the bag. She pointed to herself and then out and held up two fingers…

When the poor haggard mother nodded Adalyn returned the nod and grabbed Khalil's satchel to trot back out.

The sun still beat down on her, baking her head and back, but the sooner she got back to the trucks the sooner she'd be saved from the blistering sun.

Near the truck, two tents had been erected, but none of the men were within sight now. Maybe they'd moved on to the water system.

Once in the truck, she located the saline quickly, then dug her dictionary from her bag and grabbed a few other supplies they'd need.

Her walkie-talkie crackled and she heard Khalil—Zain—through it.

"Where are you?"

Right. Of course he'd come back as soon as she'd stepped out, so he'd think she'd abandoned them.

Grabbing it off her belt, she pressed the button and spoke back. "The fluids were running out and he hasn't had to... No urine output so far or indication that he needs to go. I came out to the truck to get another bag and see if you had a cooling blanket, which you do, so I'm taking that to them, too. He kept down the antiemetic and fever reducer, but his fever is still higher than I'd like it to be."

"You should have called."

"It wasn't an emergency."

"You're my responsibility while we're out here, Adalyn. You could get hurt wandering about by yourself."

She could get hurt?

That's why she should have called? "You didn't say that before. You said emergency. But I will let you know before I go to the truck again. Anything else?"

"Come back." There it was again, the irritated tone that had dominated everything he'd said to her when not conversing in front of their patient.

As if it had even needed to be said. What kind of idiot would she have to be to stay outside and bake in the sun or the back of this darned truck—which might actually be hot enough to fire bricks?

"Ten-four," she muttered, because that's what people said in the movies when they used these things, and using the slang felt just bratty enough to make her feel a tiny bit better about her situation.

Which was worse? Dealing with the man who swung back and forth between acceptance and annoyance, or dealing with the entirely unfamiliar and therefore unsafe surroundings? She should be the one having mood swings, because she couldn't judge from one second to the next what his mood would be. If she'd had to guess earlier, she'd have said that her going out to get the fluids and supplies to take care of his patient would have made him happy. And she'd have been wrong.

With her supplies gathered up, and a couple of bottles of water from the cooler added to her loot, she headed back out of the truck, which she'd found imminently more pleasant without the motor running, even with the heat.

Maybe she could sleep in the thing later when night came and everything cooled off. There probably wouldn't be any stinging or biting critters in the safe confines of the truck.

By the time she got back her shirt was plastered to her back, and she'd developed a thirst so keen she could've downed both bottles of water.

Kha— Zain looked at her with a sharpness that confirmed his pendulum as being firmly on the annoyance side of the Sahara right now. "Here." She handed him the bag of fluid and then crouched down beside Nadim and his mother to shake out the cooling blanket. The look of alarm blasted at her from the mother made her pause. Zain offered her no assistance, not explaining what the blanket was, just looking on. Adalyn did the only thing she could—laid the material against the bare skin of the mother's hand to let her feel the difference between this and a regular blanket.

When she smiled, Adalyn took it as consent and laid the material on the boy's chest then tucked it around his legs. He opened his eyes and looked at the strange material with wonder, then pulled it up to his cheek and smiled over the edge at Adalyn. If nothing else, he was more comfortable.

"I forgot we had that," Zain murmured, after changing the fluid bag and sitting beside her again. "You look about ready to fall over."

"I thought that our heat would be comparable. Guess I was wrong. The sun just feels so hot. I should have tied my hair back. I didn't even bring any hair ties."

"We could use the tourniquet."

"Maybe later. I'm not so far gone right now that I'd like my hair ripped to shreds by uncovered rubber."

He took one of the bottles and drank deeply from it, prompting her to do the same thing. Hydration was even more important when they were probably going to use all of the saline in their inventory to take care of little Nadim.

When he'd drained the whole bottle he capped it and asked the mother something. Soon she was laying the boy on the mat and tucking the cooling blanket back around him. With a quick trip to the side of the tent, she came back with a comb and a piece of thick ribbon.

"She's going to braid your hair for you," Zain said.

Adalyn looked up at him. "Why? Do I look that bad?"

"You look hot and miserable, but keep in mind that she understands how hot it can be where the sun hits black." He went to check the filtration of Nadim's IV, then sat beside the kid, who was now actually awake enough to look miserable.

Adalyn opened her mouth to say something, but the soft cadence of Zain's speech to the boy stopped her. He spoke gently. Not understanding a word, she could only guess from the way the conversation remained one-sided and the way Nadim watched Zain with interest that he was telling the boy a story. Another glimpse of the kind of man she could see her brother being friends with?

When Nadim's mom pulled a short stool behind her and gestured, Adalyn sat down and pulled her hair free of her collar to flop down her back in a heavy thump, helping as much as she could.

Soon the comb was sliding through her hair, working through the tangles. It all happened very quickly. One moment her hair was baking her and the next it had been braided at the neck and coiled into what she could only assume was a bun, though how the woman managed to secure it with only the ribbon, she couldn't say.

"Thank you." She said it in English, then remembered how to say it properly to her in a tongue she would understand, and repeated the words.

Zain said something else to her and gestured to the boy. "She's going to get their supper started, and I told her we'd stay with him while she cooked."

By the time the tents were set up the afternoon had turned to evening. With the sun low on the horizon, Adalyn was no longer quite so hot, but then again getting her hair off her back had gone a long way toward lowering her body temperature.

Nadim had taken the whole of the second bag of fluid before needing to relieve himself. He was on the mend, or at least helped as sufficiently as they could do in the desert. There wasn't any cure for rotavirus—and while it wasn't usually fatal, it could be. Especially in this climate where proper hydration was a daily battle even when someone wasn't vomiting and worse.

Zain herded Adalyn from the small tent to one of

those the men had erected that afternoon. He said very little, at least very little she understood. He must have bought a truckload of the walkie-talkies, because the family was given one to call for help in the night, though it didn't look as if they'd need it.

"One of us should set an alarm and check in on them during the night," Adalyn said.

With the sun low on the horizon, the temperature was dropping, but the large white tents looked like heaven from the outside.

"Someone will."

She would have gone into the first tent, but his hand landed at the small of her back to steer her past it to the second.

Once they stepped into the white tent she felt immediately cooler. Just not cool enough to keep standing up. The short nap the night before had pretty much only been enough to keep her on her feet, and the weariness she felt screamed for her to sit and conserve energy at every opportunity. She scanned the tent for the optimal place to sit down, one that would allow her to remain awake a little longer.

There were bedrolls on the ground, a lantern and a simple rug that spanned the vast majority of the floor of the moderately sized domicile, but it was all terribly ordinary.

"This is where you sleep?"

"This is where we sleep." He stepped past her and folded himself down onto one of the bedrolls, his legs pitching up at lazy angles so that he could lean his forearms on them. And the look on his face... She couldn't identify it. She'd have said smug if those hooded eyes didn't also travel down her body and then back up again...

Adalyn had sometimes been on the receiving end of almost tangible looks before—usually during high school when baleful looks from popular classmates had sometimes felt as real as a slap in the face. She'd just never have guessed a simple look could feel like a caress, but her skin prickled with awareness.

It took effort to think, let alone speak. She had to get this under control.

"Just us two here? What about the...medics?" Whom she'd only so far seen at a distance, and who looked like anything but medics. "Or are they really security?"

"Hakem and Suhail are both trained as security, but Hakem is also trained as a paramedic. Good eye. What gave them away?" His intimate look faded, though his eyes still showed an interest she couldn't begin to wrap her mind around.

"They both look like they could bench-press a car." She folded herself down onto her bedroll opposite to him, but then spotted her bag and crawled to it to open it and dig out a protein bar. Distraction. Plus, she hadn't eaten anything all day and had no taste for the adventure that would be required to eat whatever food these strangers gave her. Sustenance was a necessity. She tore one open and settled back on her roll.

"They sleep in the other tent."

She glanced around the tent and back to the bar while working on the wrapper. She'd come up with a plan during the hours with Nadim, and it was the only idea she had on how to salvage this situation.

Win Khalil over so he'd let her help him. Good plan.

Think of him the way she thought of Jamison. Treat him the way she treated her brother.

"We should sleep in Khalil's tent." She said his name quietly but kept on with her plan. Teasing and joking around. That's what she usually did with Jamison. "I bet it's fancy. And golden. With air-conditioning. And maybe a pool. Too bad we have to stay in Zain's tent." Would he get that she was teasing him? Any friend of her brother would need a good sense of humor. "I thought that other tent was the clinic."

"It is," he said, only confirming that he'd heard her going on about Khalil's tent with the tilt of one corner of his mouth... Half a smile was all that had got her. "We don't leave it empty once it's got supplies inside. The vaccines, needles, gloves and alcohol are not irreplaceable, but I don't want anyone coming to harm because they tried to use something without knowing the proper way."

Khalil's eyes were still fixed on her—and more specifically on her protein bar—in a way that made her feel nervous, but for once it didn't seem as if they were about to quarrel. "Did I do something wrong?"

"You brought food?"

Or maybe they were about to quarrel.

"I…" She looked at the thing she'd planned on eating in privacy somewhere that would minimize the amount of offense not wanting to eat their food could cause. "I packed them and water tablets because, you know, you hear horror stories about people eating something lovely in a foreign place and then getting terrible gastrointestinal distress or some other illness. I just wanted safe food." And before he could say anything else, or before she said something wrong, she crammed one end of the sawdust-flavored gritty protein bar into her mouth and broke off a chunk.

Attempting to chew the thing required water, and if she didn't get some fast, it might suck half the moisture out of her body.

"Good, is it?"

She looked back at him, grinning around the mouthful as she chewed and chewed and chewed…one finger up to signal to him that she would speak when her mouth was not full of wood chips and fake chocolate.

"I bet we could build something out of those. A barbecue pit maybe," he said. So he did have a sense of humor.

If she laughed now, she'd definitely choke to death. Just a little longer, and maybe one bite would be enough for her. Once it was clear, her jaw burned from the effort and she was seriously reconsidering having another bite. "I guess I wasn't shopping for flavor."

"Just safety from villainous foreign foods."

She sighed, nodded, and he leaned behind him to grab a water bottle to pass to her. She took it and drank eagerly. Foreign villainous water… "Thank you."

"It was either that or watch you turn into a pru—"

The loud sounds of her swallowing drowned out the last of what he'd said. But somehow… "Did you just call me a prude?"

"Is that what it sounded like?"

"Yes." And something she'd heard before, back in the days when she'd actually cared enough to try to fit in with other people. When she'd had aggressive and hurtful words lobbed at her regularly. Fat. Prone to hysterics. Nerd. Prude… "I'm not a prude. I just don't…"

Khalil watched her cheeks go pink to the point that the rosy hue surpassed the mild sunburn she'd gotten on her window-side arm during their drive and the bridge of her nose and apples of her cheeks from her short trips through the camp earlier.

He kind of wished he had called her a prude now. "I said prune. You know, a plum that has dried out? From that sawdust brick drying you out."

Even her ears had turned red. She looked at him long and hard, as if he was going to lie about that.

"Well, I'm not. I'm neither."

"Good. That is actually good. Because I need to speak to you about something." It may have been an accident, but it was an opening, and he'd take whatever opening he could get. "The village men were asking about you. Who you were. I've never brought a woman with me before."

She folded the top of the bar's package closed and carefully laid it beside her, the kind of slow meticulous actions that screamed wariness. "What did you tell them?"

"I told them you were my mistress."

He delivered the news matter-of-factly and waited for her reaction. If the label didn't distress her, he'd have to look for another weapon. Her reaction would have to inform the next move.

It took a couple of seconds for the words to register, and he knew as soon as they had. Her mouth fell open and she looked toward the exit and back, confirming the power of the attack.

"Why did you do that?"

Khalil let his gaze do the wandering again. He'd been fighting to control his desire to look at her since their meeting in her room the previous night. The image of her in her underthings had burned into his mind and helped inform him now as he took in supple limbs, the light freckling of her normally pale skin, the way the white cotton top clung to her from the heat and the sweat moistening her skin. He remembered what white cotton looked like against her flesh.

"Khalil?" She whispered his name, the heat having found a way into her voice, as well.

She'd asked him why. Right.

"Because we're sharing a tent, and when they asked about you it was with lust in their eyes." Lust he could understand.

Adalyn looked at the door again but seemed to shrink into the bedroll. "How did that mistress thing help? Now they're going to think that I'm a… I'm… That I'm…"

"That you're mine." He filled in, "It was either mistress or wife. You were the one determined to come with me."

She fidgeted with the top of her water bottle, unscrewing and screwing the cap over and over. "Then you should have said wife. At least then they wouldn't think I was a woman of…low morals. I know that in this part of the world that sort of thing really matters." She tightened the cap and dropped the bottle beside her. "I'm trying to help you, and you're making it hard again."

"Am I?" Hands on the rug, he leveraged himself over to sit beside her on her bedroll, the desire to stretch her out and pretend she really was his nearly overwhelming all reason.

But there was always that wariness about her.

"What is it costing you if some people you will never see again think that you and I will be naked in here together later?"

"I'll be embarrassed," she whispered, but a blush continued down her neck and over the small patch of exposed skin on her chest. Embarrassed she might be, but the idea excited her, too. "And I won't be able to understand what they say about me. They'll say harsh things. Or they'll laugh and clap you on the back maybe. Way to go, Zain! You got yourself a travel-sized floozy to keep you warm on those chilly desert nights."

He could still make this work. It might even be better if it excited her. Then she could leave on friendly terms with him. Just not as friendly as they'd both like. The forbidden quality could work in his favor. They must think of Jamison after all. And if they couldn't control themselves, she'd have to go… "And you like that idea." He leaned in just enough to feel the heat pouring off her.

"No, I don't! I don't… I haven't dated much… I have…" She couldn't even bring herself to say the words. Either that or she was flustered enough by the fact that he was coming on to her that she didn't know what to think.

"Have past lovers complained, Adalyn?" Knock her off-kilter, then make a move…

CHAPTER FIVE

"THAT IS NONE of your business!"

Her voice pitched up into a higher register, enough to cause Suhail—cooking outside—to call to him for a security check. He shouted back that everything was fine and cupped a hand over her mouth, and an ache formed in the center of his palm where her plump lower lip brushed his skin, hot and moist…soft. "Don't scream. It will alarm everyone."

She jerked her head back, lowering her voice to an angry whisper. "I don't need to explain my sexual history to you. I am here as your doctor. And this is very inappropriate behavior. You should sit on your pallet. Not here with me. And not… You know what? You're right. It is nothing to me what these people think of me. I'm just an American trollop. I'm sure that they'd have thought that regardless. But don't think for a second that I'm going to…"

The angrier she got, the pinker she got, the more heated her whispers. And despite the tirade, with his close proximity, she kept looking at his mouth as she made her displeasure known. When she looked at his mouth, subconsciously she'd lick her lips or for a fraction of a second lose her train of thought.

He wanted it to. His train of thought hadn't gone this far when he'd been plotting earlier. For once he'd had no idea how she'd respond to a kiss. Would it scare her off? Make her agree to go back to the palace and then home? Make her want more?

What reaction did he even want? For her to kiss him back or run for the hills? Theoretically, and for entirely different reasons, either reaction would do. Only, now he wasn't all that certain he could follow through on the idea to kiss her senseless and send her away for the sake of his friendship with her brother.

All the planning didn't give him what he needed. Curling his hand around that bun her hair had been worked into, he dragged her to meet him and caught her with her mouth open. That plump little lip that had tormented his palm, that he'd watched her repeatedly dampen with her tongue, he caught it with his lips. A tiny sound of surprise and alarm sounded in her throat, but it took very little for her to relax into his grip. Her head fell back and it took no coaxing at all for him to gain entrance into her mouth.

Suddenly, it was no longer about scaring her away. It was about the feeling that rolled over him as his hand left her hair and he wrapped his arms around her. He'd wanted to taste her since that first night when he'd caught her in her underwear, the first time she'd blushed for him. It was pure. It might be pure lust, but she wouldn't let him kiss her if she saw him as a monster or a villain.

Small hands fisted the material of his shirt as if she wanted to tear it off him but could only manage to twist and tug, helpless in the face of unexpected need that might ruin them.

Her kisses went from timid and accepting to wanting to ravenous in the space of heartbeats.

Despite the heat, she still smelled sweet. He pressed her back into the blanket, rolling with her until he could feel more of her soft body against his.

He could forget like this. Forget everything—the world, his responsibilities—just revel in what she could give him. Wrap her around every painful part of him.

Except it was a lie. One he wanted more than anything to be real in that moment.

She wasn't really his. This was a cover story, maybe a dangerous game of chicken…but nothing more. She wasn't his, she was Jamison's sister.

He heard a manly throat clearing and reluctantly broke the kiss to look toward the tent flap.

Suhail stood there with two dinner bowls, and not even a hint of judgment on his face. Both men Khalil traveled with were loyal to the core and had been with him almost all the time since the coup, and Hakem longer. For years. Since before the coup. Through it. Khalil still didn't understand why Hakem stayed with him— and stayed loyal—after that…

They were the only ones now outside the Quinn family who knew what he got up to when he left the palace.

He nodded and Suhail put the bowls down at the foot of the bedrolls, and though he still held Adalyn in his arms, she'd grown tenser since those heady moments when she'd rolled pliantly back onto the bed with him.

He slid his arms from beneath her and sat up while his willpower remained.

"You kissed me," she whispered, slow blinks and speech sounding just the slightest bit drugged.

Not so hard to understand, though he'd rather put it

down to sleep deprivation than some kind of real connection. "You kissed me back," he reminded her. Yes, he may have started it, but she'd participated as feverishly as he had. If Suhail hadn't come into the tent, could he have stopped himself?

Whatever the answer, Khalil didn't even have to question whether he could maintain that control when she was close enough to grab again.

He scooted back over to his bedroll. A quick lean to the side and he grabbed the bowls and set one in front of her. "It's nothing fancy. Rice and some cooked meat. Eat it. It is better for you than that thing you were eating."

She looked at the bowl for a long moment, lightly brushing her lower lip with her fingertips as if she couldn't quite figure out what had just happened.

"Stop that," he muttered, looking at the food instead of her. If she kept stroking her lip that way, even unconsciously as she seemed to be doing, he was going to go right back to her bed and do things she'd—

"Stop what?"

"Touching your mouth. Just…eat."

She pulled her hand away and focused on the bowl. "How do you know it won't make me sick?"

"What's exotic about meat and rice? Nothing. I wouldn't give you food that would make you ill." He sat opposite her again on his own bedroll, hungry enough to not wait for her.

"I'm not sure I believe you."

"You should believe me," he said. "What kind of man purposefully makes his mistress ill? Not one who wants—"

She kicked him.

Not hard, but one of her feet popped out from her cross-legged position and bounced off his shin.

Yeah, he'd deserved a kick.

A soon as her foot had flown, she tucked it back under her knee and began eating what he'd given her.

Adalyn grabbed the bowl and took a bite. Any consequences were preferable to sitting there, savoring the taste of his kisses that still lingered on her lips.

As the first bite went down she had to admit the food—simple as it was—tasted good. Much better than those nutrient-dense monstrosities she'd been intent on eating, just not as good as he had.

Next time she traveled, which she hoped would be *never*, she'd have to have some kind of test phase where she actually tried to eat different kinds of bars until she found one moderately edible. And she'd make some kind of rule about kissing the countries' royalty, if she managed to stumble across them.

Stupid.

"Tell me something," Khalil said, breaking back into her thoughts even as she tried to banish him and the taste of him with the rice and meat.

Once more his gaze felt tangible, like a touch, as if he was still feeling hot and heavy over her. She kept staring at her dinner, not trusting herself to watch him putting food in his mouth.

Tell him something? Like…that no one ever kissed her like that before? That the few times she'd gone out on dates they had been an utter disappointment. None of the fireworks she'd read about in books. Not even a sparkler or a single match's worth of passion. But here, in this tent, with this man who infuriated her,

her toes had curled and her back had arched from the current zipping down her spine and everywhere he'd touched her.

"Anything. Tell me what you're thinking."

"No." The word launched from her with the same force she'd felt zinging through her at his touch. She took another bite to give herself time to think and slid back to the subject of him. His sleep problems. Though talking about sleep or thinking about sleep made her want to just go to sleep and try to work out what his angle was tomorrow, when she'd have a handful of functioning brain cells. Which would have to be after she'd filled her belly and fallen into the coma she planned to fall into. "Tell me about your sleep thing."

"Talking about you would be more interesting. You're a late bloomer."

"You mentioned that I didn't look like my picture. How old was I in the picture? It couldn't be all that recent because I've seen Jamison in person once in the past two years."

"When was that?"

"Last week." She sighed, shaking her head. "We were having bread pudding at my favorite restaurant when you called him. That is how I got wrangled into this." Yes. Talk about Jamison. Talk about how Khalil had caught them during the rare visit when Jamison could apply pressure in person. It was easier to dodge promises and brotherly manipulation when you were only speaking on the phone or in email, but in person? He could be extremely annoying. And persistent. And, if she made it back alive, she'd be sure to tell Jamison it wasn't "good for her," as he'd said it would be about twenty million times.

"I think you were in college," he said, bringing her focus back to the topic.

She looked up and caught him grinning, a lopsided smile that didn't look at all as if he was making fun of her. "So, before medical school. You saw the pudgy me."

"You were a bit rounder than you are now," he confirmed. "Not unattractive, just different."

"Medical school was hard, but the dietary courses helped." She pushed past the subject before he worked around to calling her a prude again. Not that he had before—according to him—but it surprised her how much that had upset her. Not that the kissing hadn't made up for it, but...that really wasn't the topic. She wasn't here for kissing. This was not a vacation fling in the Caribbean, no matter how nice those sounded in books. Two different kinds of sandy destinations. "I want to know why you sleep better in the tent."

"I told you..."

"No, you didn't. You just said that you have insomnia at the—"

"Don't say that word," he said, cutting her off before she said *palace* where anyone might accidentally overhear and understand.

"Sorry." She took the final bite of her rice dish, amazed she'd eaten it all, and set it aside. "Tell me what you think about when you're going to sleep."

"I don't know. What I have to do, I suppose." He definitely didn't want to talk about it. And that was too bad.

"When you're here that's what you think about?"

"Yes. When I'm on one of these medical missions I think about the people. The patients, and what they need... What I need to provide for them."

His words didn't really convey any emotion, but there

was a tension in his voice, a tenor of deception among the mundane words. "And that's different than when you're home?"

"I guess."

"You don't think about your other duties in the same way as you think about your medical duties?"

"Would you?"

"I don't know," Adalyn said, shrugging as she untied her shoes and slipped toward the head of the bedroll. The more she immersed herself in the riddle of his sleep issues, the easier it was to stop thinking about the way his mouth had seared hers. "I've never done anything but my medical duties, not since finishing my training." Because that didn't sound extremely lame. But she liked her quiet life. She liked the safety of it. Not like here, where at any second… "Hey, what will keep things from coming into the tent while we're asleep?"

"What things?"

"People. Critters that are poisonous. Snakes and spiders and scorpions."

Khalil grinned, finishing his dinner and reaching for her bowl. "Netting will keep the 'poisonous critters' out." He rose and took the bowls out, presumably to have them cleaned.

When he came back, she was retying her shoes.

"Going somewhere?"

"Just want to make sure I'm ready to run away in the night if a snake gets in."

"You think you can sleep with the threat of a snake hanging over your head?"

"I think I could sleep through a tornado right now." She crawled into the bed and pulled her blankets up to her chin, no matter how warm she already was. Her exhaustion was increasing the closer she got to sleep. "Tomorrow. We'll start observation tomorrow. For real. And talk more. I think you should try to think about the differences in your sleeping situations. See what might be causing you stress back home."

He made some sound of affirmation, but she didn't open her eyes to try to see what his expression could tell her. Or what he was doing as he moved around the tent. Preparing for bed? Making them safe from poisonous creatures that might bite or sting them?

This would be just like sharing a room with Jamison or her roommates in college. So he was handsome. So even thinking now about his kiss made her lips tingle and gave the sensation of movement…of hurtling forward without any semblance of control.

She wanted sleep. Her body craved it, her mind felt dulled by exhaustion and wrung out from riding that crest of fear for days straight. No doubt the reason she could only think right now about the physical sensation of his mouth on hers. That was easier than more intellectual pursuits.

The sound of his blankets came so close by… If she opened her eyes, he'd be just there, within arm's reach. In the stillness, if she listened closely, she could hear him breathe.

That shouldn't comfort her.

She rolled over, putting her back to him in the hope of calming her mind enough to drift off. She needed sleep. Lots of sleep. She could probably sleep for the rest of the week and not feel recovered…

CHAPTER SIX

Khalil knew this blasted landscape. He knew every movement, every sound. He knew what he said. He knew what he did...

And this time he had to stop it.

To his left, he could see the stooped form of his brother, running in the night.

Already there? Already running?

Khalil pushed himself in the direction Arash had run, weakness crawling through him, dragging his effort down into sluggish half steps. It was the poison he knew he carried. It made him into something he didn't want to be.

The farther he ran, the faster he moved, even beyond reality.

Before Arash took that final step Khalil reached him, grabbed his arm and spun him around. As he opened his mouth to speak something lashed forward from behind him, a segmented limb tipped with a barb that dripped poison.

One quick movement, right through the heart, and Arash crumpled to the ground at his feet.

He didn't need to turn around to identify its source.

He was the poison. He was the betrayer.

He was the scorpion who'd killed his brother.

Khalil knew he was in a dream before he pulled himself out of it. It was different this time, but the message remained. All his fault. All his fault.

His thundering heartbeat in his ears, sweat drenching his clothing more than it had even during the day's construction, he sat up and climbed immediately out of the bed, as if it were something that hurt him. As if he'd find it full of scorpions.

When he'd moved the few steps away from it that he could while remaining inside the tent, he remembered that Adalyn was there. With the darkness inside the tent he was lucky he hadn't stepped on her. Had she awakened? Had he said anything to make her wake up? When he found the light, would he find her looking at him? Find those lovely green eyes full of compassion, or something worse?

One thing was certain, he couldn't face that until he got control of his body, slowed his heart and breathing, but it was harder to banish the nightmare images when all he could see was the darkness. The blackness made a perfect projection screen to revisit his crimes.

To hell with her reaction to his nightmares. He had to get a light, get real images to fill his vision again.

He stretched his arms high over his head to feel the top of the tent, and from there and the slight breeze at his back that placed the door, he followed the tent to the side, where he'd find his lantern.

The battery-powered lantern clinked softly as he picked it up and fumbled about, searching for the switch.

Soon the tent interior was cast in low blue LED light.

He looked toward Adalyn's bedroll.

Not sitting up. Not looking at him.

He stepped closer, moving around to her side of the tent so he could see if she was actually awake. It also put her between him and his abandoned bedroll—the thing that held approximately the comfort for him as a briar patch in a sandstorm.

Her features were relaxed in sleep, soft breaths, the slow rise and fall of her chest as she lay there, now sprawled on her back. The blankets she'd covered herself up with had been strewn to the side, revealing her in the khaki pants and top she'd worn into the desert that day, her boots still on.

Since it had been later in the day when they'd gotten the tent erected, the sand where they'd set up still carried heat from days baking in the sun. The tent walls held in this heat—gentle to the air but warm beneath, like a morning bed after a night with your lover.

She hadn't heard him. She hadn't witnessed anything. He pulled his shirt over his head and went back to his bag, intent on at least changing into something dry. Get rid of the reminders of the dream.

Now that his heart had slowed and ceased bruising his chest from the inside, he could think about it. This one had been different. Where had that scorpion nonsense come from?

It hadn't happened that way, of course. That wasn't how he'd—

Adalyn. She was afraid of poisonous desert things getting into the tent in the night. But she'd gone to sleep with the most poisonous thing in the desert lying an arm's length away from her.

Ignorance was bliss for a reason. It certainly made it easier to sleep.

Think about something else.

What would she be doing if she were at home right now? The time difference meant…she'd probably be asleep. Sleep specialists tended to do most of their sleeping in the afternoon so that they could observe patients at night.

Did she live in a house or an apartment? Did she walk to work every day?

Did she spend her time with someone special?

Khalil had never doubted Jay's devotion to his little sister, though the way he spoke of her had led Khalil to think of Adalyn as the most boring woman in the world. He didn't even know what state she lived in.

Admittedly, this opinion of her as boring had probably been formed when they'd been teenagers and she had probably still been in pigtails.

Boring didn't fit her at all now.

The next time anyone tried to send him to a medical professional of any sort he was going to have to ask for a picture and maybe a phone interview before he committed to it.

And definitely not take anyone else into the desert with him to disturb his sleep.

Something had made the nightmare come to his safe zone. It couldn't be that he'd been thinking about it to summon it, because he thought about that night all the time.

Guilt maybe? For failing to come up with a story that would keep her safe before he got her to the desert? For not outright forbidding her from coming with him?

For kissing his best friend's little sister?

For the way her bed with its cast-off blankets looked like heaven, and his wet mess looked like some special kind of spiky hell?

Would the nightmares come back if he crawled into that soft, cotton paradise beside her and slept?

She'd wanted his kiss…

She might even welcome him into her bed…but the best she could give him would be a bit of oblivion. She could offer him no absolution.

He plowed his hand through his hair and pushed his blankets to the side of the tent so he could sit there.

No more sleep tonight, and he couldn't bring himself to check the time. It was still dark, so what did it matter how long the rest of the night was? Hours stretched before him any way he looked at it.

If he could just get through tomorrow, when night came again he could drug himself. The pills were in the truck because he hadn't expected to need them. If he went banging the doors around now to get them, he'd wake everyone in the camp.

With the battery-powered lantern in hand, he fished a book out of his bag and settled in to read. Staring at her peaceful sleep wouldn't do him any favors. Too little sleep had left his willpower shot, and if he watched her much longer he'd crawl right in beside her. The idea of sleeping with his nose buried in her hair and her soft body against him… God help him.

He found where he'd left off and began to read. At least this way he could get into someone else's head for a while.

When they got back to the palace he had to send her home. And tell Jamison this was all something he had to work out on his own. It was foolish to think anyone could fix this for him. Even if the nightmares were gone tomorrow, it wouldn't change the past.

And, besides, maybe they were a gift. Something to

keep him doing what he was supposed to be doing. To be the leader that Arash would have been.

A good man wouldn't need reminders, but maybe he did. At least these nightly remembrances kept in the front of his mind the kind of man he was, and the kind of man he needed to become.

Forgetting would only make his crime worse.

Sounds of life outside began to seep into the tent. In the desert people were early risers—outdoor work was best done before the sun reached its hottest and that suited Khalil's sleepless schedule. Fewer hours alone with his thoughts. The sounds actually began before the first rays of the sun hit the tent, before even the diffused predawn light made it inside.

He should wake Adalyn.

Her bed and the peaceful expression on her face had tempted him every minute of the long night.

Still not daring to return to his bedroll, he finally dropped the book he'd read and reread all night, his reading comprehension not the greatest when his mind had been focused nearly entirely on the desire to sleep, or the desire to sleep with her.

The heat from the sand no longer really warmed the rug beneath him. But if he lay there long enough he'd fall asleep. At least for a few minutes. And when the dreams came again, since they'd finally found him in his safe haven, this time someone would notice. She'd wake, find him sweaty and panting, or worse—maybe he'd say something in his sleep.

Getting up and getting moving was the only way to get through this day.

Pulling himself up from the rug required nearly more

strength than he had in him, but once he was up he dressed and fished a caffeine bean from his bag to pop into his mouth. He needed to get water to wash, tell the men to set up for vaccinations, check on Nadim again… and then he'd wake Adalyn.

Twenty minutes later Khalil set down a jug of water beside a basin where a towel and washcloth had already been placed, then went to crouch beside her.

She hadn't moved an inch in hours. Did she always sleep that deeply, or was this just the effects of jet lag? Maybe she had some magic pill to make sleep better. Something other than the ones he'd been using to self-medicate and hold on.

"Adalyn." He said her name before touching her hand, then said it a few more times, each repetition increasing his frustration, until he finally gave up the gentle approach and shook her arm until she opened her bleary eyes. "It's time to get up."

Sleep jealousy, what next?

"What time is it?"

"Early. Just after six." He gestured to the basin and stood. "Wash up and meet me in the other tent. We'll have breakfast together before we see patients. And we need to run two line-ups today—one for examinations and one for vaccinations. I will run examinations, you can do the vaccinations. We need to make sure every-one's healthy before they have the injection."

She nodded and sat up, her hair still smoothly braided from the day before… She really hadn't moved much last night.

"Did you sleep last night?"

Khalil nodded, even as his conscience made him aware that he was only answering the literal truth, not the truth she was looking for. He had slept—you didn't have nightmares without sleeping—he just hadn't slept much. "I slept." Not a lie. Technical truth was all he had going for him. Tonight he'd get the medicine from the truck before everyone bedded down, and he'd have a whole dreamless night to catch up on sleep.

"How is Nadim?" she asked, apparently satisfied enough with his answer to move on.

"Much better. He even ate a little last night and everything stayed down."

A sleepy smile was his reward, and he turned to leave, intending to give her privacy to wash, but his foot caught on something and he felt himself falling but couldn't work out what to grab to steady himself. He crashed into the trunk, the corner smacking him in the solar plexus before he bounced off.

"Kha— Zain! Are you okay?"

He rolled onto his back, sucking in a painful breath and staring hard at the top of the tent, which spun in dizzying fashion.

Well, that had woken her up. Adalyn scrambled to his side and reached to touch his forehead. "Can you breathe?" His hair was mussed, and though it was already warm outside it wasn't hot, but he was sweating more, compared to the way he had been yesterday when he'd come in from tent construction. "Are you sick? Did you drink some bad water!?"

The shrill note in her voice startled her and she took a breath and held her tongue as she watched him work his way back into a normal breathing pattern.

If he got sick, she would just have to make Suhail and Hakem call for a helicopter to take him away to the hospital. And she'd have to ride back with one of them.

For possibly the first time in her life Adalyn regretted never having learned to drive.

"I'm not sick," he mustered after a long, tense minute. "I just got…wobbly. Got up too fast."

"You weren't sitting. You were standing the whole time."

"I crouched beside you to shake you awake." The words came out gruffly as he rolled to his side first and slowly sat up. "I am probably a little dehydrated."

"Then you should drink something." She looked over at the jug he'd directed her to. "Is that water clean for drinking?"

"Yes, but I'll get some. You wash and meet me there."

He didn't look good or even moderately steady, but Adalyn didn't argue as he shuffled toward the tent entrance and through it.

Shuffled was the right word. His feet barely left the ground as he walked, which was probably why he'd fallen. Nothing to do with standing up too fast and getting dizzy. He walked like a zombie, the mindless locomotion of someone truly exhausted.

He'd lied to her. If he'd slept at all last night it had only been for a few minutes—maybe an hour at most—but she doubted it.

Great. She should have tried to stay awake long enough to observe him. She'd just been so tired, which made her all the more sympathetic to his current state—as if she didn't already have years of experience with the aftereffects of sleepless nights.

Adalyn washed and dressed with record speed, and headed for the other tent to eat and observe Zain-Khalil.

As sleep-deprived as he seemed to be, he really shouldn't be seeing patients.

* * *

With the small population of the village Adalyn reck-
oned they could've gotten the vaccinations done in a
day by just running one line, but this was Khalil's show,
his decision.

His sleep-impaired decision.

Giving shots didn't take much brainpower, and her
mind wandered along with her gaze over the tent. Not
many men had turned up, mostly mothers and their children. One set in particular concerned her. The little one
lay against her mother's shoulder limply, asleep. She
couldn't have been more than five—if she was that—
and she was definitely ill.

So when Adalyn turned back from the station where
she'd prepared the next vaccination and found that same
mother and the now awake child waiting, she began to
realize just how impaired he was from sleeplessness.
Putting down the vaccine, she went to Khalil's station
a few feet away, picked up his thermometer and stethoscope and headed back to the mother and child.

Khalil gave her a look but she ignored him. After
a few short motions to explain to the mother what she
was doing, she put the thermometer to the child's head
and had her suspicions confirmed. Fever, low grade for
now, but signs of infection. With her borrowed stethoscope she listened to the child's belly and sighed. Had
he even listened? From everything Adalyn had heard
from Jamison, Khalil was observant and conscientious,
not the type to be lax in his duties to patients.

Motioning for the woman to wait, she took the instruments back to Khalil and leaned in to whisper to
him, "That girl is sick. She can't have the vaccine. Did
you listen to her belly?"

"She's hungry."

"And the fever?"

"It's hot outside."

"No," Adalyn said, tilting her head toward them again. "Ask them to come back over. I don't want to look like I'm questioning your authority, but that girl can't have the vaccine." She paused for a heartbeat, but before she could really think about whether it was right to do so in front of others she went on—they probably couldn't understand her anyway. She whispered, "I think you should have a nap in the tent while I'm here. Let me handle the examinations and inoculations. Hakem can help me with translation."

Khalil frowned, but rather than arguing with her about the girl he took his instruments and had a listen to the child's belly again. After confirming her quick diagnosis, Khalil spoke with the woman and sent her out of the tent with an electrolyte-enriched drink for the girl and medicine for nausea. While not as ill as Nadim had been, she'd still need to be watched.

That frown stayed with him as they finished up the last of the vaccinations, which took considerably longer than the first half—which told her he was slowing down and trying to pay more attention.

The problem was that trying to pay better attention didn't amount to much when you were severely sleep-deprived.

As they were packing up the instruments Adalyn heard some commotion outside and before she could ask Khalil what they were saying a man with a head wound came rushing in with a little girl in his arms.

Hakem moved before she could even ask what was

going on and had a table out for the man to lay the child on.

Adalyn met Khalil at the table, grabbing instruments as she went in the hope of helping.

The girl's skin had a blue cast to it. Adalyn's throat seemed to close up. This was an emergency, far more so than the one they'd had with Nadim.

Words flew back and forth as questions were asked and answered.

The girl's top came off and the bruise on the right side of her chest really brought the situation home for Adalyn. She didn't even need to palpate that bruise to know the ribs were fractured in two places—a section sucked in slightly with every labored intake.

Flail chest.

Khalil listened with the stethoscope, but the girl's breathing was so loud and wheezy Adalyn could hear it without the stethoscope.

She needed surgery. That was it. That was all that could help her...

So when Hakem handed Khalil a large-gauge hypodermic, it took her a couple of seconds to react. "What are you doing?"

"She's got a tension pneumothorax."

"No." Adalyn grabbed his hand to keep him from puncturing the girl's chest. "She's got flail chest. That needle isn't going to help her. She needs surgery, Dr. Zain. She needs surgery. Look." She gestured for him to look at the girl's side, where at least two ribs were cracked in two places, creating a floating section of chest wall and messing with her ability to inhale. "Do you have sedatives?"

"Yes." He looked confused for a moment, so Adalyn

stepped between him and the table and said to Hakem, "We need to ventilate her. And one of you needs to call for the chopper. Now."

She left Khalil standing, looking even more out of it than he had, and went to his drug cabinet. Her hands skimmed over the glass bottles, causing them to clink and clatter as she found her way to the right drug. Grabbing a syringe and alcohol preps, she got to the table, found a vein and injected it. By the time she'd completed the shot and the girl started to drift off, Khalil had gathered his wits enough to retrieve the right sized intubation kit for her.

He didn't even try to do it himself, just prepared the instruments and handed them to her one at a time.

It had been years since Adalyn had intubated anyone, let alone a child. She began murmuring the steps to herself, making sure she remembered, and Khalil added a couple of tips as he tilted the girl's head back, doing everything he could to help her complete the intubation.

Less than a minute after she'd ordered Hakem to call the chopper she attached the bag and began forcing oxygen into the girl's lungs. Within seconds her color began to return to normal.

Hakem returned, taking over the bag. "You have to go with them in the helicopter, keep her breathing. She can't do it on her own. I'm going to set up an IV for her and send you another dose for when she starts to rouse."

Not her job. This was not her job. She wasn't built for emergencies. Her knees wobbled, but her hands stayed steady enough to surprise even her.

"You've got things under control," Khalil murmured to her. "I'm going to go…to the tent."

Adalyn nodded, tying the tourniquet around the girl's

arm and threading the catheter into the vein. "What happened to her?" she asked Hakem quietly.

"Car crash," he said, shaking his head, his voice lowered as he said, "It is harder to do out here... Unless you are reckless."

Cold shot down the back of her neck, as if this was the Arctic, not a Middle Eastern desert.

"I see." Her voice wobbled, just like her knees. She taped the IV port in place and then packed him a small kit with a couple of saline flushes, another two doses of the injection, because she didn't know how long it would take to get to the hospital, and she also didn't know how quickly they'd take the girl in even if it was an emergency. The best she could do was to overprepare, for safety. Grabbing a notepad from the back table, she made some quick calculations and wrote down the times Hakem could give the other doses needed to keep her under, then led him through it to make sure her instructions were clear.

"Is he her father?" She gestured to the man still at the foot of the table.

Hakem nodded.

"Tell him what is happening. Can he go, too?"

Hakem nodded again, and before he could start talking she said, "Broken ribs, and maybe a bruise on her lung."

Since she was there, she got together the supplies to bandage the man's head—butterfly closures would have to do, since he refused stitches. And Adalyn was kind of glad. She really hadn't stitched anyone in ages. Today had been a day for revisiting too many old, rusty skills.

And she still had Khalil to deal with.

CHAPTER SEVEN

How HAD ADALYN become the village surgeon?

Sweat—having nothing to do with the heat—still plastered her shirt to her back.

Hakem had called for the helicopter to pick up Adila and her father, which did relieve her a bit. At least now she knew Hakem would have someone to mind the bag if he needed to give another dose of the sedatives she'd sent with him. But having the tent free of patients meant she was now obligated to find Khalil and choke him to death.

She barged through the flap in the tent and found him sitting with his back against a trunk, the only solid thing in the tent, staring into space.

"Zain." She snapped her fingers and he lifted exhausted eyes to her, but the shell-shocked expression in them sucked the anger right out of her. "Did you sleep at all last night?"

She grabbed the bag he carried on his visits to Nadim and went to kneel in front of him.

He sighed and nodded. "I did. I just don't know how long."

With the sun still high, the white interior of the tent was bright enough for her to examine him.

"Are you having memory lapses?"

He watched her as she dug the stethoscope from his bag and put it around her neck. In his satchel, she spotted the plastic bag full of coffee beans but didn't comment on it. Yet. She knew all the tricks to staying awake.

"How would I remember that?"

"Don't be cute, Khalil." She whispered his name to keep it from traveling. Khalil was her patient, not this Zain alter ego. She needed him to really hear her and would use whatever weapon she had at her disposal. "How much did you sleep?"

"Not much."

"What woke you?" She pressed the listening end of the stethoscope to his chest to listen. Elevated heartbeat. "You're chewing the coffee beans, right?"

He sighed, waited for her to listen to his heart and then nodded.

"Your heart is going like a horse at full gallop. You can't have any more of those."

"They're helping me stay awake."

"Yes, and that isn't helping you." She dropped the instrument beside her and repeated the question he'd not deigned to answer. "What woke you?"

"Adalyn…"

"No, Adalyn didn't wake you. Adalyn slept through the whole night and probably didn't move once or make even a single sound." She was speaking about herself in the third person, which was kind of even annoying her. "Something woke you. Bad dream? You need to tell me the truth now." She snatched the bag of coffee beans from his satchel and shook it at him. "People who have insomnia don't need help staying awake."

"Bad dream." The two words came out softly, but

perhaps not by choice. His words rasped, as if they had been forced out, and he had only barely managed to get his voice working at all.

She stuffed the coffee beans into her pocket and laid a hand on his cheek so he'd look at her. "About the war?"

"About the war."

All he'd done was repeat her words, but the haunted look in his eyes told her everything she needed to know. She wouldn't ask him for specifics about the dream. They weren't important at this point anyway. What was important was getting rid of all his crutches. "What else are you using to keep from them?"

Whether he took comfort from her hand on his cheek or just didn't have the energy to push her away, Adalyn couldn't say, but it became too much for her—the dark stubble on her palm sent electricity scratching up her arm. She slid her hands to one of his and took it instead, keeping the connection but trying to lose some of the intimacy that made it hard to think.

"You mean to stay awake?"

The fact that he needed to ask for clarification on what he was using to keep the nightmares at bay told her he was doing more than just trying to stay awake.

"To stay awake, sure, but anything else?"

"Just normal things."

"Pills?"

"Not really. I've randomly taken a steroid or two in the past couple of months, but nothing…nothing regular or, you know, prone to cause addiction. I didn't need to. I was leaving for the desert every few days. Exercise, extreme doses of caffeine, keeping busy…they all helped until I could get back out to the desert again. Frequent short trips."

He was talking and she needed to keep him talking, so she prompted him whenever he even hesitated slightly. "But last night was different?"

"I guess. I really don't want to talk about it, Adalyn. I just want to try to sleep again. Maybe you could sleep in the other tent. Or maybe I should sleep in the other tent—your being in the tent with me is the only difference I can think of."

"No. You're staying with me." She'd had at least enough sleep to carry her through one night, so she'd be the one awake tonight, making sure he didn't stay up or sneak more coffee beans.

She stuffed the stethoscope back into the bag. There had to be some way to help him through this out here. They couldn't leave tonight. They should leave tomorrow, early if they could, but she wasn't letting him drive anywhere, and she didn't know how to drive, so she couldn't do it. He had to sleep tonight. She'd seen the aftermath of badly driven vehicles just half an hour ago...

"You need at least four hours tonight, and we're going to swap out some of your crutches for others."

The flap opened and Suhail came in with the night's dinner—a repeat of last night's, but made freshly, thank goodness. Before leaving, he wordlessly handed a bottle of pills to Khalil and left.

Khalil opened the bottle and shook one out, then reached for his water.

"What are those?" Another crutch? She set her bowl down and grabbed the bottle of pills, and then the hand he'd shaken one into so he couldn't take the darned thing while she was investigating. Flipping the bottle around, the logo on the cap made her stomach bottom out. "Have you taken these before?"

"Not often. Once per visit at home, that's it."

"So the last time you had one?"

"Three or four days ago."

She set the pill on the other side of her and shook her head. "You're not taking them."

"I need to sleep, Adalyn."

"Yes, you do, and you also need to wake up again. These never passed FDA approval, which I know means nothing to you here outside American review panels and such, but the reason they didn't pass is present, no matter where we are. You know the trials? You know how many people died? If you're suppressing dreaming, I can understand that, but you can't do it with these pills. There are others. There are some that are almost through trials and much safer."

He pulled his hand free to take it anyway, and Adalyn did the only thing she could think of…and tackled him to the ground. "You're not taking these!"

The shock of her leaping on him and knocking him on his back worked in her favor. Khalil dropped the pill…and spilled his water. With reflexes enabled by rest, she scrambled off him, snatching the pill from the bedding before he could recover.

Without pause, she darted out of the tent with the pills in her hand. The heat sucked the life out of her, like always, but she found Hakem and thrust the pills into his hands.

"Zain—" she said the fake name, getting his attention "—cannot take these. Even if he asks you for them, don't give them to him. In fact, please get rid of them somehow."

Hakem looked at the bottle, a frown pulling down his heavy brows. "He needs them for his insomnia."

"He needs them like he needs a hole in his head." She shook her head, took a breath and rubbed a hand over her face. "They're not safe. They can cause uncontrollable bleeding. So, even if he asks you, don't give them to him. You're here to protect him? Save him from these. Get rid of them."

Hakem answered with a slow nod, enough that she took it as a win for now, and turned to head back into her tent.

She found Khalil sitting on her bed—since she'd doused his in water—scowling.

"Eat. Then I'm going to examine you again. And then you're going to sleep." Let him scowl. He could look however he wanted as long as he listened to her.

"What did you do with them?" he asked, ignoring her orders.

"I buried them in the sand somewhere you'll never find them—even if you dig a thousand and one Arabian holes in the desert."

She kicked off her shoes, grabbed fresh water to hand to him and then sat beside him to eat.

"You think something has changed in the past five minutes since you examined me before?"

"I wasn't looking for signs of bleeding before. Bruising. Or what I'm really afraid of..." She looked at the top of his head and then looked him in the eye again.

"I'm not having a hemorrhagic stroke. There would be symptoms."

"We'll see. Those things have a ridiculous half-life. If you had them three or four days ago they're still in your system enough to mess you up. Not enough to help with the dreaming, obviously, but that kind of bleeding isn't something that can even be controlled. Why did you pick that particular drug? There are safer ones that are almost through the trials."

"They wouldn't ship them here."

"Why?"

"They thought we were trying to steal the formula or something. Make generic ones. Who knows? I couldn't get an answer, and I didn't raise enough of a fuss to get one, because I didn't want the attention. All they had to do was leak something to the press and—"

"And you wouldn't be able to hide this." Adalyn understood hiding nightmares, and when she'd done it she hadn't had the weight of an entire country riding on her shoulders. Somehow, sharing fears brought a kind of vulnerability unlike anything she'd experienced in her life. That was a big part of why she wasn't digging further into his nightmares. Well, that and it wasn't her job.

Generally, she was the first step in getting someone to a good therapist to deal with whatever trauma was causing their nightmares. And although she knew Khalil wasn't going to go to a therapist, she didn't feel equipped to help him on that front. All she could do tonight was treat the symptoms and try to get him some sleep before he suffered some kind of psychotic breakdown.

Whatever he was thinking, he gave up speech and focused on eating. At least she didn't have to tackle him again to make him eat.

They ate in silence, and once the dishes had been removed she fetched a jug of water, a couple of washcloths and a basin, and came back inside.

The sun sat low on the horizon, and the white tent

no longer glowed with light. She set her washing supplies to the side, grabbed his kit again and fished out the penlight.

Khalil had moved the trunk to her bedroll so he could lean against it again, and she knelt in front of him to shine the light in his eyes.

"This is unnecessary."

"Says you, and your judgment is terrible today." She made him look at her and checked pupil reactivity. "Good. Okay. Take off your shirt and your pants."

He lifted one brow.

"I'm going to look for signs of bleeding. Bruising. I'm going to feel your belly. And you're going to tell me about your bedtime rituals. What do you do when you're trying to fall asleep? Do you think about it? The nightmare?" She avoided referring to the cause of the recurrent nightmare for now. And in order to keep herself from staring at him as he stripped, she went about moving his wet bedroll and opening hers up so that it lay flat and they could both lie on top of it.

"I try not to think about it." Despite the looks he'd been giving her, he followed her orders. The shirt came off. Then the T-shirt beneath it. And finally he stood and unbuckled his pants and let them fall away. "What are you doing?"

She shook the sheet out and laid it to one side. "When you're trying not to think of it, you're actually thinking about it. Your brain doesn't remember the 'no' part of the thoughts. It just focuses on the nightmare. You're priming yourself to have it by trying not to have it. You need distraction, and we need to change your sleep environment for that."

When she'd futzed with the bed until she could futz

no longer, she grabbed her perfume and sprayed once over the blankets.

"What are you doing?"

"You said you liked the way I smell, so I'm… I thought it would be nice. We're going for comfort and things that please here," she said quickly, then tossed the bottle onto her bag and focused on him again. "I'm going to look for bruises. You can wash your face and whatever. Get rid of some of the grit. It'll feel nice. And that's the whole point, to feel nice and comforted and different. Oh, yeah, I didn't mention it before… You're going to be sleeping in my bed with me."

The other brow joined the first, halfway up his forehead. "You think that's a good idea?"

"I'm not offering sex. And your bed is wet, besides. Do you… When you…" She cleared her throat, grabbed the light and went to shine it on his arms first, tracking over the skin to look for darkening. Clinical. This was an examination, not a sexy striptease or whatever. *Think of Khalil as a patient. No. Think of him like Jamison.* That should be sufficient to keep her from having inappropriate thoughts during the examination of his admittedly really, really nice body.

Not something she should be noticing. *Focus. Get the stupid question out and then get on with whatever didn't require enough concentration to talk.* "Have you been…with anyone, you know, since they started?"

"You mean have I slept with a woman since I've had nightmares?"

"Yes." Of course it was easy for him to put the sentence together, and he was the one who was sleep-deprived. She moved on to his chest but looked much more quickly so she could move around to look at his back. "Have you, and…has it helped or…you know…anything?"

She sounded worse than her idiotic twelve-year-old self when she'd gotten around a boy she'd liked. Adults talked about sex without getting flustered and stammering.

"I haven't been with anyone since then, no."

"Okay. Well, I guess it will be an experiment. I'm going to be a stand-in…bed friend. But not in a sexy way." She sighed and dropped to look at his feet, then his calves. Calves got banged up all the time. The dusting of dark hair on tan skin made her job harder, never mind the dips and bulges of muscles casting shadows. Bruises stood out better on her, being so pale. That was why this was taking so long. Not her distraction. She was just being thorough.

"So, anyway, just…we'll do that and see how that goes."

She looked at his thighs even faster than she'd looked at his chest…because she wanted to slow down and look longer. When she was satisfied he wasn't bruising randomly, she made him lie down and did a quick examination of his abdomen for any hardness or signs of bleeding. Nothing. Nothing but a knot in her throat and a headache from the way she couldn't force her eyebrows to relax.

Pulling away, she poured water into the basin, washed her face and then handed him the dry cloth and towel. "I'll sit with my back to you if you want to wash a bit…and then I'll wash a bit…" Good grief, this desert trip was such a mistake. Hotel. She was supposed to get a hotel room with a bathtub and air-conditioning!

And she was supposed to see Khalil only in a clinical setting with machines…and cameras…and colleagues!

And now that she knew what he was up against, she couldn't even enjoy wishing she hadn't come. Those if-only gateway thoughts to more pleasant mental vistas even made her feel guilty.

If she hadn't come, would little Adila have survived today? Would Khalil really have been able to sleep last night if she hadn't been there, and been more clear-headed today? If she'd caused his lack of sleep, then that mistake was only because of her being there.

Maybe she had made things worse.

Or maybe he'd keep taking those pills and would suddenly bleed to death while bending over to pick up something from the floor because the slight pressure change made a blood vessel in his brain burst. That drug was a nasty thing. Foolish. Desperate…

Khalil watched Adalyn sit with her back to him, as she'd announced she would, and went to the basin. The sooner he got this over with, the better. Thanks to his performance today, the idea of her figuring it all out no longer seemed like the worst thing in the world.

Maybe she would figure out what he'd done, or maybe having her soft skin against him would bring the kind of comfort that had tempted him all last night… Tonight, at least, his guilt had nothing to do with her and everything to do with his own choices. Being in the desert might be his biggest crutch, but he never would have relied on it if he'd even suspected he wasn't providing good care to these people. Now he had to ask himself how many other faulty diagnoses he had made while this mess had been going on. How many bad decisions was he making regarding the kingdom?

That meant more than his pride.

Besides, what could it really matter what she thought about him? It's not as if he'd ever see her again after she left here.

The thought made his shoulders tense, and he had to roll them a couple of times as he washed, the tension itching deep in his bones.

"Do I have doctor-patient confidentiality with you, Adalyn?"

She didn't turn around, though her head tilted slightly, an indication that she was not only paying attention but examining everything he said.

"Of course you do."

"I don't just mean with the press and strangers, I mean with everyone. Jamison. Or even my men here with us."

"You don't have to worry about it," she said, and then fell silent in a way that said she was chewing on something else. He let her chew on it, got dressed in fresh clothing and went to sit beside her on the bed.

When he sat, she looked at him. "I asked if you're dreaming about the coup. The war zone you went to. You don't have to tell me what the dreams are about… but are they about something that happened there? I'm not going to ask for any other details, even though I do think you should find someone to talk to about the dreams and their cause. And that's all I'll say on the matter tonight." She twirled her finger around and pointed at the tent wall in the same direction she'd been facing.

She was going to wash.

And that'd undoubtedly involve taking her clothes off…

"Yes." He said the word quietly, swiveling as instructed to face the tent wall. It was just as well. Knowing his luck, he'd fall asleep in the middle of making love to her, and she didn't need him giving her more issues.

"Do you remember when I told you that I had nightmares after the crash?"

She was going to talk to him…while he was supposed to be watching the wall. Made it harder to stop himself from turning.

"I remember. How long did you have them?"

"About two years. At first, I didn't want anyone to know. Because I knew they were wrong. The things I dreamed weren't what happened at all. And at the time people said I became hysterical all the time. I really hate that word, by the way. They need to come up with another one that doesn't imply big emotions being related to ovaries, or negative traits associated with having ovaries."

He grinned at the little tirade, but something she'd said earlier stuck with him. "What do you mean, you dreamed what didn't happen?"

"A couple of weeks before their wreck there was a very close call and I was in the backseat of that one. But in my dreams the two events somehow got mashed together. My imagination played a big part, because I remember being in their accident. I wasn't in it, but the memory I have is so emotional, it feels real…"

He felt her sit behind him and turned to look at her. She'd stripped down nearly as far as he'd done, tiny white cotton shorts and a matching top with straps. There it was again, the look of an oasis, cool and refreshing.

"Does it bother you to talk about it now?" he asked, trying to focus on what she was telling him rather than the way he wanted to mash himself against her and lose himself in her scent.

"Not really. I talk to patients about it, but I don't… I've never really told Jamison. He was away at school, and he seemed to need that separation. I felt like if I told him he'd come home to be with me and it all felt very selfish. Now I don't tell him because I know he'd feel guilty for not having come." She lay down and patted the bedroll beside her in invitation. "I don't know how you usually…you know, lie with a woman. And you probably shouldn't lie that way anyway. We're making things different but still comfortable and comforting. So I feel like I should be touching you somehow."

Khalil looked at her a moment longer, then stretched out the opposite way and rested his head on her belly. "Touching." But any wayward erections in his sleep wouldn't traumatize her.

And it wasn't enough. He pushed the hem of her vest top up enough to expose her midriff and laid his cheek on her belly again, and this time the cool, soft skin against his face was enough to pull that tension from his shoulders.

Her breathing came a little shallower, and Khalil was glad he'd turned so his gaze was down toward her feet and not up at her breasts and face. "I'm not sure this is going to work if you can't be comfortable."

"I can," she argued, and then he felt it, a tentative touch at first, but she began to comb her fingers through his hair and he nearly fell asleep right then. "Feels kind of like a scene out of *The Arabian Nights*."

"Why's that, Scheherazade? Going to tell me a story?"

"I was thinking about it," she said, and then firmed up her answer, the combing continuing. "Actually…yes. You need something new to think about when falling asleep, and I know a good story for that."

It was true, he did need to think about something else. He didn't tell her that he'd been thinking new, consuming things since she'd lain down beside him. Hearing her talk could only help—he was tired to the point that it wouldn't keep him awake, but her voice had a soothing quality. She probably did this with other patients, maybe not exactly this, but changing their sleep schedule, maybe even the gentle, distracting conversation while they fell asleep. And there was something altogether sweet about her telling him a bedtime story when any other woman who'd made it to his bed would be angling to dazzle him with sex.

"So, I'm going to tell you a story about the dream warriors and the dragons…" she said, the gentle tone of her voice fading as he immediately began to drift off, one thought sticking with him: whatever dragons lurked and waited for him, she was ready to charge into that battle in his stead.

CHAPTER EIGHT

ADALYN BECAME AWARE that the big warm body that had been close to her all night was gone. And there was a sound of movement in the small tent.

She opened her eyes to pitch blackness and fumbled around at her side for the lantern, flipping it on.

Khalil was on his hands and knees, his shoulder stretching out the side of the tent, he'd moved so far away from her.

His eyes were open...and his T-shirt stuck to him, drenched in sweat, but he didn't look awake. People could do all sorts of things in their sleep, but over the years Adalyn had cultivated the ability to spot the differences. Acting strangely aside, there was something missing in the eyes when consciousness was an illusion.

Would he respond to his fake name if she said it? Probably not.

Normally she wouldn't wake someone in a nightmare, she'd just let them go through it and monitor what happened with her equipment. But she'd promised to stand guard tonight. She had to risk saying his name and hope he didn't come out of it swinging.

"Khalil?" She said it low, crawling toward him in what she hoped was a nonthreatening manner. The way his muscles strained and the wideness of his eyes said that whatever he was going through was bad enough.

She said his name again, and then just started talking, picking up the thread of the story she'd been telling him, the one that she'd listened to herself repeat a thousand times when wrestling with her own night dragons. Every instinct in her said to touch him, ground him to reality and the moment with her, but that instinct was wrong. Dangerous, until that hyperalert expression faded to the inevitable confusion that would follow when he actually did waken.

"Khalil?" She said his name softly again.

Nothing. If anything, he looked more strained than he had. Even in the low light and with his soaked T-shirt rumpled on his skin, she could see the muscles down his spine and over his ribs bunched and tight.

She couldn't risk saying his name louder, so she tried something else. "Adalyn." She said her name, once… twice…and this time she did touch him. First just stroking her fingers over the back of his hand, then up his arm, then to his cheek… By the time she'd combed her fingers through the damp black hair, he'd fully woken up.

The confusion she'd expected wasn't there, but he did go from looking dazed to grim before she could think of anything to say.

Pulling away, he stood and walked to the opening of the tent, unfastened it and stepped directly out into the cold night air and the open sand in his wet shirt and shorts.

Adalyn gave him a moment. He was awake now, and not in any danger out there.

The danger was in his mind, and she'd promised to

protect him from it. Despite her assertions that she'd had sufficient sleep to stay awake the whole night, she'd failed. If she'd stayed awake, maybe she could have gotten him out of it before he'd become soaking wet and panting.

Her plan to change Khalil's sleep experience by changing his surroundings and rituals had seemed to work, at least partially. Probably until she'd fallen asleep and had stopped talking to him. Which was why she should never have told him the story she'd conditioned herself to go to sleep to—her brain took it as a sign that it was time to sleep.

Right.

Cold air blew through the opening…enough to cool her down. He must be freezing. And maybe embarrassed. She couldn't just leave him standing out there indefinitely.

She stood and followed. He'd not moved from the opening, just stood outside the tent. "Hey, come back inside." She touched his arm again, and he turned to look at her.

The moon, bright and full, illuminated the landscape, and her eyes adjusted quickly enough, having been in complete darkness before. "I'm sorry, this was my fault. I fell asleep on you. It's probably not much comfort, but I'm fully awake now. You can try again…or we can just get you out of the wet shirt and you can come inside, relax an—"

A low tone came from nowhere, stopping the words in her throat, almost like a bell that just kept ringing. "What is that?" she whispered, stepping slightly closer to him.

When he didn't immediately answer she stepped

fully out of the tent and up beside him, slipping her hand into his.

"It's a dune," he said finally, and even if it didn't make sense to her, him talking about anything was a good sign and she wanted to keep him grounded there with her. Help him let go of all the bad feeling that tended to cling after a particularly bad dream.

"I didn't know they did that. They don't do it in the daytime?"

"They do." He flexed his fingers so that hers settled better between them. Piece by piece, word by word, that's how she could help him right now. And besides that, her curiosity was roused.

"But they weren't ringing yesterday."

"They only do it when there's a slide. Like an avalanche but smaller and of sand. Happens when the wind blows the top ridge off a steep dune and the sand spills down one side."

The bright moon made it possible to see him, but she couldn't see his expression as well as she had with the blue lantern. And she really needed to look into his eyes right now, figure out whether he was upset about the dream or angry at her for failing him. He moved his arm, pulling out of her hand, and looked out over the desert and the outskirts of the village where they'd set up.

The tone finally started to fade, and she was starting to get cold. "Please, come back inside." His name was on the tip of her tongue, but she managed to keep it there while outside the tent, even in the middle of the night. "You're going to freeze in that wet shirt."

Khalil turned to head back inside, pulling off the shirt she'd objected to once he stepped into the tent again.

Two nights running he'd have to down another bottle of water before morning at this rate.

Adalyn closed the tent behind him and went to feel the bedroll. "It's pretty much dry. You must have gotten up before you really got drenched." She rolled onto her bottom and sat, cross-legged. "Do you want to talk? Do you want me to shut up? I promise to stay awake this time. I'm really sorry…"

"Don't be sorry," he finally murmured, and went to sit beside her, not bothering with another shirt this time. He had only one clean shirt left and if he put it on and went back into the dream, he wouldn't have an undershirt for tomorrow. "It's not your fault. You can't control my subconscious."

"But I don't think you were having a bad dream when I was talking. Only after I fell asleep." She turned her arm toward the light to read the dial of her watch. "You did very well for the first two hours. The last time I looked at my watch was about an hour ago. So it was after I fell asleep that the dream returned."

"Circumstantial evidence," he said, then leaned to the side to grab a bottle of water. "I'll try again. Maybe we can change things. I'd rather lie up beside you, but I've no intention of pawing you."

The word *intention* made that statement the truth. He had a strong *desire* to paw her, and kiss her, and blot out all the ugly thoughts still lurking at the black edges of the tent, but resisting that had to be his number-one priority.

He tilted the bottle to his lips and drained it in one go. Definitely dehydrated, his throat felt like the singing sand.

"But if I lie down, I might fall asleep again."

"We'll risk it." He screwed the cap on again and

then gestured to her. "Lie on your side, whichever side you prefer."

She lay on her right side, and then looked at him... brows up and perhaps a tiny bit of nervousness showing in her eyes. Khalil crawled over her to lie down behind her and tucked her smaller body against him. If she was as innocent as all the blushing and stammering suggested, she probably didn't have much experience of spooning with a lover. For some reason that thought pleased him even as he doubted it could possibly be true. That stupid inner caveman of his.

"Just relax, go back to sleep. We both need it. It takes a few days to get over jet lag. If you managed to stay awake for a couple of hours, you did more than your part." He slipped one arm under her head so that her head rested on his biceps and the other around her waist, but what he really wanted was more of her scent.

He hadn't been talking about her perfume when he'd complimented her scent before, even if that's how she'd chosen to take it. The perfume was nice, it had been distracting at first—which had been the point—but it was that special Adalyn smell he wanted. She had some earthy sweetness he'd never be able to define beyond pale, generic words. She smelled good. Fresh. Maybe a little salty even. He burrowed his nose in her hair and closed his eyes.

She smelled like a cool breeze blowing off the sea.

Good God, she smelled good.

"Isn't my head going to crush your arm?" She whispered the words, as if they were going to get caught and get into trouble. As if he hadn't already told people she was his mistress.

"If your head gets heavy, I'll move my arm." Her

back was stiff against him. "Is this uncomfortable for you?"

"No. I'm just…not used to being touched a whole lot."

Of course she wasn't. He let his hand fold over her hip and pressed her back against him, squeezing in a way he meant to be comforting, and maybe a little flirty. "Want me to tell you a bedtime story so you can sleep?" With her pressed against him, it was hard to remember she wasn't what he'd told everyone.

The tease made her chuckle. "No. I'm going to sleep on my own like a big girl."

"Got it, no story." He could sleep like this. Maybe she'd relax better after he'd gone to sleep. "Don't move away from me when I fall asleep."

"I won't," she whispered, and with slow, deliberate effort began to relax. He could track her thoughts as she did, almost hear the muscle groups echoing in her brain as she focused on them one at a time, starting with the neck and letting his arm support the full weight of her head. Then down her shoulders and back. When she'd willed her body into submission, she laid her arm over the one at her waist and squeezed his hand, "Sweet dreams, Khalil."

It sounded like a blessing when she said it.

He stretched his fingers back until she took the hint and slipped hers between them.

With their fingers linked, he fell back to sleep.

Adalyn treated sleep like a cross between a business and a holy experience. People who'd had sleep issues in the past—the kind that left a mark—tended to do that.

Don't stay in bed when you've woken up or it teaches you to lie in bed awake.

Don't do anything in bed but sleep. Well, maybe one other thing, but she hadn't branched out into that other bedroom activity.

Though now, waking with Khalil behind her, his arms around her and his slow gentle breath fanning her neck, she had to wonder why.

The second thing she noticed? He was still asleep.

There was nothing she could do to keep the smile off her face. It may be unconventional medicine—and even that was minimizing how wrong it generally was—and while she'd truly never want to do this with another patient, it felt nice with Khalil. It felt natural.

A quick look around informed her that the sun was rising, even if it hadn't yet fully risen—the tent had taken on the soft gray cast of indirect light filtered through white canvas.

She should let him sleep a little longer.

Slowly, she shifted forward, intending to slip out of his grasp, but his arm tightened, pulling her back against him.

"No."

He said one word, then pressed his nose back into her hair and the deep breathing resumed.

How to deal with this?

Adalyn checked her watch. Not quite six in the morning. People started the day early here—she could already hear movement in the village—but it felt mean to make him get up so early.

"Are we driving home today?" she asked softly, since he'd had the rule about getting on the road at six. And if they had to take the tents down, they'd never make it before ten if they didn't get up immediately.

His legs stretched out behind her, but he kept his arm anchored around her waist. "Yes."

As he nuzzled closer, she felt the brush of lips and stubble against her neck.

Had he kissed her neck?

She stilled, her breath stopping as warm, feathery kisses moved up the side of her neck and chills crashed over her.

Did he remember it was her sleeping with him?

Was he really awake or did he think he was in bed with one of his past lovers?

Heaven only knew what was going on in his mind. If she'd had him hooked to her equipment, she'd at least be able to tell if he was dreaming or if this was a conscious action.

But this was a no-equipment zone, and with him behind her she couldn't even look him in the eye to tell.

She shifted beneath the weight of his arm until she was on her back and could see him.

His eyes were open, and a little amused.

"Are you awake?"

"As far as I know," he murmured, and then slid his hand up from her waist to cup her jaw, tilting her head just so… Leaning in, he continued those featherlight kisses over her jaw to capture her mouth, light and teasing until her breathing sped up and her lips parted, then the gentle kisses became something altogether more insistent. More luxuriant. More sinful.

His bare chest right there, hot against her side, his long bare legs tangling with hers.

One second she was thinking about getting up and

getting to work, and the next her arms had crept up and around his neck, holding him to her so he wouldn't stop kissing her.

Again she had that sensation of movement, but unlike every ride in a vehicle of any description that she'd ever taken since she was twelve this movement only brought a rush of excitement.

His hand slid up her ribs and cupped her breast through the thin jersey knit of her tank top, the gentle kneading building another kind of tension in her belly. An ache that started as a squirm, then got needier.

His two-day beard growth scraped her cheeks and chin, hot and rough against the smooth softness of his lips.

They could be a little late…

It took every ounce of willpower Khalil had to keep from stripping off those tight shorts, ripping off the top that separated him from her breasts and the hard little nubs begging for his mouth.

Last night his exhaustion had overridden everything else—it had felt like heaven to have her against him, but now that his exhaustion had been battled back somewhat, his mind and body craved more of her sweet sanctuary, whatever form it might take.

Her hands plowed into his hair, holding his head to hers, while one of her legs tracked up the outside of his—an unspoken invitation. He could have her. She wouldn't want him to stop… He just had to get the material out of the way.

His hands shook as he slipped them under her, squeezing her soft cheeks as he lifted and hooked his fingers in the waistband of her shorts. One little tug and they slid past the curve.

Where was the sheet?

They'd been warm enough in the tent, tangled together to forgo the sheet, but he felt blindly behind him now and dragged it over them so at least, if anyone came barging in, she'd be covered.

"Khalil…" From her lips his name sounded like a plea, and his heart thundered harder, faster.

She hadn't called him Zain and he didn't correct her. Zain wasn't the one invited into her embrace.

He dragged her shorts the rest of the way down soft supple legs, dropped them and immediately went for her top, as if it was a race. As if every second that a barrier existed between their flesh might actually kill him.

He needed her. He needed this.

He pulled the top off, exposing to his gaze small, perfect breasts with desperately pink, erect little peaks. The need driving him kept him from looking longer. Leaning in, he took a nipple into his mouth and sucked hard. She arched into him and he let his hands roam, learn her curves, pull her closer.

"Dr. Zain," a man spoke. They weren't alone…

Something else was said, and he didn't catch it, his attention immediately focusing on covering Adalyn. He grabbed the sheet and dragged it up, and only then did he look for the person who'd spoken.

There was no one in the tent.

But that had been Suhail's voice. Outside the tent flap but very close.

Hell.

In a louder voice Suhail spoke again, and the tenor

told Khalil he was repeating himself. Time to take down the tent. Everything else had been done. Time to go...

"What's he saying?" Adalyn's soft question pulled his attention back to her and the dazed look in her lovely green eyes. Right, she didn't speak Arabic.

"We need to get up." A short summary was all he could manage, still leaning over her, their flesh pressed together from torso to toes. Still hard and heavy against her hip.

Her dazed expression was the sexiest thing he'd ever seen.

Wide eyes, pink cheeks and an impossibly throaty whisper. "We were going to have sex, weren't we?"

Okay, it was the first time he'd ever been asked that...

Khalil nodded, not sure how to take the question.

Adalyn swallowed, licked her lips and focused on his mouth with demanding intensity. "I still want to."

Thank God.

"Me, too." The words came even as he dragged himself away from her. "But it's bad timing. I'm sorry, but Suhail may have saved us..."

Get up. Get dressed. The longer he lay there with her, the less likely he'd get out of that bed for a few more hours.

"But you said you wanted to." She sat up as he stood, clutching the sheet to her chest as she did.

"I do. But I don't have any condoms with me. We weren't just about to have sex, we were about to have unprotected sex."

Adalyn's gaze fell to his erection and whatever arguments she'd been about to make died in her throat.

There she sat, clutching the sheet to her chest, and he strode around without a shred of shame.

Lord, it was sexy.

Was this what he felt when he looked at her?

She dropped the sheet, letting it pool at her waist. Not quite so far as strolling around the tent completely naked, but a step.

His eyes slid down with the sheet, and she watched the muscles in his abdomen squeeze, the proud member bobbing in response.

She'd done that to him and it made her want to do more. To stand up. To test his resolve to get back on the road today. All bad impulses, but all she really wanted to do.

At least at this moment he wanted her as she wanted him. He may have been with a whole caravan of women in his past—she really had no idea and had no desire to ask—but right now he wanted her.

Her.

Plain little Adalyn Quinn, easy to overlook and even easier to forget.

The realization came in a heady rush that made it even harder to ignore the brand-new ache low in her belly.

The whole situation overrode all logic and rules about safety—things she prided herself on and used as her first and most important guides in life—but if he came back to the blankets with her she'd take the risk. She'd revel in the risk, if it was even only just as good as being kissed by him.

If he hadn't turned away and begun getting dressed, she might have even begged... How was that for risky and vulnerable?

Her weakness really should worry her more than it did.

"Don't go out there yet," she whispered as he approached the tent flap, shoes in hand, and she scrambled out of the sheets to come up behind him.

"Adalyn, I can't. We can't. I can't be in here with you." He turned, and though he glanced down at her body, it was quick and he locked onto her gaze again.

"Do you regret this?"

"No." His denial came with enough force to banish those niggling voices. "But I have to go." A soft sigh came and he looked back at her. "You look…"

What? Sad? Turned on? Terrified?

"Since the moment I found you dressing you've looked like an oasis to me." He shook his head, taking his time and looking at her now, and as his eyes skimmed over her body he reached out and let the back of one finger track down over the small swell of her belly, a brief touch that caused a fresh wash of goose bumps. But when he once more looked into her eyes the heat there banished any lingering fear or chill. "This isn't over."

Three little words kept hope alive…

Before she could find any words to say he slipped out of the tent.

It took another several breaths before she calmed down enough to wash up. If he could get on with the task of packing up, she could, too.

She just couldn't do it with the scent of him clinging to her and keeping that flame burning bright in her chest.

CHAPTER NINE

ADALYN SPENT THE ENTIRE drive back to the palace alternating between two conflicting emotions: fear and arousal.

With Khalil there beside her, the air-conditioning may have cooled the actual air but the current running between them still sizzled and popped.

Though she might not want to admit it, picturing him standing proudly naked before her, flushed and panting and looking at her as if he could do things to her that she couldn't even imagine, was entirely too good a substitution for the usual bloody, awful death scenes that filled her mind when she travelled.

And right now that meant she'd fixated on his shoulders and the strong, lean arms that stretched to the steering wheel. He had nice shoulders. Wide and sturdy, without being overly bulky. Was it weird to obsess over shoulders?

"Stop it," Khalil said, his eyes on the road.

"Stop what?"

"You keep looking like that, and I'm going to pull over and finish what we started this morning."

Because she was staring…

"I can't help it," she whispered, smiling despite her

breathless confession. To play down the want running her ragged she laughed a little. "You're better to picture than broken, twisted bodies in burning metal carnage."

"Well, that's a relief."

She grinned wider. "Not by much, but..." This feeling. This was why people flirted and played with one another. And to think, all this time she'd kind of thought she was just...not interested in any of this.

Khalil heard her breath hitch. It'd be easy to think that it was just because she was replaying their morning and not that she was afraid of the drive still, but he really couldn't tell which way her attention was going. She had a thing about using the right crutch at the right time to deal with painful situations. Sitting there, staring at him, could be a crutch.

And he was going to mess it up.

"Not that I want to make you suffer by reliving bad memories, but something about what you said about your nightmares has been bothering me."

She looked back out the side window, the playful tone going out of her voice as she said, "I can talk about it. It's okay. It doesn't really hurt me now. Other than, you know, the worry that someone will think I'm a little unhinged if I tell them the truth about the situation. But I think you understand..."

But she'd stopped smiling.

He understood being ripped apart by nightmares, if that's what she meant. But rather than dig into that, he asked the question burning in his mind. "What did you mean when you said that you remembered their wreck?"

"Well, memories are thoughts, right?" she said, and when he nodded continued, "If you picture something repeatedly, your brain learns it just like it learns a memory. It can't tell the difference. That's the whole basis behind brainwashing—manipulating the natural manner of learning and memories."

"Yes." Something still didn't gel. "So your nightmares were you reliving these false memories you'd given yourself?"

"Yes, but I didn't know they were false. I still…" She paused long enough for him to look at her. Whatever it was she wanted to say wasn't coming easily. Maybe he shouldn't make her do this.

"It's hard to explain." She gripped the seat belt and tightened it as she spoke. "I know I wasn't there. I know it. I know exactly where I was when it happened. I even remember being there. But…I also remember being in the crash, even though I wasn't there. All I have is emotion, and the emotion of that memory is so strong that it overrides reason and what I know to be true. It even seems clearer to me before I start looking for details."

Khalil knew there was something in what she said that he was supposed to get, but he didn't. "You don't have details in your fake memory?"

"I have some details, but… In the real memory I can tell you exactly where I was, who I was talking to and even what we were talking about when the police came to tell me about the crash. But it feels distant. I know now that's because of shock, but the fake memory feels more real because it came later, when the shock had worn off. It has the fear and emotion but it doesn't have the details."

"What details?"

"We always listened to music in the car, but I couldn't tell you what was playing. I couldn't tell you what my mom was wearing before the crash, or where it happened. I couldn't tell you the color of the other cars involved. And when I realized that, that's when what really happened started to seep back in, contrary to what I'd pictured over and over. It was there, but even today it feels less real to me."

He nodded. "Why did you picture it over and over?"

"I don't know. Because I was twelve? Because of the smaller wreck a couple of weeks before? I'd been in that one, but we were on the periphery of it. Other cars got the worst of it, and our car only got knocked on the front left wheel well, and the driver's window shattered beside my father's head…but we didn't get hurt. Not really. Sore for a few days, but not hurt. The other cars, the ones that actually caused the wreck? There were several people inside those vehicles, and only a couple survived." She looked back out the window, and Khalil could tell that the fear was starting to replace whatever mellow mind-set she'd made by looking at him.

"Look at me," he said, reaching across the cab of the truck to take her hand.

"No… No, you need both hands on the wheel!" She pushed his hand back to the wheel, the pitch of her voice rising.

"Okay, but look at me," he said, taking hold of the wheel with both hands now, in the ten and two positions, as he'd been taught. "You don't have to tell me anything else. I think I get it. You saw what happened to those cars, and then, when they wrecked, you knew enough about how it would play out to picture it."

"And I couldn't stop obsessing over it. I couldn't stop wondering how long they'd lived after the crash. Had they been waiting for help to come? Had they been praying and trying to comfort one another? Wondering who would take care of me and Jamison? Had only one of them been awake, or alive? Had one seen the other slipping away before they succumbed, and known they couldn't do anything to help?"

She'd said it couldn't hurt her, but her voice got weaker the more she led him through those questions, breathless. Sounds of pain…

"I had so many questions, and they were all terrible. My aunt and uncle—that's who took us in after it happened, my mother's sister and her husband—well, mostly they took me in, because Jamison was away at school except for the summers. Anyway, they thought that by not answering those questions, not talking about it, they could save me from it. But they couldn't."

"Did you let them help any other way?"

"Yes. I asked them to send me to therapy. There had been a couple of visits with a grief counsellor for two weeks after, but it was only enough to make even my twelve-year-old self know I needed someone better," she answered, and then shrugged. "Because I knew it was wrong. I knew I was messing up somehow, but I didn't know how else to handle it. By the time I'd gotten in to see the therapist, I'd already picked the vision of the crash that best appealed to me and reinforced it to the point of madness. In my memory now they died at the moment of impact. But I can see their bloodied bodies, I can see…glass shards piercing their faces, the engine pushed up between them, crushing them. I see it like a picture, a snapshot. Like it's real. No suffering. Just gone. At the same time. Whenever I started to worry or wonder…that's what I pictured. It was a terrible thing that happened, but…"

She stopped in mid-sentence, then fumbled for her water to take a long drink. *Wash it away, the emotion, the images...* It definitely still ate at her. That kind of emotion was impossible to fake. She really did feel she'd been there, even though she knew she hadn't been.

He didn't know what to say.

"So I messed myself up by trying to picture the only scenario that made it the tiniest bit better. The way the mind works is amazing, and sometimes terrible."

"Did you ever find out how it actually went?" He shouldn't keep making her talk about this, but he knew she hadn't told Jamison any of it. Her brother, the person she was closest to, didn't know. If she didn't tell him, had she told anyone but that therapist? Did she talk about it at all anymore? Maybe she needed to.

A soft sniff demanded he look at her again, but she'd closed her eyes and was busily swiping her cheeks with her hands.

"I... No. I didn't. I don't know what would happen if I found out and it was worse. Sometimes you just have to let go of things that you can't change. I can't make it a kinder story, and I accept that, but I'm afraid that if I find out it was worse...the dreams would come back. That I'd obsess, that I'd trigger some kind of psychological avalanche. So I walk softly around it. I saw a therapist until we got through the constant nightmares. She was the only one who knew, so you can believe I know all the unhealthy tricks to hiding nightmares."

"How long did it take?" he asked, brushing past that little warning she'd given about hiding his own.

"I don't consider myself cured, Khalil." The words came softer than the others, the same voice he'd use to break bad news to a patient or their family. "I'm...I'm in remission. Sometimes I relapse, and I have a CD I play when I'm sleeping for when that happens. Posthypnotic suggestion has been the best maintenance plan for me. And it took me two years to get through the worst time."

"What's your CD like?"

She smiled again, shaking her head. "It's me telling myself a bedtime story."

"Dragons and dream warriors?"

"Yes. That's part of the CD. The first part. The last part is me repeating what actually happened that day for me, not them… One's kind of soothing, and the other is me trying to bolster the signal strength of what actually happened. Beef up my own real memory with the repeated words… It goes on for about twenty minutes. When I first got the idea for that I was already practicing. Every morning when I went to bed after a shift in the sleep clinic I wired my head up with electrodes and ran them to a monitor. Then the next evening I reviewed it all, came up with an average time that it took me to fall asleep and built the recording times around those averages. And now I only use it until a nightmare phase passes and things return to normal."

"Why doesn't that trigger more nightmares?"

"I don't know. I think because it happens when I'm asleep. If I'm having trouble falling asleep and that part of the CD begins to play, I stop it and get up for a little while, then go back to bed and start it from the beginning. I don't listen to the suggestion part when I'm awake. Not since I recorded it."

"I don't understand what any of this monitoring is going to tell you. We've already established that I have nightmares that interrupt my sleep."

Khalil sat on a high stool as Adalyn painstakingly placed electrodes on his chest. The closer the actual time to sleep approached, the more he hated this idea. The only acceptable part of the whole situation was Adalyn standing so close and constantly touching him as she applied one monitoring device after another. Every innocent brush of her fingertips distracted him enough to keep him sitting there…at the tipping point between falling asleep where he sat and dragging her to bed to make damned sure he had a good night.

"I want to know at what point in your sleep cycle your nightmares are occurring," she said, pulling his attention back to the fact that she was cocooning him in wires. "You can't tell me that, since you never seem to know how long you've been asleep before they start."

Her sweet breath fanned his skin as she leaned in close for different steps in her task.

Touching her would make him feel better, but he was now awake enough to recognize that wasn't a great idea. It was both a fantastic idea and a terrible one. They'd both agreed to cool things down when they reached the palace, so his sleep could be as normal as possible. Adalyn wasn't the type to have a fling, and hurting his best friend's little sister—especially when she'd come all this way to help him—didn't sit right. His libido was less than convinced it was the right thing to do, but he was ignoring it.

"You need to monitor my heart for that? I can confirm for you that it does race when I'm in the nightmare."

She looked up at him, making eye contact only long enough to confirm that her thoughts were also somewhere else. The closeness affected her, too. That shouldn't please him.

"I know it does. That's why I need to monitor it. Increased heart rate is an indication of fear, as is the amount of sweat on your skin—and I have monitors for that, too. As well as respiration. Your heart will speed up before you start to sweat, but it's all valuable data. Indications of when your nightmares are starting. What point in your sleep cycle."

He didn't need to ask about the EEG, the cap with all the wires she'd hung on the camera until it was time to strap him into it. "Do you do this to people with insomnia?"

"Yes."

"They're already having a hard time getting to sleep. All this discomfort…" His complaining started to scratch along his own nerves. When complaints turned to whining, it wasn't a good look for anyone. Just take the wires and electrodes and get on with it.

"I know. You aren't going to have that problem, though. I bet I could put a dancing monkey in the corner and you'd still be able to sleep within minutes of hitting the pillow, you're so sleep-deprived."

"I slept a few hours last night," he reminded her.

"And you have a sleep deficit. You can't make up for all that missed sleep and the stress it puts on your body in a couple of hours. Now hush. This is to help you. You want them to go away, don't you?"

"Yes," he muttered, and closed his eyes as she shook out the cap with the leads and tugged it onto his head. What he must look like. Ridiculous.

She buckled the strap under his chin, tested the tension and then dropped one finger to the waistband of his pajama bottoms, tugged it out a few times as if testing the stretch of the waist.

"What are you doing?"

"Just checking to see if you've got your cranky pants on."

Khalil wanted to glare at her, but he captured her hand instead, his thumb pressed to the pulse point on her wrist. "Do you want me to take them off? I'm happy to take my pants off for you, Adalyn." He could play games, too. Only, his were more fun.

Her cheeks immediately went pink and she gave a little tug to free her wrist from his grip. "Not unless you like to sleep pantsless. This is all about your comfort. That's why I'm making with the cap instead of loose electrodes that I have to hold on with tape and a wad of conductive goop. It's much more uncomfortable." She turned and picked up a large, blunt-tipped syringe. "Almost done, and this is less goopier than the other EEG getup. Just one more thing after I'm done with the cap."

"That is?"

"Straps around your belly and chest to measure respiration, and an electrode on your legs to measure movement. Oh, and the sensors that track eye movement."

"That's three more things."

She tilted his head this way and that, the needle going into the cap at regular intervals…hitting all the different electrode ports on the cap with a conductivity compound. Not only was he wired up, he was gooey. And gooey was anything but sexy.

He should get some kind of reward for putting up with this.

When that was done, she performed the last three quick steps and then carried all his leads to the bed so he didn't trip on them. A camera on a tripod sat at the end of the bed, along with some panel that received the other end of all his wires. She ushered him into the bed before plugging him up.

"If you need anything, just say my name and I'll come running."

"You're going to wake me when they start?"

Adalyn paused as she looked at him, trussed up like a Thanksgiving turkey. If she said no, would he still go to sleep? Probably not. She could tell him yes, but it would be a lie. She needed as much data as she could get, and that meant she needed him to stay in the nightmare as long as he could. He might be having small warning nightmares that led up to the big one, kind of like aftershocks to an earthquake, but before. If she woke him from the small ones...

"I'll wake you if you look like you're in great distress. That's really the only way that I'll know that you're in a full-blown nightmare. Otherwise you might be having some other exciting dream. Because there are different phases of dreaming, and the phase you're in when you have them is important to treatment."

"Why?" Despite the scowl he wore while lying there, his eyelids had already started to droop, and the word was no sooner out of his mouth than it stretched into a wide yawn. Poor baby really was so tired...

"Because different cycles of dreaming have different jobs. It's all your brain trying to process memories and new experiences and make sense of what information you've been feeding it, and when those dreams occur matters. It helps identify what your subconscious is trying to figure out. If we can provide those answers when you're awake, then we have a much better chance of controlling those dreams."

It was true, but not the whole answer. And he still

didn't look pleased about it. But, then, when did he ever look pleased about anything when he was being forced to go to sleep? Only children and adults with nightmares fought sleep, the rest of the adult world fantasized about lying in bed for long lazy hours, a reward for the exhausting trials of modern life.

"Let's just get on with it." He closed his eyes and rested his hands on his belly. When she went to pull a sheet over him, he waved it off. "I don't want it."

Rather than making him even an iota crankier, she turned on the camera at the end of the bed, turned off the lights, turned on her flashlight so she didn't trip and headed to her suite…where all her monitoring equipment was set up.

Adalyn wasn't a liar. She didn't sugar-coat things. She was honest, and damn the consequences.

Usually.

She also wasn't the sort of person who spent vast quantities of time with other people who were actually awake. There were a few people at work, those who spent enough time with her to know her quirks and like her anyway, but other than that she leaned much harder toward straight talk than gentle reassurances.

And, still, given all that, she'd lied to Khalil.

Nothing was ever conclusive where dreams were involved, but his nightmares while in the palace were so predictable, there was an extremely good chance that she could tell when he began having those dreams again. People dreamed almost the whole time they slept, but the worst offenders happened during REM sleep. That, coupled with his physical reactions, should be enough to let her know when they started.

Had she told him the truth, he'd be up chewing coffee beans and refusing to cooperate. It all left a bad taste in her mouth. As did her entanglement with him. There was nothing professional about the way she looked at him. The way she felt. But for all she knew, maybe this was just how it was for most people when they were attracted to one another. There could be nothing special about her feelings, except that as a romantically underdeveloped adult she just didn't have enough data to categorize it all.

Quietly, she sat through the ninety-some minutes it took him to get there. As soon as the brain waves changed she picked up her flashlight, moved everything out of the way and waited. She didn't want to go in until he was waist deep in it…

The other part he would have objected to: she wanted to wake him only when he was so immersed that his defenses were down. It was the only way she'd get answers.

The sensor began picking up sweat on his chest, and she prematurely silenced the alarms there, clicked on her flashlight and tiptoed into the suite so she could stand in front of the camera and actually see him go through it.

Not that she actually wanted to witness it. His frequent anger and grumbling was a bit more understandable to her than it probably was to anyone else.

The sympathy she felt for him probably made him more attractive, too. And she really did want to wake him now, but who knew if he'd give her another chance to observe him?

People with sleep issues tended toward heavier activity during sleep. The usual sleep paralysis didn't always fire right with them. His legs were moving, as

were his arms…and his breath sounded so loud in the
cavernous dark.

Her eyes began to burn.

So loud, so fast…she couldn't wait anymore. Stepping around the camera, she came right up to his side
of the bed. She switched the flashlight to her other hand
and did what she shouldn't do—she touched him. Just
one hand, gently lighting on his shoulder. "Khalil?"

He came instantly out of the bed, wild-eyed and
shouting words she didn't understand. The next instant
he'd sprung from the bed and knocked her to the floor.
Her breath whooshed out of her as he landed on top of
her and sent the flashlight flying from her hand.

As she struggled to suck in a painful breath beneath
him, the light—wherever it had landed—flickered and
went out.

He flattened himself over her, pinning her to the
floor, and said something else.

Her lungs burned now, too. "Khalil? It's me. It's Adalyn. You're okay."

He shushed her and whispered, finally in English,
"Stay down."

The weight of him wasn't inconsiderable, and he'd
captured her hands to hold them down, too.

She'd seen people come out of nightmares swinging,
but she'd never seen them come out of nightmares…
like this.

He was protecting her…

"Khalil, it's a dream. You have to wake up." She tried
to pull her hands free from where he'd pinned her, but his
hands gripped her wrists tighter. In the utter darkness she
couldn't even see him. She couldn't tell if he was wak-

ing up or not. She tried something else. "I'm safe. I'm down. You've got me."

The grip on her wrists loosened and she slid her arms around his shoulders as a deep, terrible trembling racked him. "It's okay." She whispered now, too, petting the back of his neck, uncaring about the wires she'd trussed him up in. For a moment he pressed his face against the side of her neck and let her comfort him.

She was supposed to be asking him questions, but she'd already learned so much.

He was definitely dreaming about the war.

He was trying to save someone…

And then she knew… In his dreams, every night, Khalil tried to save his brother.

CHAPTER TEN

FOR SOMEONE SO unused to physical affection it was remarkably easy for Adalyn to pet and console Khalil.

He needed her and, having seen his face in the throes of his nightmare, she needed it, too.

The shoulders that so enamored her shook with the tension lingering in him, but her hands glided over smooth skin, stroking and kneading as she whispered assurances.

It was a dream.

Everything would be okay soon.

They were safe in his bedroom, where things were soft and sweet, not the war she didn't mention, even if her always overactive imagination supplied her with images of explosions, searing heat and flying metal. Of Hell.

But it was more than that. Touching him, holding on to him, felt more necessary than anything she could ever remember. It was important. And not just that, but it roused equal parts of protective instincts and need. And the small taste she'd had of him wasn't enough. Might never be enough.

Even this wasn't enough, but she'd stay there beneath him as long as he wanted.

Something brushed the side of her neck and awareness shot through her. It was an accident. Someone just
out of the throes of a nightmare wouldn't be kissing…

His head moved, his mouth glided up her neck with
featherlight brushes to that hollow beneath her ear. Then
something hot and wet… His tongue.

Adalyn's heart surged into a dizzying pace and her
lungs, only just recovered, sped up in concert. She
opened her mouth to say something, but all that came
out was a breathy stutter, all sounds and no pattern.
Thoughtless sounds.

Khalil took the sound as a request, and soon his
mouth was on hers, hot and vibrant, firm and needing.
Strong, despite that terrible wound he carried.

He wanted her, and it felt right. It felt fierce and free
and absolutely necessary if she wanted to maintain her
sanity. She'd heard that hormones could make people
stupid. And she didn't care. She was going to do something stupid, and it felt brilliant.

Moving her hands from his glorious back to his head,
she pulled him back long enough to fumble off the chin
strap and pull off that ridiculous wired cap.

Khalil took this as an invitation and she felt him lean
off her, the darkness of his bedroom so complete that
she couldn't even see his outline in the dark.

But she heard wires pop free from his electrodes.

She heard the plastic click of the strap on his chest
and then his belly.

He was stripping.

She rose to her knees and felt his face, pulling off
the taped-on sensors.

No sooner had they freed him from the monitors than
strong arms came around her hips, clamping her to his

chest as he rose. Even in the dark, even after his lips once more found hers, he managed to get them onto the bed. She felt the softness give beneath her as his firm heat pressed her down.

One of his hands, strong and just slightly roughened by his labors in the desert, slid under her shirt and up over her ribs. It started as a tickle that made her smile into his kisses, but ended in a full-mouthed moan as he dipped beneath her bra and stroked over her puckering nipple.

"I can't see you." He whispered the words against her lips. "If you want me to stop, you're going to have to say something out loud."

Adalyn shook her head and then managed to get some words out. "Don't stop." That was all she could manage. He leaned away and before she knew what was even happening in the dark he'd dragged her slacks and panties off. She ripped off her top and the bra beneath, and by the time he'd leaned back into her on the bed she could feel the length of him down her body, and everywhere they touched her body bloomed with sensation.

It seemed he touched her everywhere, his hands, his mouth, and she felt the nip of his teeth over her hip.

As his lips and tongue passed over her thigh he murmured something in his own tongue. She didn't understand, the only thing she picked up on was the sensuality weighting the word.

"Come back…" she whispered, blindly groping for his shoulders to urge him back up over her. Adalyn had read the medical texts, she was familiar with the mechanics. She expected pain, and she didn't care about that, either.

He settled between her legs and she slid her hands to

his hips to pull him against her, certain that if he didn't take her soon, the ache that had steadily grown since the very first touch of his lips days ago might consume her.

Khalil wished he'd turned the light on. After a nightmare the dark had always been a canvas to continue his mind playing out the nightly torment. It didn't have a chance with her touching him, beneath him, but he still wanted that connection… To see the look in her eyes when their bodies finally joined.

Next time. He couldn't stop long enough to find the light.

Gripping himself, he brushed the head of his erection along the heated folds of her sex. Finding her ready and his patience at its end, he found her entrance and sheathed himself inside her.

She made the smallest sound and froze, her sex clamping down on him like a toe-curling vise.

He wanted to move but couldn't when the realization came that she was in pain. For all her blushing and shyness he'd never really thought that the innocence about her was actual innocence. "Adalyn…" He whispered her name, then started to pull away from her. Light. God, he needed the light.

"No…" she said, grabbing his arms and pulling him back to her. "Don't go. I'm sorry. I should've…"

He leaned back into her and settled. It took every ounce of will to give her the time she must need to become used to him.

"I'm okay," she whispered, pulling his head back down to hers, her sweet mouth moving against his.

"Tell me when the pain is past…" It felt wrong to say the words out loud when the room blanketed them in darkness and he was so attuned to her that her every sound broke the air like a shout.

She flexed her hips against him. "I think it's gone already." She tested her control of those sleek internal muscles, each squeeze driving him closer to the edge of madness.

He began to move. Too fast, no doubt, and too hard... His control was shot. His conscience, overused of late, reminded him that this was wrong. Wrong for her, wrong for him...and he ignored it. He'd take whatever wrongness she deigned to give him, and thank her for every second of it. For every touch. For every whimper. For every sweet touch that gave him relief. That made him feel alive.

Whatever remained of his willpower gone, he could've cried for the joy of feeling her climax begin to ripple through her. Before the last spasms faded, his own erupted and he emptied himself into her. His pain. His grief. His seed... The last realization came with another ping of his conscience. Something he couldn't think of now, it would have to be tomorrow's burden.

She still lay trembling beneath him, and he wanted her to stay with him in the bed. Hooking one arm around her waist, he dragged her up to the head of the bed, letting himself slip from her so he could stretch out beside her.

"Khalil..."

"Stay." He said the word that mattered to him right now. He needed her to stay. Not to hook him back up, not to wait for more nightmares to come. He just needed her.

Somehow the nightmares didn't enter into it. They seemed so far away at that moment, no doubt some of her light spilling over him...even in the darkness. And he'd take that, too.

She turned to face him and snuggled in at his side. The abandoned electrode on his chest bothered her cheek and she flicked at the corner, ripped it off and then nestled her cheek on the smarting patch of skin.

"Sweet dreams." From her lips, would those words always sound like a benediction?

"Khalil..." Adalyn said his name, focusing her mind on the subject she needed to talk to him about just as he turned the truck off the main road and into the unpaved desert. This drive was already better than the last one. Since he'd gotten men in to replace the glass she'd broken, the air-conditioning actually worked.

It had been nearly a week since that night she'd woken him. A stretch of nights in which he'd slept some every night. Although he had never slept the full night through, anything was better than the sleepless purgatory he'd been exiled to before her arrival. She knew he slept not because she monitored him but because she was always right there beside him. And when he woke up in the middle of the night he woke her, too.

"Zain," he corrected her, his voice remaining light as he reminded her that they were leaving the world of her patient for the world he used to escape his problems...

"Zain." She tried again—what to call him wasn't a fight she could afford right now, especially when she was still determined not to blow his cover. It wasn't exactly fair of her to make him have this conversation while he was driving—and the strictly rational part of her mind most strongly objected because making him talk would take his attention away from the road, where he should be focused. But talking would be the distraction that kept her from focusing on the fear in her belly. "I've been trying not to pry into the subject of your dreams, but I don't feel like that's something I can keep doing."

"Sure it is," he said, and slowly looked over at her in the seat beside him. "We have other things we could talk about. How delightfully hot and snug that…"

"Stop." She groaned over his words, "That's…distracting. I'm not going to talk dirty to you while you're driving in the desert." She wasn't good at dirty talk anyway, and that was part of his delight at her trying, amusing and arousing at the same time. And her ability to turn him on was like discovering some heady new superpower. She could get so distracted by him, so easily. She had to focus. This conversation needed to happen.

"You like to talk when we're in the car. It's a pattern with you. I'm just trying to help you think about something besides the truck."

"No, you're trying to make me think of something besides the subject of your dreams." She would stay on topic. She would stay on topic. "We're heading back to the camp…"

"Different camp." Another correction, though this time the levity in his voice had faded.

"Okay, we're heading to a different camp and you're not avoiding sleeping, but when we're together…"

"It's working. Us being together. I'm sleeping, I'm making better decisions than I was—I see that now. Having you with me…"

"But I feel like I'm your new crutch." She blurted the words out and let them hang there for a second as she watched his jaw flex and all traces of his playfulness disappear. "I'm not going to be here forever." Even as she said the words some emotions she didn't want to face twisted inside her.

Khalil was a very intelligent man, he knew that without her reminding him, but he'd been avoiding that subject. Which just proved her status as the new crutch.

She'd think about that later. She turned in the seat, enough to look at him without abandoning her seat belt. "I know you were trying to protect me when you tackled me. You thought I was Arash, right? You're reliving the war when you couldn't save him?"

He drew a slow breath, before releasing it in a rather irritated way.

"Please, tell me. You need to talk about it, and I know you're not going to go to a therapist. You probably also aren't going to talk to your family about it. So that leaves me, Hakem, Suhail or Jamison. And I'm here now…"

"And you won't be soon," he said.

"Right," she confirmed, and then stopped. "But I'm not on a time schedule. I mean…I'm on indefinite leave, which is not to say that I can stay for months but we do have some time. And a couple hours' drive, right?"

Time when he didn't have any demands being made on him to run the country or save lives. Time he could use to save his own.

"I don't want to talk about it."

"Of course you don't, it's unpleasant, and sweeping it all under the rug is another crutch."

"A crutch? Like you distracting yourself from your fear of cars by talking? You want me to talk? I want you to drive." He took his foot off the gas and let the big truck slow on its own.

"I don't know how to drive."

"I don't know how to talk about this."

"Khalil…"

"Zain," he corrected again, turning to look at her as he applied the brakes and slowed the beast down. "You drive, I talk. That's the deal."

"It's a bad deal. I won't be able to pay attention to you because I don't know how to drive! I'll have to spend all my attention steering and—"

"There are no roads out here. You can't go off the road if you're already off the road."

"And we might not ever get there. What if I go over a big dune the wrong way and then the truck gets off balance and turns over and rolls down to the bottom and bursts into flames?"

"That won't happen. This isn't Hollywood. Cars don't burst into flames just because they roll over." He shifted into Neutral, then reached over and flipped open her seat belt.

"This is ridiculous."

"Well, this is the way it is."

The way it was… Him once again counting on her to not have the courage to do this. And if they had been back in New Orleans, or even in the city here, she probably wouldn't. If she'd not spent so much time traveling the past ten days, she probably wouldn't. She knew exposure therapy helped people, but she just had never been able to force herself to do it.

He stared at her, one hand on his seat belt, ready to fasten the thing again and get back to driving.

Normally, she'd never agree to this deal, but the longer they sat with the truck not moving, the warmer it became. The air-conditioning only worked so well out here. And he was counting on all these things to make her give in.

"Fine," Adalyn said, forcing a lightness to her tone that she didn't feel, and turning as she stood, removing herself from the seat so that he could slide into her space and she could step over into his.

The look on his face said he thought she was bluffing, and he slid over easily and fastened himself in.

She twirled and sat beside him, then scooted to the driver's seat.

Did he know how this pushed at her nightmare? Had she told him that being in the car wasn't enough for her imagination, that what came with that false memory was the kind of guilt that could only be called self-blame? As if maybe she could have changed the outcome if she'd done something before... Or false survivor's guilt... But guilt all the same.

The truck's engine still rumbled as she went through adjusting the seat with Khalil's help to slide it forward enough to reach the pedals. This, unfortunately, cramped his leg room, but that was just tough. If he was bound and determined that they both suffer as much as possible, then that's what would happen.

"Okay, how do I shift and make it drive?"

This led through a somewhat less eager period of instruction as Khalil began to realize she was really going to try to do this. That didn't mean that she'd be able to split her attention and talk or ask the right questions at the same time, but at least she was going to try to hold up her end of the deal. If this was the only way he would talk about his dreams...

Hakem and Suhail, who'd left a little later than she and Khalil, finally reached them and pulled up alongside.

Another conversation she couldn't take part in, and they pulled ahead, leaving them to Adalyn's driving to get them to the village.

"How far before they're outside the range of the radio?"

"Several miles."

Her stomach bottomed out. "Great…" No one would see if she crashed and they exploded. "Tell me how to get the gear to shift again."

It took another twenty minutes for her to get the truck up to enough speed to get it into the proper driving gear, and her nerves were well and truly frayed by the time she did it.

And she was supposed to talk to him now. Now that she couldn't remember what the heck she was supposed to be talking about. About his dreams. Confirming if her conclusions about what had actually happened were anywhere close to what had happened. And mostly… providing him a safe place to talk about it all.

Safe place. Hah. As if this was safe.

"You're going the wrong way."

"You said there wasn't a road so not to worry."

He tapped the GPS doodad on the dashboard. "We still have to end up at the proper coordinates to find the village."

She couldn't figure out how to manage one other thing, and navigating was it. "Screw it." She took her foot off the gas. "Downshift it for me and I'll get back over in my seat and you can drive the darned thing. You win. Let's hope you don't win the whole stupid war, because you'll definitely be the one to lose if you do."

Khalil did as requested, and once the terrifying vehicle stopped moving she unbuckled and climbed over him again, this time not bothering to stand and let him slide over—she just climbed over his lap after he slid a few inches toward her.

The maneuver had her straddling him at one point, hands on his shoulders for balance, but before she could lift the other leg to complete her walkover, he grabbed her hips and focused her attention back on him.

Suhail and Hakem wouldn't come looking for them anytime soon. No one else was going to roll up and catch them, but doing what they both wanted to do right now would just be rewarding his bad behavior.

Even someone as minimally experienced as she was could see desire flare to life in his eyes as he captured her in that vulnerable position.

"I swear to God, if you try to kiss me…" she muttered, but even as she said the words she had to wrestle with that little excited wiggle in her belly that wanted him to kiss her. And in order to make herself get on with moving, she pushed at his shoulders until he let her continue over him and he slid toward the driver's seat.

Once they were fastened in and he had the truck moving, and once again back on course, she said, "I drove for…lots of minutes. You owe me like…ten questions answered."

"No."

"Eight."

"No."

"You don't get how bartering works, do you?"

"You're in no position to barter, Adalyn."

"Seven, and I will state clearly here for you that you're definitely the bigger coward if you don't even try. If I'm the one more committed to your recovery than you are. Just so long as we're clear on that."

He looked at her, the corner of his jaw flexing. "One."

"Six."

Another of those long-suffering and irritated sighs escaped him. "Two."

"Five." She should probably be happy with two, but she was greedy for this information.

"Two."

"You're supposed to say three."

"You're supposed to just ask the questions."

"Fine." She twisted slightly in the seat again so she could look at him. "You tried to protect him, and when you couldn't you tried to triage… You tried to save his life. But he was already gone, and you're reliving it in your dreams."

"That's not how it happened."

"You didn't try to save him? You just let him bleed out?"

"*No.* Of course not!" he said, and tacked on a few expletives that let her know how close he was coming to losing control of his temper.

"You tried to treat his wounds but couldn't save him," she summed up instead, her eyes fixed on his hard profile.

It took him a few seconds to respond. "Yes." He glanced at her. "That's your two questions."

She turned in the seat, staring at him longer—and, as much as she actually liked to look at him, it wouldn't help dissipate the negative emotion in the truck. From his answers she could infer that he felt guilt at being unable to save his brother, but trying to save someone in the field was never easy. Sometimes you could stabilize them enough to get transport, but even in a big city with ambulances spread out and close to any location at any time people died before they could get to a hospital all the time.

In a war zone, that level of availability was far-fetched at best.

Would he have felt that way if it hadn't been his brother?

Two questions weren't enough. It didn't give her any real tools that would allow her to help him. And his story didn't jibe with him tackling her and trying to protect her with his body. That wasn't the action of a doctor crippled by the loss of a patient, it was the action of someone who would rather die than lose the person he was trying to protect.

She looked back out the window, and it dawned on her that she'd been sitting, contemplating, brooding, all while looking through the front windshield… Something she never did without panicking.

Paying attention to that brought the fear swimming back, though maybe not as strongly as it had been before. Was the lesser reaction due to her impromptu driving lesson? Or had she just burned through so much emotion since coming to this country that she was becoming numb to it? Maybe it was just the repetition of being in a vehicle over and over while it *didn't* explode… or wreck…or both…

Maybe she could benefit from exposure therapy…

CHAPTER ELEVEN

THEY ARRIVED IN the new village camp as the sun hit mid-sky and really started to heat up. Since there was no sick child to tend, and because Adalyn really couldn't spend that much time in the super-intense sunlight, she stayed in the truck with the doors open and a book in her hand.

She'd have never pegged Khalil for a fantasy reader, but that's what she found. Epic journeys, men with swords and horses, magic and dragons... Maybe reading was another crutch—though she'd hate to label it so. It could be the kind of escape that took him out of the palace, which she was increasingly certain was what he wanted. She saw him at the palace only when it was time for sleep, and that time got pushed back as far as she'd let it be pushed back before coming to track him down.

By the end of the second chapter the first tent had been erected—the clinic where Suhail and Hakem also slept at night. She could start carrying in the less heavy pieces, which would still necessitate a walk across the camp at this distance, or she could close the truck up, start it and try to maneuver the thing over to the tent.

She would have to go around, because if she went through she would probably hit and kill someone.

News traveled faster than they did, even between these separated communities. Even though this one was different from the last—and Adalyn believed it was because the people were different even if the tents and configuration all looked remarkably the same to her from the outside—the people had heard the mistress cover story.

She saw it in their eyes when the men looked at her.

Later she'd have to ask Khalil. But for now she approached and touched his arm to get his attention. "If the truck could be moved around to the first tent, I could start unloading some of the supplies."

"Do you want to do it?"

Being generally independent, Adalyn suddenly wanted to say yes. But the more honest answer was no. "I'm afraid I'll hit a tent or a person..." Or that somehow it would go off into the desert at top speed while she tried in vain to stop it. Ridiculous as the idea was. "Will you move it over?"

He nodded, said something to the men and walked back with her to the truck in silence.

That meant she had a small opening to start asking questions. "Are we sharing a tent again?"

Khalil looked down at her and actually smiled, a teasing light in his eyes. "Are you asking to sleep with me?"

Now that they weren't at the palace and she wasn't grilling him about his dreams, his humor had started to come back. No doubt helped by the amount of sleep he'd actually had since the last trip. It was never eight hours, but even a few hours per night was better than what he'd been doing to himself before. And the night she'd woken him…they'd slept more than eight hours afterward, until he had eventually been dragged out of bed to see to some kind of bureaucratic or diplomatic crisis.

Adalyn would've said she was as warm as she could get but, still, with the question and the flirting, she felt her cheeks heat. Yes. Yes, she wanted to sleep with him. "Are you propositioning me?"

"You were propositioning me," he said. "You were the one asking about sleeping together."

"I asked about the tent," she corrected him, but felt herself smiling. "I'll just assume we are. I can't imagine that Hakem or Suhail would want me to crash in their tent."

"I wouldn't be too sure about that, either," he said as they passed a younger village man and watched him eye Adalyn like candy.

The truck sat a few feet away, and she scrambled to it and into the passenger side, letting Khalil get in and get the thing started. "Don't wear your seat belt," he said, stopping her from fastening it.

"Why?"

"We're going a tiny distance."

"Most crashes occur within five miles of home."

"Adalyn, you're trying to overcome your fear of cars, right? Be brave. Take a baby step, and I'll go very slowly around the village. In this flat area I'll make a thirty-second drive take two or three minutes, okay? That's how slow we'll go. So slow that if we managed to hit someone they'd have to be legless and asleep in order to not have time to move out of the way."

She looked at the belt she'd already crossed over her

torso and was ready to push into the lock. These little concessions…maybe she could use it as currency again. "For an answer," she said, still holding the warm metal in her hand.

He started the engine and then looked at her, the humor fading a little bit. "Okay, but you sit here beside me, and I get a kiss for my trouble."

"Someone might see…" He was always pushing her boundaries.

"We'll park with the back toward the tent and put up the windshield screen to minimize people seeing…"

Dropping the belt, she slid over on the bench to his side and kept her feet well away from the pedals. Once he got the truck backed up enough to start the creepingly slow trip around to the other tent she asked, "Who were you protecting when you leaped on me in your dream?"

"Arash," he answered, keeping his voice level, though she could see that he was working to hold on to his good mood by the way his knuckles turned white as he gripped the steering wheel.

"But earlier you said you weren't trying to protect him."

"That's not what I said." He peeled one of those white-knuckled hands from the steering wheel and laid it on her knee, squeezed and then slid it between her legs to do the same to her inner thigh.

She was definitely going to sleep with him again. Obviously. They'd been at it a week, but that had been with Khalil, not Zain. This type of behavior felt riskier outside the palace and would require sneakiness she didn't really possess. And patience. They'd have to wait for darkness and the village to get quiet.

But, God help her, the first brush of his fingers on her thighs and her legs actually parted a little to let him do whatever he wanted. It was like watching someone else act, were it not for the inferno that roared to life in her belly—hotter than the sun baking everything and everybody.

By the time they'd made it to the tent she'd forgotten all about the seat belt or her fear. He turned the truck and backed it up to the side of the tent, grabbed the windshield screen, and once that was in place Adalyn's arms shot up to tug his mouth to hers.

Whatever it was that Khalil had, it made her reckless. But it also made her feel alive.

She'd have to think about his answers. Later. After she turned his simple reward kiss into something for him to think about the rest of the day, just as she'd be doing.

And the unspoken agreement she suddenly knew they'd come to.

The early light before dawn had begun to light the tent where Khalil and Adalyn slept.

He lay with her tucked in against him, awake but unwilling to move for the time being. The dream had come, though it hadn't been nearly as bad as before she'd come to Merirach and him.

Yesterday he'd been shorter with her than he'd intended, but he wasn't just putting on a front when he said he didn't know how to talk about the dreams.

Did he need to talk about them? Yes. Even a fool knew that sometimes you had to open a wound and debride it before it could heal. And sometimes an open wound healed better than one that was closed, as contrary to logic as that sounded.

The air was cooler in this part of the small country, and she huddled against him in the bedding, her dark brown tresses fanned out over his arm, which she used as a pillow. Most times when she looked at him it was with the light of challenge in those warm green eyes. Even when it was because he was taking advantage of the peace she brought him. The only time he'd felt even a little peace in the past few months had been since she'd shown up, challenging him.

And sometime over the past ten days her opinion of him had become more important than Jamison's, his closest and longest-standing friend. The man who'd sent this prickly angel to heal him, to keep him sane.

The distinctive bang of a gunshot yanked Khalil out of his reverie and woke his angel.

"What was that?" she asked, sitting up, the sheet clutched to her chest.

He didn't need to ask what it was. He just needed to know why. "Gun. Get dressed." He leaned to the side, grabbed clothes he'd set out the night before and began stuffing himself into them as she did the same.

"Why would anyone be shooting a gun at this time of night?" She looked at the tent canvas and amended, "Morning..."

"No good reason I can think of." One of his lessons from residency had been revived since he'd become regent of Merirach. He knew how to come fully awake and alert fast. "Finish dressing, and stay in the tent. Lie down again on the bedding, low to the ground. I'll check things..."

"Khalil, shouldn't Hakem and Suhail be the ones to check?"

She was worried about him. Well, he was worried about her, too. "It came from that direction." He pointed toward the center of the village and then looked at her. "If you hear anymore gunshots, take the keys, get into the truck and get out of the village. Do you understand?"

"I'm not leaving you here."

"I'll still have the other truck with Suhail and Hakem. Don't argue for once." He grabbed the keys to the truck and tossed them onto the bed, then exited the tent at a crouching run.

Suhail and Hakem had just come out of the clinic tent, and each man had a gun in hand, ready to defend their prince. He switched to Arabic, since Suhail's English wasn't the greatest. "Do we know what's happening?"

"I heard a disagreement earlier when I made a morning sweep of the village."

Khalil looked at the lightening sky from where the three of them crouched out of view. "Did it sound like it could turn violent?"

"I wasn't expecting it, but these days…"

Another couple of shots sounded and he grunted. "Right. Time to go." He'd have to take it on faith that Adalyn was going to do what he'd told her to do after those other shots.

The three of them moved together, Khalil without a gun, through the winding paths between the tents until they got close enough to hear men arguing over the irregular gunfire.

The next shot came and immediately afterward a woman's screams told him someone had been hit.

"We'll check. You stay here," Hakem said, but Khalil

shook his head. He wasn't going to let anyone run off on their own without him again, that lesson he had managed to learn, at least.

"We'll go together."

Several more shots were fired and Khalil swore. The tents were no kind of protection. At least in the capital they'd been able to crouch down behind stone walls and cars to keep from getting shot, but here, even standing out of sight around a tent, a carelessly fired bullet could still slice through layers of canvas and kill him, or anyone else. People in their homes. Children.

The safest option left to him was the one that would ruin his desert forays, but Khalil raised his voice and began to shout who he was. Not Zain. Prince Regent Khalil of Akkari, son of Sultana Ghada, Daughter of House Merirach. When he'd given his full introduction, he ordered them all to stand down.

All sounds of the argument fell quiet, and the only thing he heard was the sound of the woman crying.

Shrugging off Hakem's attempt to keep him back, Khalil stepped into view, continuing to order the violence to end as he made it to the cleared patch of earth where the men had been fighting. A woman knelt over a downed man, and Khalil stopped beside her to look at the man. He was still conscious, but he had a rapidly expanding red stain on his torso. Hakem followed, and he gestured to the man to apply pressure to the gunshot wound before the man bled out.

It had all happened so quickly—those shots, him blowing his own cover. He had proof back in his belongings if need be...but he hadn't thought to bring any with him when they'd begun chasing gunfire.

People slowly filtered out of their tents to see him for themselves.

"I'm taking him back to get surgery. My men have orders to shoot to kill any citizen who fires another shot while I'm seeing to this man. If it takes violence to end the violence, so be it."

No one argued or demanded proof. No one even dared to speak. But as quickly as it had started, things came to an uneasy calm.

These people who had laughed and joked with him on all his other visits now averted their eyes.

When his mother and aunt had come of age, the culture was different—accepting of a line of succession through the daughters, since the king had no sons. Khalil suspected that situation would've never been questioned had the man who'd married in and become Sultan of Merirach ever tried to earn his people's respect.

But Khalil's line through his mother was of the royal line they'd been ruled by for centuries. They knew her name. He and Malik carried the blood, so they'd accepted her son as the regent and accorded him due respect. The very same reason that those who'd revolted hadn't killed his young cousin, Prince Taariq, even if they'd executed both of his parents.

He left Suhail and Hakem to keep the peace and drafted three men—those who hadn't been fighting—to carry his patient to where he could be treated. Hopefully before it was too late.

Khalil and his entourage rounded the corner to the clinic tent. Adalyn stood outside it, fretting and blatantly disobeying his orders.

The people in the village had obeyed, but she just hadn't been able to do it.

He'd deal with her later.

Yesterday's clinic needs hadn't been sufficient for him to unload the supplies he now needed. They were in the truck. His truck.

Switching to English, he barked at her, "Get into the truck. Get it started."

Then, in the language that the men would understand, he led them to the back of the truck and inside. They placed the man on the floor of the truck and stepped back as Khalil climbed in.

Adalyn was in the front, and she started the engine, as he'd ordered. No arguments, thank God.

"Drive in any direction, Adalyn. I don't care where you take us, just get us out of here."

"Don't you want me to help you?"

"Yes. But I'm not trusting that the people will hold their truce. Hakem and Suhail are there to keep them peaceful, but the one who shot this man could decide to come and finish him off. I'm not risking your life or his. Just drive."

Adalyn didn't put her seat belt on. She had to back the truck up and get the gears to work, and she'd had only one stupid lesson yesterday when she'd been more concerned with the conversation she hadn't been having with Khalil.

With some grinding of gears she found Reverse and soon they were moving. *Just go straight back, and then when clear of the tents go forward. The lower the number, the lower the gear...* What else? Something about the clutch when she was shifting?

She got the monstrosity moving forward, but she'd be

surprised if it didn't need a whole new transmission by the time she got them out of range of the village camp.

When she began to have trouble, Khalil talked her through her nerves, and after they'd been moving a while he called from the back, "Far enough. I need you. Shut it off."

That was easier. Even dealing with surgery would be better than driving more. She opened the door and climbed down, and then immediately went back inside through the rear door. "Tell me what you need."

"I need…" His pause made her pulse rocket up even higher. Any second and she'd be the one needing help. Opening trunks, she grabbed gloves and some sterile pads. "There are coagulants in the medicine chest. Get those, too. And the dressings."

She watched him turn the man to get a look at his back. "No exit wound."

That was bad. Even she knew that was bad. With the inventory requested tucked under her elbows and the coagulants in hand, she knelt on the other side of his patient, set down the supplies and grabbed the gauze scissors to cut through the man's shirt.

"We need to stop the bleeding. And I want to sedate him, so we need an IV kit. Which—" he looked at the trunks and shook his head "—is in the clinic. So bleeding first."

He wasn't trained as a trauma surgeon, Adalyn knew, he was cardiothoracic by training—just as Jamison was. But with all the time they'd spent in the field on missions, she could bet that he'd had a good deal of experience with trauma and field surgeries.

As they worked together the tension from the past few minutes slipped away. He alternated between speaking English when it was to give her instructions and Arabic when he spoke to his patient—the man he was trying to keep talking as they worked and, she prayed, stopped him slipping too far into shock.

About ten minutes later they had the bleeding controlled, and their patient was slipping in and out of consciousness. "We have to go back. He's lost a lot of blood, and all I have to give him to hold him over until the chopper comes is saline." He stood, leaving her with the patient. "I'll drive us back. If he exhibits any change, yell."

"Is it safe to go back?"

"We're about to find out," he said, climbing over the seat and into the front, where he started the truck. "Or, actually, I'm about to find out. *You* are going to stay in the truck, like I told you to do before. We're going to have words about that later, Adalyn."

Later. They always had to schedule words for later. At least right now they had more pressing concerns.

When they rolled back into the village the situation seemed to have been brought more or less under control. His men had confiscated the firearms of those who'd been shooting, and they'd stay confiscated until tempers cooled.

Since the situation was more controlled now, Khalil didn't argue when Adalyn asked to go with him and the patient.

As she stood in the tent beside the unconscious man Khalil let her set up the IV and check the man's blood pressure while he stood a short distance away, speaking to a group of several men, the instigators, she'd wager, and Hakem and Suhail.

She gleaned that the men had had some kind of disagreement they wanted Khalil to arbitrate.

And that they no longer called him Zain.

They called him Sheikh. They used honorifics. They bowed, when they weren't quarreling with one another.

Despite the rising heat, her cheeks went cold. They knew.

Khalil stepped over to her with a walkie-talkie, which he tucked into her pocket. "I'm going to go with them, but I won't go far. Call if you need me."

"How'd they find out?" she whispered, looking past him to the men now waiting outside the tent.

A fleeting frown etched between his brows, and he murmured, "I had to tell them who I was in order to stop the shooting. It was the only way to get him out of the line of fire to where we could treat him."

To save a life, he'd given up his haven. No matter what nightmares he was nursing, no matter how caustic and aggressive he could be when confronted with those nightmares, he was an exceptional man. And she had to find a way to help him and get out of there before she lost touch with her life…and what it would be without him in it.

If she didn't leave soon, she'd never want to go.

CHAPTER TWELVE

By the time Adalyn heard the helicopter she had just about given up the idea that help was coming. Khalil and his men left her in the clinic with the patient—and his inconsolable wife, she assumed, because communication was impossible.

Moments after she heard the spinning blades beating the air Khalil came back, and soon his men had bundled their patient onto a stretcher and carried him out. "Come on," he said over his shoulder. As little as she wanted to get near another helicopter, she followed. Being in his presence made her feel safe, something she never felt when fending for herself in this country. For all her fears before coming to Merirach, and all that she'd worked through in the meanwhile to get the job done, being alone and unable to communicate with anyone was quickly becoming a big enough fear to compete with vehicles.

The sun had well and truly risen now, and as she stepped out of the shade of the tent the heat on her head and neck baked into her, and she had to scramble to keep up.

Burning, stinging sand whipped through the air from the force of the propeller blades as the chopper landed.

Her lungs reacted with a coughing fit that stopped her cold. Why did he need her to go to the helicopter anyway? She could stand a safe distance away and wait for him.

She turned away from the dust, which helped a little.

Khalil couldn't have heard her coughing above that blade, but he must have sensed that she'd stopped. In an instant he was at her side with a cloth to hold over her mouth so she could breathe and his insistent arm around her shoulders, guiding her toward the chopper.

The closer they got to it the better it got, but before she knew what was happening he'd grabbed her by the hips and put her into the helicopter.

"Wait…" She pulled the cloth away from her face, forcing her eyes open to look at him.

"You have to go with him."

Go without Khalil? Far from his presence? Alone? The barren landscape behind him seemed to spin. Was it because of the coughing she'd been doing and the drop in oxygen saturation? Or was it the mountain of fear pressing at her chest?

Adalyn grabbed his hands to keep him from getting away. "Please, don't make me go in the helicopter. I want to stay! You need help!" Even as the words came out she knew how desperate she sounded.

"I have Hakem and Suhail."

"I can't go to some whole other place without you. I don't speak the language!" He had to know how much the idea scared her. He'd been with her nearly two weeks now, and more than a few of her neurotic fears had manifested in that time.

"They're going to the hospital to take him to surgery, and then they'll take you to the palace. I have to stay and clean up this mess."

Did he always sound so distant? There wasn't even a hint of playful flirting or even gentleness in his eyes as he said the words, ignoring her pleas.

She couldn't think of a suitable argument other than that she didn't want to. All she managed was to shake her head. "I'll stay in the truck, I'll wait in the truck."

"I need you gone, Adalyn," he shouted over the beating blades, then pulled her head to his mouth to say, "You're my mistress…"

And then it all became clear. The people in this village knew who he was, and they believed her to be his mistress. And she didn't even know if that was inaccurate anymore, but this had become somewhere possibly not safe for her.

There was no argument for this situation. She nodded dully and edged back into a seat to buckle in. What would she find when she got to the palace? Would his staff be willing to accept her without him at her side? Did they look upon her as his mistress, too? They'd not done an especially good job of hiding the turn their relationship had taken over the past week, even if right now it all felt like her nightmares…more emotion than substance, some kind of fantasy she'd played out in her head.

They'd happily slept in his bed, and she knew those details…the scent of his rumpled sheets, the way the morning sun hit the east windows and little shafts of light peeked past the heavy curtains and turned his warm tan skin to gold. She could barely remember the bed in her suite—it had sat untouched since her first night in Merirach.

Details that made it real.

In a remarkably short period of time the men had all

retreated to a safe distance and the helicopter began to lift. Unlike the last time, she didn't avoid looking out the window.

Details she could remember later, and know this was also real. The way the helicopter smelled slightly of fuel and fumes, the feel of the headphones thrust into her hands and soon cushioning her ears. The way Khalil marched back to the village without a backward glance.

This was real. He could just send her away without it putting even a small chink in his armor. Without worrying about her or dreading her absence.

Because it wasn't nighttime. He didn't need his crutch unless it was time to sleep...

If she'd wondered what his feelings for her were before, she now knew.

She was the only fool who'd managed to fall in love.

Emotionally battered from the turn the day had taken, by the time Adalyn reached the palace all she wanted to do was climb into her neglected bed.

No, if she was honest, she wanted to climb into Khalil's bed. She wanted to burrow into his sheets, press her face in his pillow and breathe in the last of him. Whatever they'd been, it certainly felt over.

The car from the airport pulled into the palace, and she got out. Exposure therapy was definitely working for her. After the nightmare of a helicopter ride she'd had a remarkably dull reaction to yet another wheeled vehicle to spirit her to the palace.

As soon as she stepped out, dread prickled at the back of her neck. The man who managed the house staff stood alone to receive her.

"Hello…" she said, gesturing to the car. "The sheikh isn't with me. He—"

"I am aware, Miss Quinn. Your suite has been prepared," he said, but then looked uncertain for a moment before he lowered his voice. "Sultan Khaliq Al-Akkari has arrived with the Sultana Ghada. They await the return of their son."

Adalyn blinked, and the emotion that had left her for the drive up to the palace came roaring back. Did she need to talk to them? Was she supposed to explain where Khalil was?

"Do you know why they've come?"

"I do not," he answered, but had the look of a man not used to lying. He knew. Adalyn would stake her passport on it.

But she couldn't very well call the man a liar. And she also couldn't count on him to give her good advice on how to handle this situation.

"I suppose I will go clean the grit off myself and then go meet them."

"Very good," he said, turning to lead her to her suite, as if she didn't know how to get there. He felt more like a prisoner escort than something for her benefit.

"Do they know that I'm…?"

"They know everything."

Great. They knew everything, and she didn't even know what her reaction was supposed to be, or if she was supposed to try to smooth things over before Khalil got there.

She passed through Khalil's bedroom. All her equipment still littered the suite, but when she passed the camera stand a wave of cold crept over her scalp and down her spine.

The tripod remained, but the base where her camera had sat? Empty. No camera.

And she hadn't touched it since the only night of proper monitoring…

She hadn't had the focus to remember it was recording and turn it off when he'd taken her to bed. Or when he'd stripped her clothes off, torn wires and electrodes off his own body and kissed her senseless.

The only video on that camera started out with Khalil sleeping and ended with a night-vision capture of the two of them sleeping together.

No sooner had Khalil returned to the village after sending away Adalyn than his satellite phone rang.

Only his parents, his minsters and staff had the number to the phone.

He glanced at the number calling and let it go to voice mail. He'd already rung his head of staff to let him know that Adalyn was returning and to arrange transport for her back to the palace, and she couldn't be there yet. He had a little time, and he had to deal with the situation that had prompted a sunrise shooting before he could do one more thing.

Within the next hour he gathered all the men together, decided who had the best reputation among the people and appointed an official to hear these sorts of disagreements and resolve them peacefully. How would that work out? He had no idea. The lessons in leadership he'd had growing up had never really centered around bureaucratic issues. Arash's had. Malik's had, too. But they had been the ones meant to lead. He was just an extra spare who'd messed up the line of succession when he'd let his brother die. All he could do was use his best judgment, and hope it was a better judgment now than it had been two months ago.

As Hakem and Suhail worked with the village men to pack up the tent and supplies, Khalil adjourned to the truck to return the call.

The voice that answered...

"Father..." he said, his mind whirring now as he looked at his watch and started calculating the time it took to fly home versus how long ago he'd sent Adalyn off.

She was there by now, God help them both.

There was no way for her to stay with him now, unless his father took the tack he expected—the one that removed him from the regent position and replaced him with Malik.

He'd be failing Arash for a third time if he lost the regency, forced his father out of retirement and his elder brother to clean up his mess...

And the day had started out so well, when it had been just her lying in his arms, looking like an angel...

But he couldn't fail again. Even if that meant losing Adalyn.

When it came down to it, he didn't deserve her light anyway.

Adalyn lay in the bed in her suite, staring at the carved floral reliefs on the ceiling, an untouched dinner tray sitting on the table beside her.

After showering and making herself presentable, the sultan and sultana had refused to see her.

They hadn't even wanted to meet her, and she was so mortified about the missing camera that she couldn't even bring herself to try to sweet-talk her way in to see them—if she even knew how to sweet-talk.

Another new experience she could add to her own personal travelogue.

She hadn't visited ancient monuments...unless the palace counted, but it didn't look all that ancient.

She hadn't gone to the beach.

She hadn't gone on any fancy shopping sprees, hadn't even gone to some chintzy souvenir shop.

Despite the initial rockiness, by the time they'd made it to the first village Khalil had made her part of his daily life, part of his obligations...

And then there were the other things she'd done that you couldn't really put into the travelogue.

Fallen in love with the regent of a country? Yeah, that was probably not fit for publishing.

Accidentally made a sex tape with her patient, the same regent? That was also right out.

Had they watched it? Was that why they wouldn't see her? Would it be better or worse if the sultan had it, or if one of the staff had taken it to later blackmail Khalil with?

She'd come reluctantly to the Middle East, then had sullied her name among the people as a—well, she wasn't sure what they thought of the word *mistress*, but, considering how distasteful she found it with her liberal Western upbringing, she could only imagine.

This was exactly why she should've just stuck with her travel books. The next time Jamison came calling to make her travel to help out one of his friends she'd— well, she'd say something rude and then slam the door in his face. Or the phone in his ear, as most of their communication happened on the phone.

She felt Khalil standing there more than anything else. The door didn't squeak. The floor didn't squeak.

The plush rugs on the floor also muffled footfalls remarkably well.

"Someone took the camera," she said immediately, bolting upright. He looked dirty and exhausted from the road, and now he had to face all this insanity at the palace. "I'm sorry. I should have said hello first." Pulling herself up from the bed, she covered the few feet separating them but couldn't bring herself to touch him. The fear that she was alone in these new emotions might have been worse than the fear she'd felt getting into the helicopter.

Khalil didn't touch her but lifted a hand to rub the back of his neck, then turned to prowl to the window. Did he not even want to look at her?

Suddenly trying to figure out how he felt about her seemed like the most important thing, more important than the camera or the publicity debacle. Before he'd sent her away she'd have said he felt the same, but in that moment—when he'd excluded her from his life and obligations—any sense of security had vanished. She'd just given him an opportunity to remedy that—one small touch would've done it. Or at least gone a long way toward doing it, and he'd walked away.

"Say something. Please, say anything."

With his voice bouncing off the glass, he said, "I'm here to take you to the airport."

"What?"

"You're going home."

"Because your parents wouldn't see me? Because of the missing camera?"

"No…"

The way the word hung there she knew it to be a lie. Of course the camera mattered. Of course his parents had seen it. Once again that cold settled into her spine as heat washed over her face. A body at war over how to feel, embarrassed or scared?

"What does that mean? Are we... Are we breaking up?"

"What did you think was going to happen when you had to go home?" Khalil asked, finally turning to look at her. Those beautiful golden-brown eyes now looked hard, like sharp bits of glass ready to slash at her. That she was even making an argument about their relationship was like handing him her wrists or exposing her jugular.

"I don't know. We haven't even tried to figure it out. We could do that. There has to be something. Isn't that what you're supposed to do when you love someone? Work it out? Be together...?" There, she'd said it. She'd said *love*. She'd taken that brave first step. All he had to do was...

"It was never going to work out."

"It could," she said, trying to ignore that he hadn't denied he loved her. He hadn't confirmed it, either, but he still could. "It should. It's supposed to work out. That's how this goes in the stories, when two people— good people—find each other, it's supposed to work out. They're supposed to make it work."

"What makes you think I'm a good person?"

The question sounded so ridiculous to her that it took Adalyn a moment to even figure out if she was supposed to answer it. Was he so eager to get rid of her that he'd say anything? She already knew that she was weak enough to say anything to avoid it.

"I know you're a good person. I see the way you take care of your people. I'm a good person, too."

"I'm not a good person. I'm not the hero here, I'm the villain who should never have won the crown, let alone the woman. I'm not one of your dream warriors. Adalyn. I'm the dragon."

It always came back to that, to the nightmare that he never shared.

"Why do you say these things about yourself? You wanted to save him, Khalil. You wanted to and you're still trying. Every night." Or the nights when he hadn't been with her. The nights he'd spent alone with his grief and his penance...

"I didn't try to save him." He blurted the words out, all but yelling them as he stormed for her. "I killed him." The words came out sharp and hard, and when he finally touched her it was with cold hands gripping her shoulders just a little too tight. "Is that real enough for you? You want to make things work with a man who killed his brother for power?"

"I don't believe you," she whispered, mentally replaying everything he'd said to her about his brother.

"Why? You think you're going to redeem me with the power of love?"

In all her interactions with Khalil she'd seen him sad, she'd seen him happy, she'd seen duty and caring on his face. She'd seen stubbornness and authority. But she'd never seen him like this. She'd never heard such malice in his voice. With his hands still gripping her shoulders, she lifted her own to cup his jaw, making him look at her.

"I don't have to redeem you," she said, but she was already starting to doubt. Maybe she didn't know him. Maybe all that she'd thought she'd learned about him was a front, a disguise. Maybe she had fallen for Zain, not Khalil… But she wasn't ready to believe that, either. If he was sending her away, she'd have the truth first at the very least. "I already know you too well to think that's necessary. If you killed your brother, tell me why. What was your motive?"

He let go of her so he could pull back far enough to be out of reach, breaking the small contact she'd felt blooming beneath her palm. But in the wake of it, if anything, he seemed angrier. "Jealousy. I wanted to lead. But they already had an heir and a spare, they didn't need me. I was never meant to reign, but I wanted to. That's why."

She'd come here scared of her own shadow, someone who avoided knowing others, who avoided pain and danger, but she was now ready to fight. "You wanted to be regent, that's what you're saying? You killed Arash so they'd be forced to send you here instead?"

"Why else?" He threw his arms in the air, the look on his face tortured and angry, but beneath that she could see a plea—that she save him from it somehow.

That look was the only thing that kept her going. "That's such a lie. You regent as little as you can before you escape back into the desert. For a man who thinks he wants to lead, you spend a heck of a lot of time running from it."

"Because of the nightmares."

"No. You're lying to yourself. Stop blaming the nightmares!" She grabbed his hand again, needing to touch him, needing him to feel her hand in his—as if by touching him she could help him see what she saw. That the feeling that always raced through her body would be mirrored in his, because it was love. It was love and she needed him to know it.

"This is about you. You could go into the desert and not treat anyone if you simply wanted to get away from the palace. There's a whole wide desert out there where you could hide in a tent with that satellite phone for emergencies and read. Or you could shun responsibility and go off to some fancy hotel and find some woman who's actually good at being a trollop, and let her soothe your tortured royal brow. But you don't. You go into the desert to help people. You take care of them."

"I take terrible care of them. I make bad decisions."

"Only when you're sleep-deprived. And you suffer for those bad decisions."

"Stop trying to make me the good guy!" He wrenched his hand from her touch again, throwing up walls. And every one made it harder for her to keep fighting. "And, since we're on the subject, stop tearing down your own skills as a trollop. You did a fine job."

Adalyn's newly freed hand flew, her palm connecting with his cheek before either of them seemed to know it was going to happen. His head snapped back but he didn't move away. Didn't touch her. Didn't do anything but stare at her, any trace of love she might have imagined during their tender moments…gone. Just gone.

Her chest burned, along with her palm and her eyes. At any second her heart would tear itself from her chest.

She'd be the one to walk away this time. If she didn't, she might hit him again. Or he might touch her and that connection she all but lived for would turn sour, and it might take all the sand in the desert to fill her chest back up.

"You're not a dragon," she muttered. "You might be mean enough when you want to be, but dragons aren't cowards. Get out so I can pack."

"You don't need to. I'll have it all packed and sent to you on a separate flight."

Right. He couldn't even let her have enough time to pack, he wanted her gone that badly. Had the sultan ordered her out of the country? Or was this entirely Khalil's doing?

Whatever. It didn't matter whose idea it was, the result was the same. "Don't strain yourself. I can live without it for a few days. But if you're looking for a good use of your time, see if you can find your courage, because you need to figure out what really happened. Talk to someone. If not your family, then talk to Jamison."

She put her shoes on, grabbed her purse to make sure that her passport and keys were inside and gestured for him to go.

"I could say the same thing to you."

"You could, but it would be redundant. I'm already going to. The world's biggest scaredy-cat has more courage than you. Live with that."

She wouldn't say goodbye. Even if she wanted to, she doubted another word could get past her lips without making her sick.

There had never been a longer day in Khalil's life. A fresh stone of guilt had sat putrefying in his middle since he'd said those ugly words to Adalyn. Even the small amount of pride he'd felt when she'd slapped him for the ugly lie wasn't enough to help.

Not bothering to clean up or to change into the robes his position required, Khalil headed to his parents' suite and through the double doors. Behind him, flanking him on either side, were Hakem and Suhail, his everpresent escorts. Who, technically, worked for his father.

Despite the violence that the palace had seen only two months earlier, it had been well reordered. A few bullet holes still pitted the walls here and there, but you had to know where to look for them. It had mostly been put right now. The furniture that had been irreparable had been replaced. The evidence of the repairs greeted him: a large-screen television with the eerie, frozen, night-vision-green image of him sleeping, covered in wires and electrodes, his limbs caught in mid-motion and his sleeping face contorted. Nightmare face. Beside him, Adalyn stood, hand outstretched, ready to wake him.

His parents sat on a sofa together, always together, reading a newspaper and paying no attention to the television. But only a second after he stepped in they looked toward him and his entourage.

Khalil stepped forward, bowed deeply, as he'd been taught, and straightened. Get it over with. A quick glance around confirmed that his elder brother would be back in Akkari—he was now running the country full-time, since his father had decided to step back and ostensibly retire, to spend more time with his wife. Which was why Malik wasn't the regent of Merirach, and it had fallen to Arash previously, and then Khalil.

Without speaking a word, his father reached for the remote and set the video playing.

When Khalil didn't look anywhere but at his father he said, "Look at the video, son."

Son?

He didn't need to look. He knew what had happened next. He just didn't know why his father would want to play it, except to drive home the notion that he'd let them all down, and then…sullied the palace by bringing in a lover. It was the fact that Adalyn would soon be nude on that screen that put him into motion.

Three big steps and he made it to his father, took the remote and stopped the video just at the beginning of his leap from the bed, which had ended with him tackling her and…

"I don't need to see this. She doesn't deserve to be shamed."

"That's not what we're going to look at, Khalil," his mother said, and he met her gaze for the first time. Tears wet her eyes.

"There's nothing else to see," he whispered, and stepped back, keeping his head up even if his will to fight was fading.

"You were having sleep disturbances," his father said, avoiding any wording that would make the situation more personal or emasculating. Something he'd be grateful for if he had an ounce of feeling left to spare. "You had her here to help you."

"Yes."

"She woke you and you leaped on her."

"Yes."

"Just as you screamed for your brother to come back."

Khalil opened his mouth to say yes, but then frowned and looked back at the frozen screen. He didn't remember shouting anything.

This wasn't about his lie to the people that Adalyn was his mistress, and it wasn't about his secret trips into the desert under a different identity or shirking responsibility.

They wanted to talk about the dream, not what had come after the tackle.

That was really the way he'd let his family and his country down.

Khalil looked at the remote in his hand...found the button and pressed Play.

CHAPTER THIRTEEN

ADALYN STOOD IN her apartment, the upper floor of an old Victorian that had been widely refurbished since Hurricane Katrina, staring at her bookshelf.

So many travel books.

A stranger would look at her bookcase and think she'd traveled the world, but Jamison was the world traveler.

She was just the kid sister who read about all the countries he traveled to.

Initially, she'd done this to understand the sorts of dangers he could encounter so she could warn him of all the things he needed to watch out for. He wouldn't have done that research on his own after all.

But somewhere along the way it had become a way for her to see the world without leaving home. Some way to scratch that itch to know more. She had books about places Jamison had never gone. They might even outnumber the ones she'd had a real reason to purchase, at least by her way of thinking.

It had started out noble and had turned into something sad without her even realizing it.

The people at the bookstore knew it was strange. They'd always asked questions designed to lead her to the same conclusion—not-so-subtle hints for her to actually go somewhere that she'd always understood but had viewed through the lenses of *Other People's Opinions* and everyone being entitled to theirs. Even if they were wrong.

Her reading proclivities had seemed entirely normal and rational to her before Merirach.

Now her life seemed small. And what she'd once deemed safe? Lonely.

Jamison would be there soon, and she had to figure out what to tell him about all this, but she didn't even know where to start.

She'd been home for eight long, rainy days now, and it suited her mood. A mood she couldn't hide, which was why her brother was coming for a second in-person visit in as many months. She'd been dodging his calls since she'd gotten home.

Apparently texts hadn't been enough to put his mind at ease.

So, what could she tell him to explain things without involving the whole mistress affair or the accidental sex tape? If her current mood had been because of any man other than his best friend, she'd just tell him the truth. Everything, save for the sexy details. Straightforward. Honest.

The doorbell rang and she got a sinking feeling in her stomach. If she wasn't going to tell him about Khalil, she should finally tell him about her nightmares. *Straightforward* and *honest* weren't really words she could claim for their relationship for the past fifteen or so years.

And that had to change.

She drew a deep breath and went to answer the door.

Time to follow her own advice and talk to her family about her problems. Let her big brother look out for her for once…

Jamison unfolded another sturdy banker's box and set it beside Adalyn where she sat cross-legged on the floor.

"You know, I want to keep some of these," she said, looking at the piles of travel guides circling her. "I've sorted them. Those are the ones that will be donated for sure. These are the ones I want to keep—the ones I think I'll use."

Jamison lifted a brow and squatted down beside her. "When?"

"Sometime…"

His brow rose higher.

"Sometime soon." She tried again.

He turned and sat cross-legged on the floor opposite her, the books piled between them. "I'm sorry, the judges won't accept that answer. When?"

She groaned. In the five days since her confession Jamison's interest in her general homebody tendencies had become extremely annoying, but it was her fault. She was the one who'd told him she responded to exposure therapy…because of that stupid truck.

"All right. How about this? You pick the place you're going to go to first, and then we'll start working on when. Seasons matter in travel." He picked up the books from the rejects pile and put them into the box. "And tomorrow we're going to the amusement park."

"No, we're not." She stopped looking at the books, trying to figure out a city to go to. One within the United States. Maybe one she could get to by train. A good train adventure sounded like just the thing. They hardly ever crashed, unless it was wintertime. Or maybe if there was an earthquake.

So maybe she shouldn't go west…

"Two words," he said, holding up his closed hand. "Bumper. Cars." He ticked off the words by extending fingers.

Adalyn smiled and then laughed a little. "I don't think that's necessary."

"You're going. Whether you want to or not."

"I really don't think I have a problem with amusement park rides."

"Good. You're going." He looked at the maybe pile. "You have to pick so I can pack them up."

The doorbell rang, buying her a little more time. "I think your pizza is here."

"God, I hope so." He levered himself off the floor and left her to look at her books.

At least him fixating on her exposure therapy was better than him continuing to grill her about what had gone on between her and Khalil. She'd managed not to say anything up to this point, which was why she'd definitely give in and go to the stupid park tomorrow. It might save their friendship.

She went through the maybe pile again, considering each destination and whatever local attractions she could remember from whenever she'd read the book. This resulted in five more books being plucked out of it to go into the donation box, neatly dividing the maybe stack in half.

Then it occurred to her. She went through the stack of books before Jamison could get his pizza at the front door, maybe thirty steps away, flight of stairs included?

She stood up and went to the door. Jamison was not

at the bottom of the stairs. Pizza nowhere in sight. No delivery person, either.

A worrier couldn't learn to stop worrying overnight. After double-checking to make sure the door wouldn't lock behind her, she trotted down the stairs and out onto the porch.

Jamison stood, holding his right hand protectively.

A few feet away a man lay sprawled on his back.

"You hit the pizza dude?" she barked at him as she slowly processed the scene.

Only then the pizza dude sat up, and it was Khalil.

Khalil was on her front porch. Without pizza. But he did have blood on his mouth and cheek.

The air felt even soupier than normal suddenly, and she had to force deep slow breaths if she wanted any chance of keeping that fear-tinged hopefulness from showing. He'd knocked the air out of her before, but really she'd prefer a tackle.

"Why in the world would you hit Khalil?" she shouted at Jamison, but didn't move toward either man.

"Because he messed with you. You mess with your best friend's sister, you take a punch. It's simple math," Jamison said, now shaking his hand out, as if that would dispel the smarting.

"I didn't tell you anything that happened between us."

"You didn't have to," Jamison muttered. "You've been inexplicably teary-eyed at different times of the day since I got here. I might be dense sometimes, but I know heartache when I see it."

There simply was no argument to be made against that. Her eyes burned, that inexplicable teariness threatening to return. She muttered, "For all your insight, you probably broke a knuckle, Einstein." When she transferred her attention to Khalil, though, words completely failed her.

"It's okay. It's fair," Khalil said, defending the man who'd probably just split his lip, and slowly climbed back to his feet.

Behind him, down on the street, the delivery car pulled up, finally giving her something else to focus on. She turned her attention back to Jamison and snapped her fingers. "Wallet. Then go upstairs. Both of you. I'll get the stupid pizza."

The transaction took no time at all. She took the money from the wallet, handed it to the young female driver, apologized for the chaos and then stood on the porch for a couple of minutes, box in hand.

Khalil was there. Upstairs. In her apartment.

And he hadn't looked as if he'd come to see Jamison.

She stood there, staring at the front door, until her heart slowed into something resembling a normal rhythm.

It had been two weeks and she'd just gotten to the place where, as Jamison had said, she wasn't inexplicably teary at different points throughout the day. Today it had happened only twice.

If the wound had been physical, she'd have said it had finally begun to heal. But it wasn't strong. A stiff gulf breeze could break those stitches.

And she was taking as long to get the pizza as she'd thought Jamison had.

Just go upstairs. Get it over with...

She pushed through the door and with slow, measured steps climbed to her apartment door.

* * *

Khalil stood in the middle of the living room, a paper towel held to his lip, waiting for Adalyn when every inch of him wanted to go make sure she was coming.

To control the instinct, he looked at his best friend on the couch, a bag of frozen vegetables on his knuckles.

"She's probably right," Khalil said, trying to ignore the lump in his throat he just couldn't swallow down.

"About?"

"Your hand. It's at least sprained."

"I'll be fine." Jamison said, smirking up at him in a way that relieved at least a tiny bit of his tension. "Your face is soft like a pretty-pretty princess. Couldn't have done too much damage."

Khalil laughed, a small nod to hope—hope that the other Quinn was as quick to forgive. She certainly wasn't as quick to come back upstairs.

By the time the door opened Khalil had given up waiting and started forward to go to check on her. They met at the door.

"Are you leaving?" she asked, glancing up long enough to make eye contact, and then stepped around him.

"I… No." He didn't explain, just waited as she took the last few steps to Jamison. "Not until I say what I came to say."

She thrust the wallet and the pizza at Jamison and said, "Don't eat this in my living room." When she had been relieved of her cargo she looked back at Khalil.

If she wanted to do this in front of Jay, he'd do it. He'd faced down his parents, he could do this.

Even if he got an ulcer afterward from the acid eating through his stomach.

He stood straighter.

She didn't look at him again, just gestured for him to follow her and headed back out of the living room in another direction.

They came to a simple white-paneled door and she held it for him.

Bedroom. He knew what it was before he even got through the door to see. It smelled of her so strongly that a wave of homesickness unlike anything he'd ever experienced slammed into him.

Instinct said to go to the window, look out, compose himself… Protect his emotions. He'd done that before to her, until he'd gotten control. But this couldn't be about control. It had to be real.

He swallowed, and though his eyes felt damp he turned to look at her. She stood close enough that he could have touched her. He wanted to touch her. Skip the words, take her to bed, let his body say what he was uncertain his words could.

The small tan she'd picked up in Merirach had faded with her days home, freckles had come out on the bridge of her nose and a smattering on her cheeks…almost the exact color of the desert sand. Close enough that he had to fight the urge to run his thumb over her cheeks to brush them clean.

She looked down again so that her dark hair fell forward and concealed her eyes from him. "You have to talk. I don't know what to say."

He stuffed his hands into his pockets to keep from reaching for her. "I need to talk to you about the camera."

"I don't have it…" She breathed the words in a rush, her eyes lifting with her hands as she shrugged. "I don't have any of it. The equipment isn't here yet."

"I brought it with me," he said. "It's at the airport, awaiting delivery instructions."

"So the memory card…"

"I…" He withdrew his hands from his pockets, opened his jacket and fished out the small blue card and held it out to her. "That's it."

She didn't reach for it but stared at it hard, probably to keep from looking at him. "Don't you want to destroy it?"

"No. I want it. I'm hoping that you'll let me keep it. That we can…we can keep it." Together. He should say that. Together.

It was enough to get her to make eye contact again. For the moment the look of imminent tears was replaced with a spark of the sass and sarcasm he'd missed in her. "It's that good, eh? You think I want a copy to remember you by?"

"No." He swallowed, still holding it out to her. "I'm hoping that you'll let me keep it as a record of…my journey."

Adalyn looked at the card but looked harder at the way his hand shook. Fear? Nerves? "Your journey? What journey?"

He dropped his hand down, curling the card back into his palm as he shook his head.

"That's not the right word, but it sort of is," he said, "because it shows where I was before I met you, and where I want my life to end. This video could be my whole story." He paused to swallow.

The vulnerability in his voice nearly undid her. At any second now the tears she worked to keep at bay would spring forth again. "I don't mean to be dense, I just don't—"

"Adalyn Quinn woke me up from my nightmare, and I loved her for the rest of my life," Khalil said, cutting off her question. "That's what I want my story to be. Because my whole life was a nightmare when I met you. It just got easier to recognize as a nightmare when I was sleeping."

Her chest constricted and no amount of willpower could keep away the tears burning her eyes. She gave up fighting them and simply reached up to swipe them away. It couldn't be that easy. It was never that easy. He ran a country. A faraway country… "But what about our lives being too different?"

"Shouldn't we try to figure it out? That's what people do when they're in love."

He'd used the words she'd said to him, so he *had* been listening, and he'd remembered. It would be so easy to say yes, and inside her the word echoed and bounced off her heart, but she still ached from the last time she'd opened herself up to him. Every day. All the time…

"Because I love you," he added.

Don't listen to that. Not yet.

"But your people think I'm a brazen harlot," she said, and then remembered. "Your parents! Your parents think—"

"My parents only watched the first part of the video, until my mother realized what was going on. Then she turned it off and explained the situation to my father. She said it's what young people do in the West when they're in love. Apparently my mother thinks sex tapes are all the rage. Like digital engagement rings."

She'd never even met them, but the little story tickled her. Adalyn covered her mouth, hope surging through her at the twinkle of amusement in his eyes.

But he sobered quickly enough to remind her that this wasn't a joke. It was everything important.

"It was the first part of the recording they were concerned about."

Yes. His sleep study. The tackle. Him trying to protect Arash... Words she was still desperate to hear. Dropping her hand, she shifted a half step closer to him. "Your nightmares?"

"And what I said when I leaped on you." Khalil nodded, holding his hand out to her again with the memory card on his palm, still offering it to her. But she'd definitely have to touch him to take it, and there were things she had to know first. She had to be safe.

"I didn't understand what you said, and I didn't remember enough of what it sounded like later to look it up."

"It was a warning. For Arash. I'd seen the man with the gun pop up from behind a car and take aim at him." He rubbed his upper lip, a nervous fidget.

"So you tried to get him to take cover?"

He nodded.

"So you didn't kill him."

He shook his head. "When I heard what I'd shouted it triggered a memory. Like you said, a memory with more detail than my dreams. I've been working on it. Made a timeline. Wrote it down... Am still writing down any details as they come to me. But I don't think I'm in remission yet. The nightmares still come, not every time I sleep but they're still there. Even though I'm out of the palace now. The change in sleep environment might be what's helping, or the memory details I'm getting back. I'm not sure which."

He was out of the palace. Did that mean he could stay here?

"Did they fire you?" Adalyn swallowed and took another step, close enough that his clean masculine scent wrapped around her like a hug. Every word strengthened that feeling. If she didn't get hold of herself, she was going to either lean against him and sob...or leap on him and kiss his split lip.

"Fire me?"

"Your parents. From being the regent?"

"Ah. I believe it would be closer to medical leave. My father has a greater capacity for compassion than I gave him credit for. He stepped back into active leadership of Akkari so Malik could go to Merirach in my place. Because...I need help with this."

If she breathed too deeply, his fingertips would press against her breasts, but there it was, that card still settled on his palm between them, hers for the taking.

Adalyn leaned back enough to wrap his hand in both of hers, then curled his fingers back over the card. "So you were thinking of staying for a while?"

"And about begging you to tell me..." His words trailed off and he had to take two breaths before he could finish his thought. "Tell me I didn't break us in a way that couldn't be mended."

Adalyn felt another rush of tears on her cheeks, and before she could reach for them he lifted his other hand and ran the pad of his thumb under one of her eyes.

She wanted to lean into his hand but managed to speak first. "You didn't. But we still have some things to work out." Several, but none of them seemed quite so pressing as kissing him right now. "Which we should do. Later," she said, finally letting go of his hand so she could fling her arms around his neck.

He caught her with both arms, squeezing her to him as his mouth came down on hers, heedless of the split in his lip.

Unlike in his bedroom, Khalil couldn't navigate hers with his eyes closed. His arms still tight around her, he lifted until her feet left the floor, broke the kiss just long enough to orient himself and returned his lips to hers.

Unlike the first time he'd carried her to bed, and despite the need she knew was coiling in him as it did in her, he followed her onto the pillowed duvet and slowed everything down. No need-fueled rush to completion, just kissing for the sake of kissing. Thorough. Playful. Loving.

Hungry and devastating, anointed by the coppery ping of his blood and the salt of her tears but somehow still sweet and full of promises.

"I don't hear any arguing in there!" The sound of her irritating brother's shouted words filtered through the door. Adalyn chuckled against his lips and Khalil leaned up enough to look at her as they shared a smile, both shaking their heads.

When they didn't answer, another shout came. "If you're having sex, I'm gonna have to burn the house down! Just sayin'."

They both laughed for real then and called back in unison, "Shut up, Jamison!"

As she breathed him in, a wave of peace washed over her and she could almost hear the dunes in her ears. The sound of all that sand she'd packed that hole in her chest with draining away, and something altogether sweeter refilling her.

If he was brave enough to face those nightmares haunting him, come to find her and take a punch from her brother but still remain friends, he was the kind of man worth fighting for. Her faith in him had never been misplaced, even when she'd doubted.

Khalil was her oasis. Her safe place.

Everything else they could work out.

Because that's what two people did when they loved each other...even if they had to ban Jamison from the house until then.

EPILOGUE

ADALYN AL-AKKARI SAT in a window seat in one of the family planes, the seat belt stretched around the swell of her belly.

It had been seven months since she'd flown home, her heart in tatters, on that very same jet. But this flight was different; this time Khalil sat beside her, his hand in hers.

"Breathe through it, love," Khalil said, alerting Adalyn to how hard she was gripping his hand.

From across the aisle Jamison laughed. "Get used to saying that. You have two more months to practice. Though I expect it's more likely that you'll say it once and then pass out while Adalyn and I deliver that baby."

A quick chuckle was all Adalyn could spare for her brother's antics. Teasing them—but Khalil especially—never got old for him. Even after they'd exchanged vows and she'd got a new, exotic last name, and a lot better at traveling.

But descent still had the ability to scare her.

"I'm delivering the baby," Khalil countered, not rising to Jamison's baiting for once, though she could still hear the amusement in his voice contrasting with the tenderness he channeled to her through the slow back-

and-forth motion of his thumb on her hand. Steady. Strong. Comforting. Protective. "Besides, you're going to be too busy traveling to the camps to be there for the birth. We'll send you a picture, though, on the satellite phone."

"Then I hope it looks like me. You want a handsome kid."

Not long after Khalil had shown up on her doorstep, even before his lip had healed from Jamison's punch, she'd realized their desert shenanigans had produced a baby. And for some reason birth was one thing she wasn't afraid of.

Khalil resuming his regency? That could cause her a little flare of nerves… But he'd come so far that even the sultan and his elder brother believed Khalil ready to return to his position. And, more important, Khalil felt ready, too.

The nightmares had grown infrequent for both of them, but when they flared up neither of them needed a CD to coax them back into peaceful slumber. Instead, they took turns whispering words of healing comfort to one another in that suggestible period of early slumber, and it worked even better.

Five years wasn't so long to serve the people and do right by his family. He needed to do it, and she needed it for him. In a few years, the young heir would finish school and come of age, and they could return to practice, along with the many children she'd decided in the past few months she wanted. A huge family, with as many people to love and worry about as she could manage. Jamison had even agreed to spend at least a year taking over the mobile practice Khalil had started, so she'd even have her often absent brother near her.

The plane set smoothly down and Adalyn breathed her way through the landing and taxiing to the recently reopened terminal at Merirach's airport.

No more living through books and travelogues. No more hiding herself away to stay safe.

But she would wait until the plane stopped to unfasten her seat belt.

* * * * *

MILLS & BOON®

Buy A Regency Collection today and receive FOUR BOOKS FREE!

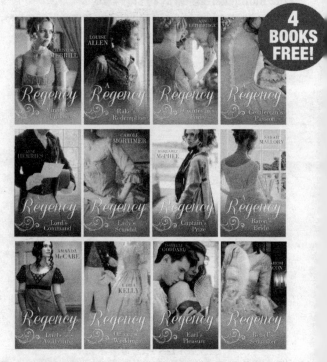

4 BOOKS FREE!

Transport yourself to the seductive world of Regency with this magnificent twelve-book collection. Indulge in scandal and gossip with these 2-in-1 romances from top Historical authors

Order your complete collection today at
www.millsandboon.co.uk/regencycollection

0915_ST19

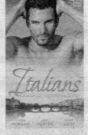

MILLS & BOON®

& MEDICAL ROMANCE™

THE ULTIMATE IN ROMANTIC MEDICAL DRAMA

A sneak peek at next month's titles...

In stores from 6th November 2015:

- **A Touch of Christmas Magic** – Scarlet Wilson *and*
  Her Christmas Baby Bump – Robin Gianna

- **Winter Wedding in Vegas** – Janice Lynn *and*
  One Night Before Christmas – Susan Carlisle

- **A December to Remember** – Sue MacKay

- **A Father This Christmas?** – Louisa Heaton

Available at WHSmith, Tesco, Asda, Eason, Amazon and Apple

Just can't wait?
Buy our books online a month before they hit the shops!
visit www.millsandboon.co.uk

These books are also available in eBook format!

1015/03